"Watch!" he shouted aloft. "What do you see?"

"It's dragons, sir!" the watchman called back. "I can see them clearly through the spyglass."

On the main deck, the sailors paused in their work to grumble among themselves. Darius hardly needed to be reminded of the danger. A dragon and a wooden ship were a deadly combination. A ship was too vulnerable to flame, and dragons were swift and could easily stay beyond the range of any weapons that could be carried at sea. He wanted no part of this fight, and he fully intended to avoid it if he could.

But he doubted that he had much choice. . . .

THE DRAGONLORD CHRONICLES

Thorarinn Gunnarsson

Dragonlord of Mystara

Dragonking of Mystara

Dragonmage of Mystara
Summer 1996

BOOK TWO:
THE DRAGONLORD
CHRONICLES

Dragonking of Mystara

Thorarinn Gunnarsson

To the memory of Ayrton Senna da Silva
1960-1994

To the heroes who prove, by the events of their lives and sometimes their deaths, that some dreams are worthy of any price and bring adventure back to a world with knights in armor

Random House and its affiliate companies have worldwide distribution rights in the book trade for English language products of TSR, Inc.

Distributed to the book and hobby trade in the United Kingdom by TSR Ltd.

Distributed to the toy and hobby trade by regional distributors.

Cover art by Danilo Gonzalez. Map by David C. Sutherland III.

First Printing: July 1995
Printed in the United States of America.
Library of Congress Catalog Card Number: 94-68144

9 8 7 6 5 4 3 2 1

ISBN: 0-7869-0153-5

TSR, Inc.
201 Sheridan Springs Rd.
Lake Geneva, WI 53147
United States of America

TSR Ltd.
120 Church End, Cherry Hinton
Cambridge CB1 3LB
United Kingdom

PROLOGUE

A warm fire flickered and snapped in the hearths at either side of the wide chamber, filling the nearest portions of the darkened room with a warm, golden light. The gold dragon, Marthaen, slipped quietly into the chamber, leaving the massive wooden door open behind him. He paused for a moment to sit up on his haunches to release the buckles of his harness, slipping out of the leather straps that held his weapons and pouches. The winter night was long and bitterly cold, and he was glad to retreat to the comfort of his lair. For the moment, he laid the harness on the wide bed in the center of the room, which was in the darkest part of the room, midway between the two fires, where the few furnishings cast long shadows. He stretched his long, slender back, then crossed the room to seat himself in the warm glow of the fire.

The winters seemed as long and cold as death in the Wyrmsteeth Range, and here it was all the colder for being so high in the forbidding mountains of that northern land. Marthaen turned his head, staring out the wide, low bank of windows looking out from the heights. The night was misty cold, and snow danced on the fitful wind. Through the storm, he could see only a few pale lights in the distance. The hidden city of Windreach seemed almost deserted. Many of those who dwelled there returned to their own lands during the depths of winter, or else retreated into the comfort and seclusion of their own lairs. Game was scarce, and hunting was poor. His one compensation was that winter was a quiet time.

He glanced toward the bed in the center of the room. Pale light shone from the fires, but it was enough for him to see the black form of some immense creature, curled up as if asleep, in the center of the bed. The dark figure moved, and a narrow head rose slowly on a long, powerful neck, turning to peer up at him. The slender, triangular face was crowned by the horns and crest of a dragon, with large eyes glittering in the darkness. Then the dragon glanced briefly aside, silently casting a small spell, and the enchanted lanterns that hung in brackets along the walls began to glow with a soft golden light. The warm light revealed a gold dragon, a young female who was still somewhat small for her breed, slender and graceful. She blinked, then yawned hugely.

"Did I wake you?" Marthaen asked.

"I was only waiting for you to come," Daresha insisted.

Daresha rose, stepping down from the bed, and Marthaen candidly admired her beauty and grace. Her face was long and narrow, with large, dark eyes glittering above a slender muzzle. Her crest was deep and full, sweeping down a delicate neck that was exceptionally long and thin. Her body was small and lithe, and she carried her broad wings tightly against her back. She was, Marthaen reflected, the most beautiful female of all her breed, more beautiful than even his own sister, Kharendaen. But while he appreciated her beauty, her deepest and most cherished appeal to him was her quiet charm and almost understated cleverness.

She brought her head forward to rub her nose lightly against his breast, and Marthaen responded by stroking his own muzzle along the side of her neck. Dragons did not often live with their mates, preferring solitude, and even Daresha kept her own lair. She was a queen, like himself the leader of her own band of dragons that looked to her for guidance and protection. But Marthaen was grateful that she elected to spend at least a part of her winters in his company.

"Were you out in this cold?" she asked, sitting back on her haunches close beside him.

"There was no moon at the lower altitudes tonight," he said. "I had to fly up above the clouds to see it. That led me to think of Midwinter's Night, and how things used to be years ago, before the Great One went away. We would feast in the evening, then go out upon the mountains to sing the ancient songs in the darkest part of the night."

"I am not so young that I do not remember," Daresha told him, quietly amused. Because she was small, even her mate sometimes underestimated her age. The Great One was the Immortal spiritual leader of the dragons and as such the only patron and advocate of dragons among the mysterious and powerful Immortals. But the Great One had been gone for nearly a quarter of a century, which was actually a rather brief time in the life of a dragon.

"Why have we forgotten the old ceremonies?" Marthaen asked, looking out the window into the snowy night. "Is it that the dragons have completely lost heart since the departure of the Great One?"

"Or is it that we fear the Dragonlord so much?" Daresha asked in turn.

Marthaen glanced at her, his ears laid back. "It is not just the Dragonlord. The dragons know that we live at a moment lost between times, cut adrift from our past but not yet a part of our future. I suspect that the Dragonlord will serve, as the prophecy decrees, as the instrument of our fate. Whether for good or ill depends upon our own impatience and fear."

"You have never feared the Dragonlord," Daresha said.

"No . . . I've come to trust him," Marthaen said slowly. "I believe that he will not deliberately act against us without provocation. What I do not trust are the oddities of fate that might make enemies of us in spite of our best intentions. I have long suspected that the first war with the Dragonlord was largely a result of misunderstandings that nearly destroyed our race, and I would not see that happen again."

"It may well be as you say," Daresha agreed. "All that most dragons know is that we have unfinished business with the Dragonlord and we have waited nearly five years now for the inevitable conclusion to our intertwined fates."

"All we can do is wait," Marthaen said, staring at the cold stone floor. "We must await the coming of our fate. And as the leader of the Nation of Dragons, it is my duty to do anything I can to insure that fate is kind to us. That is why I dare not trifle with the only power in this world that can destroy us."

Daresha moved closer to his side, rubbing her cheek along the side of his powerful neck. "At least do not allow it to concern you this night. You have been out flying in this bitter cold. Come lie beside me in bed for a time so I can keep you warm."

Marthaen sighed, dismissing his concerns. He might have to wait years for the fate of the dragons to unfold, and even then he might have no better idea of what he should do than he did now. He sat up on his haunches so that he could put his short forearms around the small dragon, drawing her close. He would have preferred to have given himself over to the warmth and comfort of his lair and his mate, yet he could not entirely escape the sense of unease that had driven him out above the winter storms. There was more to his mood than just the lament for a time when the dragons had felt more secure in their fate, but there seemed to be nothing he could do about it now. Daresha settled into his embrace, laying her head lightly on his deep chest.

The gentle moment was brief. Above the howl of the icy wind came the sound of powerful wings, followed shortly thereafter by the rustling noise of a dragon landing on the ledge outside. Daresha opened her eyes, and her ears pricked upright as she lifted her head. Marthaen glanced down at her, smiling with wry amusement, then released her. Their visitor was already knocking anxiously at the door on the ledge by the time Marthaen left the sleeping chamber, pacing quickly into the large main hall of his lair. He couldn't imagine being interrupted at this time of night unless it was extremely important. The hour already approached midnight.

Daresha remained behind, sitting back on her tail near the entrance to the sleeping chamber while Marthaen crossed the central portion of the chamber, climbing the steps to open the wide wooden door leading out onto the ledge. Although he had been expecting the worst, he was still surprised to find that his visitor was Gheradaen, a fellow member of the parliament. The older gold dragon did not speak as he slipped quickly inside the door. Marthaen was more alarmed than ever, for he had heard the roars of dragons calling in the night.

"Trouble?" he asked.

"More trouble than I would have ever expected," Gheradaen said as he shook the dusting of snow from his back. "Invaders within Windreach itself. Even within the Hall of the Great One, or so it would seem."

Marthaen was so shocked that he had to sit back on his haunches, his head bent nearly to the floor. Enemies of the dragons weren't even supposed to know of the hidden city of Windreach; the possibility of actual trespass within their most guarded citadel was almost beyond conception. After a brief moment, he looked up at the older dragon. "What has happened? Surely not war."

"Not war . . . not yet, at least," Gheradaen agreed. "Beyond that, I honestly do not know. The alarm was raised a short time ago. Jherdar has already summoned the red and black dragons to assist in a search for the invaders, although I doubt that they know just what they seek. It seemed best to me to let them have at it, since finding the intruders and dealing with them are the most pressing concerns. But I thought that the cool heads of the gold dragons should prevail before anything else happens. The response to this act should be the decision of the parliament, not the vengeance of rogues."

"Yes, of course," Marthaen said, then glanced toward Daresha. "I need you to gather all the dragons of your band who are within the city, and also those of my own if you can. Then come to the Hall of the Great One. It would be best to know what we seek, rather than merely flying about in the night looking for trouble."

"I will be there as soon as I can," she promised.

Marthaen hurried back to the sleeping chamber to collect his harness and hurriedly buckled the straps. Dragons did not commonly carry any weapons but their natural ones, and indeed the harness and weapons of a Dragon King served most often as a badge of authority. Marthaen's harness, however, bore six knives as large as a man's sword. Over his long back, he carried a sword whose blade was longer than three men. He returned to the main chamber as Gheradaen opened the door, following the older dragon out onto the cold, dark pocket of stone that served as the inner ledge. Daresha was still buckling the straps of her own harness as they left.

Marthaen paused a moment on the broad tongue of the outer ledge, open to the sky to accommodate the outspread wings of a dragon. There was little to be seen through the wind-whipped snow. Lights glittered dimly in distant windows. He could sense many dragons all about him, could hear their calls in the darkness and the snap of their wings as they passed in the black sky.

He spread his own wings and leaped out into the night. A few long, deep strokes of his powerful wings brought him to nearly full speed, and he glided swiftly and silently toward the center of the city, through darkness too deep even for his keen eyes to penetrate. Guided by some strange, magical instinct, he made his way unerringly around obstacles as he tried to spot his destination. The higher edifices of Windreach were kept dark at night, so that no light would betray the presence of the hidden city outside the ring of stone. But that night all the lower halls and passages of the towering Hall of the Great One were brightly lit.

For now, Marthaen held back, allowing his companion to lead him to their destination. He could see that the massive main doors of the hall stood open, and many dragons had gathered in the snow-swept plaza before the broad steps. To his surprise, Gheradaen circled down steeply, and they flew right through the open doorway, gliding slowly a short distance between the marble columns of the large entry hall. They landed before a gathering of dragons centered about Jherdar, Speaker of the Red Dragons. Marthaen was surprised once more. He would have thought that the hot-tempered dragon would have been among the first to venture out into the cold night hunting for enemies to slay.

"First Speaker," Jherdar said, acknowledging Marthaen's arrival even before he had folded his wings.

"I appreciate that you have been so quick to respond to this threat," Marthaen said, honestly grateful that the red dragon appeared to be handling this crisis in a reasonable manner. "Can you tell me what has happened?"

"The Collar of the Dragons has been stolen," Jherdar explained simply. The other dragons turned their heads to watch the First Speaker.

Marthaen was shocked and sat back on his haunches. The theft of the Collar of the Dragons was a dire matter indeed, almost as devastating to the Nation of Dragons as the loss of the Great One. Small wonder indeed that every dragon in Windreach seemed to be turning out to assist in the search.

Marthaen looked up, knowing that they were waiting for him to act and aware that he must not appear indecisive or frightened. "Jherdar, I am dependent upon you. Every band of dragons within the city must be gathered for the search. Spread out in all directions. Send scouts on ahead in case the thieves have the means of flight. Then take your own band and at least one other directly to the Great Bay. Watch any ships you may find there, and prevent any from departing unless you are certain that they do not have the collar. Watch the settlements of the Alphatians as well. They could well be behind this."

"Why not just attack their settlements and be done with it?" Jherdar asked.

"I am not yet ready to take such action," Marthaen told him. "Attacking their settlements would only draw attention to us, leading others to wonder why we so jealously guard these mountains. I am not yet certain that the secret of Windreach has been betrayed to the outside world."

"And if we should encounter the Dragonlord?" the red dragon asked guardedly.

"If you do find the Dragonlord, then he has probably come to help us," Marthaen insisted. "I do not believe that the Dragonlord has had any part in this, although I do not have the time to explain myself just now. Remember, be swift but be discreet. I beg you, do nothing to make our situation worse than it already is."

Jherdar bowed his head, saying nothing, and departed without argument. Considering the desperateness of the circumstances, Marthaen thought he could trust the red dragon to do exactly as he was told. All but a few of the other dragons, mostly members of the parliament who had been awaiting instruction, went with Jherdar. There were nearly four dozen hidden kingdoms of dragons in the world, but only eight of their kings or queens were at Windreach at that time. Most were accompanied by only portions of their bands. Fortunately more than two hundred other dragons, unattached to any particular band, were also present in the city. Marthaen fervently hoped they would be able to get themselves organized into a proper search party without delay.

Marthaen turned and paced across the stone floor of the Hall of the Great One, seeking the inner chamber where the Collar of the Dragons had been held in safekeeping. He hoped the scene of the theft might provide some clue to the identity of the thieves, and that would in turn tell him where to look.

Unfortunately, while he preferred to suspect the Alphatians, he thought he knew already the identity of the only thieves in the world capable of stealing the Collar of the Dragons.

Marthaen hurried back to the center of the chamber, seeking the intertwined double spiral staircases whose wide, deep steps would lead him up to the next level. The Hall of the Great One was a massive structure even by draconic standards, easily the single largest building in the world. The treasury of the dragons was located on the second level. It was not a treasury in the conventional sense, but rather a repository of all the most important artifacts and small, special treasures gathered during their long history.

The second level was in most ways like the one below, although the ceiling here was too low for a dragon to fly. It was almost entirely open from wall to wall, supported by a stone forest of massive columns. The chamber that had held the Collar of the Dragons was one of the few enclosed areas and stood near the central stairs. Walls of white stone had been set between a cluster of the supporting columns to form a large six-sided enclosure that was open on opposite ends. The enclosure was more for decoration than for security. The defenses that should have guarded the collar were within.

He was glad to see that three of the clerics of the Great One were at hand near the chamber, one of them a senior cleric he knew quite well. At least he would be able to get some of his questions answered. The clerics saw him as he approached and bowed in the manner of dragons, pressing one hand to their breast and bending their long necks in a graceful curve until their noses almost touched the floor.

"Lhorandyn?" Marthaen said, and the oldest of the three gold dragons lifted his head and nodded. "How did it happen?"

Lhorandyn frowned, glancing toward the inner chamber. "The fault was our own, I fear. Or perhaps I should say my own. The clerics are charged with guarding the Hall of the Great One, and we had sentries stationed at the main doors below, at the only two ledges leading into this level, and at the stairs above. But no outsider has invaded Windreach in centuries, and there seemed even less cause for concern on such a hostile night. Also, I fear, there are not so many clerics in Windreach at this time as perhaps there should be. Clerics seem to have little place here of late."

"That is not their fault," Marthaen assured him. "I can understand how this came to happen. What I need to know is if you have any idea of who has taken the collar and how."

"All we know for certain is that perhaps two dozen dragons have been here in the last four or five hours, which was the last time any of us actually saw the collar. It might have been taken at any time during that period."

"Rather later, I should think," Marthaen said as he began to ascend the steps. "If the collar had been missing, I daresay that the visitors would have remarked upon it."

He entered the chamber and paused. A second low dais was raised two steps above the floor and surrounded at the top by a rail of white stone. In the center of the dais stood a bust of a noble dragon, delicately carved in some sort of transparent crystal that looked like blue ice. The Collar of the Dragons should have been fastened about the neck of the statue, as it had been for centuries, but now the neck was laid bare. The collar had been a gift of peace and appeasement from the wizards of ancient Blackmoor after the war in which the first Dragonlord had nearly destroyed the dragons. It had been made for a king of dragons who had never claimed it. It was said to possess enchantments that granted vast powers to its wearer.

The collar had been protected by powerful spells, deadly enchantments laid down by the Great One himself when it had first been brought to the hall for safekeeping. Only Marthaen, as First Speaker, and the most senior of the clerics had the right to approach the collar. All others who attempted to pass within the encircling rail should have been destroyed at once. Any thief capable of stealing the collar would have needed the protection of a wizard more powerful than even the Great One himself. It seemed unlikely that any mortal wizard could possess more power than an Immortal.

Perhaps the thief enjoyed the protection of another Immortal, Marthaen reflected. That was an even more frightening prospect. The First Speaker knew that he could never hope to fight an Immortal for possession of the Collar of the Dragons no matter how much help he received.

"How did they get past the barriers?" he asked.

"That might not have been as difficult as you might think," Lhorandyn said. "As you know, the Collar was protected by enchantments placed there by the Great One himself. Those enchantments did not fail when the Great

One withdrew, but with the passage of time, they have become weaker than they once were. I fear that any reasonably competent wizard could have diverted the barriers long enough for someone else to slip inside and take the collar. We have never spoken of such a possibility, for it seemed to us that the best protection for the collar was the dire reputation of those enchantments."

"Then you think the thieves might have known about the weakened barrier?" Marthaen asked.

Again the cleric looked perplexed. "I cannot imagine how. Only a very few of the senior clerics know, and we have kept that to ourselves. If we had told anyone, it would have been you."

Marthaen sat back on his haunches, laying back his ears. For a moment, he looked utterly dejected, even defeated. "An Immortal would have known. I fear what we may face. What do the clerics know of this matter? Has the Great One spoken to you of anything?"

Lhorandyn drew back his head. "First Speaker, you know the Great One has been gone for many years."

"You must be candid with me now," Marthaen told him sternly, rising and lifting his head so that he stood above the other dragon. "There is too much at stake here. My own sister is a senior cleric, and by inference, I know beyond any doubt that she has received instructions from the Great One. If he were truly gone, these enchantments of protection would have failed completely. So tell me now what you know."

The cleric glanced aside. "I know no more of this matter than you do, and that is the truth. If the Great One had been free to tell us anything, do you not suppose that he would have warned us?"

Reluctantly, Marthaen had to agree. "Do what you can to find answers to this mystery. Also, I must ask you to summon Kharendaen here to Windreach, as you have done for me in the past. Have her come alone. There have already been suspicions that the Dragonlord was involved, and she will be required to account for him."

* * * * *

The response to the theft of the Collar of the Dragons was unprecedented in all the long history of Windreach. Every dragon who could fly turned out to take part in the search. Bands of dragons passed quickly eastward to the Great Bay to prevent the thieves from escaping by sea, while others began a more careful search of the surrounding mountains in all directions. News of the theft was traveling as fast as a dragon could fly through the Hidden Kingdoms of the Dragons, the bands that lived alone in the wild. Soon every dragon in the world would know that the collar had been stolen and would join in the search. The thing Marthaen feared most was that dragons beyond the reach of his immediate control might take some dire measures in their efforts to find their lost treasure.

Morning came, but it brought little promise. The patrols that Jherdar had organized to cut off the retreat of the invaders had found no sign of anyone traveling in those barren lands, even when they searched once more in the light of day. The snows of the night had been heavy and the winds had been desperately cold. The storm continued on into the morning so that the lands of the Wyrmsteeth Mountains lay beneath a gray gloom of icy mist and blowing snow. Although such weather was a small concern for a creature as powerful and well protected as a dragon, it was deadly to other folk. The possibility existed that the thieves had underestimated the fury of the storm they had used to cover their retreat, and they already lay dead, hidden somewhere within a deep drift of snow.

The various members of the parliament who had led their bands in the search began to return by later the same morning, which suited Marthaen. He needed to establish a general understanding of just what had happened, and especially in what ways the dragons should and should not act in response. Just the same, he saw no reason to convene a formal discussion in the Hall of Parliament. Dragons continued to arrive until they filled his private chamber across from the Hall of Parliament almost to overflowing.

"I confess that I fear the worst," Marthaen admitted when the others had made their reports. "Either our enemies have already fled, meaning that they have the same speed and mobility as we do, or else they are dead or stranded somewhere in the wilderness nearby."

"And you expect that they have fled," Jherdar observed. It was not a question.

Marthaen sat upright, with his long tail looped around him. "We seem to have no clue to the identity of the thieves, but there is much that we can infer about them and their abilities by what they have done. First, they must have possessed powerful magic to safely penetrate the enchantments that protected the Collar of the Dragons. That in itself says a great deal about them. But how did they know of the Collar of the Dragons in the first place? How did they know of the location of Windreach? Obviously they are aware of even our deepest secrets. Finally I ask this: How were they able to come within our city, enter into the Hall of the Great One itself, and escape again without being seen? These are great mysteries indeed."

"It is no mystery to me," Jherdar declared. "The Dragonlord would possess the power to break the protective enchantments."

"But how did he know about the Collar of the Dragons?" Marthaen insisted. "Do you suggest that Kharendaen has betrayed our secrets to him? Do you believe that she carried the collar away for him? I do not believe it, although I have already summoned her here to testify for herself and the Dragonlord in this matter. Kharendaen would have had no part in this. The Dragonlord is her companion, but he is not her master."

"Unless the Great One himself ordered the theft," the red dragon conjectured.

"If the Great One directed Kharendaen and the Dragonlord to take the collar, then there must be good reason, and they are welcome to have it," Marthaen declared. "The rogues turned against our clerics once before, but I cannot believe that any of us would contemplate turning against the Great One."

Jherdar sat motionless, staring downward, and said nothing. Although he had no direct part in those dark events, he was still not entirely blameless in the matter.

"If not the Dragonlord, then who?" Marthaen continued. "The Alphatians? I must suspect them, considering their recent incursions into the lands surrounding the Great Bay. If they have somehow learned our secrets, then they could be fully capable of planning the theft of the collar, providing the spells necessary to enter Windreach unseen and penetrate the protections, and even finding the means of carrying away the collar."

"A plausible explanation," Gheradaen agreed, raising his head in interest. "Yet perhaps you have an even better interpretation."

"I suspect that I do," Marthaen agreed. "The renegade dragons know our secrets already. They could pass into Windreach unopposed, mistaken for rightful inhabitants of the city."

Jherdar lifted his head in indignation. "The renegades would never dare such a thing."

"The renegades have never dared such a thing before," the gold dragon corrected him. "But they are mad in their craving for power, and there is no limit to what they may dare to do. Also keep in mind that the renegades may have supplied our secrets to other enemies."

Jherdar considered that momentarily, then nodded. "I will admit to the strength of your arguments. Even so, I am not entirely satisfied that the Dragonlord has not had a part in this. I believe that I speak for other dragons in this matter. We must have a thorough accounting from Kharendaen. Also, I want more assurances of our safety. Unless things go better for us, then we face a time of great troubles. I want new assurances that the Dragonlord will, according to his promise, take our part when we have not been the aggressors in breaking the truce."

"I have already summoned Kharendaen to tell us what she knows about this," Marthaen replied. "I still do not believe the Dragonlord was involved in this, and I trust him to help us recover the collar if we call upon him to do so. Even so, I do not wish to involve him in our affairs until we are certain we have need of him. But if I am not completely satisfied by what my sister has to say, then I will speak to him myself."

Jherdar nodded. "Perhaps that would be best. I understand that you are his friend."

"I prefer to have him as a friend, since he would make a particularly dangerous enemy," Marthaen insisted. "But he is a friend best kept at a distance all the same, as long as Kharendaen is there to keep watch on him for us. My own suspicion is that either the Fire Wizards of the Flaem or the Air Wizards of Alphatia are behind this, and I frankly do not consider the Flaem competent enough to have managed the affair. Kharendaen can report about the Fire Wizards to us, but I feel that our attention would best be directed toward the Alphatians. If the thieves were not renegade dragons, then only the Air Wizards would have possessed the magic required to take the collar and escape unseen."

The weather began to improve by early that afternoon. The snow finally came to an end, and the clouds began to break up, although the winds remained fierce and the sky still looked threatening. The improved visibility made the search of the lands surrounding Windreach somewhat easier, although it also made escape easier for the thieves. Marthaen disliked having to ask the dragons to continue their search, but the matter was too important. If the Collar of the Dragons was to be recovered quickly, it had to be found while it was still within their own lands.

The situation with the Alphatians become somewhat more critical at that same time. During the night, the winds had broken up the ice that had closed off the Great Bay, sweeping it eastward into the open sea. A couple of ships had left the Alphatian strongholds on the coast with the noon tide, taking advantage of the clear passage. A band of dragons had discovered the ships once they were well out into the bay and had circled slowly to investigate. The Alphatians themselves began the fight, shooting arrows and bolts from crossbows. Then the dragons attacked in fury, ripping apart the vessels in their search for their stolen treasure before leaving the wreckage in flames.

Marthaen had to admit that he would have done the same, though perhaps not in such haste. Without a better idea of where the Collar of the Dragons might be, he could never have allowed those ships to escape. Granted, ships were a good deal slower than dragons, and there would have been all the time in the world to do something about them. Unfortunately, Marthaen now had a problem to handle with the Alphatians, whether or not they had been a party to the theft.

Even so, he had to admit that trouble with the Alphatians had been brewing for some time now. The halfling settlement at Leeha was one thing, but the Alphatians had been building strongholds and expanding their holdings uncomfortably close to the lands claimed by the dragons. Marthaen had already known that he would have to find some way of encouraging them to withdraw, preferably without involving the Dragonlord.

When there was no sign of the presence of the invaders or even their manner of escape by that evening, Marthaen felt obliged to greatly reduce to extent of the search. Hundreds, even thousands of dragons from Windreach and the surrounding lands had been flying back and forth through the mountains and along the coast since the middle of the previous night, and they were tired and hungry. It seemed best to permit Jherdar to organize the younger dragons into patrols and begin a more calculated and less conspicuous search. That would in turn allow him to organize the more powerful and learned dragon sorcerers and clerics for a more stealthful search. Since the thieves seemed to have already made their escape, he suspected that such an investigation would now be a more effective approach.

Now that the initial fury of the search was past, Marthaen was beginning to feel desperate. How much more would the dragons be asked to take? Indeed, how much more adversity could the Nation of Dragons endure before it collapsed in anarchy? It had been a fragile entity in the first place. First there had been the loss of the guidance and protection of the Great One and the fearful prophecy, then the dreaded return of the Dragonlord. Now the most ancient and sacred of their treasures had been stolen. But even more alarming, the most closely guarded secrets of the dragons had been betrayed. Windreach was the only city of the dragons, and its greatest security hadn't been in the fact that it was so remote and unassailable, but that its very existence had remained unknown.

Marthaen was becoming very fearful of the future, all the more so because the responsibility for so many of the decisions that would shape the future of his people was his own. He felt as if he were guiding the dragons through a treacherous and increasingly confusing maze of challenges and threats. The last thing the dragons needed was to find themselves at war, and yet war with the Alphatians, and possibly other enemies as well, now seemed inevitable.

Above all, he had to keep the dragons from putting themselves at odds with the Dragonlord. He knew that he had to the right to call upon the Dragonlord to defend the dragons from their enemies, and yet he remained fearful of such involvement and how it might end. In addition, he had to deal with the prophecy that warned of a permanent change in the destiny of the dragons. With no idea of what to expect, he somehow had to insure that such a change was to their benefit.

His first bit of good fortune in all of these dire events was that Jherdar, the leader of the red dragons, had been rather shaken, even subdued by the theft, and he was willing to follow Marthaen's calculated guidance rather than fly off in fury. The leaders of all the wilder breeds of dragons, the reds, greens and blacks, were usually willing to follow Jherdar's lead in such matters. As a result, Jherdar's deference to Marthaen helped to keep the entire Nation of Dragons under control.

The other bit of good fortune was that Kharendaen made the flight from the Highlands to Windreach in rather amazing time, arriving that evening even as Marthaen was conferring with the others about changing the manner of their search. She had received the summons in the middle of the previous night in the form of a dream, a curious trick that the more talented clerics were able to manage, and she had flown without rest ever since. She was clearly hungry and at the end of her strength when she pushed her way past the startled dragons into her brother's private chamber, but the time of her arrival could not have been more critical. Many of the dragons still needed some assurance that the Dragonlord had not been involved in the theft, and

Marthaen himself wanted some assurance that the Fire Wizards were not involved before he turned his fury against the Alphatians.

"What has happened?" she asked. "Windreach appears to have been stirred up like a nest of hornets."

"Then you do not know?" Jherdar asked before Marthaen could speak.

"I have no idea," she insisted, sitting back on her tail in obvious weariness. "I was instructed to come at once, and the tone of the message was so dire that I was startled awake and did not receive the remainder of the dream of summoning."

"Windreach has been invaded," Marthaen told her, speaking directly. "The Collar of the Dragons has been stolen, and we have no idea who has done such a thing. What we need from you is assurance that the Dragonlord was not involved in any way."

"I assure you that he was not," Kharendaen said, too weary to be shaken by such news. "He and I have an understanding. I have never told him any secrets of the dragons, and he does not ask. As far as I know, he has never even heard of either Windreach or the Collar of the Dragons."

"And you can account for his whereabouts yesterday, up until the time of your departure to answer the summons?"

She nodded weakly, closing her eyes for a brief moment. "The Dragonlord was in Braejr all day yesterday. He was still at home when I left. I have not been parted from his company for more than a few hours at time, and never by any great distance, for the last several weeks. I can guarantee that he was not involved in the theft."

"What about the Fire Wizards?" Marthaen asked pointedly.

Kharendaen had to consider that for a moment. "I do not see how they could have known of the Collar of the Dragons or its location, and I doubt that they would have the skill to take it by themselves. Still, I would not put anything past them. They are desperate for power, and the Collar of the Dragons is an artifact of great power. When I return to Braejr, I will learn what I can."

"Try to be discreet," Marthaen said. "It is the will of the parliament that no one, not even the Dragonlord, should be told of these events at this time."

"I understand."

Once her own part was done, Kharendaen left the chamber wordlessly. Marthaen wasn't able to leave for several minutes, not until he was satisfied with the plans that Jherdar and the others were formulating for continuing the search in a more methodical manner. Even then, he still had to speak with Gheradaen and Lhorandyn about other ways that they might seek the identity of the thieves.

Some time later, he found Kharendaen waiting in the hall outside his private chambers. She was sitting back on her haunches and yawning hugely as he approached. Her weariness was a matter of wry amusement to him, for she was otherwise always careful to carry herself with the quiet dignity of a cleric. She lifted her neck to rub her cheek lightly against his own, their first private gesture of greeting since her arrival.

"What do you believe happened?" she asked simply.

"I believe that renegade dragons took the collar," he admitted frankly. "I suspect that they may have been in league with either Alphatian or Flaemish wizards—most likely the Alphatians, who have been expanding their holdings in our lands lately. I will have to deal with them on that account under any circumstances, whether the Dragonlord likes it or not."

"I believe that he would understand if you explained the situation to him," Kharendaen told him.

"I am sorry for the need to call you here, but we very much needed to know about the Dragonlord's intentions," he said as he sat down on the cold stone floor, facing her. "We've already had one encounter with the Alphatians earlier today, which cost them a couple of their ships. I need to be able to prevent the dragons from doing something reckless that could lead to war."

"I understand."

"I am also concerned for you," Marthaen continued, choosing his words carefully. "I appreciate receiving your reports concerning the Dragonlord. They have done much to help the dragons contain their fear of him. Just the same, you have been in his service nearly five years now."

"My service to the Dragonlord is a matter of my duty as a cleric," she said. "But it is also my own choice. He is my friend and companion."

"Just so," Marthaen insisted. "I know that you are close to him, but I do not want your love and devotion to him to get in the way of your duty to the Great One and to your people."

"The prophecy states that the Dragonlord will play an important role in the destiny of the dragons," she countered. "Is it not better for us that he should know us and think well of us? I feel that I am also serving my duty by being a friend to him."

"That is not what I mean," her brother insisted. "The Dragonlord is the greatest danger that our people have ever known. Although his intentions may be good, I fear that we may yet find ourselves at odds with him over some misunderstanding. My concern is for you. If I must yet deal with him as an enemy, I would not like to see you caught between us."

Having spoken her piece, Kharendaen lowered her eyes and retired for some much-needed rest.

CHAPTER ONE

"Captain Glantri! There's smoke on the northern horizon!"

Darius Glantri glanced up at the watchman, perched high atop the mainmast, then hurried to the port side of the deck for a clear view. He could just barely see it, but it was there, a vague, gray trail of smoke rising from some unseen point just beyond the horizon. The steersman had already responded by swinging the tiller around, bringing the great war galley slowly from a northeasterly course to due north. The other galleys in the Thyatian fleet were responding as well. Many of the sailors were watching from perches in the rigging. After a moment, the marines began to hurry up on deck to see for themselves.

"We're not on holiday here!" Darius shouted across the deck. "Prepare the ship for battle. We may be in for a fight, and I want to be prepared for one. Get water buckets ready, in case we have fires of our own to deal with. Be prepared to cut away any burning sails or rigging."

There was hardly any need to hurry. The sleek Thyatian

war galleys were already racing before a brisk southerly wind, and the marines were busy unshipping the long oars for even more speed. The trails of smoke were at least ten miles away, perhaps more. Thyatian galleys were the fastest ships at sea, but even they could not cross such a distance in less than an hour, even with the favoring wind. If those fires meant that friendly ships were in trouble, he couldn't hope to come to their aid in time to do anything more than search for survivors.

The captain paused, staring at the horizon. Unfortunately the bow of the galley came around at that moment, obscuring his view. Frustrated, he hurried down the steps and past the long main deck of the ship, climbing into the high forecastle well above the copper-plated ramming prow. By the time he could see clearly from the point of the bow, he was certain. Already he could make out the shapes of the unknown ships in the distance, a cluster of perhaps half a dozen tiny objects many miles ahead. Other dark shapes, like tiny birds, circled slowly above the burning ships or dived down at them. But those ships were too far away yet for him to have possibly seen birds circling above their broken masts. From this range, they could only be dragons.

Darius hesitated. He had heard rumors that the dragons had seemed especially agitated since the middle of the previous winter, prowling the lands in great numbers from Wendar to the Steppes in the east and south to the great desert of Ylaruam. They seemed almost to be searching for something. If they were attacking someone, he had to know.

"Watch!" he shouted aloft. "What do you see?" he shouted aloft.

"It's dragons, sir!" the watchman called back. "I can see them clearly through the spyglass."

On the main deck, the sailors paused in their work to grumble among themselves. Darius hardly needed to be reminded of the danger. A dragon and a wooden ship were a deadly combination. A ship was too vulnerable to flame, and dragons were swift and could easily stay beyond the range of any weapons that could be carried at sea. He wanted no part of this fight, and he fully intended to avoid it if he could.

But he doubted that he had much choice, in spite of his inclination to turn his fleet about and flee while he could. If dragons were attacking Thyatians or one of his country's allies, he had an obligation to do whatever he could. And whether friend or foe, he had to know why the dragons were attacking in the first place. Dragons generally kept to themselves, and he had to know what had set them off.

It was obvious that the dragon attack would be over before he could ever get there. He only hoped that they chose to go their own way when their grim work was finished. Whatever complaint they might have, he had no idea whether or not it involved him.

The battle lasted longer than he would have expected. As he watched the dragons in the distance, he could see that they were not attacking in concert but were harassing the ships in a methodical, even cautious manner, never exposing themselves to danger while they picked away at the remaining defenders. They knew that they possessed every advantage, and they weren't going to risk being careless. The Thyatian warships were racing before a strong breeze. Darius now suspected that they might arrive before the battle was done.

Darius stayed atop the forecastle, watching the fight progress almost lazily for the better part of an hour. He had fetched a second spyglass from his cabin, and he had grown familiar with the tactics that the dragons were using. They had long since disabled all the ships, largely by setting fire to their sails, forcing the sailors to cut loose the burning sheets and rigging. Then the dragons would cut out one ship after another, like a pack of wolves separating individual sheep from the main herd. They would carefully destroy any remaining defenses, then board the ship and push any survivors over the side. Next they would search the interior of the ship, an act that Darius found curious and incomprehensible, before they left finally the wrecked hull in flames.

"They're Alphatian, Captain!" the watch called down at last. "Two Alphatian war galleys, escorting a small fleet of supply vessels."

Darius had already seen the warships, although he hadn't yet been able to identify their type. All of the ships were badly damaged, no doubt from the initial phase of the attack that had left the fleet unable to defend itself. Even as he watched, the dragons turned their attention to the war galleys. The Thyatians were still some five miles distant.

It was all over soon after that. The dragons circled for a short time over the last two flaming ships, then turned as a group and flew directly toward the approaching Thyatians. Darius waited tensely, watching them for any hostile move while the crews of his ships prepared to defend themselves. His fleet consisted of six of the largest warships in the Thyatian navy, but they were no match for a dozen red dragons. And yet the dragons did not attack at once. Instead, they circled the ships slowly just out of bow range. At last, apparently satisfied their ships were not part of the Alphatian fleet, the band of dragons turned lazily and soared off toward the west.

Darius sighed, unaware of just how tense he had been for the last several minutes. Whatever the dragons wanted, their complaint was obviously only with the Alphatians. A mutual enemy often made for unlikely allies, or at least it had in this instance. Once the danger was past, the sailors hurried back to tend to the rigging and the soldiers on deck lowered their bows. Darius turned his attention back to his own ship, aware that his marines must be tiring after an hour of hard rowing.

"Ship the oars," he called. "The wind will have us there soon enough. Relay the orders to disperse the fleet to search for survivors."

Another mile or so brought them to the edge of the area of battle. The last ship had since slipped beneath the waves with a loud hiss of steam. A great deal of wreckage floated in the water—crates and barrels and charred sections from the hulk of the Alphatian ships. The sailors hurried to take in most of the sails, cutting the ship's speed to a crawl so that they could search the area carefully for survivors. A skiff was already being prepared to lower over the side.

A centurion joined him at the bow, saluting smartly.

"Captain, I can speak Alphatian. I thought you might want to know in case we find any survivors."

"Good man," Darius exclaimed. "We've got to find out what those dragons wanted."

"I'm just glad they didn't want us," the centurion admitted with a sheepish grin. "For a while there, I was wishing we had the Dragonlord aboard."

"Yes . . . the Dragonlord," Darius said, mostly to himself. "When I saw that the ships were Alphatian, I thought they must have done something to deserve such treatment from the dragons. If that is indeed so, the Dragonlord might actually have taken the side of the dragons."

The last sail was furled, and the galley crawled forward, carried only by the slow sweep of the last four pairs of oars, the rest of the oarsmen being involved in the search. Darius saw that all the ships in the fleet were beginning to take aboard a fairly large number of survivors; apparently the dragons had been primarily interested in taking and destroying the ships, not in slaying the crew. When the first Alphatians were brought aboard, the centurion spoke with them in turn. While he waited, Darius thought about the Dragonlord and his companion, Kharendaen. He counted both of them as his friends from their occasional visits to Thyatis over the years. Kharendaen had always been pleasant company, civilized and intelligent, hardly a fierce monster of legend. He kept that in mind now as he considered the cold, calculating tactics the dragons had employed during this attack.

* * * * *

The first clear light of morning was just touching the night sky as Thelvyn slipped quietly out the kitchen door of his house, closing it quietly behind him. The large gray stones of the courtyard felt cool beneath his bare feet, a condition that would change quickly once the early summer sun had risen. He paused a moment to watch the dawn sky, growing a dull silver behind the dark line of the Colossus Mountains far to the east. The roofs and chimneys and towers of Braejr stood black against the pale light.

So far, there was hardly a sound to be heard in the city, only a cart or two rattling along the cobbled streets somewhere in the distance and the perfunctory barking of a dog challenging some imagined nighttime threat.

Thelvyn paused a moment to listen to a cart rattle slowly along a nearby street, which turned the stream of his thoughts in a new direction. He had grown up in a remote frontier village, and even after five years, he was still used to the sounds of the forests and the mountains and the cool, fresh scents of the northern pines. These southern lands of the realm were flat and warm, and the city as often reeked of smoke and a thousand other smells. The streets were crowded and noisy. He missed his old home in the north, the comfortable house that he had shared with Sir George, and the life of simple adventure that the old knight had always lived. It was the life Thelvyn had always wanted, that of a trader in antiquities, traveling throughout the world seeking lost treasures. And that was where he would have preferred to have been now.

At least the enclosed courtyard of his home served as an island of peace in this strange place. The yard was large, with a wooded garden at one end, and a high wall surrounded the entire estate. He crossed the courtyard to the massive block of the warehouse. The first owner of the estate had been a Thyatian merchant who had returned to his own land during the time of the dragon raids. He had obviously valued his goods so highly that he had built a warehouse on the grounds of his mansion. For that reason, it was no simple structure but solidly built of brick, plastered and painted with bright trim so that it rivaled the opulence of the house.

Indeed the warehouse was the main reason why Thelvyn had made this place his home. It had served as Kharendaen's lair for the five years that they had lived here. Thelvyn was about to open one of the two heavy wooden doors of the front entrance, but before he did, he paused to look around. Suddenly it seemed that every dog in the city had begun to bark and howl. A moment later a dark form began to circle over the yard, black against the pale sky. Thelvyn squinted into the semidarkness. It certainly wasn't a dragon, judging by its shape. As it came closer, he realized that it was a griffon, mounted by a Thyatian rider bearing what could only be an important message. Kharendaen opened the door behind him to glance outside, then drew back and closed the door quickly so that her own presence wouldn't startle the griffon as it landed in the courtyard beside the house.

Thelvyn hurried to help with the griffon so that the rider could dismount. Griffons were smaller than dragons, but they were also mere beasts, fierce but stupid and extremely dangerous to approach. Their advantage lay in the fact that they were as fast as a dragon and also willing to be mounted, whereas dragons generally didn't allow themselves to be used as transportation. Although the griffon was steered by reins, it could be controlled on the ground by a large brass ring attached through the nostrils of its beak.

"Never mind me," the rider insisted. "The emperor sends word. You are needed at once in Thyatis on a matter of great urgency."

"Do you know what the problem is?" Thelvyn asked.

"There is concern about war with Alphatia."

Thelvyn nodded. "I'll be on my way at once. If you can keep your griffon away from the grounds until my dragon and I have departed, then you can come back here and rest for your journey home."

The rider leaped back into his saddle, and Thelvyn released the nose ring. With a jerk of the reins, the great beast hurtled into the morning sky. There wasn't much that Thelvyn needed to do to prepare, although as a matter of courtesy, he hurried to Kharendaen's lair to ask if she was prepared for such a long journey. The dragon had overheard what was said through the door and was already preparing her saddle. Thelvyn helped her with the saddle, then went into the house for a few minutes to make his own preparations.

There wasn't much that he required. He needed to tell his housekeeper that he would be gone, then leave a written message to be taken to the king later that morning. Unfortunately, he was rather uncertain about just what he should say when he knew so little himself. Ever since he had raised himself from the title of archduke to that of king, Jheridan Maarsten had devoted himself to preparing the Flaem for their long-awaited war with the Alphatians. More accurately, it would be a return to the ancient war that had destroyed their own world long ago. Jherridan had been enlisting the support of allies for some time, often quite aggressively. Thelvyn thought it best that Jherridan and his Fire Wizards did not begin making ill-advised plans of their own until they knew more about the situation with the Alphatians.

His solution was to leave the briefest, vaguest message possible, stating only that he had gone to Thyatis to learn what he could. He strongly implied that it was only a simple matter, although he knew that Emperor Cornelius, a cautious and courteous ruler, would not have sent for him with such urgency unless it was a matter of dire importance. Kharendaen was waiting in the yard by the time Thelvyn was ready. She lowered her deep chest to the ground so that he could climb into her saddle, then leaped into the air. They were climbing into the sky over Braejr even before the sun had risen above the Colossus Mounts to the east.

Thelvyn settled back into the saddle, making himself as comfortable as he could. The journey from the Highlands to Thyatis was a matter of hours for a dragon, but it would have taken weeks on horseback. The dragon saddle was comfortable, with a high back, shaped to support and hold the rider securely. The constant flood of fresh, cool air was more than enough to keep him awake on such a long journey; indeed, at times he had to struggle to draw a breath against the force of it.

Kharendaen endured such long flights well, better than Thelvyn would have expected. She hardly even needed to use her wings for anything more than soaring, for she had an uncanny instinct for locating currents or rising columns of air. Mostly she propelled herself by magical means, inherent to the nature of all the greater dragons, invoking a spell not unlike levitation. She seldom flew straight but instead shifted directions almost constantly, often drifting left or right while banking her wings sharply, or else rising or falling to avoid contrary winds. The winds of the heights offered the dragon the fastest speeds, but they also kept her busy as she sought the most advantageous drafts, leaving Thelvyn to endure a sometimes quite unsettling ride.

Now that Thelvyn was feeling a bit more awake, he was becoming even more apprehensive about the reason for his journey. It wouldn't come as a surprise if Thyatis and Alphatia found themselves involved in a major war after so many years of plotting and skirmishing. His own worry was that a war of such vast proportions would be bound to involve the dragons before it was done, especially if King Jherridan and the Fire Wizards were able to win the support they had sought for so long with an alliance of nations against the Alphatians.

It also worried Thelvyn that the king apparently believed that he could win even under the most adverse conditions. Five years ago, when Jherridan Maarsten had faced certain destruction against with the rogue dragons, the Dragonlord had fortuitously come to his rescue at the very last moment. Thelvyn hoped that the king hadn't come to expect victory even in the face of impossible odds, just because of the rightness of his cause.

Thelvyn's problem was that he detested politics, which was what his life had mostly turned out to be concerned with. His titles of captain and advisor were hollow; he was the captain of no part of the Highland Army, and to be perfectly honest, he didn't have the experience to advise the king on much of anything. His present duty as Dragonlord was to keep the peace by subduing renegade dragons, but the renegades had been unusually well behaved these last five years.

Through all that time, Kharendaen had been his constant companion, as well as his teacher and advisor. She had helped him to better understand his duties and abilities as a cleric as well as to persevere at his studies in magic. Dragon clerics were also magic-users, the result of their dual nature as both mortal and magical beings, although the situation was almost unprecedented among other races. Kharendaen had lived uncomplainingly in the city of Braejr for five years, confined to her refurbished warehouse and the enclosed yard beyond, yet she was always willing to fly for hours at a time on such errands as this.

Kharendaen bent her long neck around so that she could watch Thelvyn out of one huge eye. "What are you thinking so hard about?"

"What makes you believe I'm thinking about anything?" he asked in return.

"When you are thinking, you stop wiggling in your saddle."

Thelvyn had to concede the point. "I was wondering how much trouble we might be in. If Thyatis and Alphatia finally declare open war, I'll have to try to keep both the dragons and the Flaem out of it."

"I do not necessarily believe that Alphatia and Thyatis are about to go to war," the dragon said. "Unless Alphatia has suddenly prepared for a massive invasion, this all seems very unexpected. I suspect that the Alphatians have other enemies to concern themselves with."

"Who else is powerful enough to give Alphatia a serious fight?"

Kharendaen looked back over her shoulder at him. "Ask yourself why the emperor considers this to be a matter for the Dragonlord."

Thelvyn looked surprised. "You mean the dragons might be making war with the Alphatians? Do you know something I should know?"

"Perhaps there is something you should know before you speak with the emperor," she said, looking uncomfortable. "The Alphatians have been making extensive settlements and fortifications in lands the dragons guard jealously as their own. If there is conflict between them, the dragons were not the aggressors."

"Then you believe that I should not interfere?"

"I am only warning you that this might be a difficult situation," she answered, choosing her words cautiously. "The dragons have the same right as anyone to protect their own lands, and the Alphatians may have committed other dire acts to provoke the dragons, things that I cannot speak of to you even yet. But if others believe the dragons to be the aggressors, especially after the events of five years ago, they may also fear that the dragons will attack their own lands and the war could spread. That is what you must guard against."

"I'm not overly concerned," Thelvyn assured her. "If the dragons are successful against the Alphatians, it would probably earn them the goodwill of everyone in this part of the world."

Kharendaen found a secluded valley, and they rested for a short time near the eastern edge of the mountains of the Altan Tepes. The next leg of their journey led them across the desert lands of the Ylaruam, and the gold dragon flew high above the harsh, dry expanse of dunes and barren hills. Kharendaen had come from the cold mountains of the north, and Thelvyn knew she often suffered when their duties took them into hot southern lands during the summer. Soon their course brought them back into the long southeastern arm of the Altan Tepes as it looped down below the desert.

Beyond that lay the flat, green lands of Thyatis. Thelvyn had been raised in the northern mountain forests of the Highland frontier, and even now he found flat, featureless lands of fields and pastures to be as dreary and desolate as any desert. At least he didn't have to endure the sight of it for long, for the City of Thyatis lay hardly twenty-five miles from the southern edge of the mountains. The sky had turned heavily overcast even before they came down from the mountains, and Kharendaen flew high to stay above the clouds and avoid the rain below. If it were also raining over the city, they would have a wet time of it.

Kharendaen found their destination with uncanny accuracy, considering that she could not have seen it through the clouds. Seemingly without cause, she suddenly let her speed fall off and banked her broad wings as she began to descend in a wide, slow spiral. They dropped down into the clouds almost at once. They were so dense and dark that Thelvyn was barely able to make out Kharendaen's head and crest just ahead of him. The air grew wet and heavy as the cloud began to condense like dew on his clothing, and he braced himself for the rain that would be falling at lower altitudes.

They descended blindly through the gray clouds for what seemed like a very long time before the thick mist parted grudgingly and they emerged just above the roofs of the city. Thelvyn could imagine the effect on the citizenry at the sudden appearance of a gold dragon, the largest of breeds, although this time the event went largely unnoticed. Most of the shops had been closed because of the heavy morning rains, and the streets were nearly deserted. Kharendaen took her bearings quickly and looped tightly back to the northwest, toward the center of the city and the great mansions and palaces of white stone and colorful slate roofs.

Thyatis was the largest city Thelvyn had ever seen, larger even than the capital of Darokin, sprawling across the low hills on the west bank of the Mesonian River. The simple, solid buildings of Braejr seemed crude and impoverished compared to the delicate palaces of Thyatis, and the entire walled expanse of the Highland capital was no larger than a market center of this teeming city. Thelvyn couldn't help but think that King Jherridan had never journeyed to such places as this, or else he would realize that he was the ruler of only a simple, rustic land.

Kharendaen found the emperor's palace quickly, using powerful backward thrusts of her wings to lower herself into the paved courtyard in the center of the garden. Thelvyn began to release the buckles on the straps that held him in the saddle. The rain had stopped momentarily, and the air was cool but felt heavy and very damp. A brisk wind was shaking the tall, slender trees that bordered the garden. The clouds were dark and heavy, threatening a resumption of the rain at any moment. Out of the corner of his eye, Thelvyn spotted one of the emperor's captains, Darius Glantri, descending the wide steps in the center of the long, covered patio that looked out over the courtyard.

Darius was a young man, only a few years older than Thelvyn. He was also one of the few people Thelvyn had met who was taller than he, powerfully built and dashingly handsome. Darius was the hero of the day in Thyatis, a renowned commander in several encounters with Alphatia. Rumors were rife in Thyatian political circles that Darius was being groomed for far greater duties, for his almost carefree, amiable nature did not hide the fact that he was also a capable natural leader, easily trusted and beloved, as well as a brilliant strategist.

"How were you able to sneak in between the storms?" Darius asked as he approached. "The rains have been nearly continuous since last night."

"We must have been lucky," Thelvyn replied. "We came straight in."

"Good afternoon to you, Lady." Darius bowed to Kharendaen, then reached up to rub her nose as she brought her head close. He knew the great dragon well and did not fear her, although the two bodyguards who accompanied him were obviously less certain.

"You seem to be having a bit of nasty weather, Darius."

"And there is more of it to come, to be sure," he said. "We should get you under the shelter of the roof before the rains return."

Kharendaen folded her wings tightly and climbed the broad steps leading up to the patio. The open area was easily large enough to accommodate her, although she had to be careful not to hit her head against the ceiling, and that made her fretful. She was in a better mood as soon as Thelvyn, with Darius's assistance, finished removing her saddle. The rain had resumed by that time, a great downpour driven by fierce winds that often carried a cold spray deep within the shelter of the patio.

"Is this what you call a hurricane?" Thelvyn asked. He had always associated violent weather with the northern mountains he called home; he did not easily associate these warm southern lands with storms.

"Indeed it is," Darius agreed. "Of course, this storm is strangely out of season, and as such it should be relatively mild. Most hurricanes come later in the year, at or just after the end of summer. At any rate, we never take the pounding they are likely to get on the east coast."

"The wind seems to blow the rain in beneath the roof,"

Kharendaen observed.

Darius smiled. "I've already ordered bedding to be laid out in the hall behind the patio. Don't be concerned. You will not have to spend the night in the wet and cold."

Thelvyn followed Darius through the darkened passages of the imperial palace. The rains had brought on the gloom of evening early, and the lamps hadn't yet been lit for the night. Of course, Thelvyn could see well in the dark, and such matters didn't greatly concern him. What he did notice was that the palace seemed strangely empty and silent. The heavy boots of the captain and his two bodyguards echoed endlessly through the stone chambers and passages, not unlike the rumble of thunder from the storm.

"Because of the storm, we have only a basic staff and guard on duty at the palace," Darius explained, as if anticipating his thoughts. "Most of the advisors and aides have gone home for the duration of the storm. I fear that we cannot treat you to any great diplomatic pomp."

Thelvyn said nothing, but Darius's words reminded him that, because of his armor, he could never dare to dress in the finery that would have befitted someone of his station. The enchanted armor of the Dragonlord possessed one serious liability that he hadn't yet been able to overcome. He couldn't teleport into the armor as long as he was wearing any weapon or article of clothing such as shoes that would not easily fit within the magical suit. He would have had to remove such items first, and he couldn't expect to be allowed that much time if he was threatened by an assassin. For the sake of his safety, he had remained weaponless and barefoot since he had first taken up the armor, wearing nothing more than a shirt and trousers.

At least, everyone he dealt with regularly was aware of this problem, and he wasn't expected to present himself at court in traditional attire. He did the best he could, wearing fine silk shirts with deep, full sleeves and a vest of rich leather.

They came presently to a chamber Thelvyn recalled with

wonder from previous visits. In most ways, it was only a circular courtyard enclosed within the palace, large enough to contain small trees and other lush plants, which grew about a fountain and pool in the center of the courtyard. Overhead, above the second-floor balcony with its railing of carved white stone, rose a great dome of glass set within a framework of some bright metal. Thelvyn paused a moment to watch the torrent of rain pouring over the doom, curious that the glass didn't break during the violent weather this city apparently experienced from time to time. Darius led him to a group of seats set on the lawn beneath the largest of the trees, where Emperor Cornelius rose to greet him.

Cornelius was a tall, mature man with chiseled features and a great lion's mane of hair as white as snow. He was wise and dignified, but also very patient and kindly with Thelvyn, who looked upon this regal man as everything he could have wished his own father to have been. Cornelius had never sought to betray his trust by prying into secrets or attempting to influence Thelvyn's judgment. Cornelius was the kind of ruler that Jherridan might have been if he had been less obsessed with ancient hatreds or less anxious of the authority he had fought so hard to win.

"Welcome, Dragonlord," the emperor said, clasping Thelvyn's wrist in the Thyatian manner. "It was good of you to come so quickly."

"It sounded important," Thelvyn replied. His travels in the last five years had taught him to speak the languages of both Thyatis and Darokin; his association with Kharendaen had taught him the language of the dragons.

"It is important," Cornelius agreed as they took seats on the benches. "But young Darius witnessed the start of this, and he should tell the story."

"I was leading a fleet of six galleys on a patrol into the Alphatian Sea northeast of Dunadale, on the upper tip of the Isle of Dawn, due east of southern Norwold," Darius began. "We saw smoke on the northern horizon, well away from land, and it was well over a hour before we could get there. As we came nearer, we could see a small band of dragons attacking a fleet of Alphatian supply vessels escorted by a couple of warships. The dragons were very cautious in their attacks, crippling the ships and then disabling the defenses of each in turn before searching the ship and sinking it. They looked us over when they left, but when they saw that we weren't Alphatians, they departed toward the west.

"I moved my ships into the area of the wreckage, and we picked up over a hundred survivors. We questioned them all, and in the process, we learned that the dragons have been attacking the Alphatians for most of this year. The Alphatians don't seem to know why, but I learned that they've been up to something in the area about Norwold."

"The Alphatians have established some large holdings and fortifications in the area around the Great Bay," Thelvyn said. "They've been seeking some large holdings on the continent, and they must have decided that they could escape Thyatian notice by settling so far to the north. It seems that the dragons claim that region as their own, and they're prepared to defend it. There are also indications that the Alphatians have done something else to make themselves especially unpopular with the dragons."

"Then you already know about this?" the emperor asked.

"Only what I've told you," Thelvyn said. "And I did not know about it until very recently. Kharendaen thought I should be aware of the situation. The dragons apparently believe they have the right to defend their lands and avenge some unidentified crimes against them, and I'm inclined to agree with them. But I also want to learn more before I decide anything, which I imagine is why you sent for me."

"I'm glad now that I did," Cornelius said. "You have just helped to put the pieces of the puzzle together for us, and I admit that I feel better about the whole situation. I wanted to be pleased with the dragons for kicking around the Alphatians, but I was fearful of the extent of their involvement. Under any circumstances, I knew you'd want to be aware of this."

Thelvyn nodded. "Even if I stay out of the situation

and let the dragons have their way—within reason, of course—I still have my own problems to deal with. My first concern is that, like yourself, the leaders of other lands cannot help but be alarmed by the thought of dragons going to war again. I don't want anyone doing anything stupid that might cause the conflict to expand into places were it doesn't need to be. Unfortunately, I can imagine Jherridan drawing his sword and rushing off to invade Alphatia with every fool in the Highlands behind him. It's a good thing I'm in a position to keep a close eye on the Flaem."

"Then you expect this to be a relatively brief conflict?" Darius asked.

"I suspect that the dragons are in a very difficult position," Thelvyn explained. "You see, dragons are not territorial. Their hidden kingdoms are more like associations of dragons under a leader. The boundaries of their kingdoms are never fixed. Not only do their kingdoms exist within our own lands, often without our even being aware of it, but they may even overlap each other's kingdoms. Now, I've always suspected that they do indeed have a homeland somewhere in the northeast, but that's one of their secrets, and they're happier if I mind my own business."

"Except that the Alphatians have now invaded their lands," Darius said. "Perhaps not even intentionally, at first."

"Exactly . . . and that has created a dilemma for them. They want to keep their secrets by not calling attention to the region, but they also want the Alphatians to leave. I believe that they will fight only until they get what they want, and then they'll back off. I don't believe they have any real interest in the destruction of Alphatia, although I suspect that Jherridan might want to take advantage of the disruption to mount an allied invasion of Alphatia."

"And he may well be right," Cornelius remarked. "That depends upon whether the conflict with the dragons will leave Alphatia vulnerable to an invasion, and whether we can work out an alliance and assemble an invasion in time to take advantage of the disruption."

He paused, sitting back in his chair with his arms crossed as he considered the matter carefully. Thelvyn couldn't anticipate what he was thinking. He might actually be considering the merits of attacking the Alphatians if he found support for an alliance against them. Thelvyn waited in silence, taking advantage of the moment to watch the torrents of rain as the winds hurled it in sheets against the glass dome. The sound was distracting.

"I must confess to wishing we could put an end to the threat of Alphatia," Cornelius said at last. "I have tried to interest other nations into becoming our allies in such a war, but the inland nations do not anticipate that they could ever be in danger from Alphatia, Darokin, or even Traladara, would be valuable allies, but they are far to the west and removed from Alphatian aggressions. The emirates of the deserts to the north and the folk of the Heldannic lands and the Northern Reaches are too preoccupied with quarrelling among themselves to be of any use in foreign wars."

"That was the same problem Jherridan himself faced in seeking allies when the rogue dragons were attacking five years ago," Thelvyn said.

"I wonder what influence the Dragonlord might have in gathering support for an alliance, especially considering that the dragons are already involved."

Thelvyn seemed rather surprised by that question. "If Thyatis is willing to commit itself to an allied effort against the Alphatians, then I suspect that Darokin would take the matter more seriously and offer their support. I'm respected enough in Rockhome that King Daroban would commit at least a part of the strength of the dwarves if I were to ask."

"Does anyone else hold you in especially high regard?"

"The Ethengar have always been fond of me," Thelvyn said. "I'm sure they would send warriors, for what it might be worth. The emirates hold me personally in high regard, but Thyatis and Alphatia are already fighting for possession of those lands, and they don't much like either side. The elves of Alfheim and I are on uncertain terms, since there is some question about whether or not I might be the legendary half-elf. But if Darokin commits itself, Alfheim may send some support."

"And what about the dragons?"

Thelvyn had never considered that question. But at that moment, a messenger entered the garden and waited anxiously at the door. The emperor turned his head and nodded, and the messenger approached quickly and bowed his head.

"My lord, the harbormaster sends word that the storm surge will be approaching some three or four hours after nightfall," the messenger explained. "The tide will follow shortly afterward, and he is concerned with the possibility of flooding. He says that preparations should be made at once."

"I could attend to this matter for you if you wish," Captain Darius said, rising. "I need to check the condition of my own ships."

The emperor nodded. "If you would."

Darius saluted smartly and departed at once with the messenger. Cornelius sat in silence a moment longer, deep in thought. Then hailstones began to rattle against the glass panes of the dome. He glanced up briefly, having noticed that Thelvyn had done the same. "It hasn't broken for as long as I can recall, and we've had worse storms than this."

Thelvyn smiled. "I was just wondering what it must look like after a snowfall."

"We rarely get snow," Cornelius explained. "As to my question about what part the dragons would play in this matter, I am keeping in mind that the dragons have already demonstrated their anger toward the Alphatians, although they were equally annoyed with the Flaem five years ago. Could they be persuaded to commit their strength to a war with Alphatia? Or perhaps more to the point, could the Dragonlord demand that of them?"

Thelvyn was appalled at the idea. "I suppose that I could knock their heads together until they submitted to my demands, but that would violate the conditions of our truce. I believe that they would be far more likely to commit themselves to war with me than submit to such a demand. I cannot guess whether or not they would consider war with Alphatia to be in their own best interest, but I would never attempt to force them."

Cornelius nodded. "Perhaps it would be more to the point for me to ask if Jherridan understands that."

Again the question caught Thelvyn by surprise. "I have an agreement with King Jherridan that defines what I can and cannot do for him."

"And I suppose that he must understand your relationship with the dragons better than anyone," the emperor said. "But keep in mind that Jherridan has been trying to forge an alliance against Alphatia for years. I think you should not underestimate your part in this, nor should you underestimate just what Jherridan might privately expect of you in his obsession over defeating the Alphatians. He is in a position to believe that the Dragonlord is subservient to his will, and he might expect you to fight his wars for him as long as you have allies to consolidate your victories. The Dragonlord has the power to fight dragons; he certainly has the power to defeat nations."

"Yes . . . I see what you mean," Thelvyn agreed. "I never believed King Jherridan could convince other nations to support his plans, and I can see that I've only taken for granted that he understands my position in this matter."

"Which is not to say that he does hold such expectations," the emperor insisted. "I feel that I am interfering in Jherridan's affairs, but this matter is too important. The Dragonlord may be giving his service to the Highlands, but his duty is to the world. The dragons are a far greater danger than Alphatia will ever be. While I have much to gain by involving you in a final conflict with Alphatia, I would not wish that at the risk of destroying your truce with the dragons."

"My first duty is to maintain peace with the dragons," Thelvyn said solemnly. "Indeed, my duty is to the dragons themselves. In some way, I am to be the key to their future."

"Then perhaps it would be wise for each of us to attend to those problems we are best able to manage," Cornelius said. "I will deal with Alphatia, and you deal with the dragons."

"That would be best," Thelvyn agreed, pausing as a servant came to the door to announce dinner.

"We will speak more of this later," the emperor said as they strolled together toward the door. "Other nations will be looking to Thyatis in this matter, gauging their responses according to my own. Perhaps it would serve all of us best if I had more specific statements for you to report when you return to the west."

CHAPTER TWO

A cool, heavy rain was still falling steadily when Thelvyn came out to the patio the next morning, and it seemed likely to rain for some time to come. He had been disappointed when he had seen the rain out the window of his room, because he felt there was a great deal that needed to be done at home. Kharendaen was lying at ease along the far half of the patio so that she could look out down the steps and across the garden. Small branches and leaves had been ripped from the trees and vines by the force of the storm to litter the paving stones of the court.

"Are you finished with your business here?" Kharendaen asked, lifting her head as he approached.

"I am," Thelvyn agreed. "Are you ready to leave?"

"I would prefer to leave, if you do not mind. The rain is irrelevant to me, and you can wear your armor until I climb above the clouds."

Thelvyn could imagine that Kharendaen was rather bored, being forced to crawl within the shelter of a covered patio during an endless torrential rain. This place did not compare to her own home, which was large enough for her to move about and where she had books and other diversions.

He hurried to get Kharendaen into her saddle. Because of the confining space, she wasn't able to help him much, and the massive leather saddle was difficult for him to lift all the way up to her shoulder. Once the straps of the saddle were tight, Thelvyn teleported himself into the enchanted armor of the Dragonlord, including the helmet. Kharendaen moved slowly out into the court, obviously more annoyed with the rain than she had admitted. Thelvyn pulled himself into the saddle, and the dragon spread her wings and leaped into the dark sky. She ascended at a steep angle with long, quick sweeps of her wings.

The rain through the helmet's crystal visor was so heavy and the sky so dark that the city of Thyatis disappeared quickly below them. Kharendaen reached the bottom of the low clouds almost at once, but then several long minutes passed as she ascended steadily up through the dense mass of storm clouds. The bluish gray mist was so thick he couldn't even see her head or most of her wings, and he could only wait patiently until they came into clearer air. Kharendaen's sense of direction was flawless; she could fly blind for miles and still go straight to her destination.

Thelvyn had been flying with Kharendaen for years and his trust in her was complete, and so he remained unconcerned even when he couldn't see where they were going. For the time being, he was too occupied with his own thoughts even to notice. His discussion with Emperor Cornelius had given him a great deal to think about.

Thelvyn was reminded uncomfortably of his first days as Maarsten's new captain and advisor, when the archduke had subtly intimidated the dukes into surrendering much of their own authority and independence. Thelvyn had been concerned then that his own presence was being used as an unspoken threat, suggesting that the powers of the Dragonlord might be used to enforce Maarsten's authority. Jherridan had questioned his loyalty at the time, accusing him of being ambivalent in his duty. Thelvyn realized now just how shocked and hurt he had been by that accusation, so much, in fact, that he had felt the need to prove his loyalty to the king. Now he began to realize that he might have made a mistake, trying entirely too hard to prove his loyalty. In doing so, he may indeed have appeared to make himself subservient to the king and therefore a very powerful weapon under Jherridan's command.

This was all disquieting in some vague manner. Thelvyn realized that he had begun his service to King Jherridan with these same concerns, but then he had put such worries from his mind and had quietly done everything that was asked of him. The king had always seemed to recognize that there were limits to the terms of his service. Now Thelvyn wondered if the only one with a mistaken impression of these matters was himself, in the erroneous belief that everyone understood that he could carry out his duties without being personally or politically involved.

As Emperor Cornelius had pointed out to him, the problem now was that such misunderstandings may have been allowed to grow until Thelvyn's perception of the limitations of his duty and Jherridan's expectations may have become two entirely different things. Thelvyn had thought of himself as a defender without political ties, his duty to the king nothing more than a matter of running messages and acting as a diplomatic arbiter during a time in his life when there was little call for his primary duty as the Dragonlord. Now he had to admit that, intentionally or not, the king had been using the prestige of the Dragonlord to persuade and subtly intimidate his neighbors.

The Highlands had certainly prospered in the past five years. Other nations had deferred to Jherridan, and Thelvyn now began to wonder if he had been too inexperienced to realize that they might be fearful of being excluded from the protection that the Dragonlord gave them from the attacks of the rogue dragons.

It wasn't his place to judge whether or not war with Alphatia was a good or necessary thing, but he did have a duty to be certain that neither the dragons nor the Dragonlord became involved. The fate of the dragons, whatever it might be, was such a volatile matter that the involvement of either himself or the dragons could easily spell disaster. He had to be certain that he wasn't becoming too involved in these matters.

Kharendaen broke through the cloud cover at last, moving through a wild landscape of deep canyons and towering peaks of dense storms. Thelvyn could see that they were very high indeed, perhaps as high as they had ever flown together. He waited a minute more for the dragon to dry out in the wind after her passage through the clouds, then teleported out of his armor. The air this high was cold and thin, so thin that most folk couldn't have endured it for long. The fact that Thelvyn didn't find it much of a bother proved that he had come from a remarkable race indeed. Even dragons preferred not to stay at such a high altitude for very long.

Kharendaen glanced back at him briefly. "You seem in a hurry to return home."

"I have something important to think about," he answered. "I've discovered something that I never anticipated, but which I should have expected."

"Then I suspect that I know what the problem must be."

"A most astute dragon," Thelvyn commented. "And why are *you* in such a hurry to return home?"

She glanced back a second time. "I am a gold, a dragon of the mountains and the northern lands. Warm, wet weather penetrates inside my armor."

It was a rather succinct way of admitting that she had been literally itching to leave. Thelvyn had heard a good deal about dragon "scales," yet all the dragons he had ever met were in fact protected by large plates, like hardened leather armor.

The thought led to other misconceptions about dragons. Kharendaen never talked much about her past or about how most dragons lived, having once explained to him that there were many secrets that she could not yet reveal. Even so, Thelvyn knew enough to be aware that the image of a dragon sleeping in a cavern amid its hoard, coming out only to feed and pillage and to do battle with an occasional hero was a rather simplistic notion. Only the renegade dragons—mad, violent creatures who were forced to exist in exile from all other dragons—lived that way. Thelvyn had been required to fight half a dozen renegades since becoming the Dragonlord, according to the terms of his truce with the dragons, and Kharendaen had been his companion in battle each time.

Still, he was aware that the dragons possessed a vast, ancient, and complex civilization, with a history of collected wisdom stretching back into the depths of time. They had been ancient even before the coming of the first nation of men or elves. They had faced destruction once before, long ago, in the time of the first Dragonlord during the age of Blackmoor, and Thelvyn had no idea how they had fared during the Rain of Fire and the destruction of Blackmoor. But he was determined that they should not face destruction again, and they were already in a desperate state over the apparent disappearance of the Great One, their only patron Immortal. Thelvyn knew something that even most dragons did not—that the Great One was not gone but had only withdrawn for a time as a part of a greater plan known only to himself.

Thelvyn was fearful of what would happen when the Great One either failed to return or decided to set his plans into motion. Although he was only guessing, Thelvyn suspected that the real reason he had been made Dragonlord was to protect the dragons, even from themselves, during what would surely be a very dangerous time for them. And he was certainly not about to allow Jherridan Maarsten or the Wizards of the Flaem or anyone else to involve them in some war in which they had no part.

His thoughts came back to the hidden identity of his own patron. For five years, he had been trying to figure out which one of the Immortals would find the Great One's secret plans for the destiny of the dragons important enough to become so deeply involved. His research into the matter had only shown him that there were many more Immortals than he had ever suspected, many of whom apparently had no cleric followers. Some apparently hadn't involved themselves in the affairs of the mortal world for centuries, and may have even gone on to other worlds and planes.

With such thoughts to occupy him, Thelvyn discovered that they were home again sooner than he expected. Kharendaen descended into the court just past midafternoon, and Thelvyn hurried to help her out of her saddle. The dragon stretched from her long neck to the end of her tail, then lumbered slowly toward the door of the warehouse.

"Do you mind if I join you for dinner?" Thelvyn asked.

She looked back over her shoulder. "Dinner? How romantic!"

"There is something that I need to talk about," he explained quickly.

Although she had implied no criticism, Thelvyn still felt guilty for not spending more time with her. She endured a good deal for the sake of her duty to the Dragonlord, not the least of which was being exiled from companionship and conversation with other dragons. Her older brother, Marthaen, had once told him that Kharendaen, as a senior cleric of the Great One, was loved by all dragons. Thelvyn didn't know anything else about her friends or family, even whether she had left a mate for the sake of her present service. Dragons of legend were said to be fiercely solitary, but he had often found legend to be inaccurate on many points.

He could understand her loneliness very well, for it was something he shared. He had been raised as a ward of the village of Graez when his mother had died within an hour of his birth, leaving him an orphan of unknown race and origin. His features were vaguely elvish, yet he was too tall and powerful of build to have been an elf, taller even than most men. He had black hair and large, dark eyes, which were blue where they should have been white, although most people failed to notice that oddity.

There had always been a possibility that he was a half-elf, since he obviously was neither human nor elf but seemed to possess the best qualities of both races. Of course, there was no certainty that he was indeed a half-elf, especially considering the fact that no such thing had ever been known to exist. There remained the possibility that he was descended from the lost race of Blackmoor, which might explain his being chosen to be the heir of the Dragonlord. His mother had died when he was born, and she had spoken no known language, so she had been unable to tell anyone of his true heritage. Thelvyn suspected that the true story of his origin would remain a mystery until he was finally reunited with his own people. He didn't expect that to happen any time soon.

Thelvyn wished Sir George were there to advise him, but the old knight had been gone for weeks now and was unlikely to return soon. Now that his responsibilities as Dragonlord were again becoming more pressing, he found that he missed his old friends more than ever. Sir George still shared Thelvyn's large house in a wealthy neighborhood of Braejr, but the old knight was on the road most of the time. Solveig White-Gold was now more Sir George's partner than merely a hired sword, although she hardly ever came to the Highlands but held up her share of the business from Sir George's residence in Darokin. Korinn had long since returned home to attend to his duties as King Daroban's younger son, but Thelvyn's responsibilities took him to Rockhome periodically, and so he saw the young dwarf fairly frequently.

Despite the absence of so many of his longtime friends, Thelvyn didn't lack for either companionship or guidance. Kharendaen had been his friend and advisor for as long as she had been in his company. She seemed to do everything she could to be all the companion he could need. She gave her affection and devotion fully and without hesitation, as if she could never want for a better friend. He had often wondered about that, recalling that she was a dragon, a race with a fierce and aloof reputation. Completing the unlikelihood of their friendship was the fact that he was the Dragonlord, making him the most feared and hated enemy her people had ever known.

Thelvyn did not fault Kharendaen for not warning him earlier about the state of affairs between the dragons and the Alphatians. In her service as a cleric of the Great One, she had been assigned as his companion. Politically, her relationship to Thelvyn was more that of an ambassador, an intermediary between the Dragonlord and the Parliament of Dragons. Her task was to assuage the fears her people had about the Dragonlord. She was obliged to keep her secrets, and Thelvyn had never expected nor wanted her to betray her own kind. Indeed, his impression had been that she may have transgressed the bounds of her trust with the dragons in telling him what she had.

The cook had dinner prepared for them shortly after they returned, including a haunch of venison from the market. Like all dragons, Kharendaen preferred elk. Since there had not been time for her to hunt since her return, she had no opportunity to indulge her taste for her favorite food. Thelvyn's own dinner was brought out to the table kept for him in Kharendaen's lair, while the dragon reclined in her bed of immense leather cushions.

"Your visit to Thyatis seems to worry you, but you have not yet spoken to me of what you learned," Kharendaen said after several minutes.

"It's very much what you seemed to expect," Thelvyn told her. "Captain Darius witnessed an attack by a band of dragons upon a fleet of Alphatian warships. They seemed to search the ships before sinking them. Darius recovered quite a few survivors, who said that the dragons have been harassing the larger Alphatian settlements in the north for some time now, although they either did not or pretended not to understand why."

"I did not know that the issue had become an open conflict," Kharendaen said. "I have been aware of the situation, so I was able to guess the nature of the trouble when we first received the summons to Thyatis."

"You do not need to explain yourself to me," Thelvyn insisted. "I'm aware that you are often caught in a difficult position due to your conflict of duties to myself, the Great One, and your own people. I've always been willing to allow the dragons to keep their secrets, and I wouldn't ask you to betray your confidence to others no matter how desperate the situation."

"I appreciate that," she assured him. "But to speak candidly, I am rather annoyed with the parliament for their failure to include me in their confidence in this matter, knowing how volatile the situation could be. Even if they are right, the dragons cannot expect to go to war without dire consequences. If they expect me to protect them from the wrath of the Dragonlord, they must keep me informed of such things."

"I told Emperor Cornelius that I believe that the dragons have been provoked into this war," Thelvyn continued. "Considering how unpopular the Alphatians are, he was willing to accept the fact that the Alphatians are only getting what they deserve. I told him that I am inclined to stay out of it and allow the dragons to solve their own differences with the Alphatians, provided their vengeance is not unjustly extreme and the war is not likely to expand into other lands."

"Perhaps that would be best," Kharendaen agreed. "I expect Marthaen will handle the matter swiftly and justly."

Thelvyn nodded. "I'm sure that the dragons won't want to continue this conflict any longer than they must. I'm aware that they don't want to be involved with the outside world, if for no other reason than to protect their secrets. But I'm still concerned about the fear that could result when others begin to learn that the dragons have gone to war. I feel I need to send you to speak with your brother. You can tell him everything that I've spoken about to you. I don't expect him to reveal any of the secrets of the dragons, but I do need assurances from him about the intentions of the dragons, so that I can relate those assurances to others if I must to maintain the truce. Explain to him that I am doing this for the sake of the dragons, to protect them from undeserved retribution."

"That is fair."

"You might remind him discreetly that the dragons violated the truce in going to war without consulting me," he added. "I don't expect Marthaen to answer for that. I only wish to remind him of the wisdom of avoiding possible misunderstandings. If the dragons have a just complaint with anyone, I am required by the terms of our truce to take their part, and I am still willing to do anything I can for them."

Kharendaen looked doubtful. "I do not think that the dragons are ready to take you so fully into their confidence."

"No, I don't expect they are," Thelvyn agreed. "I just want them to understand that I will be supportive of them when they have been wronged. I need to build all the trust I can between myself and the dragons, and in this case, I thought it best not to interfere in their affairs."

"Then I will depart in the morning," she said, shaking her head when he seemed about to protest. "I will be rested, and the matter is urgent."

"More urgent than you may know," he told her. "Jherridan might finally get his alliance against Alphatia. Cornelius immediately saw the possibility that the trouble the Alphatians are having with the dragons could leave them vulnerable to invasion. If that happens, the best thing that Marthaen and I could do is to insure that the dragons are not involved. While you are away, I'll be busy making certain Jherridan understands my position in this matter."

"What do you mean?" Kharendaen asked, cocking her head inquisitively.

"I had an informal talk with Emperor Cornelius," he explained. "The sum of it all is this: I had always assumed that King Jherridan had little hope of finding foreign support for his war against Alphatia, and that my errands on that matter were wasted. Now I'm told that Thyatis would be supportive of such an effort. More than that, Cornelius says that he and I together could gather the necessary forces if we were to ask for support."

"The Dragonlord commands a high degree of respect," she said.

"And a certain degree of fear," Thelvyn added. "I've always been determined that Jherridan will not get his way, either with his own people or with foreign leaders, by using me. However, I never considered that there is an implied threat, that others might be concerned I might withhold my protection from the rogue dragons from any land that does not defer to the Highland king. The matter is hardly relevant. Whether war with Alphatia is desirable or not, I honestly feel I dare not involve myself. I am certainly not about to ask for the support of the Nation of Dragons."

Kharendaen made a derisive noise through her long nose. "If Jherridan tries to involve the dragons, he will find trouble that makes his complaint with Alphatia look tame."

Thelvyn shook his head. "That's not the problem. What does concern me is the terms of my duty to Jherridan, or, more precisely, what the king has come to expect of my duty. I'm afraid a large part of the blame must be my own. Perhaps I've tried entirely too hard these last five years to prove the loyalty I promised when I accepted Jherridan's offer to bring me here. Now I'm no longer certain just what he might think he can reasonably ask of me. The only thing that I can say in my defense is that a great deal of power and importance was thrust upon me without warning, and I was never prepared for such a life. The good villagers who raised me expected to make a smith of me."

Kharendaen nodded. "Stating your own position firmly and holding to it is the best answer for a variety of problems. You have not said so, but your concerns imply that you suspect Jherridan will try to involve you deeper in this affair than you can allow. What I wonder is whether I should warn the dragons of this, with the understanding that we only suspect that the king may wish to involve them in his war with Alphatia."

"There is one other point I have to keep in mind," Thelvyn added. "I can't forget for one minute those weasely Fire Wizards. You can be sure they'll be scheming and plotting something to suit their own desires and ends. They want power for the king, they want it for themselves, they want to destroy the Alphatians, and they want a Flaemish empire. I'll have to be careful that Kalestraan isn't filling the king full of ideas about what I or the dragons could do for him."

Kharendaen departed early the next morning, leaving Thelvyn with the promise that she would return as soon as possible. He suspected she meant to have some very stern words with her brother Marthaen about his failure to inform either the Dragonlord or herself before the dragons had undertaken actions that might have vast and dire consequences. Thelvyn meant to go to the palace early that morning to speak privately with the king before the day's business began. He hoped Mage Kalestraan wasn't there to meddle in matters meant to remain between the Dragonlord and the king.

The archduke's palace was a sprawling structure of cold gray stone on the western side of the city. Indeed, like the School of Magic on the east side of Braejr, its massive back wall formed a long portion of the outer city wall. Like most other Flaemish designs, it was solid, functional, and rather plain compared to the palaces and mansions of other lands. The larger halls and chambers were located in the center of the palace, where the main doors opened from the enclosed court. The king's private residence and chambers for the aides, officials, and servants who dwelled within the palace were located on either side, along with suites for visiting dignitaries.

Thelvyn had hardly stepped inside the door when he was intercepted. The archduke's own valet, Taeryn, a young boy with the deep red hair of his Flaemish ancestors, had obviously been waiting to greet him. The boy was barely in his teens, eager to please and possessing an openness and lack of duplicity that reminded Thelvyn rather uncomfortably of himself when he was younger. Such simplicity was a welcome delight in a personal servant, but it could be a fatal shortcoming in the Dragonlord.

"The archduke sends his greetings," Taeryn began, the usual polite introduction to the verbal correspondence he bore. "He begs you to come to his private chamber as quickly as you can."

They moved quietly along the wall, avoiding the crowd that already thronged the entrance hall. Soon they came to the corridor leading north into the private residences. Taeryn hurried along, his boots echoing through the empty passageway. His pace would have been far too quick for the dignity of most of the lords and wizards of the realm, but he knew that Thelvyn wasn't concerned about such things.

Taeryn led him directly to the archduke's private chamber and opened the door for him. The room was large, paneled in dark wood with many bookcases, with a massive desk for the archduke and chairs for his visitors. Maarsten wasn't there, but the senior Fire Wizard, Byen Kalestraan, was seated in one corner reading his spellbook. Like all wizards, he was required to spend every free moment consigning his spells to memory.

The Dragonlord hesitated for a moment as he entered. He couldn't forget that Kalestraan had conspired to send Thelvyn and his companions to what had seemed certain death, giving them a false artifact of power to use against the dragons. Yet politics now dictated that he must pretend such an event had never occurred. He took one of the other chairs, almost far enough away from the wizard to be impolite.

"The archduke says to tell you he will be here very soon," Taeryn insisted, bowing respectfully to the wizard. "Is there anything I might get for you, Master?"

"Thank you, no, lad," Kalestraan said kindly, much to Thelvyn's surprise.

Taeryn bowed once more before he withdrew and closed the door carefully. In the next moment, the echo of his boots could be heard running along the stone floor of the hall. The wizard paused to listen before he looked down at his book with a fond smile. Then he glanced quickly at the Dragonlord, as if he were embarrassed to have been caught entertaining a kind thought.

"You shake things up rather badly around here when you take off like that without explaining yourself," Kalestraan began sternly. "Under the circumstances, I hesitate to say that I hope that you haven't worried us for nothing."

"The dragons are at war," Thelvyn told him plainly, to satisfy his own curiosity about how the wizard would react. "But it seems that they're only defending themselves, and I'm not inclined to interfere."

"But no one can hope to fight dragons . . ." Kalestraan began, looking confused and even a little frightened.

"The Alphatians are invading their land."

That caused the wizard to fall silent. The prospect of the dragons going to war was a frightening one, and Thelvyn was encouraged to see that even Kalestraan recognized that, even though the Fire Wizards had used dragon attacks as a part of their political ploys in the past. The thought that the Alphatians might be getting trounced by anyone was appealing to anyone of Flaemish descent. At that moment, the door opened, and they both glanced up as the king entered.

"So there you are," Jherridan said as he hurried to his desk, obviously eager for news of Thelvyn's journey. "Your message was rather vague."

"I had no idea of what the problem was myself until I arrived there," Thelvyn said.

He quickly explained what he knew of the war between the dragons and Alphatia. He also repeated Emperor Cornelius's speculations about the possibility of an alliance against Alphatia. He would rather have left out any mention of that last part, knowing how eagerly both the king and Kalestraan would leap upon such a possibility, but he thought it best to make them aware of his position on the subject from the first. The wizard sat motionless in his chair and listened in silence, almost as if he found none of this alarming or surprising. But Jherridan grew increasing excited; he began to pace nervously in his growing enthusiasm.

"Of course, Cornelius was only speculating about such possibilities," Thelvyn reminded them both pointedly. "He gave me this message, which he wished for me to relate to you. He says that Thyatis is already committed to containing the expansion of the Alphatian Empire. Alphatia's own aggressions require that of Thyatis, for the reason of their own security if for no other. If other nations were willing to commit their strength to a war against Alphatia, then Thyatis is willing to join such an effort. But he wishes to remind you that he is not willing to make war against Alphatia simply because of hatred, and by no means will he be a part in the utter destruction of the Alphatian race."

Kalestraan looked offended at that statement of conditional support, but the king apparently found it agreeable and nodded. "That is fair enough of him."

"I must disagree," the wizard interrupted. "War with Alphatia is a cause of the highest honor, and I wish his commitment were more complete. I cannot believe that it is wise to trust an ally who is not willing to give his absolute loyalty."

Jherridan remained unconcerned. "I can appreciate that Cornelius does not want to commit himself to leaping into an invasion of Alphatia unless he is certain that the dragons have weakened them enough to leave them vulnerable. A man who speaks his mind is telling the truth."

"But why would his commitment be less than absolute?" Kalestraan asked. "I must insist that we know whether Thyatis or any other ally fears Alphatia, for such fear may undermine their support at some desperate time."

"That is expecting more of your allies than you expect of yourself," Thelvyn said. "I was under the impression that your reason for fighting the Alphatians in the first place is that you have reason to fear them. Otherwise you have no just complaint with them. Keep in mind that, to some degree, Thyatis has been at war with Alphatia for centuries before your people even came into this world."

Kalestraan looked at him as if he were a child who had spoken out of turn; his expression was more of surprise than anger. Still, Thelvyn was determined that he would not allow the wizard to force him to consider himself wrong or out of place.

"That is fairly stated, I must agree," the king said. "Did Cornelius have anything to add, rather than just a general statement of intent?"

"There are certain practical matters that concern him," Thelvyn added. "When we discussed it later that night, he pointed out that if a combined force of allied nations should gain control of Alphatian lands, then we must determine in advance just who will then claim those territories. He said that fighting Alphatia together is one thing, but we must not fight among ourselves."

"The Alphatians are our ancient enemies," Kalestraan

declared immediately. "Their lands and property rightly belong to us."

"That would be asking a great deal of our allies," Jherridan replied. "I've considered the matter myself, and I already came to the conclusion that the problem of what to do with Alphatian territory is almost as complex as knowing how to defeat them in the first place. We cannot hold a nation as large as Alphatia ourselves, and I would never expect our allies to simply give it to us. My proposal would be that an allied force would continue to manage the Alphatian holdings in trust for the foreseeable future."

The wizard looked perplexed. "What would be the value of that? I say we should take the most we can and hold it ourselves."

Jherridan made a hopeless gesture. "I cannot ignore that we happen to be the weakest nation of the west in military terms. We can't very well hold any part of Alphatia from here. But if Alphatia is open to us, would we necessarily want to stay here? As long as no one else is claiming Alphatia, we can begin to quietly send groups of settlers to establish colonies before anyone else is aware of it. That seems to be our best hope to claim Alphatia as our own."

Thelvyn elected to say nothing; he had always known that the Flaem were a scheming lot, often as impractical in their schemes as they were grandiose. He even wondered if it might actually be a good thing to have the Flaem and the Alphatians move in with each other. Then they could proceed to destroy each other without involving the rest of the world, although he still doubted that matters would ever proceed that far.

"Well, that's getting ahead of ourselves a bit," Jherridan continued as he began pacing the chamber. "Right now I'm most concerned about acquiring allies who will help us in our war with Alphatia. Did Emperor Cornelius have anything to say about that?"

"As a matter of fact, he did," Thelvyn said, choosing his words carefully. "He relayed what is possibly some very encouraging news in that regard. He believes that his influence would be enough to encourage several other nations to join the alliance against Alphatia. He said nothing about actually doing so, but I doubt that he would have said it if he weren't considering it seriously."

"That is encouraging," the king agreed. "I wonder if we might be able to exercise any influence of our own. . . . I don't flatter myself that I am held in especially high esteem in other lands, but the Dragonlord is."

Thelvyn tried to hide his immediate sense of guilt. It was time for him to take a stand, but he realized now that he had been hoping to avoid this issue.

"I suppose that I do command considerable influence," he answered guardedly. "The problem is that I don't dare use my influence for the wrong reasons. As the Dragonlord, I have a responsibility only to the dragons and to making certain that they keep the truce. I don't dare let the dragons get out of hand or do anything that might upset them. You must recall how desperate we were five years ago when it seemed that there was nothing we could do to save ourselves."

"Yes . . . I remember that entirely too well," Jherridan agreed. "Are you telling me that your involvement in a war with Alphatia could upset your own balance of trust with the dragons?"

"That's exactly the point," Thelvyn agreed. "Like it or not, the dragons are a greater danger than Alphatia could ever be. At least you would have a chance against the Alphatians."

Mage Kalestraan was immediately suspicious. "Are these your own opinions, or are you just letting the dragons frighten you?"

"Kharendaen has agreed that I must not become involved," Thelvyn insisted. "I consider her opinion on this matter one to be respected."

"I must agree," Jherridan said thoughtfully. "I understand the importance of your position, and I dare not interfere. Therefore, that is all to be said on the matter."

Kalestraan looked dissatisfied, but he said nothing. For his part, Thelvyn felt relieved that it had gone so easily. Apparently the king really did understand the importance of Thelvyn's duty as the Dragonlord, as long as he was reminded from time to time. Mage Kalestraan obviously did not understand, but Thelvyn had expected that. Even during the time of the dragon raids, the wizard had been willing to use any tool or ploy that might work to his advantage, no matter how dangerous the consequences.

Kalestraan rose and bowed low. "If you will forgive me, I really must be getting back to the Academy. I am sure the two of you can make sense of this matter without me."

Thelvyn thought that Kalestraan sounded rather put out with the situation, which had not gone quite as he wound have preferred. But he was trying very hard to conceal his annoyance, and King Jherridan seemed not to notice. He was consulting a map that hung over the mantel, no doubt contemplating each of the nations of the west and whether Thyatian influence might draw them into the alliance. Thelvyn waited in silence, even after the wizard had gone. He wasn't used to exercising political influence, much less winning his point in debate. This round had been easier than he had expected, but he knew better than to think that future conflicts would be as easy.

"Well, that is encouraging," Jherridan said at last. "Now I wonder what we should do next."

"I'm not sure, but I should think that the next move is up to Emperor Cornelius," Thelvyn ventured. "I'm sure there isn't very much you can do to encourage him to make up his mind, and I know that it wouldn't be wise to try to pressure him. Cornelius is a clever and subtle man, but very open and direct for a man of such power."

Jherridan smiled. "If you're discreetly trying to tell me not to try to bully or manipulate this man, I will consider myself warned. Frankly, my thoughts are aimed in quite another direction just now. I was thinking that, as the king of the Flaemish Realm, I bear a certain responsibility to our allies to do more than merely shout and plead for war with Alphatia and then sit back and allow our new friends do our fighting. You have carried diplomatic messages on such matter for me in the past. Has such an accusation been made?"

"Not to me," Thelvyn said. "But I daresay that some of our would-be allies must have considered it. I myself have wondered just what the Flaem could actually contribute besides a token presence."

"We must think of something," the king said. "To speak practically, for the sake of our own honor and prestige and to prove our willingness to fight this battle, we must do something to prove our usefulness. There must be something we can do that will either make the efforts of our own forces more effective or else leave the Alphatians more vulnerable to attack."

"The Alphatians are your ancient enemies," Thelvyn reminded him. "Perhaps the time has come to send your wizards to search through all of your old books. Just don't, for pity's sake, let them do anything that might destroy this world. It would also be useful if those wizards could find some way of keeping the Alphatians from doing the same."

"You needn't be overly concerned about that," Jherridan explained. "Much of our more powerful magic was lost in the time of exile. That's why the Fire Wizards assembled that great library of theirs, to try to rebuild some of their former power. I suspect that the Air Wizards of the Alphatians must find themselves in much the same situation. So far they've used only the most simple of magical weapons in their conquests. I know how hungry they've been for power, and I believe that they would have used any weapon they had."

"That's a great relief to me," Thelvyn admitted. "Aside from my duty as Dragonlord, I have no wish to participate in events that might lead to such great destruction."

Jherridan laughed. "I hope you trust me to have better sense than that. My complaint with the Alphatians is not so great that I want to see them destroyed at any cost. My first duty is to the protection of my people."

Thelvyn said nothing more, but he was somewhat reassured to hear that. He had lived among the Flaem all his life, and he knew just how obsessed they were about their hatred of the Alphatians. In truth, he had always suspected they would do anything to defeat their ancient enemy. He had already known that they didn't possess very dangerous powers. If they had been able to command such magic, they would have certainly used it during their desperate battle with the dragons five years ago.

CHAPTER THREE

Pale morning sunlight was beginning to color the sea far to the east, but the encircling walls of the Alphatian stronghold would remain in the shadows for some time yet. The Alphatians had built the largest of their hidden strongholds on the shore of a small bay, in the shape of a horseshoe with its narrow inlet facing northeast. The bay was sheltered and deep enough for ships to come right up to the newly laid stone piers. Large portions next to the natural cliff lining the bay had been enclosed in grey stone quarried from the nearby mountains, the deep caves of the cliffs serving as chambers and cool storage rooms. A massive chain could be drawn across the entrance of the bay, forbidding the passage of enemy ships.

Farmlands had been cleared in the fields and meadows above the bay, although most of the folk who had come to live in that cold, desolate land harvested timbers to feed Alphatia's insatiable need for ships. Shipwrights worked in the shelter of the large caverns along the bay, sliding the finished hulls out onto the beach for fitting before they were launched into the icy water and sailed away to their homeland in the east. At any time, even in the dead of the long, bitter winter, no fewer than two dozen ships were under construction, ranging from round-bellied merchantmen to long, sleek galleys for the Imperial Navy.

Norwold had suddenly, albeit secretly, become an important part of the Alphatian holdings because of the abundance of timber in the ancient forests and the rich ores to be mined from the mountains. The settlements were fortified and heavily defended strongholds. The Alphatians had worked hard to firmly establish their colonies before the inevitable day when the hated Thyatians discovered their work and contested this new incursion on the continent of Brun.

Given time, the Norwold settlements could supply the wealth of material needed to support Alphatian conquests farther south, drawing in the Northern Reaches and the Heldannic lands to form a new Alphatian protectorate. The empire would finally possess a firm hold on the mainland, next drawing in the Steppes before finally crushing the despised Flaem far to the west. Darokin, Rockhome, Alfheim, and Traladara would each fall in turn, forming a ring of conquest that would leave Thyatis cut off like an island.

The one thing they had never counted upon in all their carefully laid plans was that the seemingly empty lands they claimed belonged to an enemy they had never anticipated and in fact had never yet seen, an enemy infinitely stronger and more dangerous than they.

Marthaen crouched in the hills above the stronghold, watching patiently as the dragons crept into position. The Alphatians were not to be caught completely unprepared. Dragons had been attacking lesser settlements and ships all that spring, so the Alphatians in Norwold had known they were under siege for some time now. Marthaen had his own purposes in destroying one of the major holdings, mostly to prove just how dangerous and determined the dragons were but also perhaps as a means to get the Alphatians to talk.

He turned to Jherdar, who was also watching over the

top of the hill. "We might as well wake them up. Lead your dragons around and create a diversion. When the wizards raise their defenses, I will lead our own sorcerers against them."

The red dragon nodded. "We will keep them occupied."

Jherdar drew back, then turned and withdrew into the dark forests behind them. Marthaen watched him for a moment until he became invisible among the thick stand of trees. He would have expected Jherdar to be wild and fierce, eager and impatient for the destruction of their enemies. Instead, the leader of the red dragons had been subdued, even deferential, since the theft of the Collar of the Dragons that previous winter. Jherdan had apparently recognized that this was not merely a fight but a war, something almost beyond the experience of the dragons and something they had never done particularly well. The big red dragon was always ready for a battle, but he knew that he was dependent upon Marthaen to guide him in finding the wisest course of action.

Only a few short minutes passed before Jherdar and a score of young red dragons began their diversion. They flew in low over the waves, hurtling as swiftly as they could fly along the coast before turning sharply and sweeping down within the circle of the small bay. Although they were relatively few in number, the dragons seemed to fill the sky like an invading army as they darted back and forth in a quick, unrelenting attack. For the moment, they ignored the two small galleys tied up at the main pier, turning their flames against the newly constructed ships lining the beach awaiting their final fitting. Next they directed their flames against the flat stone walls of the outer face of the stronghold itself, but to no effect. The doors and shutters of the windows, made of stout timbers lined with sheets of bronze, were meant to keep out the fierce cold of the northern winter.

But this first assault was only a feint. Scouts had been watching the Alphatian settlement for some time, and the dragons knew that wizards had arrived from their distant homeland to help with the defense of their colonies. The Air Wizards needed a brief time to prepare themselves before they could summon the full strength of their defenses. After several minutes, the gentle sea breezes grew quickly into a fierce gale, whipping the water of the bay into a storm-tossed spray of mist. The terrible winds began to converge over the center of the bay, forming swiftly into a great vortex that expanded outward until it formed a wall encircling the ring of the bay, raising with it a sheet of sea-water whipped into a fine mist.

The dragons tried to escape while they could, but the winds were too fierce for them to fly through, threatening to snap their wings and sweep them away. The curtain of water had frozen into tiny splinters of ice, as sharp as knives. Far above, the encircling winds drew inward, eventually enclosing the entire bay within a great cyclone. The attacking dragons dived at the wall of spinning ice, raking it with their flames, but the magical winds were so swift that the wall of ice instantly resealed itself.

While Jherdar's young reds kept the Alphatian defenders distracted, scores of dragons moved stealthfully out of the shadowed forests into the open lands on the cliffs above the bay, watching and waiting patiently. In their company were several of the largest and oldest dragons to be found in Windreach, among the most powerful of all dragon sorcerers and possibly the most powerful masters of magic in the world.

Once they were ready, the dragon sorcerers joined their wills and magic into a single entity under Marthaen's control. They began cautiously at first, exploring the spells of the Air Wizards, beginning with only the lightest and most elusive touch but then with increasing authority as they came to understand what they faced. A spell such as the defense being used by the Air Wizards needed constant tending, and that power could not only be followed back to its source, but also turned back upon itself. Dragon magic was more like that of the Immortals, offering their sorcerers the ability to accomplish things that other wizards did not dream possible.

A new battle began for the possession of the stronghold, an unseen battle of magic and will. Marthaen had been impressed at first by the skill and power of the Air Wizards, but after all, they were only mortals. Like all folk who tried to measure themselves against dragons, they were vastly overmatched. Once Marthaen had explored and understood the web of magic the Alphatians had raised to enclose their settlement, he summoned the will of his companions to wrest control of their magic away from the Air Wizards. The struggle was brief and the end inevitable as Marthaen seized command of his foe's own magic. He did not break the spell but sent it hurtling like lightning back at the Air Wizards. Within minutes, most of the Alphatian wizards were slain by the powerful blast of the counterspell.

With the magical defenses stymied, the wall of wind began to break apart, scattering a deadly hail of the splintered ice in all directions. The dragons had anticipated this and kept close to the ground until the deadly hail ceased. Then they moved swiftly to the attack before the Alphatian defenders could regroup. Marthaen leaped into the air with long, powerful strokes of his wings, circling around tightly as he descended swiftly into the center of the small bay. Jherdar and the first group of warriors were just ahead of him, directing their fury against the central portion of the Alphatian stronghold. They landed on the piers and, standing upright on their hind legs, employed the powerful whip of their tails to batter the stones of the fortress before using their foreclaws to rip it apart. The dragons belched blasts of flame through the openings, sending archers and pikemen scattering.

Finally Marthaen himself landed on the main pier. Standing on his hind legs, the gold dragon was an immense and majestic vision of terror to the Alphatian defenders. Slowly, ponderously, he approached the double main doors of the stronghold, then reached over his shoulder to draw the massive sword he wore between his wings. The blade glittered in the stark brilliance of the morning light, a twin-edged length of bright steel as long as three men. The other dragons paused momentarily in their destruction, turning to watch their leader in cold expectation. The only sounds were the snapping and crackling of burning timbers.

Then Marthaen lifted his great sword in both front claws and swung it with all his tremendous strength against the main entrance to the fortress. The massive timbers shattered in an explosion of sound as the iron bands that had supported them twisted and snapped, leaving the ruined doors hanging loosely upon broken hinges. Marthaen bent his long neck to peer inside the wrecked doorway. Alphatian defenders now drew back fearfully from the gaze of his glittering eyes.

"Send forth your leader!" he boomed.

A tall man in armor of leather and steel stepped out to face the mighty dragon. The Alphatian warrior did not lack for courage, even though he now confronted what was surely to him the most terrifying of all nightmare visions. Marthaen stepped back as the proud soldier came to the shattered doorway.

"I am Marthaen, the lord of dragons," he proclaimed. "Remember me well. Before we complete the destruction of this settlement, I will grant you a brief time to escape in the ships that we have spared. If any dare to return to this place, they will be destroyed as well."

"I will not refuse your compassionate offer," the warrior answered, "but I am curious why you allow us to escape."

"My intention is not to destroy you, but to drive all your people from these lands," Marthaen said. "The dragons will not accept any less. If your leaders wish to parley for a truce, then you know what we demand of them. They must not expect that we can be convinced to accept anything less. Otherwise, when we are done here, we will continue our attacks upon Alphatian ships at sea and any other settlements and eventually bring the conflict to your own lands."

"You apparently have some bitter complaint that I do not understand."

"That is not your concern," Marthaen told him. "Tell your leaders that the dragons demand all that belongs to them, and we will see if they understand. Leave now."

The Alphatians needed no further encouragement. Without pausing to collect their treasures or even many supplies, they laid down their weapons and filed out from the burning stronghold. Taking stock of the numbers of the settlers, the dragons pushed out a pair of seaworthy hulls from where they were still being fitted on the beach, pulling the ships by ropes over to the pier. The farmers and craftsmen were loaded into these ships, which were towed behind the two galleys. The surviving soldiers and many of the shipwrights addressed themselves to the oars, hauling the small fleet out of the bay and into the open sea as quickly as they could.

After the ships had departed, Marthaen withdrew to the end of the main pier, leaving the final destruction of the settlement to the younger dragons. The battle had ended sooner than he had anticipated, and there had been more survivors than he had expected. He was secretly glad that the dragons continued to be subservient to his will by permitting so many of their enemies to escape.

"Do you believe that the Alphatians will be prepared to parley after this?" Jherdar asked, stepping out onto the pier to join him.

"I do not expect it," Marthaen admitted. "They will probably need to think about it for some time, which is why I am making my demands clear now."

"Then we will continue our attacks on their ships and settlements?"

"That is the best way I know to encourage them," he said, then glanced up as he saw a young gold dragon circling down swiftly toward him. He sighed as he saw that it was Kharendaen. "Please excuse me. A storm approaches that I must somehow endure."

"Then I take leave to seek my own shelter," Jherdar said, glancing over his shoulder cautiously. There were few dragons he feared, but he had a deep respect for the young cleric.

Marthaen wished he could have fled as well, but he knew an accounting was due. Indeed, he was well aware that the matter was better handled sooner than later, before the dragons were trapped by their own actions into consequences they did not foresee. Kharendaen landed on the pier like an eagle descending upon its prey. Quickly she folded her wings, then paused a moment to glance about at the destruction surrounding her. Dragons were busy pulling apart the burning wreckage of the settlement, and dark smoke poured from the caves where ships had been assembled and timbers stored.

"I looked for you at Windreach," Kharendaen said at last as she approached her brother. "They told me that you were teaching the dragons to make war."

"I am not prepared to argue the matter," he replied, standing firm. "We are well within the rights granted to us by our truce with the Dragonlord. You know the circumstances well enough to understand that."

"I am not arguing your *right* to make war," she told him sharply, arching her neck in a fierce gesture. "I am arguing the *wisdom* of going to war without discussing the matter with the Dragonlord to insure there will be no misunderstandings. And without warning me. You left me with a monstrous problem. I had to answer for your actions, even though I could only guess what you were doing."

"And so the Dragonlord has sent you to demand an accounting?" Marthaen asked.

"Actually, he is willing to be more generous with you than I am," she answered. "He is prepared to be understanding, but you must realize that you have also placed him in a difficult position. If the Alphatians should ask him to defend them from your attacks, he has to know they are at fault before he can refuse them."

Marthaen looked uncomfortable with that. "I feared from the first that we would be unable to completely protect our secrets."

"The Thyatians learned of your attacks upon the Alphatians," Kharendaen continued. "Others will also be hearing of the news by now, and the thought of the dragons going to war with anyone is a frightful concern to them. They want assurances from the Dragonlord, and for that, he must have certain assurances from you. He is prepared to consider this a matter between the dragons and the Alphatians, as long as you can explain your intentions. He needs to know about the extent of the war you propose to make, and how long he can expect it to last. He needs to be able to assure others that your war will not involve them."

"That is fair enough," Marthaen agreed. "You can tell

the Dragonlord that I will come to speak with him myself in a few days."

* * * * *

Kharendaen needed only a few short moments to prepare herself for the short predawn flight from Braejr to the mountains east of the city. She slipped into her dragon saddle, settling it over the short plates of her crest at the base of her neck and buckling the straps about her neck. As he watched, Thelvyn reflected with wry amusement that one advantage of a dragon over a horse was that a dragon could saddle itself. He opened both doors of the warehouse that served as Kharendaen's lair so she could slip through. Then she crouched in the center of the open court while he climbed into the saddle. Although the morning was somewhat cool, he didn't think he would need to wear the armor of the Dragonlord. He could teleport into it in an instant simply if need be.

Kharendaen leaped into the air with a thrust of her powerful hind legs, climbing slowly into the morning sky with long sweeps of her broad wings. Once she got up to speed, she settled into a more relaxed flight, rising steadily as she headed north over the city before turning eastward to pass over the Aalban River and on toward the distant mountains. The full sleeves of Thelvyn's shirt snapped in the wind, but the air was fresh and cool.

"What do you think?" Thelvyn called out. "Is Marthaen prepared to be reasonable? He must understand that his recent actions might result in consequences he could not desire."

Kharendaen bent her long neck to look back. "Marthaen has been ensnared in a conflict of duties. He must protect the secrets of the dragons at all costs, yet he is also the defender of the Nation of Dragons. Secrets have already been compromised, and actions he must take to protect his people will only compromise those secrets even more."

"I can appreciate his situation," Thelvyn said. "But those secrets could become too costly to protect."

"That is the decision he must now make."

They had risen so high that the morning sun suddenly lifted above the great Colossus Mounts to the east. The warm light startled Kharendaen, who had been flying with her head bent around while she climbed steadily with long, slow sweeps of her wings. For a moment, she faltered, then resumed her pace.

"That should teach me to pay better attention," she remarked, then glanced back once more. "Marthaen would not have asked to speak with you unless he has something important to say."

They were approaching the forbidding heights of the Colossus Mounts, still dark in the shadow of the morning sun, when a second gold dragon rose suddenly from the high cliffs to join them. Marthaen looked a good deal like his sister, although as the older of the two, he was somewhat larger and his face was more full. He came in close beside Kharendaen, and they flew together for a time, soaring on the cool winds of the heights. They seemed to enjoy each other's company, almost as if they were at play. Mindful of her passenger, Kharendaen refrained from the more adventurous tricks that her brother tried. Thelvyn watched them with interest, thinking once more how dull Kharendaen's life must be in his company. Dragons were meant to live free.

After a brief time, Marthaen began to circle downward toward a ledge high up on the side of a steep, rugged mountain. Kharendaen landed on the ledge beside him, folding her wings and then pausing a moment to allow Thelvyn to drop down from his saddle before she sat back up on her haunches. Thelvyn stood facing the larger dragon, who had been watching him closely. Somehow Thelvyn had the impression that Marthaen didn't approve of the company his sister was keeping.

"I have been told—rather sternly, I might add—that my actions may have placed the dragons in a difficult position," Marthaen began.

Thelvyn nodded. "I understand your need to protect your secrets, even if I do not know what those secrets are. If it helps, tell me only what I must know to understand this matter, and I will promise to keep your secrets.

Rather than repeat them to anyone else, I will simply use all the influence I have to assure others that the dragons have been acting justly and in their own defense."

Marthaen frowned. "We have guarded these secrets since the fall of Blackmoor."

"That may well be," Thelvyn said, "but just the same, if the Alphatians come crying to me to protect them from the dragons, I have to know why I should refuse them."

The gold dragon considered that for a long moment. In spite of himself, he had always liked Thelvyn, and he trusted his sister's judgment of the Dragonlord. While he did not show it, he was very impressed that Thelvyn had been speaking the language of dragons with him, and speaking it well.

"Very well," he agreed at last, frowning. "The first issue is one of security. The Alphatians have established extensive settlements in our lands. I suppose it must be obvious by now that the region you know as Norwold is in fact the core of our own homeland. It is a secret we have guarded for a long time. Although we have ignored the Alphatians these last few years since they first arrived, they began the actual fighting early this spring when they began attacking not only the dragons of that region but also the frosthomes of northland elves who dwell in those forests and who are under our protection."

"That might have been in reaction to certain events of the previous winter," Kharendaen reminded him pointedly.

Marthaen glanced at her, still frowning. "Last winter, invaders entered our hidden city of Windreach, among the greatest of our secrets, and succeeded in stealing the Collar of the Dragons. The collar is the most ancient and powerful heirloom of our people and also among our greatest secrets."

Thelvyn smiled wryly. "Your secrets have taken a rather hard knock in all of this."

"My immediate suspicion is that either the Air Wizards of Alphatia or the Fire Wizards of the Flaem took the collar," Marthaen continued. "Either could have thought that such a thing would be useful to them in their ancient war with each other. Since our lands are fairly crawling with

Alphatians already, I tend to suspect the Air Wizards. I personally do not think the Flaem are competent enough to have managed such a thing."

"And I suspect that neither the Alphatians nor the Flaem could have acted alone," Kharendaen added. "They could not have learned of the collar by themselves. Neither could they have found Windreach alone. And they certainly could not have removed the collar from the very heart of the city. Whoever took the collar almost certainly had to have been in league with renegade dragons."

"Then you really do not know," Thelvyn assumed.

"In the last five years, the dragons have been in conflict with both the Flaem and the Alphatians," Marthaen said. "That in itself is a cause for suspicion. And I have reason to suspect a renegade would not have gone to such trouble. Taking the collar would be an insult to the Nation of Dragons, even a provocation. But, like all dragons, even a renegade would know that the collar would not serve him."

"Unless he has convinced himself that he is the rightful Dragonking," Kharendaen observed. "You must not underestimate the madness of a renegade."

"I have not forgotten that," Marthaen agreed. "But I think he would have proclaimed himself by now. A renegade who believes he is the Dragonking would not have to steal the collar. He would merely claim it. Others would judge the validity of such a claim. Now you know enough to understand our actions. What do you say? Will you support us?"

Thelvyn nodded. "There is no question of my support. More than that, you can trust me to do what you cannot. I will do what I can to discover if the Fire Wizards have the Collar of the Dragons. They might be incompetent, but an alliance with a renegade might have still given them the means. And I will also do what I can to find out if one of the renegade kings has it."

"And will you remain apart from our conflict with Alphatia?" Marthaen asked.

"You must first tell me the terms and limits that you are willing to place upon yourself in this war," Thelvyn insisted.

The dragon glanced away, plainly reluctant. "Our only concern is that the Alphatians withdraw from our lands, and we expect from them either the return of the collar or the right to satisfy ourselves that they do not have it. I have already sought a parley with their leaders, but I will fight this war how and where I see fit."

Thelvyn considered that briefly, staring down at the ground, before he sighed and nodded. "I will not interfere, although it is against my better judgment. If the dragons have a just claim against Alphatia, then it only seems right for the Dragonlord to take their part. But I will tell you this: You must try to put a quick end to this matter, with the least violence you can manage. And you must not make war upon any group simply because you suspect they have possession of your collar. If you attack the Flaem on suspicion alone, I will defend them."

* * * * *

On the way back to Braejr, Thelvyn considered the matter carefully. He remained dissatisfied, even fearful, about one point. He suspected that the dragons would never be satisfied until they discovered who had stolen the Collar of the Dragons and were able to reclaim it. Marthaen might be willing to promise not to act on suspicion alone, but it was always possible that the impatient reds and the younger dragons might turn rogue once again and take the matter into their own hands. He vowed to do whatever he could to find the collar first, and at the moment he could think of only one way to attack that problem.

The morning was still young by the time they returned to Braejr.

The gold dragon came in low over the crowded streets and found the yard of the house with uncanny accuracy, descending lightly into the court and folding her wings before she settled low to the ground to allow her rider to drop down from the saddle. Kharendaen bent her neck around to rub her nose against his chest, an old, very familiar gesture of affection. Thelvyn rubbed her nose in turn.

"You seem to be running a great many errands these

days," he said. "I hesitate to ask you to make another journey."

"This is a dangerous time, and I must do my part," she assured him. "Where do you wish to go?"

"I need to stay here and deal with the king and his wizards," Thelvyn explained. "I'm going to put the matter of the stolen collar to them as directly as I can, so I can see how they react and hear what they have to say. But we're going to need help in finding the collar, and I can think of only one expert with such a talent for finding lost treasures. I need to send you alone to Darokin, to see if you can find Sir George for me."

Kharendaen nodded. "That is a wise choice. As a mandrake, Sir George is a dragonkin and he would know something of the Collar of the Dragons already. Our secret would be safe with him."

She departed at once, still wearing her empty saddle so she would be able to bring back the old knight, provided she was able to find him. She couldn't easily go into the city, so the best that she would be able to do would be to land at the court of the capitol and send someone to find Sir George for her. The journey was a fairly short one. Even allowing for the time needed to locate Sir George, she expected to return by that evening.

Thelvyn had his own task to attend, and so he hurried to the king's palace as soon as Kharendaen had left. Like Marthaen, he was more inclined to suspect the Alphatians of the theft than the Flaem, but he felt certain that the Fire Wizards would have stolen the Collar of the Dragons if they had the means. He hoped that by throwing suspicion directly at Kalestraan and reminding him of the wrath of the dragons, he might be able to judge something of the wizard's guilt by the way he reacted.

As he had feared, it was too late in the morning to expect a private conversation with the king any time soon. Jherridan was holding a public audience that morning. It provided a chance for people from throughout the realm to petition their king in certain matters or seek his judgment in others. For once, Kalestraan was nowhere to be seen in the palace, so Thelvyn sent word to the Academy requesting the wizard to join him to discuss an important matter with the king that afternoon. Since the subject doubtlessly involved the Alphatians, Kalestraan was not about to refuse, and the king set aside time for a meeting in his private chamber after lunch.

"I spoke this morning with Marthaen, First Speaker of the Parliament of Dragons," he began, careful to relate no more of these events that he had to. "To put it simply, the Alphatians have been settling and fortifying lands that the dragons claim as their own. Earlier this year, the Alphatians began attacking dragons, as well as bands of elves who live under the protection of the dragons."

"Then I would say that the Alphatians have earned their troubles," the king said, unimpressed.

"Unfortunately, that's just the beginning," Thelvyn continued. "Someone has stolen an ancient artifact of power from the dragons, and they'll stop at nothing to get it back. As it happens, they suspect that either the Alphatian wizards or the Fire Wizards stole the artifact. For the moment, their greatest suspicion is directed toward the Alphatians. But if they don't receive satisfaction in that direction, they will eventually come looking here."

Thelvyn had been watching the wizard surreptitiously, waiting to see how Kalestraan would react. To his frustration, the wizard merely listened attentively, as if this was all very new to him, and looked properly concerned. Either he was innocent of any knowledge of the theft, or else his talent as an actor had been refined by years of court intrigue.

"This is outrageous," Jherridan declared, highly indignant. "Surely the dragons don't think that they can bully us."

"That's just the point," Thelvyn continued. "The dragons have a real complaint, and according to the terms of my truce, I am required to take their part. I've convinced them to grant me some time to do what I can to find their treasure, and if I manage to recover it, then I hope to be able to convince them to accept it with no questions asked. But if they come looking for it themselves, they'll be thinking only of vengeance. And if the thieves refuse to surrender the treasure, I can't do anything to protect them."

That made Jherridan shut up in a hurry. He cast a brief glance at his wizard. While Thelvyn still felt certain that the king had no part in the theft, Jherridan obviously didn't consider Kalestraan beyond such an act. But the senior wizard only continued to appear unconcerned.

"I don't know what to say about that," Kalestraan said at last. "Obviously I did not steal this artifact. Frankly, I don't even know what you are talking about, but I can see for myself that I am better off not asking. You both know I already have command of a native source of latent magic here in our own land, though we have much to learn about how to control it. I do not require additional artifacts of power, and I would not want such a thing so near my own source of power in the first place. I have no way to prove that I don't have it hidden somewhere. If you propose to search for it, then I will certainly do anything I can to assist you."

"Thank you for your generous offer," Thelvyn said quickly. "I propose to do precisely that. Once I've done all I can to find it here, perhaps the dragons will accept my word that you don't have it."

Thelvyn had to let the matter drop. There seemed little more he could do at that time, and he still couldn't imagine how the Fire Wizards could have learned about the collar or taken it in the first place. But if Byen Kalestraan thought he could bluff Thelvyn into accepting his innocence, he was sadly mistaken.

Thelvyn wasn't able to return home until that evening. As he walked the short distance from the palace, he wondered if Kharendaen had returned with Sir George. As soon as he stepped through the gate into the yard, he saw that the main doors to Kharendaen's lair stood open and a warm light was pouring through the doorway into the gathering darkness of the yard.

Once inside the warehouse, he saw that Sir George sitting in one of the chairs speaking with Kharendaen, who reclined in her bed. Although Sir George still spent much of his time in Braejr, the only home he actually owned at that time was his comfortable townhouse in Darokin. He was a tall, powerfully built man who could, when he wished, be mistaken for being rather soft, even plump. He had a friendly and disarming face, with bright eyes, a great beak of a nose, and a long, flowing mustache, and he was fond of dressing in the flamboyant manner of a Darokin merchant. At one time, he had been an errant knight of Darokin, serving in the Order of the Roads, retiring to trade in antiquities when he lost his left hand in honorable combat. Only his closest friends knew that he was also a mandrake, able to assume the form of a small dragon as needed.

"There you are, lad," Sir George declared. "So you've managed to stir up a pot of trouble, and now you've called for me to get you out of it."

"I beg your pardon, but I don't recall that any of this was my fault," Thelvyn replied as Kharendaen rubbed her nose against his chest.

"Stop kissing your dragon and come to dinner," Solveig said as she hurried past him, bearing a large tray to the table. "We were about to start without you."

"Solveig! You've come as well," Thelvyn exclaimed, pleased.

"That was quite a ride, I can tell you," Sir George remarked.

"He rode in the saddle, while I held on behind him," Solveig explained. The tray she carried turned out to be Kharendaen's dinner, a roasted haunch of elk. In a moment, a servant arrived with their meal.

Thelvyn hadn't seen Solveig White-Gold for some time now. She was involved in her business with Sir George and hardly ever came to Braejr. He flashed a warm smile at her, remembering fondly a time when he had been much younger and she had totally fascinated him. Solveig was descended from the fair barbarian folk of the Northern Reaches, and she had been given the name White-Gold because of the pale gold color of her long hair. She was fond of wearing barbarian armor, and she was one of the few people Thelvyn had ever met who was taller than he. She was one of the most deadly fighters he had ever seen, and Thelvyn had learned most of his own fighting skills from her. She had lavished him with the understanding and gruff affection of an older sister for all the time he had known her.

"I trust that Kharendaen has explained everything to you already," Thelvyn said as they sat down to dinner at the solid wooden table set beside the dragon's bed of deep cushions.

"Insofar as she was willing or able to," Sir George said. "Fortunately, I already knew a few of those secrets. I don't suppose that you had any luck with Byen Kalestraan."

Thelvyn shook his head. "I believe the expression is something like `Butter wouldn't have melted in his mouth.' He assumed the stance of a poor misjudged soul. The good wizard asked how he can prove he wasn't involved. Of course, he offered to help us search to our hearts' content."

"And search we shall," Sir George agreed. "Of course, I think I would prefer to do my searching without his help, since my concern is about the places he won't want to show us. As soon as I can arrange things, I think Solveig and I need to have a look in the dark places beneath the Academy. I need you to find out what you can about their older stronghold in Braastar."

"Are you equal to the task of searching the abode of wizards?" Kharendaen asked.

"I trust so," Sir George answered, seemingly unconcerned. "In my time, I've been a knight, a wizard, and a thief, not necessarily in that order. That combination of skills has gotten me in and out of tight places often enough in the past. I think the first question that we need to have answered is whether or not this collar is even here in the Highlands."

"You seem to think it is not," Thelvyn commented.

"No, as a matter of fact, I'm inclined to agree with Kharendaen on that account," Sir George said. "The renegade dragons must have been involved in the theft of the collar. Only a dragon would know what it was and where to find it, and only a dragon could have carried it away. Did anyone ever give you a good description of the thing?"

"No. I simply assumed it must be some kind of a collar large enough to fit a dragon."

Sir George glanced at Kharendaen for approval to speak

freely. "It was given to the dragons by the Great One long ago. It's supposedly an artifact of great value and magical power."

"Perhaps I can explain that best," Kharendaen said, although she appeared uncertain about discussing secrets of the dragons so openly. "The Collar of the Dragons was not a gift from the Great One, but an offering of peace to the dragons from the wizards of Blackmoor at the time of their truce with the first Dragonlord. It was indeed very costly, and it supposedly granted the dragons certain powers they desperately needed to survive at a time when their race had nearly been destroyed. I should point out that a collar is the draconic equivalent of a crown, although no dragon has ever worn it as such. There is a prophecy that someday the Dragonking will appear, a mystical figure who will lead his people into a new age of greatness, and he will be the first dragon to wear the collar. I cannot dismiss the possibility that one of the renegade kings has convinced himself that he is the true Dragonking and has stolen the collar to prove his claim."

Solveig looked startled. "So if the Flaem don't have the thing, and the Alphatians don't have it, we have to start checking the renegade dragons?"

"It might come to that," Sir George agreed.

"I should add that, if the wizards did steal it, they would have needed special magic just to carry it away," Kharendaen continued. "The collar was made to draconic proportions and contains nearly an entire ton of gold and jewels. It is not something that a fleeing wizard could have simply stuck in his pocket."

"Kalestraan mentioned that he has no need to steal an artifact of power when he already has his own hidden source of native magic," Thelvyn said. "He said he wouldn't want an artifact of such power so near his own source of magic."

"What the mage says holds little weight. The Fire Wizards have never had much success controlling their secret power," Kharendaen said. "Kalestraan might have seen the collar as a possible means to contain and direct his magical source. Now that he knows that he is suspected, he might try to do something about moving it to a more remote location. If the dragons had discovered it here, he would be in a very difficult position."

"If he tries to move it, we'll be waiting for him," Sir George declared.

"Well, that does answer one thing," Thelvyn declared. "At least now we know why Kalestraan might have been motivated to steal the Collar of the Dragons in the first place. He hoped it might give him control of his hidden source of power."

"On the other hand, if Kalestraan has learned to control his source of power, he might not need to be concerned about the dragons coming to collect the collar," Sir George said, frowning. "He would already have all the power he needed to defend himself against the dragons—or the Dragonlord, for that matter. The fact that he has not yet tried to seize the throne and toss Jherridan and the Dragonlord out is the best proof we have that he either doesn't have the collar or else he hasn't been able to get it to work for him the way he expected."

CHAPTER FOUR

Thelvyn was feeling somewhat better about his situation at court when he arrived the next morning. The morning was devoted to civil court, in which the king heard and pronounced judgment, or at least took under advisement, various important petitions and other civil matters from throughout the Realm. Thelvyn was one of the king's advisors, and as such he might be called upon to offer his opinion on matters being considered. He knew that the lives and livelihood of many people could depend upon an accurate judgment, and he preferred to be on hand to hear those cases for himself.

He entered as inconspicuously as he could through a side door hidden by screens on one side of the throne room. The king was standing on the steps just before his throne as he listened to a petitioner. Jherridan was still young and impatient, so filled with excitement that he would often stand or even pace while conducting business. Thelvyn moved quietly to the end of the gallery on the side of the room. As he did so, one by one all the petitioners in court turned to stare at him, some quietly pointing him out to others. They knew him at once as the Dragonlord, the tall, black-haired foreigner with vaguely elvish features, attired simply for a figure commanding such tremendous power.

Thelvyn waited patiently through the presentation of that week's petitions, but for once he hardly heard a thing. His thoughts were still occupied with his own problems. He hadn't even noticed the morning's business was done until the herald dismissed the court, now empty of petitioners. He was surprised to find that Taeryn, the king's valet, had come up quietly behind him bearing a tray of large cups.

"The king seems quite content lately," Taeryn said in his simple manner. "He used to worry about the Alphatians all the time—whether they were trying to do something to us, or what he could do in retaliation. Sometimes I wished that the Alphatians would just go away."

"I doubt that the Alphatians will ever 'just go away,' " Thelvyn answered. "But the king might indeed have reason to be less worried about them."

"I've brought liquid refreshments," Taeryn said, proffering the tray. "The king says that you are to join him for lunch."

Thelvyn took one of the cups. He had no idea what had made Taeryn think that he should bring drinks to the throne room if lunch was about to be served, but the young valet did the best he could and everyone was tolerant of his eccentricities. Thelvyn wasn't fond of the spiced, sweetened ale the Flaem seemed to like so well, so he was in no hurry to drink whatever it was he had. He walked slowly over to the front of the dais, waiting while the king spoke quietly with Byen Kalestraan.

"Will you be staying for lunch?" the king asked the wizard as he descended the steps of the dais.

"No, I really must be getting back to my own affairs," Kalestraan said, then turned to Thelvyn. "The king told me of your suggestion, that perhaps we could contribute something important in the war against Alphatia. We have begun the search either for magical weapons or for defenses against their magic."

"Have you been successful?" Thelvyn asked.

"Unfortunately, it is too early yet to guess whether or not our efforts will bear any fruit," the wizard explained. "So much of our learning was lost in the time of exile. You have doubtless observed for yourself that we have been working exceedingly diligently to build a whole new field of specialties based upon our native fire magic. We will also be doing what we can to determine how much the Alphatians might recall from their own past, or more importantly just how powerful their magic is at this time."

"I have heard the stories of how the ancient magic destroyed the home world of both races," Thelvyn said. "I should think the Alphatians have had a shortage of powerful wizards for at least the last five hundred years, since magic has not played an especially important part in their conquests."

"Are you sure of that?" Kalestraan asked.

"I asked about it when I was in Thyatis," Thelvyn replied. "The Thyatians know more than anyone about the Alphatians since their coming into this world. You might begin your research with them."

"Yes . . . that might be an excellent suggestion," Kalestraan agreed, then bowed to them both. "Gentlemen, if you will excuse me."

Thelvyn watched as the wizard hurried away down the carpet that led from the main doors of the chamber to the throne. The young Dragonlord had the uncomfortable feeling that he had this same conversation once before, five years ago when he and his companions had come to Braejr to try to find a way to subdue a dragon. Kalestraan had seemed friendly and eager to help then, much the same as now. Thelvyn was quietly amused to think that Kalestraan's pleasant demeanor was probably intended to divert suspicions that he had anything to do with the theft of the collar. The young advisor to the king wanted to make certain the Fire Wizards sought Thyatian help by diplomatic means, rather than by resorting to their previous method of pilfering tomes of history and magic from the libraries of other lands.

Jherridan set his untasted cup back on Taeryn's tray. "It would be nice if those wizards came up with something useful for a change. They're too expensive not to get more out of them."

Thelvyn only shrugged. "I'm not so sure they will. They can't have much strong, solid magic at their command, or they wouldn't be so desperate to find more. And I know that the Alphatians aren't doing any better. If you do get your war with Alphatia, I really suspect it to be fought with more conventional weapons."

"Perhaps you are right," Jherridan said. "However, I needn't tell you how strongly our people are motivated by thoughts of ending our ancient conflict with Alphatia. That in itself might encourage our excellent wizards to greater efforts."

Thelvyn tried not to look too amused, but he had never expected to hear the king speak so critically of his wizards.

"The new ambassador from Darokin has arrived," Jherridan continued. "I consider it encouraging that they now consider us important enough to merit an experienced ambassador and a stronger diplomatic presence."

"That will permit you to discuss the subject of an alliance with a high-ranking representative of Darokin for yourself," Thelvyn observed. "If Darokin could be brought to Thyatis's present level of enthusiasm, the war with Alphatia would almost be assured."

"I have that very much in mind," Jherridan admitted. "We will be having a reception for the ambassador as soon as he is settled into his residence."

"Oh?" Thelvyn asked guardedly.

"The ambassador is apparently quite an admirer of the Dragonlord," the king added. "Not to put too fine a point on it, but I very much need for you to be there if you can."

"Yes, of course," Thelvyn answered uncertainly, thinking that it would undoubtedly be a formal affair.

Thelvyn's discomfort with such events was entirely a matter of personal embarrassment. For one thing, he was always required to attend without an escort; the Flaemish ladies had always been quietly cautious of his company since he was a foreigner, and he had preferred keeping to himself since he had come to Braejr. Another source of his dread of such affairs was that he hardly ever dared to attend them dressed in proper attire. Rich clothes, a ceremonial weapon, or even shoes would prevent him from teleporting himself instantly into the armor of the Dragonlord. Of course, everyone knew the reason for his more casual dress, and the king actually approved. Jherridan appreciated having the powers of the Dragonlord immediately at hand in case any situation developed in which they were both vulnerable to attack.

Thelvyn was glad when it finally came time to return home that evening. Darkness was already settling over the city as he made his way through the streets of the fashionable western district of Braejr, and night was coming late with the rapid approach of summer. That morning he had felt especially confident about himself and his new policy of keeping himself removed from affairs that were not an actual part of his duties. He seemed to have supplanted the wizards in the king's favor, which he felt certain would encourage the wizards in their research so Kalestraan might have something to show the king and win approval.

Thelvyn had found the situation gratifying at first, but now he was beginning to feel vaguely uncomfortable. His presence at court had been irrelevant for so long that he was unprepared to suddenly find himself in high favor with everyone and his opinions valued. His efforts at exerting his independence seemed to have worked against him, as if his greater authority and determination had only made him more desirable as an advisor. He had to admit that he would probably feel better about things if Kalestraan did not seem equally impressed with him, since it only brought to mind the wizard's past duplicity. Kalestraan was probably only echoing the king's approval as a matter of political expediency.

To his surprise, he found that Sir George and Solveig had investigated the layout of the Academy during the day, and they proposed to pay a secret visit that night to search for the Collar of the Dragons. The three of them had dinner together and then settled down to wait for the depths of night by retiring to the den, a cozy room that had been appropriated as Sir George's domain since he first moved in. Thelvyn was reminded of an older time, sitting together in the den in Sir George's former house in the remote village of Graez on the northern frontier. It had been a rather brief but still especially important and happy time in Thelvyn's memory, since that was the time of his transition from a frustrated and lonely youth to a full-fledged adventurer in the old knight's company. Still, the setting was less than perfect, for two old friends, Korinn and Parrentin, were absent, and the entire company was unlikely to ever be together again.

"Are you sure you don't want me to come along?" he asked.

Sir George shook his head. "I have a few tricks up my sleeve for escaping if we get caught. If someone sees us, we could pass for common thieves. But you're entirely too recognizable, and it would be politically difficult for you if the wizards saw you trespassing in their private quarters."

Neither Sir George nor Solveig seemed at all concerned about the prospect of breaking into the Academy. They sat in the den and traded tales of their adventures while they waited for the deepest hours of the night. The Fire Wizards had always held a vague terror for Thelvyn, although he wondered if that was mostly because of the lessons of his difficult childhood among the Flaem. In the past, he had fought renegade dragons in their own lairs, but he was happy to be going to bed when Solveig and Sir George went to collect their weapons and tools for their adventure.

The moon had set early, and the night was especially dark as Sir George and Solveig made their way through the streets of Braejr. The Academy was a sprawling structure built along the inside of the east wall of the city. The large, well-stocked library stood at the north end, the wizards' residences and the student dormitories in the center, and the actual school of magic at the south end, near the river. In formulating his plans, Sir George had concluded that the collar would not be anywhere on the main floor, since it was too large to hide easily, but he thought there was a chance it might be somewhere in the chambers and passages beneath the Academy.

He had already considered his plans carefully, and he had decided that the best way to get into the lower level was through a delivery doorway that led down into the cool cellars below the kitchens. As a mandrake, his vision was sharp enough even in the near total darkness to see the lock clearly, and his abilities as both a thief and a magic-user told him that there were no magical traps or alarms guarding the approach. That came as a bit of discouraging news, since it seemed to indicate that either there was no passage between the cellars and other regions beneath the Academy, or else the wizards simply had nothing there worth guarding.

"Have you picked that lock yet?" Solveig asked impatiently.

"I haven't even started," Sir George answered as he consulted his tools.

The lock was massive but fairly simple, as if the Academy's occupants were more concerned that it might be forced by brute strength rather than foiled through stealth. Sir George could have had it open at once with a simple spell, but he remained concerned that the Fire Wizards had placed wards to resist or at least detect the use of magic against their doors and raise an alarm. None of his lock-picking tools seemed sturdy enough for this massive piece of iron.

"Half a moment."

Sir George quickly removed the hook he had been wearing on his left cuff and handed it to Solveig, who seemed rather nonplussed to discover what she was holding. He reached inside his jacket, feeling for the small pockets that lined the inside, and brought out a small pike, bearing a short, wicked-looking hook with a narrow blade above it. He locked this in place on his cuff, then slipped the point of the blade inside the keyhole and made a couple of complicated turns. The lock snapped open without further protest.

"It pays to use the proper tools," he told Solveig, taking back his hook and reattaching it to his cuff.

Sir George brought out a pair of small magical lanterns, which he cautiously encouraged into giving out a faint glow, and they descended the long, low ramp into the cellar. He handed one of the lanterns to Solveig, and together they looked around, finding themselves surrounded by sacks of flour and bins filled to overflowing with potatoes. Onions tied together by their stems hung in great clusters from the ceiling. The cellar was fairly large, but at least it wasn't closed off from the other passages beneath the Academy. A heavy wooden door at either end led onward, both north and south. The doors were unlocked, although Sir George was careful not to open them until he had tested each for traps.

As they made their way deeper into the bowels of the Academy, they discovered that the underground level was a hive of neatly laid passages and chambers, all set between walls made of massive blocks of stone connecting the great pillars that bore the weight of the structure above. Even the floor was set with large stone blocks. The chambers obviously served as storerooms for the entire Academy. They were filled with discarded furnishings, all manner of magical apparatus, and trunks and racks stuffed with old clothes. There was even an area beneath the library with crates full of books, possibly duplicates, all carefully packed, and one chamber where old parchments and rags were kept for packing the covers and binding of new tomes.

Sir George didn't really expect to find a treasure such as the Collar of the Dragons on this level, which wasn't secure enough to protect something of such great value, nor did he find any container large enough to have held it. He was seeking hidden passages that would lead down to still lower levels or to hidden passages, trusting to his thief's ability to detect such things instinctively. He soon found what he needed in a dark corner of a dusty room. He gestured for Solveig to stand back, then cautiously approached a single large stone set in the floor.

When he held his lantern close, he saw that a small metal handle had been set into the stone itself, so that no part of the handle protruded above the level of the floor. When he examined the hidden door, he could detect only a trap so old that it was barely functioning. This only heightened his curiosity. It was as if the wizards felt they had no secrets worth guarding.

"Stand back," he warned his companion. "Since the Flaem are Fire Wizards, I have a pretty good idea what to expect."

Sir George caught the inset handle with his hook and, moving around cautiously well to one side of the trapdoor, heaved open the protesting stone. A great flash of flame shot out from the opening, curling around the stone and licking briefly at the ceiling. If the spell had been fresh, the flames might well have engulfed the chamber. But when he stepped around the stone to peer inside the opening, he found to his amazement that it had been filled completely with packed clay.

They found several more, six in all, of the hidden doors. In each case, the passage had been filled and tightly packed with clay, enclosed beneath a flagstone made to look like any other part of the floor. Sir George could appreciate hiding secret passages in that way, but at first he couldn't understand why they had all been filled in. Only when he had found the last of the sealed passages did he finally realize the problem.

The answer left him in such a bad mood that he had to sit down on a trunk and fume at his own foolishness, his chin in his hand. After a minute or so, he finally looked up at Solveig.

"They weren't able to open any secret passages or chambers below this level," he explained. "The river is on the other side of the east wall, and half the city has a tendency to convert back to a marsh as it is. It was all they could do just to keep this level dry and able to support the weight of the building. When they tried to open a few hidden storerooms, the passages would floor, and they had to seal them with clay to keep the water from flooding the cellar."

"Then we've wasted our time?" Solveig asked.

"More or less," Sir George agreed. "At least we can be reasonably certain that the collar isn't here."

"Then can I make a suggestion?" she inquired.

Sir George nodded. "By all means."

"Let's go home and go to bed."

* * * * *

Both Thelvyn and Kharendaen were amused the next morning when they heard the story of the exploration of the dark places beneath the Academy over breakfast in Kharendaen's lair. Sir George was still rather disgruntled about the matter, although he was willing to admit that he hadn't really expected to find the collar in the first place he looked. Solveig had a complaint of her own, since the others tended to discuss their secrets in the language of the dragons, which she did not comprehend.

"It makes perfect sense," Kharendaen remarked. "The land between the juncture of two rivers is a bad place to build a city. The larger buildings actually float on the wet sand, much like the hulls of ships, and opening holes in the cellar would have the same effect as puncturing the hull of a ship."

"That's an interesting comparison," Thelvyn commented. "You could destroy large parts of Braejr by literally pulling the plug on the larger buildings. But it's not very relevant to our problem, I'm afraid. Where will you look next? Their old residence in Braastar?"

Sir George shook his head sullenly. "I don't see any point in continuing to poke about like common thieves in the hope that we happen across what we're seeking. I agree with Kharendaen that only a dragon could have stolen the collar, no matter who has it now. The renegades had a hand in this, and one of the renegade kings might still have it. Frankly, I have better, more reliable ways of getting information from that source than I have here."

"The renegades are dangerous and difficult to approach," Kharendaen cautioned. "Do you propose to poke about their lairs, or will you simply ask them?"

Sir George glanced deprecatingly at her. "You dragons disdain the renegades entirely, and so you know hardly anything about them. You're also guilty of disdaining the company of the drakes, and yet the drakes remain loyal to the dragons. The point is that the drakes don't remove themselves from the affairs of the outside world, and so they know a good deal about what's going on. I propose to go straight to a source I know and trust. I'm going to ask the drakes."

"They must be good for something," Kharendaen remarked, teasing him for his criticism of the conceits of dragons.

"The problem is, I need to borrow a dragon," he continued. "Otherwise this could take weeks or even months."

Kharendaen lifted her head, surprised but not offended. "Unfortunately, I dare not leave the Dragonlord. The dragons are at war in the east, and we may be needed there at any time. But that is not to say that a dragon is not available. If the Great One is willing, I will summon one of my fellow clerics to serve your purpose."

The next morning, Thelvyn turned his attention back to the matter of the ambassador's reception at the palace, which was now only four nights away. He was determined to attend the reception in formal attire, which meant that he had to have clothing and boots made for the occasion. He took some time out that morning to be fitted for both, taking Sir George with him to help decide what would be best for him. Between his childhood as a village orphan peasant and the limitations placed upon him by the armor of the Dragonlord, he had no idea of fashion.

At first, Solveig flatly refused his suggestion that she accompany him to the reception as his companion, even though he knew that she had been raised in one of the first families of Thyatis and was perfectly able to to handle herself at even the most demanding social occasions. But she relented reluctantly by that evening, submitting to Sir George's reminder that Thelvyn really needed her company to help keep him out of trouble. In other words, keep him away from the daughters of ambitious men, she read between the lines. Of course, that meant she needed to have clothes of her own made for her, and she had some rather definite ideas about what she wanted.

That night brought another surprise, at least as far as Thelvyn was concerned. He had completely forgotten that Kharendaen had promised to summon a dragon cleric to serve Sir George in his search for the Collar of the Dragons. Therefore he was rather surprised to see a gold dragon land in the courtyard outside the house just after dinner. Kharendaen was out into the yard to greet their visitor even before the others could get there, and it was at her suggestion that they all quickly moved inside her lair. She preferred that the Flaem, especially the Fire Wizards, should not be aware that a second dragon had arrived at Thelvyn's house. She reasoned that anyone who saw the new dragon's arrival would assume it was she.

The gold dragon was a young male named Seldaek, younger than Kharendaen and also somewhat smaller. To Thelvyn, who was familiar with dragons, he looked like a boy, hardly old enough to be considered an adult. He was obviously rather fearful of the Dragonlord at first and kept a respectful distance. But he was in fact a cleric, and he deferred to Kharendaen as both his elder and a leader of his order. He quickly proved himself to be no young fool, but brave and clever and patient. Kharendaen knew him well and trusted him completely. She entrusted the young dragon to Sir George's keeping at once, and the old knight told him all they knew and had planned up until that moment.

"How soon can you be ready to begin a long journey?" Sir George asked finally.

"I am ready now," Seldaek replied, glancing over his shoulder at the dragon saddle he wore. "Now I know why I was instructed to bring this saddle. I am willing to leave as soon as you are. Am I correct in assuming we go first in search of the drakes?"

"I know where to find them," Sir George said. "The wilds of Darokin are home to several drake communities."

"Drake communities?" Solveig asked.

"When drakes are ready to have little ones, they go off by themselves into the wilds to live for some time in their true form," Sir George explained rather defensively. "There are hidden drake communities formed especially for that purpose, places were drakes can live as themselves. My earliest memories are of hunting rabbits in the woods and climbing stones outside just such a community. I was about four or five when I mastered the ability to change my shape, and shortly thereafter my parents took me to their home in Darokin."

"That must have been quite a change for you," Thelvyn commented.

"Oh, it was. Frankly, I didn't much like it at first. But my parents were jewelers and traders in small treasures, quite well off. I actually come from a line of rather remarkable mandrakes. Most are petty thieves, rather quiet, furtive folk by nature. I grew up a trader and learned that before I ever became a knight."

"How do two drakes ever find each other, when they are hardly ever in their true form?" Thelvyn asked.

"A dragonkin will always recognize another on sight, no matter what form it might take," Sir George answered, then saw that the others were staring at him. The two dragons seemed to have a dark fascination for what he said, as if they found it all strange and quite uncivilized. "Pray don't worry yourselves about it. The drakes are the least of our concerns. Seldaek, are you prepared to face the renegades?"

"I am not afraid," Seldaek insisted bravely.

Sir George and Seldaek didn't make an especially reassuring team as far as the others were concerned, and they still held certain misgivings when they watched the pair fly off toward the south in the darkness before dawn the next morning. Solveig had accepted the fact that she wouldn't be going with them, since the company of drakes and renegades was no place for one who was not dragonkin. Her place was with the Dragonlord in the Highlands. If it proved necessary, she was to continue the search for the collar in Braastar or other strongholds of the wizards.

Once they were gone, Thelvyn had to turn his attention back to more immediate concerns in Braejr. His situation at court remained much the same as it had been. Jherridan valued Thelvyn's judgment more than ever and sought his advice in all matters, yet remained careful never to presume upon him or test the limits of his duty as the Dragonlord. And while Byen Kalestraan made no apparent progress in his search for magic that might be helpful in a war with Alphatia, he voluntarily kept his word to permit the Dragonlord to search all the strongholds of the Fire

Wizards. Thelvyn was given a tour of the entire Academy, and Kharendaen took him to Braastar and other strongholds throughout the Highlands. He found nothing, as he had expected, although he now had an idea of where to send Solveig for a closer look if need be.

When the evening of the ambassador's reception arrived, Thelvyn had trouble getting himself ready and was nearly late. He had grown used to wearing nothing more than shirt and trousers for years now. His new clothes were slightly more colorful than the typical Flaemish attire, since he was certain that he would have felt even more self-conscious in the gaudier fashions of Darokin or Thyatis. Even so, the jacket gave his arms less movement than he wished, and he had to remember not to bend over too far, or else everything got out of place. He was absolutely convinced that the boots were much too small. He nearly fell down the stairs when he finally came downstairs from his room.

Solveig was waiting for him, although the only reason he even recognized her was that it was highly unlikely there was another golden-haired woman well over six feet tall in all the Highlands. She wore her hair unbraided and loose over her shoulders, complemented by a netting of gold chain inset with rubies. Her dress was long and deceptively simple. It was made of a deep green satin that had almost a metallic sheen, with wide, flowing sleeves. With the exception of the sleeves, the dress was otherwise formfitting and enhanced her slender, athletic figure. Because of her experiences as a warrior, she had several faint scars on her arms, and so she refused to wear dresses or shirts without long sleeves. A rather amazingly large area of the front of the dress's front stood below the high collar, revealing an ample portion of her breasts.

Curiously, she wore a cape of matching dark green attached to the collar of the dress, so that it could not be removed. Although that seemed an unexpected feature, it in no way diminished the dress's stunning effect. To highlight her appearance, she wore a necklace of ancient design, with gold plates bearing precious stones that spread across her bare shoulders. Thelvyn recognized it as a piece from Sir George's private collection; the Flaemish worthies at the reception would have been scandalized to learn that it was Alphatian in origin. In addition, she wore a gold belt, cinching the clinging dress at her waist and complimenting her figure all the more.

"My word," Thelvyn breathed softly.

"Put your eyes back in your head," Solveig admonished him. "Sir George told me that I'm to scare off the ladies tonight. I don't necessarily have to be a barbarian to manage that, now, do I?"

"Obviously not," he agreed. "I've apparently never had a chance to fully appreciate your true . . . versatility in the past."

Solveig reached over her shoulder, slipping one hand beneath the cape, and brought out a short sword from where it had been hidden. He didn't recognize it as one of her own. She must have had the sheath attached directly to the dress somehow, since there was no belt or harness to be seen. The cape had a heavy lining of some sort of material, which completely hid the sword so that its shape couldn't be detected through the fabric. Since Thelvyn was also planning to carry a sword of ceremonial importance, he no longer felt so concerned about assassins.

"Well, the two of you have fun," Kharendaen remarked wickedly, poking her head out the door of her lair as they left. "But that might be a bit much to expect."

Solveig had declined Thelvyn's offer to have a carriage brought around; he did not have a carriage anyway, since the palace was only a few streets away. He noticed that she wasn't wearing slippers or sandals but light suede boots of the elvish style, quite in fashion in this northern land. Thelvyn had specified a low heel for his own boots. Of course, he wasn't used to boots of any type, since they were too bulky to allow him to teleport into his armor.

"Kharendaen needs to get out more," Solveig remarked as they strolled together. "When she starts saying things that I would have expected to hear from my mother, I don't know whether to be alarmed or merely amused. After all this time, I never expected that she would start thinking that we might make a good match."

"Is that really what she meant?" Thelvyn asked, trying to

remember just what the dragon had said.

"Well? Why *weren't* we ever closer?" she asked suddenly.

"You happen to be one of three people in all the world I would say that I *am* close to," Thelvyn replied. "But I know that isn't what you mean. There was a time when I thought I was very in love with you. But I was just a boy when we met, and then I became the Dragonlord. I acquired responsibilities that made it impossible for me to travel about the wilds as an adventurer, which was the life you still wanted."

"But I knew I wouldn't want it forever," Solveig remarked. "In fact, I've been thinking a good deal lately that my time as Solveig White-Gold is coming to an end. Valeria Dorani is anxious to have a turn, but I'm not ready to go back to Thyatis. So when I began to think about home, I knew this was the place I had to come to."

"This will always be your home whenever you want it," he told her sincerely. "But I don't know just how close you would want to be with the Dragonlord. I'm not even human, and I apparently have a rather dire fate before me."

"Still, you have grown so. I like the person you've become," Solveig said, then glanced at him. "Someone else said that to you before as I recall. Do you ever think of that elf girl?"

"Sellianda? I think of her a good deal, not so much for the ties we never had but because she was the only one who ever seemed to honestly desire my company in that way. But she is an elf. She belongs to her quiet order and her deep woods, and I'm not so sure that she would really want to be a part of my life. I'm afraid that someday my duty will take me places where none of my old friends can follow."

Many carriages were drawn up in the main yard of the palace by the time they arrived, and more were still arriving. Like Thelvyn and Solveig, many of the guests who lived closer had walked. King Jherridan had cleverly conspired to have the reception for Lord Derrick Mortrand, the ambassador from Darokin, take place on the same night as the Flaemish Summer Festival, so that the entire city would be celebrating. In addition, he had invited every wealthy merchant and dignitary to be found in Braejr.

According to Flaemish custom, Ambassador Mortrand stood at the main door of the palace with his host to greet the guests as they arrived. Both Lord Derrick and the king failed to recognize Solveig in spite of her remarkable height. Jherridan didn't even seem to recognize Thelvyn for a moment, it had been so long since he had dressed formally. Indeed, as they joined the gathering crowd, Thelvyn found that many other people failed to recognize him. Part of this could be blamed on Solveig, who was so striking and compelling that she provided a considerable distraction.

Byen Kalestraan stood just beyond the king and the ambassador, looking especially wizardly in one of his finest robes, which had an especially high, stiff collar, trimmed with gilt. He looked surprised when he saw Thelvyn. "Well, lad. I hardly recognized you with shoes on. I wasn't aware that you would be dressing formally for this occasion."

"I didn't decide myself until very recently," Thelvyn admitted.

"It becomes you indeed, but I am fearful for your safety. You must take special care." The wizard seemed to notice Solveig for the first time and reacted with great delight. He bowed to her gallantly. "Pardon me, but I fear that I do not know your most remarkable companion."

"Solveig White-Gold," she introduced herself. "It's been a long time since we met."

"It has indeed," Kalestraan agreed. "I must say that the two of you make a striking couple, and remarkably well suited for each other. I'm pleased to see Thelvyn finally enjoying the company of a lady worthy of the Dragonlord."

"He has spent too much time with his dragon," Solveig agreed graciously. "And now if you will excuse us . . . ?"

She led Thelvyn away into the crowd. Thelvyn was beginning to feel a bit nervous about this evening, unsure if Solveig's interests were sincere or if she was just teasing him and the Flaemish worthies at the same time. He knew how wicked she could be, playing out her jests for hours, even days at a time, all the while concealing her amusement. Thelvyn couldn't believe that her interest in him could be serious, knowing the differences that stood between them. They had been more like brother and sister for the duration of their long friendship. Thelvyn had to admit that he was tempted; the fact that he had been avoiding female company didn't meant that he was uninterested, although he was far from certain that Solveig was the right female.

If nothing else, he was determined to be cautious. He suspected that the ultimate objective of her jest, if indeed it was a jest, was to get him to make a fool of himself.

CHAPTER FIVE

According to Flaemish custom, the reception began with a formal dinner, followed by a time of quiet conversation at the table while minstrels played soft music. Thelvyn and Solveig were seated near the head of the king's table, reflecting Thelvyn's new standing as a favored advisor. Mage Kalestraan sat across from him, having come to the table late and looking rather distracted about something. After a time, Jherridan rose to address the gathering, introducing the new ambassador to the guests with a few appropriate words. His words were few indeed, since the Flaem had never been in the habit of making long speeches. When Lord Derrick thanked them all with a few words of his own, mostly concerning the fine hospitality of his guests and his belief that his stay in the Highlands would be a productive one for all concerned, Jherridan followed the ambassador's lead and made his own concluding speech a brief one.

With such necessities out of the way, the guests retired from the dining hall to the reception hall, where music was provided for dancing. Side tables were laden with various drinks and pastries to suit almost anyone's taste. Because the back of the palace stood directly against the western wall of the city, all the courts and gardens were in the front. The reception hall was open to the court and the palace garden, so that guests could step outside for some fresh air, and later to witness the fireworks provided by the wizards for the Summer Festival. Thelvyn and Solveig retreated to a quiet corner inside the reception hall, waiting until things settled somewhat.

"Would you like to dance?" Solveig asked suddenly.

Thelvyn was surprised at the suggestion. "I suppose. I'm not very good at it, since hardly anyone ever wants to dance with the Dragonlord."

"Well, I learned in my time in Thyatis that hardly anyone wants to dance with me either," she said. "I suppose my size is intimidating. So we might as well have a dance or two together, since no one else will have us."

In fact, they danced four dances in a row, mostly because Thelvyn was so inexperienced that he needed the first three just to learn what he should be doing. After that, the musicians began to play the more complex and stately dances common to the south, and Thelvyn was forced to take refuge from the dance floor. Solveig excused herself to get a drink and also to snoop about, to get some feel for the local politics. For all her protestations that she had left Thyatis to get as far away from politics as she could, she seemed eager to involve herself once again. She had only just left when Thelvyn was approached by Merissa Mortrand, the ambassador's daughter.

"Your friend seems to have abandoned you," she observed. "Do you need someone to dance with you?"

"I'm afraid I'll have to excuse myself. I'm not much good at these courtly dances," he told her, feeling awkward. "Solveig went to get some liquid refreshment."

"She seems quite attached to you," Merissa said, speaking more directly.

"If you must know, she's showing off," Thelvyn explained, dropping his voice. "You see, she's always suspected that the king is a bit enamored of her. She stays close to me so that he respects her privacy."

"But surely the king is a desirable match for anyone."

"That's just the point," he said even more softly. "You see, the king is young and of an age when he needs to think about marriage. Solveig is just a humble barbarian orphan, her past unknown. She might be very remarkable and striking, but there would be no advantage to King Jherridan or the realm in a marriage with her. So, for the greater good, Solveig distances herself from the king so that other, more worthy young ladies may have their chance to know him better."

"Oh . . . I see," Merissa remarked thoughtfully. "Then you and Solveig are not intimate?"

"No, though we have slept together," he told her evenly. Thelvyn knew that was stretching the truth considerably. They hadn't slept together for years, and never in the same bed. Besides, there had usually been a dwarf in the room at the same time.

Merissa blushed deep red and disappeared back into the crowd without another word. She had taken Thelvyn's hint in exactly in the manner he had intended—not that he had fooled her in the least, he was sure. She put up a pretense of being silly and superficial, since that was the custom of young ladies in Darokin.

Solveig returned a moment later with a cup of sweet elvish wine for Thelvyn. "What did her ladyship want?" she asked.

"She wanted to know how matters stand between us," he replied. "I discouraged her with some tactical exaggerations and sent her after Jherridan, who seems to suit her better anyway."

"I'm not so sure it will suit Jherridan," Solveig commented. "At least I see I don't have to worry about you anymore."

She disappeared into the crowd again. Thelvyn had to agree with her that King Jherridan was so devoted to his duties as the first King of the Flaem in two thousand years that he had never been very concerned with personal matters such as marriage. A few minutes later, Kalestraan came quietly up behind him. The wizard was watching the gathering with a distant eye, the way that one would admire a painting or watch a play.

"You seem not to want for companionship tonight," he remarked.

"Too much, actually," Thelvyn said. "I made certain that Ambassador Mortrand's daughter was aware of how matters stand with me, then sent her hunting in the king's direction. That's what she wants anyway."

"The king?" Kalestraan asked, seemingly confused.

"I certainly hope there's no rule that the king cannot marry a foreign lady," he explained. "The realm needs to strengthen its ties with the rest of the world, especially if you people are serious about going after the Alphatians. Merissa may not be a princess, but I know that Lord Derrick is one of the most influential men in Darokin, and he seems to approve of the match. And I must admit that Jherridan isn't likely to do much better, being the king of a rather small and remote northland realm."

"Yes, I see your point," Kalestraan agreed, although he still looked rather puzzled. "You've done well, then. Perhaps now we should just let matters proceed as they will, so that we may weigh the possibilities when they are set before us."

The wizard wandered away, leaving Thelvyn even more bemused than ever. He had forgotten for the moment that the political affairs of the Highlands and the personal affairs of King Jherridan were not his concern. At least his intentions had been good; such an alliance probably would be to the benefit of both the king and the realm, and Jherridan wasn't very likely to do any better. A few minutes later he spied Jherridan himself coming toward him through the crowd. He realized he should have been expecting it. The game was far from over.

"There are times when I wonder why I ever wanted to be king," Jherridan said wearily.

"The ambassador's daughter?" Thelvyn asked.

Jherridan frowned. "Didn't I see her after you earlier?"

"Perhaps," Thelvyn admitted. "I suppose I should warn you. I get the impression that Merissa is not fishing in these waters entirely on her own initiative. I suspect

Lord Mortrand is interested in some kind of alliance with Darokin by marriage with his daughter, and I needed to make my position clear. When my duty as Dragonlord leads me away from here, it will be to places where someone like Merissa cannot follow. Frankly, both she and her father are more interested in an alliance with you anyway."

Jherridan sighed loudly. "I'm aware of what an alliance with a powerful nation could mean for the Highlands. Indeed, I had been thinking for some time now that perhaps I should be having you discreetly solicit for such an alliance. I suppose that this would be an advantageous union for us. I just wish she wasn't such a silly twit."

Thelvyn nearly choked to keep from laughing. "It is the custom in certain parts of the world for young ladies to attempt to present themselves as simple and innocent, which is seen as alluring."

"Do they indeed?" Jherridan was greatly surprised. "Well, it does take all types to make the world, doesn't it?"

The king sighed heavily once more and wandered back into the field of battle, although his heart didn't seem to be in the fight. Thelvyn retreated to the garden, certain that anyone would be able to find him if he was needed. He sat for a time on a bench near the fountain, watching the fireworks over the center of Braejr. As he had expected, Merissa came out to the garden only a few minutes later looking for him. In her mind, he seemed somehow to have made the transition from prey to fellow conspirator. She sat down on the bench beside him.

"Having trouble?" he asked.

"The king danced with me twice," she explained. "I've tried, but we just don't seem to hit it off."

"Well, have you tried talking to him like a reasonable person?" Thelvyn asked. "You're going to find that the Flaem are not as sophisticated, as you would call it, as the people of Darokin. Jherridan is going to judge you by you yourself, not by how well you can play some game he doesn't understand."

"So you think he finds me foolish and dull?" she asked.

"King Jherridan is a remarkable man," Thelvyn said,

deciding to butter the bread generously, as the dwarves would say. "He is sincere, devoted, and fair. But I suppose that in Darokin, such a man would be considered foolish and dull."

"It might be said, but that doesn't necessarily mean it would be believed," Merissa said, kissing him on the cheek as she rose. "You're rather unique yourself."

She hurried away into the palace, leaving Thelvyn alone once more in the darkness of the garden. Of all the things that had happened that night, he was most amazed with himself. He would have thought that a person needed to be experienced in courtly matters to play the role of the matchmaker effectively, but apparently any fool could pull it off. Perhaps the key was not being personally involved in the courting.

After a time he made his way back to the party. Neither Jherridan nor Merissa had sought him out in some time, and he wanted to see how they were getting along. He was also concerned about how Solveig was entertaining herself with the worthies of Braejr. He saw Jherridan making the rounds of his guests, with Merissa close by his side. He also found Solveig mingling among the rounds of the guests. She was being charming and ingratiating in her own barbaric way, and everyone seemed quite taken with her, although she refused to dance with anyone but Thelvyn.

Some time later, shortly before midnight, Solveig came looking for him. "It is said that in Alphatia's high society, it is considered a dishonor to be the first guest to leave a party. For that reason, their affairs often last most the night until someone finally weakens."

"I can take a hint," Thelvyn assured her. "In fact, if I don't get out of these boots soon, I'm likely to be lame for weeks."

They remained long enough to make appropriate farewells to the king and to the ambassador. Lord Derrick and his daughter both looked enormously pleased; their evening had apparently turned out very well indeed, as far as they were concerned. Jherridan was at least trying to look pleased.

"I'll get you for this, Dragonlord," he whispered softly to

Thelvyn.

Thelvyn had almost forgotten that this was the night of the Summer Festival. Small groups of revelers still wandered the streets, and all the lanterns remained lit. Solveig remained in fine spirit, obviously quite pleased with herself and the way her evening had turned out, as they walked together through the streets.

"You won't need to worry about unwanted attention from the ladies after tonight," she told him.

"Well, I do worry about the impression you must have given people," Thelvyn said. "They'll be planning our wedding after this. And then what will they think when you disappear for months at a time with Sir George?"

"You worry too much," Solveig said.

Suddenly she stopped short. They had come to a place where a joining of streets made a square in the form of a tiny wooded park. Thelvyn glanced up, startled to see a tall man in a dark cloak carrying a drawn sword step out of the small stand of trees to block their way. Even as his heart sank, Thelvyn cursed the foolishness of his own vanity. He turned to see another tall, dark man standing some distance behind them, blocking their retreat. Thelvyn knew beyond a doubt that these were not late-night partygoers, or even petty thieves.

Solveig reached over her shoulder and drew her sword as Thelvyn drew his own blade. Both were small ceremonial weapons and no match for the massive blades of the strangers.

"I'm afraid I've been caught with my pants down, so to speak," Thelvyn said softly. "I can't get into the armor of the Dragonlord with these clothes on. At least I've had some practice fencing tonight."

"They're not likely to be a match for us, are they?"

Thelvyn hoped she was right. Although he and Solveig were both tall and strong and well trained in the skills of combat, Thelvyn still felt vulnerable without the enchanted armor. Years had passed since the last time he had been required to defend himself entirely by his own talents. And Solveig was wearing a fashionable party dress. They were at a distinct disadvantage.

Thelvyn and Solveig stood back-to-back, each facing one of the two tall, dark assassins who challenged them. Apparently Solveig had thought of all possible contingencies. She grabbed the soft material of her long, full skirt with one hand and gave it a firm tug. The skirt came away in a single piece below the gold belt. Beneath it she wore a much shorter skirt of the same dark green fabric, allowing her much greater freedom of movement.

Thelvyn wished he could remove his own extra clothing as easily, but he suspected he wouldn't be allowed the time to remove even his sword belt or cape. There was certainly no chance for him to take off his boots without sitting down, and he wouldn't be able get into his armor until he had. He would have to depend upon his own abilities, without the enchantments of the Dragonlord. He felt vulnerable and uncertain, but he knew that this was no time to doubt himself.

"Something isn't right," Solveig said softly. "How much will you need to disrobe to get into that armor?"

"Too much," he told her. "I'd never have time to get out of these boots."

"If we can take out one of them, even slow him down, then I might be able to cover you long enough."

"It might come to that," Thelvyn replied. "Still, I'm not entirely helpless. Be ready. I'm going to try something."

As furious as he was for finding himself trapped like this, he knew he had other ways of defending himself. Using a magical spell at his command, he summoned a sphere of light and sent it up among the tree branches. The light was bright enough to cast a soft glow through the intersection and chase away most of the deep shadows. Perhaps someone would see it and summon help. For the moment, their attackers hesitated.

The assassins moved together at the same instant, leaping forward with their swords raised high. Thelvyn brought up his own small sword in response; his instinct was to duck and leap aside as the massive blade of his opponent sliced down, but he couldn't leave Solveig's back unprotected. All he could do was to catch the attacker's sword with his own and deflect it aside.

The sword was nearly ripped from his hands by the force of the blow. The assassin recovered quickly, turning his blade under Thelvyn's, catching him unprepared, with his arms in an awkward position. He was unprepared for the crushing strength of his enemy, who had overpowered him to his disadvantage. Although Thelvyn possessed all the height and strength of his unknown race, he was facing an opponent whose physical power he could only describe as unnatural.

Thelvyn was forced to draw back to retain his grip on his sword, bumping against Solveig's back. He had to recover quickly, but he was surprised to find his enemy gave him the moment he needed by drawing back as well. When the assassin raised his massive sword for a second powerful sweep, Thelvyn turned the blow aside before the heavy blade could gather speed. Dropping low, he passed beneath the assassin's blade and came up quickly behind his opponent. The blow he delivered with his small weapon hardly scratched the leather armor beneath his enemy's cloak, but it served its purpose.

Thelvyn had realized his only advantage was speed. He desperately needed the room to move quickly, to leap clear and spare the fragile blade of his sword. Fortunately the assassin ignored Solveig's now exposed back and followed him out onto the square. Solveig and her opponent were trading blows furiously.

The dark assassin tried to match Thelvyn pace for pace, occasionally stepping in quickly to slash with his sword. Thelvyn was mystified by his opponent's caution despite seeming to have an overwhelming advantage. He realized almost too late that he was still being tested, and his enemy was holding back until he was certain that Thelvyn was isolated from his powers as Dragonlord. That fact alone allowed Thelvyn to hold his own, but it was obvious the true contest was yet to begin.

Suddenly the assassin lunged at him in sudden fury, striking over and over again and again in an effort to break Thelvyn's sword. It was all Thelvyn could do to turn or evade the blows from his enemy's massive sword, and he grew increasingly desperate. He knew he was unlikely to win a defensive battle. He had to find a way to end this somehow.

Finally Thelvyn sensed that his enemy was beginning to tire at last. The assassin had been doing most of the work, trying to match Thelvyn's quickness despite the burden of his armor, at the same time throwing all his strength behind his blows with the heavy sword. When at last one of his strokes went a little too wide, Thelvyn rushed in beneath his reach and pushed the dark assassin backward as hard as he could. The assassin stumbled a couple of quick steps backward before falling over onto the cobblestones.

Thelvyn quickly thought better of trying to finish him off while he was down, knowing how easy it would be for something to go wrong if he tried to close with a large, stronger enemy who was also armored and better armed. Instead he leaped back, hoping to buy a few moments to rid himself of the clothing and boots that prevented him from becoming the Dragonlord. In his haste, he tripped and fell. Fearful of becoming tangled in his cape while he was down, he jerked it loose and tossed it aside as he rolled away from his enemy, then leaped to his feet.

The assassin was still struggling to rise, burdened by his armor. That gave Thelvyn a moment more to pull off his jacket and remove the massive decorative belt he wore, although he despaired of ever removing his boots. The assassin came at him, determined to finish him before he found some way to get into his armor.

The contest resumed as before. Thelvyn used his quickness as his only advantage, doing whatever he could to avoid his foe's massive blade. He forced himself to remain calm, reminding himself that he was clever enough to survive if he was careful. His enemy seemed to be tiring, but not much more quickly than Thelvyn. Indeed, he was beginning to wonder if he faced a man at all. The assassin was completely concealed in a dark cape, his face hidden within the shadows of the deep hood.

Thelvyn's sword had been nicked and bent by the unrelenting assault of powerful bows, and he knew that the weapon could fail at any time. The moment came sooner than he had expected when his sword broke suddenly just above the hilt. He leaped backward swiftly, avoiding the assassin's blade, then cast another spell of light directly into his opponent's face.

His opponent was blinded by the spell, and that allowed Thelvyn a moment to see how Solveig fared. Although the two assassins seemed identical, her adversary appeared to be less strong, an even match for the tall Northlands warrior.

Thelvyn's attention was drawn back to his own enemy when he saw the assassin somehow dispel the magical light that blinded him. The cloaked figure rubbed his eyes, his face still hidden within the hood, then reached for the sword he had dropped. He seemed unable to find it at first, as if his vision remained blurry.

Knowing he was weaponless, Thelvyn threw himself at the stranger to keep him from regaining his sword. This time the assassin wasn't taken completely off guard and braced himself. The impact knocked Thelvyn backward. He rolled aside desperately as the assassin attacked, hissing in fury. In growing desperation, Thelvyn realized he was no match for the size and crushing strength of the strange warrior. He jumped aside, nearly falling once more in his haste to put some distance between them.

The assassin failed to pursue him at once, standing in the street with his legs braced firmly, and Thelvyn realized almost too late that the strange warrior was now commanding a spell of powerful magic. Thelvyn summoned an invisible shield, the only defense he could think of in his alarm. An instant later, a great spear of intense flame leaped out from the assassin's hands, crashing against the shield with tremendous force. In his experience, only the flames of a dragon rivaled its intensity. Whoever the stranger was, he was not only a powerful warrior but also a skilled magician, a deadly combination that was almost unheard of. Thelvyn was at a loss to know how to fight him.

As soon as the flames died, Thelvyn stood ready to act quickly. He had only one option left to him, and he was acting now more by instinct and desperation than plan.

Summoning clerical powers he had not called upon since becoming the Dragonlord, powers of almost unprecedented strength, he raised his arms and began his own attack. A spear of invisible force leaped out from his hands to strike the assassin, blasting him with such intensity that he was hurled backward against the trunk of a tree. The force of that blow should have been enough to kill a horse, but the stranger shook his head and began to rise unsteadily. Thelvyn hit him again, flattening him against the tree once more. Slowly he slid down the trunk and collapsed to the ground.

Thelvyn hesitated, wondering if the fight was done, but the hesitation was nearly his undoing. The assassin stirred weakly, not even attempting to rise, then made a sudden gesture with his hand. Thelvyn felt the invisible missile strike his shoulder, smashing against the bone with such force that it hurtled him backward to the hard stones of the street. He wasn't aware at first that it had ripped deep into his shoulder all the way to the bone. When he tried to move, his shoulder protested with a fierce burning pain, and his left arm failed to respond.

The assassin knew that he had won, and he took his time as he returned to the street to collect his sword. As indestructible as the strange warrior seemed, Thelvyn's last attack had indeed left him dazed. He paused to retrieve his sword, then walked slowly over to finish his prey. Thelvyn could hardly move at first, managing only to sit up awkwardly. He was weaponless, too confused by his pain to command his magic. All he could do now was to leave himself open to the influence of his patron, hoping that the Immortal who had always watched over him would grant him the powers to defend himself.

But he was not to know if he could have saved himself. Solveig rushed to his assistance, shouting some dire Northlands oath as she came at the assassin from behind. She had managed to defeat her own opponent, and his body lay in a dark heap several yards away. But this one was by far the more powerful of the two attackers. He met her attack blade to blade, disdaining the use of magic, and Thelvyn knew he was playing with her in a battle she could not hope to win. All she could do now was to buy Thelvyn the time he needed to get himself into the armor of the Dragonlord.

With extreme effort, Thelvyn bent forward but found that he couldn't remove his boots one-handed. In his desperation, he climbed to his feet and hurried across the cobblestones to collect his discarded belt. He drew the dagger and used the blade to slice open the side of each boot so that he could kick them aside. Free to act at last, he rose painfully and teleported into his armor.

The assassin stood motionless, watching him as he drew the massive sword from its belt and hefted it awkwardly with his one good hand. Solveig moved cautiously out of the way. Then the assassin turned sharply to look down the street behind him, and Thelvyn turned to see that Kharendaen was charging to the attack, a vast dark form running in a swift, leaping gait like some immense cat.

Seeing that his own position had become hopeless, the assassin turned and disappeared into the trees of the small park. Thelvyn released a powerful bolt from the blade of the sword, which discharged against a tree trunk. The tree was shattered by the impact and collapsed, the top part slowly falling over with a loud crash. But Thelvyn knew that his one-handed aim had been so unsteady that he couldn't possibly have hit the fleeing assassin. Thelvyn returned the sword to his belt and removed his helmet, teleporting it out of the way.

Then he saw that Solveig was wounded, sinking into Kharendaen's claws as the dragon hurried to catch her. Thelvyn rushed over to her, and he could see at once that her injuries were terrible. She had been completely run through by the assassin's sword. The blade had entered between her ribs just below her left breast and emerged again from her back. Somehow she had continued to fight, drawing upon her fierce Northlands fury to give her strength, and buying him the time he had needed.

"We have to get her home," Thelvyn said desperately. "A healer might—"

"It is too late to find help for her," Kharendaen said. "She does not have much time left to her. If I cannot save her, no one can."

Thelvyn had forgotten for the moment that Kharendaen was a senior cleric. His concern was that the Great One would not look with favor upon the use of such powers for the sake of one who was not a dragon, especially at a time when he had removed himself from the affairs of dragons. Kharendaen lifted Solveig gently, sitting back on her haunches while she cradled the tall warrior in her claws like a sleeping child. The healing magic was not denied; Solveig's form began to glow with a soft light of icy blue.

"I have done what I can for now," Kharendaen said after a moment. "Her danger is no longer as great, but we must take her home and find skilled help for her at once."

She turned to walk home on her hind legs so that she could carry Solveig gently, then paused, staring. The lifeless body of the assassin Solveig had slain began to change, shifting, flowing, and expanding in shape until it became that of a black dragon.

* * * * *

Kharendaen remained in the yard outside the front door of the house, holding Solveig until the healer arrived. Under the circumstances, Thelvyn had sent a city guard at once to fetch the king's personal healer, knowing that Jherridan would not deny him. Until the healer arrived, Kharendaen did not allow the Northland warrior out of her sight, fearful that her abilities as a cleric might still be needed. But the healer arrived shortly in a carriage that had been lent to him by one of the worthies at the ambassador's reception. He took one look at Solveig and ordered her brought inside at once, allowing only his servants to accompany him. He had much work to do that night, and he needed to have everyone out of the way.

"I guess I don't need to ask what happened," Kharendaen said. "What about you, Dragonlord? I can see that you favor your left arm. I suspect there must be some reason you don't want to come out of that armor."

"I was hit by a magic projectile," Thelvyn explained. "I really don't think it's all that bad, but I prefer to stay in the armor until I'm ready to have it tended to."

"I think we should do something about it immediately," Kharendaen told him firmly. "A single strike from such a missile can be extremely deadly, and I do not trust you to know how badly you are wounded."

Kharendaen took him into her lair while a servant was sent into the house to fetch medical supplies. When everything was ready, Thelvyn teleported out of the armor. It was the first chance even he had to assess his injuries. He had been prepared for the worst, knowing that he had no movement or feeling in his left arm. Indeed, the impact had shattered his collarbone and the outer end of his shoulder blade, ripping skin and muscle apart as the missile progressed through the front of his shoulder and then tore its way out the back. A few inches to the right and it would have nearly taken off his head.

Except for the intervention of magic, Thelvyn would never have hoped to have the use of his arm again. But Kharendaen applied her clerical talents to the task in the most intense spell that Thelvyn had ever witnessed, and it seemed that the Great One was inclined to favor him. In all the old stories, there was always some magic spell or potion powerful enough that even a man near death would leap up again ready to fight. Such things did exist, but healing magic that powerful was rare, and even Kharendaen did not possess it. Her spells moved the shattered bones back into place and fused them, repairing torn muscles and tendons. Even so, Thelvyn could expect not to be back to normal for several days.

"I must return to the place of your battle," the dragon said when they were nearly done. "I need to determine whether you were attacked by dragons who had been enchanted to take human form, or if the transformation of the dead assassin to the form of a dragon was a trick to lay false blame."

"I suspect that they were real dragons," Thelvyn said. "The one I fought was extremely strong. His strength was unnatural, and he was both a skilled warrior and a powerful wizard. Everything suggests that he was not mortal."

"Not mortal, perhaps, but not necessarily dragon," Kharendaen answered. "A dragon may be a skilled warrior, but with the fighting skills of a dragon. When a dragon is enchanted into human form, putting a sword in his hand does not make him able to use it well. Yet you say that he was skilled."

"He seemed to be," Thelvyn said, trying to think. "He might have just been quick and strong, like a dragon. I suppose there's no proof one way or the other."

"I will determine the truth beyond all doubt," she told him. "You go in the house and see how your friend is doing, but I think that you should stay with me this night."

Kharendaen left to complete her task, no doubt frightening the city guard and any remaining late-night revelers half to death. She wasn't at all in the habit of going out into the streets, especially not at night. Solveig had since been taken to her room, and the healer had done all he could. Now he would have to allow matters to work on their own for a time before he could begin using new spells and potions to lead her step by step to a complete recovery.

"She has a long and difficult road ahead of her," he explained to Thelvyn. "I do not expect her to be able to walk about for at least five days, and full recovery will require a month or more. I will stay this night, in the event she takes a bad turn."

"But she will recover?" Thelvyn insisted, greatly concerned. "What I mean is, she will regain her full strength and agility as a warrior?"

"Oh, yes," the healer insisted. "Given time and the proper techniques in healing, it will be as if she had never been injured. But I will say that the dragon saved her life. You might even say, technically speaking, that she was dead, except that your dragon kept calling her back to life. Anyway, she is going to be restless for a time while the potions do their work. You can go in and see her now."

Thelvyn opened the door quietly and stepped inside. Solveig was settled back on a great mound of pillows that kept her body inclined. A small lamp cast a soft light on the table beside her. She was bandaged and dressed in a white shirt, and she didn't appear much the worse, aside from the fact that she looked very pale and tired.

"So the assassin got you as well?" she asked.

"Magic dart," he explained, sitting in the chair beside the bed so that he could face her. "Kharendaen says I should be fine in a few days."

"I'm told that your dragon saved my life," Solveig remarked. "I'm afraid I don't remember what happened. I'm . . . impressed."

"Listen, I can't say how sorry I am about this," Thelvyn insisted. "I feel like this is all the fault of my own pride and vanity."

"No, it's not your fault. I invited myself, remember. If you had gone to the reception alone as you had planned, I would have never been in danger."

"Well, I've learned my lesson," Thelvyn assured her. "I'll never wear shoes again, not even to the king's wedding."

Solveig tried to laugh, but it hurt too much. "Are you sure that this isn't his doing? He said he was going to get back at you."

Thelvyn ignored her comment, knowing it was only a joke. "The one you killed turned into a black dragon," he told her. "That was why they were so hard to fight. Kharendaen has gone to confirm whether or not they were really dragons in enchanted form. If they were rogue or renegade dragons, that was probably the best chance they will ever have of getting rid of me. It almost worked."

"I hope you realize that they couldn't possibly have been working alone," Solveig said. "Do you really expect that they just happened to make their attempt on the one night in months that you were vulnerable? Someone told them you were going to be isolated from your armor for a few hours."

"I can't believe that Kharendaen or the Parliament of Dragons could be involved."

"I don't believe it either," she said. "Kharendaen loves you too much to betray you, even if the parliament had asked it of her. But keep in mind that you have enemies who are not dragons, and some of them have attacked you before. For one thing, you can't be very popular with the Alphatians these days. They might even know how to enlist a renegade dragon in their schemes. If so, now that the attempt on you has failed, the king might be in a great deal of danger just now. At least those two are dead."

Thelvyn didn't really know whether or not the second assassin had escaped, although he expected that to be the case. But the damage to Solveig's chest kept her from speaking anymore, and so he left her to rest while he retired to the silence of Kharendaen's lair. Since the gold dragon hadn't yet returned, he settled himself into a large chair next to the cushions of her bed. His shoulder hurt and he felt tired, but he couldn't stop himself from brooding about the events of that night, especially his own mistakes. Kharendaen came in a short time later; he heard her closing the yard gate before she crouched to slip through the door, which she closed and locked behind her.

"They were real dragons," she said as she settled herself into her bed, her neck turned so that she faced him. "I suspect they were both black dragons, and I think the one you fought was an elder, perhaps the leader of a band of renegades. He did escape, by the way, although you injured him enough that he will not be back any time soon."

"Solveig thinks the king is in danger now," Thelvyn said. "She also thinks they must have had someone here who told them I would be vulnerable tonight."

"I believe she is correct on both accounts," Kharendaen agreed. "But it would be difficult to guess who the informer might be, if indeed it was anyone you know. Anyone who saw you being fit for your clothes would have been aware of your plans."

"She also pointed out that the Alphatians would have reason to be afraid of me, if they have the impression that I might be involving myself in a war against them."

"I cannot say," she answered. "Often renegades will hate and fear other dragons so much that they will make alliances with the enemies of dragons. I suspect that to be the case here, rather than the possibility of renegade dragons acting against you alone. But tonight was the best chance of defeating you they will ever have, and I suspect that the matter has resolved itself with the failure of this attempt. I have sent word to Jherridan to be especially on his guard."

"Would they have needed help in assuming human

form?" Thelvyn asked. "I've never heard of dragons doing that."

"I am uncertain about this part," Kharendaen explained. "Many dragons, especially the greater breeds like reds and golds, do possess the ability to take human or elvish form at will. But your attackers were black dragons, a lesser breed. The Parliament of Dragons fears you enough that they might attempt such an act, but they would have sent more powerful enemies against you than a couple of black dragons. The one you fought was a wizard, and he may have had the ability to transform himself and his companion into human form."

"Are you able to take human form?"

"I could," she agreed reluctantly. "However, my duty to the Great One forbids it."

Thelvyn settled himself more comfortably into the chair. "How did you know that I needed you?"

"The Great One warned me in a vision," she explained.

"It's nice to know that everyone is watching out for me," Thelvyn remarked. "My own patron seems to have let me down on that one. Still, the fault was entirely my own. I acted stupidly."

"You cannot deny all pleasures in your life for the sake of your duty or security," Kharendaen told him. "The chance you took was a reasonable one, and you could not have known that your enemies had gone to such lengths to attack you at one of the rare times when you were vulnerable. But I think you should rest now. Tomorrow will bring new problems, I am sure, not the least of which will be the complaints of your injuries."

CHAPTER SIX

Kharendaen might well have been a prophet when she predicted the next day would be a troubled one for Thelvyn, except that her prophecies were matters of simple logic. The day began with problems, the first being that there was a dead dragon in the middle of the street in one of the most fashionable districts of the city. The problem wasn't so much how to remove the body, but whose responsibility it was to do so. The city guard, the king's army, and the sanitation department were all arguing the matter, and everyone was understandably reluctant to begin cutting up the carcass to haul it away. Since black dragons were among the smallest breeds, Kharendaen offered to lift it into a large freight wagon if one could be brought to the site. As a cleric of the Great One, she felt a certain responsibility for the proper removal of dead dragons, even those who had tried to kill her friends.

Thelvyn's problems were much more serious. He arrived at the palace to find that the king's guard seemed to be preparing for war. Of course, he realized that the king might look upon that as a reasonable precaution under the circumstances. Taeryn met him just as he entered.

"The king wishes see you," the young valet said. "I was on my way to tell you."

"I thought I should get here as soon as I could," Thelvyn answered.

"The tall lady is going to be fine?" Taeryn asked anxiously.

"Yes."

Taeryn led him quickly to the king's chamber, where he wasn't surprised to find Jherridan and Byen Kalestraan already in the middle of a furious debate. Thelvyn was inclined to think that they were overreacting. He had been the subject of assassination attempts when he first became the Dragonlord, and it had not been considered a matter of national emergency.

"So, there you are," Jherridan declared as he entered. "I was told that you may have been wounded."

"I received an injury to my left shoulder," Thelvyn explained as he settled stiffly into a chair where he could face the others. "Kharendaen worked her magic on it, so I should be back to normal in a couple of days. I have it bandaged in a way that will allow me access to my armor."

"At least you can defend yourself," Jherridan remarked. "What about Solveig? A guard came for my healer, and he seemed very concerned."

"Solveig has had a very bad time of it," Thelvyn explained. "The healer said she'll recover completely, but it will take time."

"I'm sorry to hear that," Jherridan said. "Solveig is a most remarkable lady, and the two of you make a perfect match."

"Perhaps a little too perfect," Thelvyn replied. "I don't think you should expect too much from that. Solveig was merely entertaining herself a bit last night. She has a very subtle sense of humor."

The king rose from his chair to began slowly pacing the floor. "Thanks to the ambassador and his amorous daughter, I feel as if I were the one they tried to assassinate last night. My only comfort was the thought that the barbarian woman had caught you. But that's the least of my problems. We must demand an accounting of this from the dragons. What does Kharendaen have to say about it?"

"I don't need Kharendaen to tell me not to attach too much significance to what happened last night," Thelvyn said, for once making no effort to stand simply because the king had. "There have been assassination attempts against me before. The difference this time was that I carelessly allowed myself be caught in a vulnerable situation. Someone knew that I would be vulnerable and took advantage of that. I don't believe it was merely an unfortunate coincidence."

"No, there is no question of that," Jherridan agreed. "It appears obvious there is a traitor among us."

"I'm not so certain that there is a traitor," Thelvyn insisted. "A spy watching my movements could have observed me being fitted for clothes and boots, and it would have been simple enough to figure out what I was going to use them for. Unfortunately, I could never make a secret of the restrictions I have getting into my armor, since that explains my appearance. Otherwise, I'm not too sure just who would have known about it ahead of time and would have gained any advantage by betraying me. I recall that even Kalestraan was quite surprised at my attire last night."

"Your dragon would have known," Kalestraan said, speaking for the first time. "You were attacked by dragons enchanted into human form. Can you be certain that she has not betrayed you to dragon assassins?"

Thelvyn shook his head. "Kharendaen has no reason to betray me when she has so many opportunities to kill me herself. I slept in her bed last night. I often do. If she wanted me dead, I would not be here now."

Jherridan paused in his pacing to consider that briefly and nodded in agreement. "I have to admit that she seems unlikely to be a part of any conspiracy to kill you. What does she have to say about the attack?"

"She found out that the dead assassin was a black dragon," Thelvyn explained. "The black dragons are one of the lesser breeds, and many of them are renegades. I honestly believe that they were working alone. The renegade dragons fear me most, since, by the terms of the truce, they are the only dragons that I am free by the terms of the truce to slay. Granted, renegades may also be willing to work with other enemies for pay if nothing else."

"But someone would have had to enchant them into human form," Kalestraan pointed out.

"Not necessarily. Kharendaen told me that most of the greater breeds of dragons have the ability to assume human or elvish form, and the assassin I fought was a powerful wizard. Under the circumstances, one of them might have even been the spy, in human guise."

"It seems to me that you are going out of your way to defend the dragons," Jherridan remarked coldly.

"I don't see any evidence whatsoever to accuse the Nation of Dragons of being behind the attack," Thelvyn insisted. "And even if they were, the attempt failed, and they know I'll be too cautious for them to catch me by surprise a second time. I don't see any point in stirring up trouble with the Nation of Dragons over a matter that is ended, and which probably did not even involve them."

"We have no reason to fear the dragons," Kalestraan said. "You have the advantage over them."

"No, quite the contrary. They have the advantage over me," Thelvyn said. "They must know it, but their fear of the first Dragonlord has kept them from forcing their advantage so far. The first Dragonlord seems to have had the mobility to chase down dragons as well as the power to defeat them. I did not inherit that same mobility. I don't even know what it was. Kharendaen has provided me with a degree of mobility, but she isn't going to serve me in any war against the Nation of Dragons. And there's nothing I can do about a dragon who doesn't want to fight me when I'm standing on the ground."

"But you would still be in a defensive position," Jherridan said.

"I doubt that I would be very effective. The dragons could use their mobility against me. If they attacked this city, they could burn down a large portion before I could even get there. All they have to do is to stay beyond the reach of my weapons and they can do what they want with impunity."

Jherridan shook his head. "I can't ignore the attempt on your life. The appearance is that the dragons have broken their truce, and I must believe that until it can be proven otherwise. You've already told us that the dragons have reason to feel they have some complaint with us for having possibly stolen their treasure. As I see it, they would have to remove the Dragonlord before they could safely move against us. For that reason, I am forced to take this attack upon the Dragonlord to be an act of war. I declare that all dragons within the realm and in the Wendarian Ranges must depart, or they will be fought to the death. It is my decision that plans should be made at once for the Dragonlord to lead an army into the northern Highlands."

Thelvyn frowned, greatly displeased. "You are aware that Kharendaen will have no part in this. If we move against the dragons, then there will no question that the truce has been broken. By the terms of the truce, she will be required to depart."

"That is not our concern," Kalestraan said. "We cannot have a spy for the Parliament of Dragons in our company."

Thelvyn did not reply at once, still frowning. "You have forced me into a very difficult position. Whatever you do is entirely your concern, but I am not your subject, and you cannot order me. If I do not take part in this and remove myself from the Highlands, then I have not broken my truce with the dragons. In that way, the conflict will be confined only to the Highlands."

"Are you refusing to obey me?" Jherridan asked, standing with his arms crossed.

Thelvyn rose to leave. "Perhaps I should say that I will be taking this matter under consideration. My duty as the Dragonlord is to the world, not just to the Highlands. If I think you are wrong in your attack on the dragons, then I cannot help you. Indeed, if you get yourself in trouble, then I may not be able to defend you. I hope you are completely aware of the consequences of your actions. At the very least, you are throwing away five years of work on your alliance against

Alphatia."

He left the king and Kalestraan to reconsider their plans. He could see that they had been expecting him to handle the dragons for them, and he wanted it understood that he was unwilling to have any part in their plans and also could not hope to fight the entire Nation of Dragons alone. If they had to fight the dragons without him, he reasoned they would not be so quick to want to. Thelvyn decided not to return to the palace for a while, to make certain that they understood he was serious about exercising his independence.

Whatever happened, Thelvyn knew, he had to be very, very careful. He was suddenly in the middle of the worst trouble since the attacks of the rogue dragons five years before, potentially far worse trouble. It would be far better to have a falling out with King Jherridan and the Highlands than with the Parliament of Dragons.

* * * * *

Thelvyn was in no mood to find himself in the middle of a pointless war. He was worried about Solveig most of all, but he was also concerned for Kharendaen and whether he might lose her. More than likely, he would have to leave his home in the Highlands in order to protect his position of neutrality. Among his lesser annoyances, his injured shoulder was also bothering him. It was a constant reminder of his foolishness, a mistake that had nearly cost Solveig her life.

While he and Kharendaen both had been expecting trouble to come of the attack, neither of them had anticipated this. King Jherridan's actions were extreme, even irrational, if he thought that he could declare war against the Nation of Dragons when he had not even been able to defend his land against the rogue dragons five years before. But Thelvyn knew the Flaem well enough that he didn't find this turn of events unusual. They were typically a rather unemotional lot, but they didn't bear assaults to their pride well, especially their belief that they were superior to all others, men or dragon. Jherridan was indeed capable of driving his country to destruction, since his pride didn't allow him to anticipate the possibility of defeat.

Thelvyn needed to return home to consult with Kharendaen at once. Since he wasn't able to negotiate directly with the Parliament of Dragons himself, he very much needed her to speak for him. He found her sitting outside, beneath the trees, and she rubbed her nose affectionately against his chest the moment he arrived. He quickly explained the situation. The great gold dragon took it very seriously indeed.

"This is insane," she complained, sitting up on her haunches. "Five years ago, the rogue dragons were acting entirely upon their own. But if the Flaem plan to attack dragons living peacefully in lands they are entitled to inhabit, then the Nation of Dragons will surely consider it an act of war."

Thelvyn settled himself stiffly on the bench beneath the tree, shaking his head helplessly. "I know Jherridan is capable of being completely irrational, but I'm beginning to wonder if he had some assistance in jumping to conclusions. Byen Kalestraan was sitting there offering advice and opinions. He wants the resident dragon thrown out of the city as a spy, although that seemed to come as a surprise to Jherridan. He acted as if you were my property."

"Your king has always been aware of my advantages," Kharendaen said.

"He's not my king," Thelvyn declared. "I've threatened to leave. I pointed out to him that my only real duty as the Dragonlord is to maintain peace with the dragons, not keep them subdued no matter what. If he still insists upon chasing the dragons out of the northern mountains, then I'll leave the Highlands rather than seem to approve such plans."

"I fear that it may not be that simple," Kharendaen told him. "Your duty could become rather complicated at that point. The dragons might hold you responsible. Any attack upon them by other races will be seen as a breaking of the truce on your part, although technically that is not correct. The dragons may even expect you to defend them from attack in order protect your part in the truce. Would you be willing to go to war with the Flaem?"

"My word, that *could* get complicated," Thelvyn said thoughtfully. "But I've had to consider this once already with the Alphatians. If the dragons are being unjustly attacked, then I would have to defend them. My duty, at least as I see it, seems to be to prevent the dragons from going to war, no matter how. The Flaem are not my people, and I feel no need to take their side when they are obviously wrong."

"That's still getting ahead of ourselves," Kharendaen reminded him. "Our first concern must be how to keep this war from even getting started."

"I can only do my best," Thelvyn agreed. "I was wondering if I should send you to the Parliament of Dragons. If they could formally deny any part in the attack on me, I could use that to undermine the king's plans for war. At the least, I need to know what their reaction is going to be and what they expect of me."

"Yes, that is so," she agreed. "They will most certainly deny involvement in the assassination. And the fact that you appear to be acting in their best interests may impress them. I can only try. Do you want me to leave at once?"

"I think you should," Thelvyn said. "I need something I can work with as soon as possible. And I want you to return before I have to leave the Highlands, if it comes to that. I trust that the parliament will allow you to return. I haven't broken the terms of the truce."

"My brother Marthaen suspects that my duty to you was secretly commanded by the Great One," Kharendaen said. "He will make certain I am allowed to return. I must not be parted from you."

It was still the midmorning, and Kharendaen left for the Parliament of Dragons at once. Thelvyn watched her as she lumbered out into the yard and leaped into the sky, climbing in broad circles over the city. He knew her departure would be noticed by others, and he hoped it gave the king something to think about. Just the same, he felt very vulnerable without her. Kharendaen's company had always given him not only prestige but also a high degree of mobility, both decided advantages over his enemies. But she had also been his closest and dearest friend, unhesitating in her support and affection.

Now that Thelvyn faced the possibility of being separated from Kharendaen for the first time, he realized that he valued her company dearly. As an orphan, he had been able to assemble at least the shadow of a family. Sir George had been like a father to him, or at least a kind and devoted uncle, while Solveig had made a rather erratic sister. But none had been closer or more constant than the dragon.

Thelvyn had expected there would be time to have a brief rest and prepare himself before anything else happened, but it was not to be. Early that same evening, a griffon rider arrived with an urgent message from Emperor Cornelius of Thyatis. Thelvyn accepted the message grimly, only too aware that it implied far worse than it actually stated. Just the same, whether or not it made his own position of neutrality more difficult to defend, he knew that he had to discuss the matter with King Jherridan at once.

"I've just received a message by griffon rider from Thyatis," Thelvyn began when he sat alone with Jherridan in his private chamber. "Unfortunately, it didn't say as much as I wish it did. To put it simply, Thyatian spies have learned that the Alphatians and the dragons have been meeting together, and their discussion has resulted in an alliance. The terms of the alliance are not known, although I suspect that it was more a treaty of surrender on the part of the Alphatians."

"I gather we don't know anything for certain yet, aside from the fact that there has been some type of surrender or alliance made," Jherridan said. "Until I know more, I feel I have to treat this news as the most dangerous of all possible situations. An alliance between the Alphatians and the dragons in a war of conquest would be unstoppable, even with the Dragonlord to defend us, according to what you told me earlier."

"But an alliance makes no sense," Thelvyn protested. "Why would the dragons want an alliance with Alphatia? If they were interested in building an empire, they could have conquered all of this part of the world, including Alphatia, long ago."

"For the dragons, you are the primary enemy," Jherridan reminded him. "Obviously the dragons feel such an alliance gives them the power they need to deal with the Dragonlord, the only enemy they have cause to fear. The nations of the west can't help you fight the dragons or act in retaliation if they are tied down by a war with Alphatia. And with the dragons keeping you occupied, the Dragonlord can't hope to defend the west against the Alphatians. It seems to me that an alliance solves both their problems."

Thelvyn frowned. Unfortunately, the alliance made sense if the dragons were prepared to go to war with the Dragonlord. He realized something that he had not considered before, that the dragons could have convinced themselves he had been involved in the theft of the Collar of the Dragons. He had been so busy with his suspicions regarding Kalestraan that he had failed to consider that the dragons might look upon him in much the same way they did the Fire Wizards. Thelvyn desperately needed for Sir George to find that collar in order to divert the suspicions of the dragons away from him as well as forestall their anger against the Flaem.

"I don't know what to say," he admitted helplessly at last. "You seem determined to provoke a war with the dragons. They've kept the truce and stayed out of the Highlands, and you conceded them the right to inhabit the Wendarian Range. If you attempt to drive them from lands that you agreed they could claim as their own, then you're making war inevitable. That was the very cause of their conflict with the Alphatians, and you saw how fiercely they fought to defend their lands."

"My best hope for defending the Highlands against an enemy as dangerous as the dragons is to move quickly," the king insisted, although he appeared to be wavering. Even he had to admit that attacking the dragons in their rightful lands was an extremely provocative act.

"Kalestraan hasn't been pushing you toward this, has

he?" Thelvyn asked candidly. "You know that if he were involved in the theft of the treasure of the dragons, he wouldn't think twice about using both of us to stand between him and their justifiable anger."

This time, it was Jherridan's turn to sit for a long moment in thoughtful silence. Finally he sighed, still looking uncertain. "I don't know what to think anymore. Kalestraan is pushing me too quickly toward war. You push me away from war. My only concern is the defense of my own land, and I agree that war with the dragons would be a disaster for us. But our disadvantage is even greater if we wait for them to come to us."

"My duty is to do anything I can to prevent the dragons from going to war," Thelvyn explained. "If you give me a chance to work with you, I hope to be able to promise you the security you need without the cost of a war. And if the dragons are determined to provoke a war, then I will defend you. You may or may not be aware of it, but Kharendaen has already departed to speak with the Parliament of Dragons. We should have their answer soon."

"All the same, I feel I must prepare for the worst."

"Yes, I agree," Thelvyn said. "I just hope it hasn't come to that.

"Then what do you suggest?"

"Well, you were determined to push the dragons into breaking the truce. Now you're stuck with it. There's not much I can do to prevent this war if you continue to provoke the dragons in the lands you promised them."

Jherridan nodded slowly, still looking pensive. "I still don't see that I have any choice. Whether intentionally or not, the dragons have threatened us, both in their attack upon you and in their reported alliance with the Alphatians. I will continue to prepare the Highland Army for war, and I will begin moving forces into the frontier. For now, I want no dragon but Kharendaen to enter the Highlands, and I am still prepared to force the dragons out of Wendar as well. But I will do nothing more for now until Kharendaen returns with the parliament's reply."

Thelvyn had to admit that was the best he could hope for, considering that the situation appeared to have taken a very bad turn. He still believed that this was all a great misunderstanding, that the purported alliance involved nothing more than Alphatia's surrender to the demands of the dragons to withdraw from their lands. Considering that they had gone to war over that very issue, it was the most logical assumption. Until Kharendaen returned and could tell him more, all he could do was wait and hope that no side did anything to make war inevitable.

Thelvyn was reminded of the time, shortly after he had become the Dragonlord, when he had spoken with Marthaen on the subject of misunderstandings. Marthaen had explained his belief that the first war with the Dragonlord had begun with a misunderstanding. The more the wizards of Blackmoor fought to protect themselves from the threat of the dragons, the more the dragons fought to protect themselves from the threat of Blackmoor. Marthaen had spoken of his concern that a new war with the Dragonlord might easily begin through just such a misunderstanding, and now his words seemed prophetic. The dragons had been provoked by the theft of the collar and by the need to defend their own lands. They had made the situation worse in their zeal to protect their secrets. And they could not defend themselves, even when they had been wronged, without awakening the fears of others.

King Jherridan wasn't prepared to relent on the subject of the dragons just yet. The next morning, he gave orders to have the Highland Army prepare to march north to establish new forts and strengthen those already in existence. If the dragons did not withdraw from the mountains of the Wendarian Range soon, then the army would enter the mountains to remove them. Jherridan would have liked to send the Dragonlord at once to some of their closer allies to request support, but Thelvyn had caused an unintentional delay in that by sending Kharendaen to the Parliament of Dragons.

Of course, sending a show of force to the frontier wasn't the same as actually fighting the dragons who lived in the mountains to the north, beyond the borders of the Highlands. Whether or not war developed would depend a great deal upon the king's resolve and on how the dragons responded.

Thelvyn had hoped to be left alone, but it now seemed that everyone had plans for him. The next morning, Byen Kalestraan sent a messenger to deliver a request for the Dragonlord to come to the wizard's private chamber at the Academy. The wording was cordial enough, far more friendly than the senior wizard had been the last time they had spoken. Thelvyn thought he had a good idea what Kalestraan had in mind. The wizard either wanted to plead Jherridan's case for war privately, or else offer some secret evidence implicating the dragons, the Alphatians, or both.

After brief consideration, he decided to accept the invitation, thinking it best to learn just what Kalestraan did have in mind. Thelvyn had been to the Academy, or indeed anywhere else in that part of the city, only rarely in all the time he had lived in Braejr. He was escorted immediately to Kalestraan's private chamber, where he found the wizard to be much more friendly and helpful than he had the other night. Thelvyn was offered a comfortable chair and a cool drink. He had to decide quickly if the Fire Wizard would dare attempt to drug or poison him.

"I have attempted to prepare for all possibilities," Kalestraan began, coming directly to the point. "As you said yourself, if you were required to go to war with the dragons, you would immediately lose the assistance of your dragon, and without a dragon to carry you, you would lack the mobility needed to fight dragons effectively. You felt that the first Dragonlord must have possessed some magical means of mobility, but you had no idea what it was."

"That is so," Thelvyn agreed, surprised by Kalestraan's unexpected helpfulness.

"I have been looking into the possibility of finding you some magical means of flight, something to give you the same advantages the dragons possess," the wizard continued. "For once I can say that our research has proven to be both simple and fruitful. Rather than one possibility, we must decide upon the best of several such methods."

"That sounds encouraging," Thelvyn said guardedly, wanting to know more.

"I think we can safely assume that the first Dragonlord did not ride a dragon into battle against other dragons. A captive dragon would have been unreliable, and an enchanted one would have been unpredictable. In either case, the dragon would have been far more vulnerable to attack than the Dragonlord himself. Have you had any thoughts about the secret of his mobility?"

Thelvyn shook his head helplessly. "I always thought he must have possessed some magical flying device, perhaps something like an armored sled or carriage."

"Perhaps, but that seems to me to lack the elegant simplicity of the enchanted armor itself," Kalestraan said. "Whatever his means of flight, we can be sure it left the first Dragonlord free to use his weapons and defenses in the most effective way possible. My own suspicion is that the magical artifact must have been small and simple enough to incorporate it as an actual part of the armor. The fact that it was not with the enchanted armor when you received it does not mean that we cannot arrange a substitute."

"Then you have something specific in mind?" Thelvyn asked.

"Indeed. My hope is that the armor itself may give us a clue to the nature of the magical device by showing us the place where it was attached to the armor and possibly even its shape."

"Then you want me to summon the armor?" Thelvyn asked suspiciously.

"Summon it?" Kalestraan asked, seemingly confused.

"I really don't know what becomes of the armor when I teleport it away," he explained. "I simply will it off and will it to come back. But I have never physically removed it in the same manner one would remove one's clothing."

Thelvyn didn't add that he certainly wasn't about to hand it over to Byen Kalestraan even if he could.

"If you would simply teleport into it, then we might inspect it," the mage assured him.

Still fearful of some kind of trap, Thelvyn had to consider that briefly. The enchantments of the armor had stood against the best that Jherdar, the crafty leader of the red dragons, had been able to throw at it. He felt certain there was nothing that Kalestraan would be able to do to harm it. He teleported into the armor, then removed the helmet.

"I can see one thing right away," the wizard remarked. "There are two attachments on the shoulders, one on either side, obviously meant to hold a cape. Was there a cape with it when you received it?"

"No, there never was," Thelvyn said. "I always assumed the cape had been optional, perhaps merely a ceremonial decoration that would have only been in the way during battle. Could this cape have been the magical artifact of flight?"

"Nothing would be simpler," Kalestraan replied, obviously quite satisfied with himself. "What indeed is a cape but a large square or rectangular piece of fabric or cloth? In essence, a flying carpet."

"A flying carpet?" Thelvyn seemed dubious. "I can't imagine a flying carpet being stable enough for the first Dragonlord to have ridden one into battle, nor can I imagine trying to fight a dragon while hanging from one by the shoulders. Or are you thinking of something different?"

"More likely, I suspect, the artifact imparted the power of flight directly to the wearer, responding to his will. In a sense, flight was a part of the enchantment of the armor, although that enchantment was instilled within the cape. It seems the cape was either destroyed or for some reason was missing at the time the first Dragonlord retired his armor."

"Can you duplicate such a device?" Thelvyn asked.

"We can certainly research the matter. A modification of the spell would impart the enchantment of flight to the wearer, rather than to the carpet itself. That should be irrelevant to the spell of flight. A carpet has never been the most stable or practical vehicle of flight, but it has always been highly effective for holding a spell. That is why it would be better to adapt the spell of flight to a cape rather than attempt to infuse it into the armor itself, especially considering the powerful enchantments the armor already possesses."

"I always wondered why flying carpets seemed so

common," Thelvyn said. "However, they don't seem especially safe."

"They're not," Kalestraan replied as he returned to his seat behind the desk. "Fortunately, this aspect of the Dragonlord's armor is perhaps the only part we can duplicate. I am certain we'll be able to give you the speed and agility of a dragon soon. I understand your friend Kharendaen has not yet returned."

"I expect her back by tomorrow at the latest," Thelvyn said. He teleported from his armor and returned to his seat.

"You obviously expect the dragons to claim they had no part in the attack upon you," the wizard continued. "Is there any chance they might be persuaded to declare their support to our own alliance against Alphatia, to prove that they are not already secretly allied with the Alphatian mages?"

"I can understand your concern about an alliance between Alphatia and the dragons," Thelvyn replied guardedly, curious.

"I must consider it a very real concern. Enemies of the Dragonlord could be expected to find a common cause."

When he finally left the meeting with Kalestraan, Thelvyn felt rather confused. The wizard still seemed determined to go to war with someone, although he no longer seemed concerned whether he was fighting the dragons or fighting with the dragons against the Alphatians. The only thing Thelvyn was sure about was that war must in some way be to the wizard's advantage. Thelvyn was unsure just what he thought of the possibility of flying about with a flying carpet tied to his neck. He wished that he could ask Kharendaen for her advice on the matter.

Kharendaen returned the next evening, settling heavily into the courtyard just at twilight. Thelvyn could see she had exhausted herself by making the journey as quickly as possible. He decided not to pester her for news until she had eaten and drunk most of a barrel of Flaemish sweet ale. Then Thelvyn moved his chair closer so that he could face her as she reclined in her bed in the lair.

"How do matters stand in Braejr?" she asked.

"Very much the same as when you left," Thelvyn explained. "I'm afraid Jherridan and I have had something of a falling out, although I believe he is becoming more willing to listen to reason. At the same time, Kalestraan has his wizards hard at work making a magical artifact of flight for me. In other words, I won't need you. I just don't know if he actually means to give it to me."

"But the king has not changed his plans to drive the dragons from the mountains?"

Thelvyn shook his head helplessly. "The army is making plans to fortify the northern frontier. Whether he actually marches them into the mountains remains to be seen."

"Unfortunately, the situation is not very simple as far as the Parliament of Dragons is concerned either," Kharendaen explained. "They declared that they had no part in the attack upon you and they have not broken the truce. They will defend themselves against any attack, but they are also willing to keep the truce if Jherridan will."

"That is very much as I expected," Thelvyn observed.

"There is this to consider," Kharendaen continued. "They reminded me that Jherridan himself requested the truce with the Nation of Dragons five years ago, and the dragons now expect that he should abide by the terms of that truce. Specifically, the dragons are to be free to inhabit the Wendarian Range. If Jherridan sends his army into the mountains, it would be the same as invading another country, and the dragons will consider that an act of war. In other words, the dragons feel that the responsibility for the breaking of the truce is with the Flaem, not you. They don't necessarily hold you accountable for the king's actions, but they will attack if provoked. How you respond to that situation is entirely up to you."

"Meaning that if the Flaem ask for trouble, I have to decide whether or not to let them choke on what they've bitten off," Thelvyn mused. "Well, the best I can do for now is to try to talk Jherridan out of actually attacking the dragons."

"The Collar of the Dragons also remains an issue," she added. "The parliament is now satisfied that the Alphatians do not have it, which directs even more of their suspicion toward the Flaem. As a sign of good faith, they would like to have it returned, or else be permitted to assure themselves that it is not here, although they are not yet prepared to press that point as a requirement for peace."

Thelvyn looked grim. "I think I know how Kalestraan is going to respond to that. To cover his own schemes, he's been pressing the king even harder to make war with the dragons. Even Jherridan admits it."

The dragon replied with obvious reluctance. "The treasure of the dragons must be returned soon. We are aware that the Fire Wizards are experimenting with some source of incredible power they have discovered in this place, although they seem to have not yet been able to command it in any practical manner. All the same, they must not use artifacts of the dragons to play with terrible things they do not understand."

"I know that, but my first priority is to keep the dragons from going to war," Thelvyn insisted. "All I can do about the Collar of the Dragons for now is to hope that Sir George is able to discover some clue about how it was stolen or where it is."

CHAPTER SEVEN

Thelvyn found himself standing in a field of grass of emerald green, stirred in gentle waves by a cooling breeze. Great mountains surrounded him on all sides—towering, majestic peaks, clad in fields and forests of tall pines with crowns of gray stone and white snow. The glade where he stood was on the slopes of such a mountain, and he could look out across a deep valley where a swift river weaved through forests and fields. The sky above was as blue as sapphire, with a scattering of white clouds that clung to the tops of the highest summits.

He knew almost from the first that this was a dream. Although he had heard of dreams sent by the Immortals to influence their clerics, he had never experienced such a thing for himself. He knew that he hadn't left his home in Braejr. This land was the very image of all that was perfect in the mountain lands, too perfect to be a part of the mortal world.

A tall woman stood before him, a woman with black hair and large, dark eyes, and an almost aristocratic presence.

He knew at once that this imposing lady was his mother, Arbendael, whose spirit he had met years ago on the slopes of the mystic World Mountain. She was unlike anyone he had ever known, both in appearance and bearing. He wondered if what he saw in her was in any way what others saw in him. Somehow, by the circumstances of his dream, he didn't even think to ask her any of the many questions that would have otherwise been so important to him, and which she certainly would have refused to have answered.

"Thelvyn? Do you understand what is happening?" she asked.

"I do. This dream is a vision sent to me by my patron, to instruct me in matters that I must know of. But am I really speaking to you, or are you my patron, appearing in the form of my mother?"

"I am indeed Arbendael," she answered simply. "A time of great trouble is at hand, and you must do your best to handle it. Both you and your companion, Kharendaen, will be asked to do something you will not wish to do. You are both sharing this same dream."

Thelvyn turned to see that Kharendaen was now standing in the field beside him. He had to suppose that, as a senior cleric, she was far more experienced in this than he was. There had been times, he knew, when the Great One had given her very detailed instructions.

"I cannot tell you for certain what will come to pass," Arbendael continued. "Yet if events unfold as they seem destined, then this is how you each must respond. If the truce is broken, then Kharendaen will be required to return to the dragons. But do not despair, for you will not be separated for long. Kharendaen, when the time comes that you must leave, the Great One will give you specific instructions regarding what you must do."

"I understand," the dragon agreed obediently.

"Thelvyn, your duty is more difficult to explain," his mother said. "You must remain in the Highlands and attend to your duty as advisor to King Jherridan and a captain of the Highlands army. While the destiny of the dragons remains your primary duty, you must recall that the dragons are able to protect themselves, and you have proven your ability to defeat the dragons without doing them serious harm. At this time, it is more important that you do all you can to prevent the dragons from doing great harm to others."

"I will do what I must," Thelvyn answered. "But I feel that I have enemies on all sides, the dragons being the least. Can you tell me whether I can trust the king and Mage Kalestraan? I am suspicious that either the Fire Wizards or the Alphatians may be behind all of this, although I can only guess what they hope to gain."

"The obvious answers are the correct ones," Arbendael told him. "Your enemies would use you if they could, and everyone would rather be rid of you if you do not act to their advantage, even the dragons. But that is the way of politics. You must trust only those who have always been your friends. But you may be reassured to know that you will almost certainly be given a new advisor for the duration of Kharendaen's absence."

At this point, Thelvyn awoke abruptly. As he had expected, he found himself lying in his own bed in the heavy darkness of the deepest part of the night. The air felt rather cool, almost like early autumn. He rose and quickly put on a shirt and trousers, then slipped quietly out of his room. The house was dark and silent, although his night vision allowed him to find his way in even the deepest shadows.

When he opened the side door into the court, he wasn't surprised to see a light in the windows of Kharendaen's lair. Knowing that she was awake, he didn't hesitate to cross the court and open the door to the converted warehouse. He found her lying on her bed, although she lifted her head as if she had been expecting him. The magic lanterns glowed softly, so that they cast only a dim, cool light, and her immense blue eyes glittered as she regarded him down the length of her slender muzzle. At that moment, he thought she must be the most beautiful, graceful creature in all the world.

"I presume we both had the same dream," he began. "Such a thing has never happened to me before, so I wanted to be certain it was real. Am I supposed to take these things at face value, or are there hidden meanings?"

Kharendaen smiled, a remarkably becoming expression. "The Immortals are under such constraints that it is easy to become frustrated with them, especially for those of us who must deal with them regularly. It is easy to forget that they are not playing games but doing their very best to help us."

"I'm just worried what I'll do when you have to leave," Thelvyn admitted as he slid a chair close beside the bed. "I've always relied upon you to advise me how best to deal with the dragons."

"Sir George can advise you," she told him. "He has always tried his best to understand dragons. I will return soon enough. I do not believe that this present trouble will take too long to resolve. And do not forget that you will be given a new advisor in my absence. Perhaps you will like your new companion even better than me."

"I'd never believe that."

"You should not say that until you know who will replace me," the dragon insisted. "You may find that you no longer need me, if the Fire Wizards can give you the ability to fly. You are becoming quite experienced in matters of politics and diplomacy, although you may not have had time to notice that."

"Why do I need a practical reason for wanting you around?" Thelvyn asked.

"I suppose that you do not," Kharendaen agreed. "Keep in mind that this will not be the end of your duty as Dragonlord. We are tied together in that duty for a very long time yet to come. We simply had not anticipated that we might best serve our duty separately for a time."

Thelvyn nodded. "I shouldn't begrudge you the chance to spend some time among your own kind. I should have asked you more often if you would like some time away from me. As a cleric, you must have certain duties to your order."

"I will not be spending much of my time at home," she told him. "I will be busy with responsibilities of my own, I am certain. It might add to your frustration to know this, but I received more instructions in my dream than you did.

I had quite a long talk with your mother before you got there."

"What was she like?" Thelvyn asked, careful not to sound as if he envied her. "The only time she talks to me is when she has some portentous message to deliver."

Kharendaen considered that briefly. "Your mother is just as she has always been, as Sir George has always described her to you. She is wise and noble and kind, very much the person you are growing up to be. I might add that you also look very a great deal like your mother."

"I tend to forget that," he admitted. "The last time my mother spoke to me, the spirit of a gold dragon intervened. I only just remembered that."

This time Kharendaen looked troubled. "I must confess to you that the spirit of the gold dragon has watched over you for a very long time. But that is nothing for you to fear."

"Is the spirit the Great One?" he asked.

Kharendaen shook her head. "The Great One does not take that form. He is very ancient and does not belong to any modern breed of dragon. The spirit of the gold dragon you saw is a servant of the Great One. She was a great and powerful cleric who lived long ago, and she serves him even yet."

* * * * *

When Thelvyn went to the palace the next morning, he felt a certain ambivalence about his duty as the Dragonlord. If the dream sent to him by the Great One was any indication, even the Immortals now believed that war with the dragons was inevitable. But he still held some hope that war could be avoided if Jherridan could only be convinced to be reasonable. The dragons had stated their desire to avoid war, and Thelvyn felt sure he could meet them halfway by agreeing to keep his soldiers out of their lands. But Thelvyn also knew that the attack upon himself and Solveig would remain a difficult point. The dragons could deny their guilt, but there was still no proof that they hadn't been involved.

The king was able to meet with Thelvyn in his private chamber at once, and Kalestraan was not present to interfere. The king listened patiently to Thelvyn's arguments, but the Dragonlord could see that he remained unimpressed.

"Without better proof of the dragons' peaceful intentions, I have no choice but to continue as I have," Jherridan said. "But I am willing to strike a bargain with you, something that might make you considerably happier about the entire situation. You are still my advisor and a captain of the Realm. I would be willing to grant you command of the Highland Army and fuller authority for the defense of the northern frontier. If the dragons respond to the closing of the borders by keeping their distance, then I won't ask you to go into the mountains after them. I recognize the impracticality of trying to fight them in their own element."

"That would satisfy your needs?" Thelvyn asked.

"It suits me well enough," the king agreed. "I'm not fool enough to want to fight the entire race of dragons. If your presence on the frontier forces them to withdraw from the area of the border and behave themselves, then I'm satisfied."

Thelvyn settled back in his chair to consider the king's words. After a moment, he frowned. "Frankly, that's the best offer I'm likely to get, and I don't see that I have any choice."

"I was under the impression that you had one other choice," Jherridan reminded him. "The other day, you stated your intention of maintaining your neutrality by leaving the Highlands."

"Is that what you would prefer?" Thelvyn asked candidly.

"Would I offer you command of my army if it were?"

Thelvyn shook his head. "I'm no longer allowed that choice. The dragons have stated, as I said, that a move against their rightful holdings in the Wendarian Mountains would be considered an act of war. Since you no longer require me to chase them out of their own lairs, they might respond to that by some restraint on their own part. My presence would encourage that."

Thelvyn had decided he wasn't about to reveal that the

Immortals had now required him to remain in the Highlands to protect the Flaem from possible attack by he dragons. The dragons were supposedly far better able to take care of themselves, although Thelvyn remained uncertain that he could ever hope of establish a new truce if he was forced to harm or slay any of them. He was suspicious that Jherridan might incorrectly interpret that to mean that the Immortals were taking his side and become entirely too bold.

Still, he was encouraged. Jherridan was granting him authority to use his own discretion, which was actually a fairly generous compromise compared to his more extreme policies of a few days earlier.

"I suppose that this will require Kharendaen to depart," the king said.

Thelvyn nodded. "There is no question of that. Indeed, she has already been given other duties to attend to. The Immortals are to send me a new clerical advisor."

"I suppose that can't be helped," Jherridan said. "I am forced to agree with you that Kharendaen has not been acting against us as a spy, since she has had many opportunities to have done far more damage. I will send word to Kalestraan to remind him of your need for an artifact of magical flight."

Thelvyn came away thinking that things had taken a rather unexpected turn. Although he had always held the title of captain, he had no actual military experience. At least his duties for the foreseeable future were rather simple: He was to direct the movement of troops into the northern frontier to fortify new and existing outposts along the border. He was not to lead his forces into the mountains. If the dragons responded to the arming of the frontier by attacking, he would have to adapt his plans at that time. The dragons had said they would interpret such activities as acts of war and respond, but he still hoped that they wouldn't be so hasty.

In his experience, dragons were often both calculating and cautious in their schemes. If they weren't threatened in their own lands, perhaps they wouldn't feel the need to respond to the fortifying of the frontier. At the same time, they didn't forgive insults to their pride. Thelvyn hardly knew how they would respond. He wondered if they would feel the need to test him at least once, to prove to themselves whether or not they had learned how to fight him. His success in meeting such a test might depend entirely upon whether the Fire Wizards could provide him with the power of flight. If the dragons tested his ability to fight them on their own terms and found him wanting, there wasn't much even the powers of the Dragonlord could do to stop them.

As matters turned out, Jherridan proved to be more clever in arranging his appointments than Thelvyn had expected. Within the hour, he found that an experienced captain had been appointed to serve as his advisor and second-in-command. Thelvyn knew Harl Gairstaan, and he had always found to be him a resourceful officer who was content with his duties and had no political ambitions of his own, the very image of Flaemish dedication. Although Gairstaan was an older man, he seemed to hold no resentment at being appointed to serve the Dragonlord. Instead, he held Thelvyn in the highest regard and actually seemed rather flattered by the association.

"To tell you the truth, I'm relieved not to be directly responsible for dealing with the dragons," he admitted when Thelvyn paid him a visit in his quarters to speak with him privately. "I'm sure you know best how to handle this particular situation."

"The plan is to avoid actual battle if we can," Thelvyn explained. "By fortifying the northern frontier, we will in effect be drawing a line in the sand between the Highlands and the mountains and telling the dragons not to pass beyond it. My hope is that they won't find the prospect of war worth their trouble."

"I've always heard that dragons are fierce and stubborn, quite jealous of anything they consider to be their own," Gairstaan observed.

"They can be, and I grant that they are going to be very offended," Thelvyn admitted. "But since this stays within the bounds of the truce they have honored for five years now, I hope that they'll see that nothing is really changed."

"And if they do attack?"

Thelvyn shook his head helplessly. "That has to be my responsibility. The army will only be moving into the north for the sake of appearance, to strengthen their garrisons and establish new forts in remote areas. For now, I'm willing to leave the actual arming of the frontier to you. What preparations have you made so far?"

"Supplies and a small force of soldiers have already set out for the north," the captain explained, indicating a map on the wall of his chamber. "The Eastern Reach is already as well fortified as it can be. Dragons closed the pass of the Eastern Reach during their attacks five years ago, and Duke Ardelan has done what he can to insure that it doesn't happen again, although I daresay the dragons could close it again easily enough if they wanted to. Our main concentration of new fortifications will be along the base of the mountains in the northwestern frontier, in areas that are still mostly unsettled."

Thelvyn nodded. "I grew up in that area, and I know it well. Of course, the problem with any fortifications is that they don't really do much to contain dragons. They can simply fly over or around our forts and attack wherever they please. I think you should know that, unless the wizards can supply me with the ability to fly, the dragons can deal with me quite effectively by simply ignoring me."

"I see," Gairstaan said, appreciating the full implications. "Well, we'll just have to respond to that as best we can. There might not be much our soldiers can do against dragons, but moving our forces into the north might encourage them to postpone their plans to attack."

Thelvyn shook his head slowly. "Five years ago they were only harassing us, playing with us. If they attack again, this time it will be all-out war, and they're going to be determined to destroy everything. We can't fight that. I still prefer to avoid an open conflict if we can."

"I can now appreciate why you consider that so important," Captain Gairstaan agreed. "I confess I hadn't understood or agreed with your obvious reluctance to fight the dragons even after they had attacked you, nor did I agree entirely with the king's decision that we are not to drive them from the mountains."

"I wanted you to understand our real goals," Thelvyn said. "I am the only one who has any real power to fight dragons, and so the entire purpose of the Highlands army must be to help me to perform my duty. If we can put on a good enough show, perhaps the dragons will be more interested in talking than fighting, and none of our people will have to get hurt."

As a good Flaemish soldier, Captain Gairstaan was more interested in fighting Alphatians than dragons. All that Thelvyn could do now was to review the plans to fortify the Frontier and make any changes necessary. A train of freight wagons was due to leave for the north in a few days, and companies of soldiers to man the garrisons would follow.

Thelvyn decided that he should go along as well. Since the soldiers of dukes Aalban and Ardelan would be involved as well, he wanted to talk with the dukes and their captains in person and make certain they understood their parts in his plans. The problem was that the moment the soldiers left Braejr, whether he was leading them or not, the truce with the dragons would be declared broken and Kharendaen would be obliged to depart.

When he returned home that evening, he discovered that a package had been delivered from Byen Kalestraan. He could guess at once what it must contain, and he was rather surprised that the wizard had actually given it to him, although he supposed his decision to lead the Highlands army once again made him useful. For his own part, Thelvyn's feelings were ambivalent; the price of the cape of flight had been his companionship with Kharendaen, or so it seemed to him.

Without taking the time to open it, he took the package up to Solveig's room so she could see it. He opened the window and called Kharendaen, who came across the courtyard to watch and listen at the window. Thelvyn untied the package and removed out the cape, which was of a rich maroon so deep in color that it looked almost black. The material was thick and dense, yet soft. He felt relieved, since the comparisons to a flying carpet had made him think of wearing a great, gaudy length of Mithlondian rug tied about his neck, complete with gold fringe. One end of the cape was fitted to go around his neck, the ends slipping into the clips on the shoulders of his armor.

"What am I supposed to do now?" Thelvyn asked once they had the cape attached.

"The understanding was that the cape would respond to your will, in the same way your armor functions," Kharendaen reminded him.

With grave feelings of doubt about the abilities of the Fire Wizards, he tried to concentrate. He was as surprised as anyone when he suddenly shot straight up and hit his head against the ceiling so hard that he nearly knocked himself out. He hovered there for several minutes before he collected his wits enough to will himself to come back down. When he did, he dropped out of the air abruptly, nearly landing on the dragon's nose, protruding through the window. Solveig laughed so hard she started to cough.

Kharendaen smiled, although she tried to speak seriously. "That at least answers one question. If you are distracted using your will to command your armor or your weapons, the cape will not suddenly fail you. That is a great advantage. Dragons have to do it the hard way. If we don't keep moving, we fall."

"That's because of the inherent ridiculousness of your situation," Solveig pointed out. "It's never ceased to amaze me that dragons and rocs, two of the largest animals ever to exist, should be able to fly."

"Even a hummingbird will fall if it doesn't keep moving," the dragon reminded her. "How did the cape feel, Thelvyn?"

"The sensation was like floating in water," Thelvyn explained, rubbing his head and staring up at the ceiling. "Going up felt just like floating to the surface from the bottom of a pond."

"With some practice, I believe you will find that the cape suits your needs perfectly," Kharendaen said. "My interest now is in knowing if the defenses of your armor protect the cape as well. I would not want you to engage a dragon in battle only to have the cape destroyed by dragonfire. If the cape failed, at least your suit should protect you from being injured in a fall."

"I'm sure the armor will protect the cape," Thelvyn said. "Anything in contact with the suit, even another person, is protected by the armor's invisible shields."

He teleported out of his armor, forgetting to remove the cape first, and he was somewhat surprised when the cape went right along with it. Since the cape wasn't an original part of the suit, he hadn't expected it to be included in the enchantment of teleportation. Vaguely fearful of having lost the cape, he brought the armor back and was pleased to see that the cape remained attached to the shoulder clips. At least he wouldn't be bothered by having to carry the cape about with him or spending extra time putting it on when he needed it.

"Well, that's certainly convenient," he commented. "If the wizards of Blackmoor really were my ancestors, they certainly knew their business."

"If the first Dragonlord had ridden about on some magical device, the dragons would certainly have remembered it," Kharendaen added. "We know so many other details about him."

"That's just the point, isn't it?" Thelvyn asked. "I now have the same ability to fight dragons as the first Dragonlord. The cape makes all the difference in the effectiveness of the powers I command, from being merely an avoidable annoyance to the dragons to being an unavoidable threat. I can't escape the suspicion that Kalestraan had that very much in mind. Have I now become such a threat that the dragons must destroy me at any cost?"

"I cannot see that it makes much difference," Kharendaen told him. "The Dragonlord has always been a matter of legend and nightmare to the dragons. They fear you beyond reason already."

* * * * *

The first light of dawn was only just coming to the sky when Thelvyn opened the doors to Kharendaen's lair and stepped outside into the cool night air. The dragon would be leaving that morning, and since he had no way of knowing when he would see her again, he had spent her last night with her in the warehouse, just as he had so many other times in the last five years. Now, holding her head and neck down, Kharendaen crouched low to slip through the doorway as she followed Thelvyn out into the courtyard.

"Sometimes I wish I could just fly away with you and be done with politics and kings and wizards," Thelvyn said. "There are times lately when I've wished I were a dragon like you, although I know that's impossible."

"Even if you were secretly a dragon, you would still be the Dragonlord," she said. "And your duty would still require you to remain here. Being the Dragonlord is something only you can do, and it means too much to the entire world for you to forsake that."

"I'll do what I must," he replied. "There's no question of that, and all the wishes in the world can't change it."

Kharendaen shook her head slowly. "I know that we will not be apart for long, certainly not as long as you seem to fear. Nor should you allow the task ahead to concern you so much. The destiny of the dragons is beginning to unfold, but you are only one part of that. Their destiny is not your responsibility, as much as it might seem to be. Immortals are guiding these events. Follow the guidance of the Immortals and everything will be fine."

"That sounds nice, if only the Immortals would confide in me a little more often," Thelvyn said.

Kharendaen smiled. "If you consider, you will recall that the Immortals have always been able to make their will known to you. Perhaps not directly, but through the advice of clerics like myself, or else by guiding the path of your life in ways that made the right choices unavoidable, even when they were not obvious. Remember that a new companion has been promised to you, a cleric who will help you during the time I cannot be with you."

"Your trust must be very reassuring," Thelvyn mused. "My circumstances have never permitted me to develop such trust. Clerics have the companionship of their fellow clerics, but I've always belonged to an order of one, myself alone following the will of an unknown patron. Even in your company, I'm still alone in that respect."

"Perhaps that, too, will soon change," she told him. "I know you have been made to endure a great deal, and I either do not know or cannot reveal the secrets of your mysteries. In that respect, I feel I have failed you utterly as a friend. Unfortunately, I cannot foresee the time when your questions will find answers."

"You've never been responsible for my personal problems," he assured her. "It's enough to me that you care. I suppose I've taken it for granted too long now, but I realize you've been a remarkably good friend, especially considering who I am."

"Perhaps you have not been allowed to know dragons well by knowing only me. I am not unique in that regard, as you seem to think. Many dragons are not cold and aloof."

She lowered her head and rubbed her nose gently against his chest, the same gesture of affection she had used for as long as she had known him. Then she turned abruptly and stepped out into the center of the courtyard. Thelvyn moved out of the way quickly, taking position in the doorway of the warehouse. Kharendaen spread her wings, crouched low, and launched herself into the air. The dawn sky was still filled with stars, but Thelvyn's sharp eyes could follow her dark form easily as she circled tightly and began to climb. As he watched, she turned and disappeared into the northeast, toward home.

* * * * *

The young dragon flew as low and as rapidly as he dared over the woods and hills, so that the tops of the trees occasionally raked his belly or were snapped off by the end of his tail. He hardly even needed to move his wings as he descended quickly from a high pass in the eastern mountains of Rockhome, just above the cool, wet lowlands of the Northern Reaches. His path switched back and forth quickly as he tried to stay as much as possible within the cover of the hills and stands of trees. This was a dangerous place to be, even for a dragon, and he was trying very hard to hide his fear. The land belonged to the greatest of all the renegade kings, and it was the last place the young gold dragon belonged.

Sir George Kirbey crouched low in Seldaek's saddle and held for dear life, grateful that he was able to catch his hook firmly over the front edge of the saddle. If there was ever a place that looked like it belonged to renegade dragons, this was it. The surrounding mountains were steep, stark, and barren, all the same dull gray-brown in color. They descended into a great valley, shaped like a long oval basin set amid the mountains, filled with dense woods of tall pines with short, sparse branches that somehow always appeared wet and forlorn, as if they had just endured a terrible storm. In the very center of the valley, almost completely surrounded by a cluster of lakes of still, oily-looking water, stood a short, saw-toothed ridge of dark stone that resembled the plates of a dragon's crest.

Seldaek demonstrated remarkable and often hair-raising skill in flying as he made his way toward the center of the valley. When he left the hills behind, he had to use the taller stands of trees for whatever cover he could find, darting rapidly back and forth, sometimes dropping down into partly clear spaces in the woods. He had chosen the time of his approach with great care. The rising sun cast long shadows that concealed him almost until he reached the very center of the valley, and there was no betraying light to glint from his gold armor. At the same time, he had to watch the distant ridge carefully for sentries. If he were spotted, his only hope would be to turn and flee like no dragon had ever flown.

At last he landed on a low rise more than half a mile from the ridge, in a place where one of the bridges of dark, wooded land broke the ring of still lakes. He dared come no closer. He crouched down in the shadows, allowing Sir George to slip down from his saddle. The old knight walked a few paces to the top of the rise and looked about. Although the desolate land seemed to have remained empty and silent since the beginning of time, a forgotten city of the ancestors of the dwarves lay somewhere beneath the ridge.

"I don't think you want to go in there," Seldaek said softly.

"Of course I don't *want* to go in there," Sir George answered. "I just don't have much choice in the matter. I don't see much point in bringing the Dragonlord here until we know something for certain. If I don't find the collar, I at least need some evidence that these renegades were in league with the Fire Wizards."

"I will wait for you here," Seldaek said. "When should I expect you to return?"

"By tonight, I should hope. If I don't show up by morning, you can start to worry. And for pity's sake, don't try to come in after me."

"I know better than that," Seldaek said, shivering. "May the Great One protect you. You are brave indeed. I don't care now what everyone says about drakes."

"Just don't let yourself be seen," Sir George said as he began to make his way toward the distant ridge. Then he paused and turned back, staring. "What does everyone say about drakes?"

The young dragon said nothing, but there was a mischievous glint in his eye. Sensing that he was being teased, Sir George made a disgusted sound and continued on his way.

Although he had said nothing about it to his companion, Sir George wondered if he would even be able to get inside the caverns. Unfortunately, the drakes had been unable to tell him very much about this place. It was so old and desolate that the dragons had never learned of it, and the dwarves had forgotten it long ago. He had to search for some time before he was able to find the opening into the ancient city below. A young red dragon was sitting on a ledge far above, obviously a guard. Fortunately, the dragon's eyes were directed in the distance.

The ancient place Sir George was about to enter was the lair of the largest and most powerful renegade band in the world. The renegades were on guard at all times against attack, but they had overlooked the seemingly preposterous possibility that someone would try to sneak inside their stronghold.

Even so, Sir George took nothing for granted. The

drakes had told him that an army of orcs and other evil folk were believed to occupy the dark passages below. He was worried that the minions of the renegades might guard the entrance passage. Sir George was counting upon his suspicion that the very security of this stronghold must also be its vulnerability. Since the occupants were so confident of the city's security, there was little concern for the possibility of a spy or petty thief. Even so, he wouldn't have dared this if he hadn't had complete faith in his considerable abilities as a thief, as well a drake's ability to see in the dark. The latter came in particularly handy as he slipped along the twisted passage from shadow to shadow.

The forgotten city was not hollowed out from the great ridge of stone rising from the center of the valley, but instead it was far below. There were conflicting legends of the origin of this place among those few who knew of its existence. Some called it Darmouk, the ruins of the last surviving city of the dwarves before the fall of Blackmoor. The dwarves themselves believed that Kagyar had created their race to cope with the new world created by the Rain of Fire.

The entrance spiraled down into the depths. It was obvious that the renegades had widened the passage to better suit their own needs. The entrance passage opened at last into a series of large chambers that had once served as the final line of defense against invasion, and these in turn opened into the immense main chamber of Darmouk itself. The very sight of it was so impressive that even Sir George had to pause and stare in amazement.

The main cavern of Darmouk was so vast that it made even the caverns of Dengar seem small in comparison. Unlike Dengar, it wasn't a natural cavern but a single immense, carved chamber, perfectly oval in shape, five miles in length, and more than two miles wide. The ceiling rose more than four hundred yards above the terraced floors. Great arches of white stone supported the curved dome of the ceiling. Even as formidable as this underground city was, the great destruction of the Rain of Fire had nearly ruined it. The tall, graceful buildings had mostly collapsed in wreckage during the fall of Blackmoor, and two large portions of the ceiling had collapsed when the supporting beams failed, crushing large parts of the city beneath landslides of stone.

Darmouk had lain abandoned and forgotten for centuries. In recent years, it had been rediscovered by Kardyer, one of the largest and strongest red dragons in the world. He was also a sorcerer so skilled in magic that his abilities rivaled those of a gold. In his long life, he had sat on the Parliament of Dragons. But five hundred years ago, he had gone mad, defeating a series of young rogues and renegades one at a time and binding them to his will until a band of twenty-six dragons recognized him as their king. Moreover, he had gathered a small army of orcs and goblins to serve him, raiding westward into Rockhome, south into the Emirates, and east into the Northern Reaches to enrich his treasuries.

Sir George had only partly believed the tales he had been told, but now he saw that they must be true. Everywhere he saw dragons gliding over the ruined city or reclining on ledges in the distance. He could smell the orcs, and he could hear their talk and evil laughter in the abandoned buildings where they made their homes. Like his young dragon companion, he was becoming more and more fearful of this dangerous place in which he found himself. He could well believe that a renegade as mad and powerful as Kardyer could come to believe that he was the Dragonking.

Sir George wanted to be done with this as quickly as possible. He looked about the ruined city, deciding that the renegade king must make his own home in the ancient palace that sprawled atop the highest terrace in the center of the city. He needed the better part of two hours to make his way there stealthfully, careful to stay hidden in the deep shadows of the dimly lit cavern. The orcs were easy enough to avoid because of their smell and the sound of their evil laughter. Deep within him, the collector of antiquities raged at the sight of this ancient relic of a lost age serving as a den for renegades and orcs.

Searching the palace itself was far more dangerous, for he knew that it was the abode of mad dragons. The chambers here were massive, large enough to serve even the needs of dragons. The damage caused by the terrible Rain of Fire had been repaired, and the wreckage had been cleared, restoring the palace once more into the proper abode of a king. But there were still many corridors where a dragon could never hope to pass, and Sir George hoped to remain in those passages while he searched for Kardyer's treasury. If Darmouk had indeed been built by the ancestors of dwarves, then he hoped that they had built their vaults in much the same place as in the strongholds of dwarves he knew . . . beneath the palace.

"Sir George Kirbey, as I live and breathe!" a great, rumbling voice suddenly declared from behind him.

Sir George straightened, hardly daring to turn and face the dragon that had come up silently behind him in the darkness. He could only curse himself silently, knowing that he had waited too long to hide himself in the remote passages. Behind him crouched the largest dragon he had ever seen, a red dragon larger by far than Kharendaen or even her brother Marthaen. He knew beyond doubt that this could only be Kardyer himself.

"Come now, Sir George. I know who you are," the dragon continued, slinking forward like a cat to loom over the old knight, staring down at him possessively. "I make a point of learning about such things when I can. The Dragonlord has a one-handed companion who is secretly a mandrake. Now, just how many one-handed mandrakes would come poking about in my domain? There is really no question, is there? The only real question is why you are here, for I must confess surprise."

"I get the impression that you don't get a lot of company here," Sir George said.

"No, indeed. I think you should stay with me for a time, in case the Dragonlord himself happens to drop by," Kardyer said. "I have tried to remain circumspect since the return of the Dragonlord, yet I am a dragon of considerable fame. Perhaps a conflict with the Dragonlord has been inevitable, but at least now I won't be caught unprepared."

Sir George sighed, resigning himself to captivity. At least he could deduce two important bits of information from what he had heard already. Kardyer obviously didn't have the Collar of the Dragons, nor did he seem to have had a part in its theft. If he had, then he would have known what had brought Sir George here to spy. And the old knight apparently wasn't going to meet an untimely end just yet, although he thought it best not to trust himself to the goodwill of a mad dragon any longer than he could help it. He needed to find a way to get out of here as soon as he could manage it.

CHAPTER EIGHT

Solveig White-Gold was finally able to be up and about somewhat, although her activities were still limited to coming down to dinner and spending a brief time in the den afterward. Thelvyn was glad to have her company, especially now with both Kharendaen and Sir George gone. She had grown up as the daughter of one of the first families of Thyatis and knew quite a bit about politics and intrigues. Her experience qualified her to give him some good advice about his own situation.

"The wizards have been unusually quiet lately," he told her as they sat in the den after dinner one evening.

Solveig was sitting in Sir George's favorite chair, wearing only a silk robe that left her long legs bare. Since she was still tightly bandaged, the robe was all she wanted to wear in the warmth of early summer.

"By wizards, you mean Byen Kalestraan, of course," she said. "I would guess that he's either up to something, or else he just plans to sit back and remain as unnoticeable as possible until this business is over. He must know that the dragons have some very hard questions to put to him."

"I would think so, except that he's still quietly but firmly pushing the king toward war," Thelvyn said. "And pushing me as well, if very gently. You would think that war would be the last thing he wants."

"Then he must be up to something," she agreed. "When you take into account his past behavior, that seems even more certain."

Something stirred outside. They both listened carefully. Thelvyn heard a sound that had grown familiar in the past five years, that of the wings of a dragon making long, powerful backstrokes in the final moments before landing in the courtyard. His first assumption was that Kharendaen must have returned, and he hurried to the door, certain that some news of importance had summoned her. He hoped it was good news, perhaps some concession on the part of the dragons rather than new demands. But when he reached the yard, he could see in the darkness that this dragon was too small to be Kharendaen. He recognized the young cleric, Seldaek.

He hesitated, noticing that the dragon appeared fearful and upset. Then he realized that Sir George wasn't with the young dragon cleric. The saddle fastened about the base of his powerful neck stood empty.

"Where is Sir George?" he asked anxiously, glancing over his shoulder to see Solveig following. "The truce is broken. You're not supposed to be here."

"I had to come," Seldaek insisted. "I need your help."

"Let's get you inside Kharendaen's lair, and then we'll talk," Thelvyn insisted, hurrying to open the doors to the old warehouse. He had never seen a dragon so agitated, and he felt concern for the old knight's safety.

Seldaek crouched low to slip through the doorway, although he was so upset he bumped his shoulders against the lintel and nearly brought down the wall. Solveig followed close behind him, taking care to avoid the end of his long tail. Thelvyn hurried to close the doors, then he quickly ushered Seldaek in the direction of Kharendaen's bed.

"Now, what is this all about?" he asked. "Where is Sir

George?"

Seldaek sighed. "I think Kardyer must have captured him. Sir George went inside Darmouk to search Kardyer's treasury for the Collar of the Dragons."

"Who is Kardyer?" Solveig asked impatiently.

"He is the most powerful of all the renegade kings," Seldaek explained. "Sir George talked to the drakes, who had heard that Kardyer has been boasting that he can defeat the Dragonlord. Perhaps he was only saying that to impress a renegade queen he seeks as a mate, but it led Sir George to wonder if Kardyer might have stolen the Collar of the Dragons."

"The most powerful of all the renegade kings," Thelvyn repeated to himself.

"But we will be going to rescue Sir George, won't we?" Solveig asked.

"*I'll* be going to rescue him," Thelvyn corrected her sternly. "You couldn't rescue a kitten from a tree just now. Seldaek, can you take me there tonight?"

"Darmouk is in eastern Rockhome," the dragon said. "We would not arrive there much before morning."

"Then get some rest while I prepare to leave. I'll bring you some food."

Thelvyn began by raiding the pantry, searching for anything that would make an appropriate dinner for a dragon. Unfortunately, with Kharendaen gone, there simply wasn't all that much meat in the house. Then he hurried to prepare himself for his journey. Solveig followed him, looking concerned and impatient.

"Do you really expect to go after a renegade king all by yourself, with only that half-grown lizard?" Solveig demanded as he stuffed supplies into his pack.

"You forget that I'm the Dragonlord," Thelvyn answered calmly. "I've fought renegades before. Who do you expect me to take along who wouldn't simply be in the way?"

"Perhaps you're right," she relented, then changed the subject. "Do you think Sir George is still alive?"

"I think so," Thelvyn assured her. "My hope is that things just took longer than he thought, or else he couldn't get out again right away, and Seldaek simply panicked. He might even be sitting there waiting for us when we arrive. And even if he was caught, they would know he was a mandrake on sight."

"They might also know exactly who he is," Solveig reminded him. "They could be expecting you."

"Then I'll have to be especially careful," he said. "I would prefer to find Sir George before the renegades know I'm there."

Thelvyn left a brief message to be relayed to the king the next morning, saying only that the Dragonlord had been called away on urgent business and that he would return as soon as possible. Solveig watched from the yard as he climbed into Seldaek's saddle, and the young dragon leaped into the night sky. Solveig was obviously impatient to find Sir George, and Thelvyn understood how much she wanted to go. But he knew his decision was for the best. The enchantments of his armor gave him the ability to face an army of renegade dragons, but a companion would only be someone he would have to protect.

Seldaek was game to do his best, as eager as anyone to rush to the rescue of the old knight. But the gold dragon had just made the same long journey, and he had only a short time to rest before he was in the sky once more. They were forced to stop to rest twice during the night, during which time the young dragon would stretch himself out to his full length and sleep like a stone for a quarter of an hour before he would leap up and insist upon continuing the arduous journey.

It was still pitch-dark, well over an hour before dawn, when Seldaek glided silently down into the desolate valley. At Thelvyn's direction, he returned to the place where he was to have waited for Sir George. In spite of their hopes, the old knight wasn't there to greet them. Thelvyn dropped down from the saddle, patting the dragon on his shoulder.

"I have to go in alone," he said. "I doubt I can find Sir George and get out again without being seen, but I hope to find the old fool before I have to fight the renegades."

"I understand," Seldaek answered.

Following much the same path that Sir George had taken many hours before, Thelvyn passed through the ring of lakes and made his way along the base of the ridge. Seldaek had told Thelvyn all he knew about Darmouk, although he was drawing mostly upon the legends of the dragons. The drakes had been able to add little to that. Thelvyn hoped to discover a secret entrance or escape tunnel of the ancient dwarves to enter the city, someplace confined, where no dragon could have gone. The problem was, he soon came to realize, he could have searched days, even weeks, for such an entrance without finding it.

He resigned himself to the fact that he would have to find his way into the underground city by the main entrance, following the vague instructions that Seldaek had been able to give him. As Sir George had the day before, he was able to locate the hidden entrance by the presence of the two dragons standing watch on the ledge above it. For a moment, he drew back into the shadows to think. If he were expected, then the dragons on watch were meant only to give an alarm. Renegades were said to have delusions of superiority, even invulnerability, but Kardyer still would never expect two of his minions to be able to defend his lair against the likes of the Dragonlord. They were there only to watch and to sound the warning, meaning that Thelvyn had to deal with them before they saw him, or else he had to slip past unseen.

Caution told him that he mustn't leave enemies at his back. He hated to kill dragons, but he reminded himself that these were renegades, and thus dangerous even to their own kind. His treaty with the Nation of Dragons had made it clear that he was welcome, even expected, to slay any renegades he might find.

Thelvyn moved quickly while his resolve was firm. Teleporting into his armor, he drew his sword and raised the blade, sighting along its edge. For a brief moment, he considered his target, the dragon on the higher of the two ledges and the one most likely to escape to sound the alarm. The enchantments of the sword responded to his will with a flare of tremendous power. With the sound of lightning streaking through the sky, the weapon discharged, and the flash of the bolt tore through the night. The beam of intense force struck the dragon in the head, between its horns, with such force that it not only crushed the dragon's skull but snapped its neck. The great creature simply collapsed like a puppet whose strings had been dropped, dead even before it had begun to fall.

The second dragon rose, darted its head back and forth sharply as it probed the darkness. Unable to get a clear target at the creature's head, Thelvyn had to train his sword toward the dragon's massive chest, this time discharging a beam of the weapon's searing cutting force. The bolt was blinding in the night air, like a flash of lighting, and the beam scorched a hole directly through the dragon's chest. This time the stricken dragon lived just long enough to rear up in surprise and pain, then fell heavily onto its side and tumbled heavily down the side of the ridge, finally coming to rest in a sprawling heap at one side of the entrance to the passage.

Thelvyn ran to the entrance, aiming his sword toward the dark opening. If there were other guards on hand, he wanted to catch them before they could race back down the passage and spread the alarm. Once inside, the darkness was almost impenetrable, even to his keen eyes. He pulled off his helmet to listen, but there was no sound of anyone fleeing down the long, winding tunnel. So far, at least, his way appeared to be unopposed.

Now he faced new choices. Returning his sword to his belt, he teleported out of his armor. If the warning had not been given yet, he hoped to find Sir George before the renegades knew he was there. He thought he could be more stealthful without the armor, which was heavy and awkward. He hurried along the dark passage as quickly as he dared. Dawn would be coming only too soon, and the dragons below would awake. The tunnel was dimly lit with magic lanterns that glowed ceaselessly for as long as they lasted, although after thirty centuries or more since the Rain of Fire, many had failed.

He paused for a moment to listen, suddenly aware that dragons were moving along the passage behind him—a small army of dragons by the sound of it. His first thought was that some the renegades had been away in the night, hunting or perhaps pillaging in distant lands, and were now returning to their lair. When they discovered that their sentries had been slain, they hurried to the defense of their underground stronghold. Thelvyn considered fighting them, knowing they would be at a disadvantage in the tightness of the passage. But he knew he would be able to slay only the first two or three. The rest would retreat, closing the passage for his own escape.

Thelvyn decided it was time to sacrifice caution and turned and ran deeper into the tunnel. He knew he had descended some distance already, and he thought he might reach the bottom of the passage ahead of the dragons. But soon he realized they were moving too swiftly, coming up quickly behind him in the darkness. At last he retreated into the best cover he could find, a deep, black recess in the rocks where he could wait for the dragons to rush past him in their haste. Thelvyn knew it was difficult for dragons to run downhill; their hind legs were longer than their front, like a cat's, to help them leap into flight. But these dragons were moving along at a fair pace all the same, one almost on the tail of the one ahead of it. He watched them pass, twelve in all, and it was only after the last one had rushed past that he realized, to his amazement, that they were all gold dragons! They couldn't be renegades!

Shouting and waving his arms, Thelvyn leaped out of the shadows and hurried after the dragons, but they were so intent upon their raid of the renegade lair that they failed to notice him. All he could do now was to run after them, hoping that he wasn't too far behind. Soon he came to a series of small gate chambers, the final defenses of the original occupants against invaders from above. Making his way past these, he finally came into the main cavern of Darmouk, pausing a moment to look around at the ruins of the ancient city as it lay in the eternal twilight, illuminated by the dying light of the ancient magical lamps. The gold dragons had already taken wing in the spaciousness of the huge cavern, hurtling themselves over the terraced streets toward the sprawling palace that rose like an island in the cave's center. The renegades were only now becoming aware of the danger, a few dragons rising to face the invaders before fleeing from the wrath of the larger and more powerful golds.

Once more Thelvyn teleported into his armor, and prepared to join the golds. He hesitated as he saw another gold dragon leap through the gloom of the gate chambers behind him, and he pulled off his helmet to wait. It was Seldaek, who had obviously witnessed the arrival of the golds and hurried to join them.

"I tried earlier to summon Kharendaen magically, but I didn't think she heard me," the young dragon explained, anticipating his questions. "Apparently I was mistaken."

"They don't know that I'm here, do they?" Thelvyn asked. "Is Kharendaen among them, or did she send other golds?"

Seldaek could only shake his head helplessly. "I do not know who has come. They did not pass near enough for me to recognize who they were."

"Come on, then. I don't want any of the gold dragons to get hurt, so I'd better get over there."

"Do you wish to ride me into battle?" Seldaek asked.

"I have my own means of flight," Thelvyn said. "You warn the other golds that I'm here. And try to discourage the orcs from joining the fight."

Indeed, Thelvyn could hear the orcs shouting and cussing and rushing about, but they were either slow to get themselves organized or reluctant to join in a fight between dragons. They wouldn't be a serious threat, at least not for some time. Thelvyn summoned the cape of flight into cautious life, aware of just how little practice he had at using it. He felt himself rise slowly, arching toward the center of the city as he gained speed. The cavern suddenly seemed full of dragons darting and chasing back and forth. The golds were having their way so far, but the renegades had them outnumbered at least two to one. Thelvyn drew his sword, knowing full well that aim would be difficult while he was in flight. He thought it best to show himself to the attacking golds by putting down a few of the renegade dragons, although the palace remained his ultimate destination.

* * * * *

Marthaen landed on the dusty stones of the great plaza

of the ancient palace, folding away his wings tightly to protect them from harm in the coming battle. His sister Kharendaen landed nearby a moment later. The main doors of the palace stood open before them. They looked about for a moment, suddenly aware that this wasn't a palace of ancient kings but the forgotten sanctuary of an Immortal. Great bearded images of Kagyar stood on guard on either side of the steps leading up to the doors.

The big gold dragon knew this place was the crumbling image of an age only the dragons now recalled, frozen in time at the moment of its destruction. Marthaen allowed himself only a brief moment to glance about, quietly impressed. He could see that Darmouk was no natural cavern. In some ancient time, tremendous forces of magic had lifted the ceiling of the main cavern, at the same time pushing up the ridge of stone directly above. What he didn't know was who had accomplished such a thing, whether the dwarves had once known such powerful spells, or if it had been a gift to them from Kagyar himself, or even from the legendary wizards of Blackmoor.

He turned to his sister. "You must seek that old fool of a drake. I go to find Kardyer."

"Will you fight him?" Kharendaen asked, trying to hide her concern.

"I must," Marthaen told her. "Do not be concerned. If he is like other renegade kings, he will be too sure of himself to be cautious."

Marthaen hurried into the darkness of the passages, seeking the heart of the lair. Kharendaen followed him for a time before she turned aside, seeking the lower levels. Her brother paused for a moment, watching her as she descended a wide double stairway into the darkness below. He was worried about her, and he had not wanted her to come. He knew the Dragonlord was in here somewhere; they had seen the evidence of that outside the entrance.

The chambers and corridors of the sanctuary stood silent, as if the place had been abandoned when the renegades had flown out to meet the invading golds. But Marthaen knew that he didn't dare take that for granted. Even though Kardyer was one of the largest red dragons in the world, he had not yet come out to fight. He would wait in the darkness of his lair, knowing that the leader of the gold dragons would come to him. They were both aware that this fight was inevitable. As they stalked one another in this dark and ancient place, the only question was who would find the other first, hoping then to gain some advantage over his enemy.

Marthaen's search was a brief one, since the main corridor led him directly to a vast central chamber, which obviously served as Kardyer's personal lair. He stood for a moment in the doorway, looking around. Crudely-made cushions, fashioned from the rough hides of some great beasts, were scattered about amid discarded bones. A square dais at the back of the chamber appeared to serve Kardyer as both bed and throne, a place where he could recline while looking down upon the rest of his court. A stairway to either side of the dais led down into the lower levels.

The chamber appeared to be empty, at least until Marthaen heard the rattle of a heavy chain. Poking his head cautiously inside the room, he was able to look around the doorway into a large alcove that had been hidden from him before. A red dragon, a young female, lay chained to a bolt set in the wall, held by a massive collar of steel fastened about her neck. Marthaen moved slowly into the room, anxious to determine if she was indeed a prisoner. Suddenly she saw him and leaped up, then drew back in growing alarm.

Then Marthaen saw for the first time that her wings were gone, ripped away at the shoulder so long ago that even the wounds had been concealed within new armor. Marthaen paused for a moment, seething with fury at the cruelty of the renegades and regarding the young creature before him with pity. One of the worst nightmares of dragons was the fear of losing their wings, the loss of their great freedom and boundless joy of flight. There was no greater punishment, including death, for a dragon, and he wondered what she could possibly have done to deserve this. Perhaps her crime was nothing more than trying to flee this place of fear, the loss of her wings and the heavy chain meant to insure her loyalty.

The young dragon continued to draw back from him until she was pressed against the stone wall at the back of the room, shaking with fear. Marthaen wondered if she had ever before seen a gold dragon. He also wondered, in growing fury and revulsion, whether she had ever in her young life been approached by a male who had given her anything besides violent matings and abuse. She didn't appear to be more than eighty, perhaps a hundred years old, and every day of her life had probably been spent in this dark hell.

"Do you understand me?" he asked. "I am going to break your collar and free you. Then you can leave this place, and Kardyer will not follow you. If the Dragonlord does not kill him, I will."

She seemed to understand, cautiously moving closer to him and holding out her neck, though she still shook with fear. Marthaen inspected the collar and found it to be simple yet effective, a band of thick steel that had been bent around her neck and held in place by two massive rivets that passed through holes in two of her crest plates. The holes appeared to have been seared through the plates with a white-hot rod. It was simple enough for him to free her, casting a spell which made the metal of the rivets as brittle as ice. They shattered easily as he took the two ends of the metal band in his strong claws and bent it slowly apart.

The young female reacted to her freedom in a way he hadn't expected, smashing all of her wiry strength against him to send him crashing over backward. She was on him before he could recover, knocking the breath from him. At the same time, she clamped her jaws firmly into his neck. She lacked the size and strength to break his neck outright and began to saw with her fangs in an effort to penetrate his armor. She had never learned the meaning of kindness or trust; all she knew was that she had waited all her life to hurt someone worse than she had been hurt.

Marthaen had made the mistake of compassion, and he seemed likely to lose his life to a mad dragon half his size because of his mistake. Suddenly a bolt of power blazed out of the darkness to one side of the dais, catching the young dragon in the chest and sweeping her off Marthaen to send her crashing against the wall of the alcove where she had been chained. She shook her head numbly, then crouched to spring, snarling in fury. A second bolt of power struck her in the head, slaying her in an instant even as it hurtled her against the wall a second time. She collapsed limply to the stone floor, her head crushed, her neck broken.

Marthaen waited where he lay, afraid of rising into the path of one of those death-dealing bolts. When he was convinced the brief battle was over, he rolled over and sat up on his haunches. The Dragonlord appeared out of the shadows, putting away his sword to free his hands so that he could remove his helmet. When Marthaen brought his head close to speak softly, Thelvyn reached out and hugged his nose. The huge dragon drew back sharply in profound surprise.

"Dragonlord, please!" he declared.

"Sorry," Thelvyn said contritely. "I thought you were Kharendaen in the darkness. You do look like her, you know."

"Keep your hands off my sister as well," Marthaen grumbled, then shook his head. "Excuse my bad temper. I hate being made a fool, especially by myself."

"I can't fault your compassion," Thelvyn said. "I hated to do that. I could see she was hardly more than a child. I would have tried to free her myself."

"Perhaps you gave her the only freedom she could have," Marthaen said slowly. "I should have realized that a child raised in torment by mad dragons would have become as mad as any of her captors. But no matter. We must find Kardyer at once. Only you and I have the power to fight him, and I do not want him slaying any of my companions."

"Is Kharendaen here?" Thelvyn asked.

"I could not stop her from coming," he answered. "She has gone into the lower levels seeking Sir George Kirbey."

"What?" Thelvyn demanded in disbelief, turning on the gold dragon in his fury. "Does a dragon have to be mad to be able to think? Where do you suppose Kardyer has gone? He knows that we've come to rescue Sir George. That's where he'll be waiting."

Marthaen rumbled in anger, as much at himself as at Kardyer. "Find him, then. You can move more quickly in these passages than I can ever hope to."

Thelvyn turned and hurried back to the dais, descending the nearest of the stairways at a run even as he fastened his helmet and drew his enchanted sword. The gold dragon followed as quickly as he could, although the stairs were so narrow and steep that he had to climb cautiously. Never in his life had he sought any battle in greater fury—or greater fear.

* * * * *

Kharendaen slipped quietly through the dark passages in the depths of the ancient sanctuary. As a cleric, she was a fighting dragon only when necessary, but she had fought renegades in the past with the Dragonlord. She would fight now if she had to, although she preferred to avoid battle if she could. The only one she did not wish to face was Kardyer himself, knowing that she was no match for the renegade king. She was fearful for her brother's safety and privately hoped that the Dragonlord would find Kardyer first.

As she searched the dark passages, she tried to think just where Kardyer would be most likely to keep his prisoner, especially considering that this had been the sanctuary of an Immortal. The lower passages seemed the most secure, although not completely—not to a dragon, at least. The passage was difficult, often tight, with many blind corridors and stairways that were too small for a dragon to enter, but not a man or any of the evil creatures Kardyer had gathered for his army. He would want his prisoners where he could see them, and he would want his treasury where he could get at it in a hurry. In either case, it would be a place where anyone would have to go past him to get there, and where there were no passages to allow others to go where a dragon could not.

At first she wondered if she had come to the wrong place. Perhaps she would be more likely to find what she was searching for in the larger passages of the upper level. There was a great deal of territory to search in this place, and her time was limited. Occasionally she could hear sounds of the battle raging in the city above. The gold dragons, outnumbered but superior in size, strength, and magic, were locked in a fierce struggle against the renegades. They needed her help, but they especially needed the skills and leadership of Marthaen and the power of the Dragonlord to protect them. She wanted to be done with this, so that she could leave this dark and fearful place. The very stones seemed to echo the madness and despair of the renegades.

Then, just as Kharendaen was becoming convinced that she must search elsewhere, she discovered that she had come the right way after all. Kardyer had apparently kept his vile slaves busy through the years turning the lower levels of the ancient structure into a vault secure enough to hold his secrets. The main passage had been sealed with a great latticework of steel bands, too heavy to be broken or easily destroyed with dragonfire, set in a massive frame that was bolted into the stone walls, floor, and ceiling. Even dragons would have had a difficult time forcing their way through this, yet Kharendaen felt that she didn't have the time to seek a way around this barrier.

The gold dragon sat back on her haunches as she closed her eyes and concentrated on her spell, not her powers as a cleric but the magic that was unique to dragons. After a moment, her form began to glow vaguely, encased within a pale, shimmering light so that she appeared almost transparent. She rose slowly, careful not to disturb the spell, and began to move forward with utmost care. Her tapered nose pressed up against the lattice of steel bands and then passed through unhindered. She stepped forward cautiously, moving like a ghost through the barrier until her entire length was safely beyond the barrier. Only then did she pause once again to glance back. The glimmering light faded to leave her real and solid once more.

She continued her search, observing that all the smaller side passages were sealed off with blocks of cut stone. She didn't have to go far before she came abruptly to a large open area, with stairs on either side leading upward. The floor of the center of that chamber was open in a large, square-sided pit, with wide steps leading downward to either side. She descended once again, certain now that she must be close to her goal. The steps ended at the back of a short alcove, which opened up on a passage of tremendous proportions, very wide and just barely high enough that she could have spread her wings and flown.

She noticed that she had now descended so far that this part of the sanctuary had not been built from great stones but was carved from the native stone with an absolute precision that only dwarves could manage. The walls, ceiling, and floor were all perfectly smooth, the corners sharp and straight. As she explored, she found that the first passage only served to link two long corridors of equal proportions, each lined to either side with chambers of great size behind heavy wooden doors. The northern half of each of the main passages had been closed off by Kardyer's slaves. Thick walls of stone sealed the passages, except for a low window that was closed by steel bars. The passages leading back remained open.

Kharendaen realized immediately what this place must have been. There were storage vaults here as large as warehouses, rows upon rows of them, extending back as far as she could see. In ancient times, the ancestors of the dwarves had kept their treasures here, where valuable goods could be stored under the watchful eyes of Kagyar and his clerics. Now it served as Kardyer's treasury and dungeon.

"Kharendaen!"

She turned sharply at the sound of her name, tracing the call to its source. The voice had been that of Sir George himself, and she found him peering at her from behind the bars of the heavy wooden door of one of the cells.

"I hardly expected to see you," he said. "I thought you were in exile."

"Seldaek summoned me," she explained. "I brought gold dragons to fight the renegades, but Seldaek had gone to get the Dragonlord, and he is here as well."

"Kardyer has the keys," the old knight said. "As you can

see, the locks are all fairly new."

"I can get you out," she assured him. "The wood of these doors may have been preserved by magic or other means, but it is still thousands of years old. Stand back."

She turned, intending to give the door a snap with her tail. But as she did, she suddenly found herself face-to-face with the largest red dragon she had ever seen. Kardyer had slipped up silently behind her while she had been speaking with Sir George, waiting patiently, with an unsettling lack of concern, for her to notice him.

Startled, she drew back her head instinctively, but she had been taken by surprise, and the huge red moved more quickly than she could defend herself. One of his large, powerful claws closed with crushing strength around the top of her neck, just below her jaw, while the other took firm hold of the top of her right foreleg immediately beneath her shoulder, a surprisingly forceful grip that she could not hope to break because of his great size and strength. He tossed her over on her stomach easily. Then, walking backward on his hind legs, he drew her out into the open area at the intersection of the corridors.

Very certain of his absolute power over the young gold, Kardyer then lay down on the floor on top of her, never releasing his hold but pinning her even tighter with a portion of his weight while he bent her neck backward painfully. He lifted his head to stare at her appraisingly, still with that same self-assured lack of concern. Kharendaen could not even struggle, knowing that he possessed the strength to break her neck in an instant, even one-handed.

"My goodness, such prizes there are to be found in my vaults," he said, thrusting his head close to hers so that his breath was warm in her ear. "Now, why would a dragon want to wear a saddle? For the sake of an old mandrake who will never fly again? I've heard stories about a gold female who wears a saddle because the Dragonlord rides her."

Kharendaen did not answer, knowing it would be pointless. She was trying to summon the magic to protect herself, but her mind was confused by a fear unlike any she had ever known.

"Do you think I plan to kill you?" Kardyer asked, bringing his head around to stare into her eyes, twisting her own neck painfully so that she had to look up at him. "It seems a shame that I must, since you are too dangerous to try to keep. It's been so long since I've seen a gold, I had forgotten just how beautiful and graceful they can be."

Then Kharendaen knew why she was so afraid. Kardyer pulled himself around until he was lying with his heavy chest pressing into the middle of her back. Again he used his crushing strength to force his powerful tail beneath her own to thrust it aside. He moved quickly before she could struggle, trapping her tail beneath one of his hind legs while turning her hips so that he was pressed against her, holding her tight with his own weight.

"Kharendaen!"

Kardyer lifted his head sharply, then relaxed again into almost smug self-confidence. Marthaen was trapped on the wrong side of the barrier, able to see them both clearly through the low opening but unable to force even his head between the bars. The big gold drew back in fury and desperation, tearing at the bars and the stone that prevented him from saving his sister.

"You cannot get through, brave dragon," Kardyer said smoothly. "Do you think perhaps you can find some way around the barrier before I can have my way with this fine lady, or do you prefer to stay and watch? Either way, I'll wait for you."

"Leave my sister alone!" Marthaen roared in his anger and helplessness. "By the Great One himself, I'll make you die slowly in torment for the next hundred years!"

"Your sister indeed," Kardyer repeated. "Then by all means, stay and watch. This should give you special joy."

Marthaen drew back abruptly from the opening. Grinning in vile satisfaction, Kardyer stared down at the helpless cleric beneath him, anticipating his pleasure. He lifted his head sharply, aware that the darkness behind the barrier was suddenly filled with a stark white radiance. The stone of one corner of the barrier began to glow a dull red only a moment before it exploded in a hail of splintered stone. Kardyer was forced to turn his head away, protecting his eyes from the deadly shards of hot stone. After a moment, he turned back, hissing in fury, but in the next instant a beam of force shot through the shattered barrier to strike his hand sharply, snapping the bones and compelling him to release his death grip on Kharendaen's neck.

Kardyer roared in pain and fury, then fell silent in dread. A figure in black armor stepped through the hole blasted through the barrier, already lifting a long sword in a menacing gesture to aim the point directly at his face. The renegade was beyond reason by that time, confused by pain and fear, yet blinded by tremendous fury, even indignation, at the audacity at this puny enemy to attack him. He rose to leap forward in battle, and that gave Thelvyn the clear shot he needed. His sword glowed briefly, then discharged a bolt of intense power, striking Kardyer in the chest with such devastating force that the red dragon was hurtled backward into passage beyond.

Thelvyn was cautious enough not to be caught by surprise by the next attack. Kardyer had held his bodyguards in reserve, six of his most powerful dragons, who now leaped to the attack from the side passage. Thelvyn lifted his sword again, aiming the blade toward the charging dragons, and willed the sword to discharge the most powerful bolt that he had ever dared to summon. The bolt was blinding in its intensity, and the concussion shook the very stone of the ancient city. The blast was enough to destroy all six renegades, scattering their burnt, broken bodies throughout the passage.

Almost frantic in his fury and desperation, Marthaen had drawn back just long enough to allow the Dragonlord to break through the barrier. Now he rushed forward into the breach, pulling out loose debris with his claws and then attacking the sides where the stone had been cracked and weakened by the explosion. In moments, he had an opening just large enough to force his way through, although it was a tight fit. As he pulled himself through the break, he looked up to see Kharendaen sitting up, still shaking in helpless anger and fear, her nose pressed to Thelvyn's chest as the Dragonlord rubbed her muzzle gently.

Still feeling helpless, Marthaen walked slowly along the

dark passage to where Kardyer lay, more than a hundred yards away from where he had been struck. The renegade king still lived; although he would not survive his terrible injuries, dragons could be very slow to die. His chest had been completely crushed, so that each breath he drew was an agonizing effort. He lay sprawled across the floor, too weak even to move, staring blankly in his pain. Even so, he looked up as Marthaen approached.

"I am Kardyer . . . greatest of all . . . the renegade kings," he said, hardly commanding enough breath to speak. "I did not believe . . . that even the Dragonlord could defeat me."

"No dragon can defeat the Dragonlord," Marthaen said. "Only the Great One himself could hope to fight him."

"But I too . . . am an Immortal," Kardyer insisted, clinging to his delusions. "I cannot die."

"You have these last hours to consider it," Marthaen told him and turned away, leaving him to die in agony, suffocating slowly in his inability to draw a breath. Killing him would have been a kindness, and Marthaen felt that he was due these last hours of pain in payment for all the torment he had caused.

"If you don't mind . . ."

Sir George was watching him through the opening in the door of the chamber where he was imprisoned. Marthaen took hold of the handle and pulled until the ancient timbers of the door broke free of their hinges. The old knight stepped out, looking none the worse for his captivity.

"After so much effort to rescue you, I am pleased to see you had the decency to still be alive," Marthaen told him. "Do you know where the collar is?"

"Kardyer doesn't have it; he never did," Sir George said in disgust. "He was so full of his own delusions of grandeur that he would never have been in alliance with anyone else in the first place, even a group as impressively sneaky as the Fire Wizards. But he does have a fair amount of treasure stacked about. He took considerable pleasure in showing it to me."

"The treasure belongs to the Dragonlord," Marthaen said. "It is his right, as the slayer of Kardyer."

"Me?" Thelvyn asked, confused. "What would I want with so much treasure?"

"Lad!" Sir George admonished him as discreetly as possible.

"According to custom, you should give some thought to the dragons who have helped you," Marthaen explained. "But the treasure and the lair itself now belongs to you."

"We can worry about that later," Thelvyn insisted. "We still have renegades up above to deal with."

Still shaken by her ordeal, Kharendaen took a brief moment to settle close against her brother's breast, rubbing her cheek again his. Marthaen watched Thelvyn as he hurried away with the old knight to the defense of the gold dragons above. Marthaen knew only too well that the Dragonlord had saved both his own life and his sister's in the last hour, a debt he couldn't easily repay. And yet he couldn't help but think of the very real possibility that he would be going to war with the Dragonlord in the coming weeks. He also had a very serious duty to protect his own people, even if that meant defeating the Dragonlord any way he could.

Marthaen recalled with irony how, only last winter, he had warned Kharendaen about growing too close to Thelvyn. Now he found himself trapped by his own obligations.

CHAPTER NINE

Since both dragons wore saddles, Kharendaen and Seldaek brought Thelvyn and Sir George back to Braejr. The matter of Kardyer's hoard remained unresolved, although it was a very important issue to all the dragons, even Kharendaen. Thelvyn rewarded all the golds who had joined in the mission to rescue Sir George, even insisting that Marthaen take a part of the treasure in spite of his insistence that he was already in the Dragonlord's debt. The rest, a rather considerable amount, Thelvyn could only lock it away in the vaults where it already lay and trust that no one would discover the entrance to Darmouk, which was also considered his property. He was assured that the gold dragons who knew of the ancient city would never speak of it or return uninvited, respecting the sanctity of his hoard as they would that of any dragon. None of the renegades had survived.

On their return to Braejr, Solveig met them in the courtyard, but she feigned a complete lack of concern, at least now that she knew the old knight had returned unharmed.

Kharendaen had to leave again at once, having other duties of her own to attend to. Seldaek would stay with Sir George for a time to continue the hunt for the Collar of the Dragons. Thelvyn had his own responsibilities, which he had not forgotten. He had accepted command of the Highland Army, and he was to lead the first caravan of supplies and soldiers to the frontier the next day.

Thelvyn's problems the next morning turned quickly from being one of dragons to one of horses. Having had the services of a dragon at his disposal for the last five years had gotten him rather out of practice riding a horse. He had no reason to doubt his ability to control a horse, but the prospect of actually sitting the saddle for the next few days was daunting. He doubted that his experience riding a dragon was at all similar, since dragon flight was extremely smooth compared to the jarring gait of a horse.

King Jherridan had given him a fine young stallion, by far the best horse Thelvyn had ever owned. The horse was of the swift but tireless breed that the Flaem had brought with them from some other world. The breed was characterized by their small bodies and deep chests. They were typically brown in color, with darker manes and tails. In appearance, the young stallion was very much like the two mares he had ridden during the quest that had eventually made him the Dragonlord. Like all horses, this one refused to bear him peacefully until Sir George had worked some subtle magic with the beast. Thelvyn named him Cadence, the same as his two previous horses, since he wasn't told the name the stallion had previously.

He joined the army of the king at the main garrison at sunrise, just as the lines of soldiers and wagons were being prepared to move north. For the sake of convenience, all the massive freight wagons, the mobile catapults, and the companies of soldiers with their ordnance wagons were assembled in the fields outside the gate, along either side of the road. At first, Thelvyn overestimated the force that was being sent to the frontier, knowing only that it consisted of most of the king's army, the core of the entire Highlands forces. In times of war, Thelvyn knew, a nation such as Thyatis or Darokin could put an army larger than all the population of the Highlands into the field. Even so, Thelvyn would have thought the Highlands army had grown in strength during the years of eager preparation for war with Alphatia.

Once Thelvyn had taken command, he quickly discovered that he was expected to hold several hundred miles of the remote northern border with a mere twenty-five hundred men and five hundred elves. They would be joining some twelve hundred soldiers already at the frontier. If the conflict with the dragons did turn to open war, the dukes might be persuaded to part with another two thousand men; whether the elves would pledge additional support remained highly debatable. The elves were reluctant allies in this venture, correctly assuming that the entire business probably could have been avoided.

The army would need at least a week to reach the northern border, which worked to Thelvyn's advantage. Another week would give the dragons more time to consider the matter, and probably to discover that the Highlands forces were under his command. He hoped they would think twice about challenging him, and that might lead them to hesitate long enough to see for themselves that he would only be securing the northern border and not bringing the army into the mountains to attack them on their own ground.

Thelvyn still hoped to avoid war with the dragons, although he expected to have to prove himself again in combat. His new power of flight gave him the ability to fight dragons more effectively than ever, even to force a battle with dragons who did not necessarily wish to fight. They could no longer use their greater speed and mobility to avoid him. He could go to war with the dragons if he must, but he couldn't be everywhere at once, and the dragons would be able to inflict tremendous destruction before he could hope to force them to surrender.

The first three days of the journey north went reasonably well, and they made fairly good time. The roads in the central Highlands were well established and decently maintained, and there hadn't been any heavy rains lately to turn them to mud. That was especially important considering how many large and heavily laden freight wagons they had, wagons that would be easily trapped in any soft mud, which was why it was necessary to get them into the north before the midsummer rains.

Their pace slowed when they approached the frontier. They had left behind the wooded, rolling hills of the middle Highlands for the pine forests of the north, where the roads were narrow and often twisted steeply through the rugged land. Strangely, Thelvyn felt content; he had grown up in these forests and mountains, and to him this was home. He had never been especially fond of his life in the village of Graez, where he had always been an orphan and an outsider, but he had missed the trees and the mountains during his time in the warm, dusty plains surrounding Braejr.

"We'll need to divide up our soldiers and supplies when we come to the crossroads," Thelvyn told Captain Gairstaan as they rode together. "Half will head northeast, toward Nordeen and the Eastern Reach, while the other half goes to Linden and the northwestern border. We can fortify our positions more quickly that way."

"Which force will you be heading?" Gairstaan asked. "I would suppose that you plan to be where you'll be most likely to encounter dragons."

Thelvyn shook his head. "I've been thinking about that, and I haven't decided. We could be confronted by the dragons in the Wendarian Ranges, who will be coming straight down from the mountains. Or the Parliament of Dragons itself might chose to intervene, in which case they'll be coming along the mountains from the northeast as they did five years ago. They might be seeking me out, or they might try to avoid me. I hate being in the position of having to wait until they make the first move and then respond accordingly, but I don't see much choice."

The final plan that he and Gairstaan decided upon was to keep the army together until they were past the first crossroad at Traagen. Just south of Nordeen, sightly more than half of their forces would turn westward, following the new road that had been built to serve the remote settlements along the foothills of the Wendarian mountains.

Thelvyn couldn't help but think how much things had changed. When he had been growing up in the village of Graez, the village had been the edge of the frontier, and these recently settled lands had been wild and largely unexplored territory.

As it happened, matters took the one turn Thelvyn hadn't anticipated: The dragons attacked sooner than he had dreamed they would. The army had just moved into a large area of open ground when the sky suddenly seemed full of dragons. Thelvyn counted them quickly and realized that there were only a dozen, but they darted back and forth so rapidly that there seemed to be more. He saw at once that they were young red dragons. He was getting the idea that it was a favorite tactic of the dragons when fighting large forces on the ground to catch them out in the open, where the dragons could make easy attack runs while their enemy couldn't take cover. They had done the same thing when they had fought Jherridan's forces five years before.

Thelvyn did the only thing he could, since the dragons weren't about to allow his forces to retreat to the forest more than a hundred yards away. He moved all the soldiers forward through the files of freight wagons, which he then had form in a tight line along the rear. The wagons would comprise something of a barrier at their rear, allowing his forces to concentrate on the attacks from the front and sides. If the catapults could be made ready in time and the companies of archers moved into position, there was some reason to hope that they could hold their own against this band of dragons. The Dragonlord's presence helped to insure that.

The dragons held off their attack while the Highlands forces made ready to defend themselves. That left Thelvyn to wonder what they might be expecting. Did they hope to intimidate the Flaem? Did they already know the Dragonlord was there? That would make a difference in their plans, although he had no intention of allowing them to have their way. He would need to take control of this situation soon if he could. After a brief time, Captain Gairstaan rode over to join him.

"All units are deployed," Gairstaan reported. "What are they waiting for? It almost seems as if they're waiting to give us a fair chance."

"Dragons have a strong sense of honor," Thelvyn said, "although I suspect they have their own reasons for waiting. It depends on whether or not they know I'm here and whether they want to prove something to me. If they don't attack, they might be planning to challenge me."

"Can you fight them?"

"According to their custom, only their leader and possibly his own bodyguards will challenge me," Thelvyn explained. "But I suspect they'll be keeping in mind my battle with the red dragon Jherdar and his bodyguards five years ago, and they won't repeat his mistakes. I doubt they know I have the power of flight now and can face them on their own terms."

"So what will you do now?" Gairstaan asked.

"I'm going to give them a good scare," Thelvyn said. "For all their plans and expectations, coming face-to-face with the Dragonlord is going to unnerve them. Imagine the worst monster of legend, some creature that has frightened you since you were a small child, and then consider having to fight that monster. That's how the dragons look upon the Dragonlord."

He left his horse in the old captain's care, then donned the armor of the Dragonlord and walked out onto the field. As he had expected, the sudden appearance of the Dragonlord caused them to break off their bold display and retreat a short distance. Five of them landed on a distant hill to speak together in hushed tones, while the rest circled tightly above. Thelvyn was beginning to think they hadn't been expecting him after all.

The five dragons discussed the matter briefly, then they took to the air to join the others and moved closer to the Highlands army, still keeping a respectful distance away. Perhaps they regretted they hadn't attacked immediately while they assumed they had the advantage, rather than wasting time making an arrogant show of strength. Any initial advantage they might have had through the element of surprise had since been lost.

After a time, the largest of the red dragons landed on a low rise, perhaps a hundred yards away, and Thelvyn walked out to meet him. As Thelvyn came closer, he felt the reawakening of his instinctive fear of dragons, the old fear he had nearly forgotten because of his long friendship with Kharendaen. Dragons had been his unrelenting enemies since before he was born; his mother had died because of their desperate attempt to end his life even before it had begun.

Still, Thelvyn had to put down his growing terror, forcing himself to appear calm and confident as he approached the red dragon. His last hope of avoiding a fight was to appear as the Dragonlord he needed to be, stern yet benevolent. Dragons instinctively respected the authority of the wisest and strongest of will among them.

"This conflict is unnecessary," Thelvyn began. "I promise you that the dragons aren't threatened either by me or the Highlands army. They wish only to secure their borders, and I am here to insure that there are no misunderstandings."

"This is a peculiar way to avoid a misunderstanding," the dragon said, glancing at the army arrayed behind the Dragonlord. "How can I not take your presence here to be anything but a threat?"

"The Flaemish king has declared that he will not send his army into the mountains unless the dragons attack first," Thelvyn said. "And I will not help them to do unprovoked harm to dragons under any circumstance. If you attack the king's soldiers here in his own lands, you will make war inevitable."

"War has been long in coming," the dragon declared. "The only thing that is inevitable is a battle to the death between ourselves and the Dragonlord."

The dragon turned abruptly and spread his broad wings, then, after three long bounds, leaped into the air. Thelvyn returned to his former position at the head of the army's defensive line, putting on his helmet so that he wouldn't be caught unprepared if the dragons attacked suddenly. The crystal eyeplates limited his vision somewhat, but he observed the movements of the red dragons as closely as he could. All the dragons had returned to the sky at the same instant as their leader. Now they circled tightly, perhaps a mile to the west, as they apparently prepared to attack.

Thelvyn watched the dragons as they began to spread out, circling the besieged forces on the ground. In his first battle with the dragons, they had been aware of his limitations to his range of vision and had used that against him, several of them coming at him at a time in the expectation that one of them would be able to get in close enough to attack. But this time they directed their attack not at him but at the Highlands army, staying outside the range of his weapons as much as possible as they streaked in quickly to release a blast of flames and then withdraw. He began to wonder now if he should have ordered his forces to spread out more. Their tight formations left them vulnerable, but at least the Highlanders weren't defenseless. Although their longbows weren't of much concern to a dragon, the lance-sized, metal-tipped shafts from their catapults were another matter.

From the dragons' tactic of attacking suddenly, then retreating, Thelvyn could see they intended to destroy his army in spite of his protection by taking advantage of his lack of mobility. So far, the evasive tactics they used to guard themselves against the Dragonlord's weapons had worked well. Thelvyn knew he had to intervene quickly before his own forces lost their courage. He used the bolts of power from his sword carefully, trying his best to keep the dragons at a distance while he waited to play out his one element of surprise.

His chance came suddenly as the red dragon he identified as the leader turned and darted in to attack. He waited until the last moment, then commanded the cape by will, lifting quickly into the air at an angle that would intercept the dragon. The dragon leader was caught by surprise by Thelvyn's sudden move, but he reacted quickly, angling sharply to the side. Thelvyn raised his sword, but all he could do was sting the dragon with a glancing blow across his lower back and haunches. Then he had to turn quickly to ward off the attack of a young dragon coming up swiftly behind him.

Thelvyn knew he was trying to fight dragons in their own element, and his disadvantages were obvious to his enemy. While he could fly faster than any dragon, the weight of his armor was awkward, robbing him of maneuverability. Worse, his massive sword threw him off balance, making it difficult for him to aim the weapon effectively. He maneuvered as best he could, but the dragons only teased him, easily eluding his every attempt. Even so, he was better off than he was on the ground.

Thelvyn knew if he could have simply destroyed the dragons, as he had the renegades in Darmouk, his task would have been much easier. But if he began killing dragons, he could never convince them to keep the truce.

The sudden appearance of the Dragonlord in the sky had been disconcerting to the dragons, but it wasn't in itself enough to make them retreat. They could see his disadvantage for themselves, and they continued to dart in and strike quickly, then withdraw before he could respond. There were just too many dragons for Thelvyn to guard himself effectively, much less attempt to fight them.

The leader of the red dragons continued to circle him slowly at a safe distance, watching him and no doubt thinking of ways to put him even more at a disadvantage. Thelvyn found the actions of the red dragon curious and disconcerting. He realized too late that he had underestimated the cleverness and skill of his enemy, having made the ill-founded assumption that this was the leader of a small, inexperienced band. In fact, the red dragon had identified the hidden vulnerability of his cape even before Thelvyn did.

Suddenly the dragon turned and flew directly toward the Dragonlord, a seemingly hopeless plan of attack. Thelvyn turned quickly to face the dragon and raised his sword. Just as he was about to discharge a bolt, he abruptly found himself falling as the cape's power of flight failed without warning. While the enchantments of the armor of the Dragonlord were fully protected against the effects of counterspells, even those to nullify magic, the cape was not. The wizards who had made it lacked the skill of the mages of ancient Blackmoor, and protecting the enchantment of the cape against all magic was beyond them. The red dragon had simply rendered the cape useless. Thelvyn tried not to allow fear to control him, trusting that the armor would protect him from a fall even from such a height, although he found it hard not to give in to the instinctive terror of falling.

He was plummeting with his legs beneath him, as if he had leaped from a high ledge. The instant his boots touched the ground, he felt a powerful force rebound up through the legs of the armor, catching him and helping to break his fall. Even so, the impact hurled him violently forward, so that he crashed heavily onto his chest. He lost his grip on his sword in his instinctive response to protect himself from impact with the hard ground.

Rolling across the ground to where the sword lay, Thelvyn grabbed the hilt, then scrambled to his feet as quickly as the armor would allow. As he had expected, all the nearby dragons had rushed to the attack as soon as they saw him start to go down, sensing their best chance yet to defeat the Dragonlord. Two were already on the ground, running toward him in long, leaping strides like immense cats. He lifted the sword desperately and summoned its stun power, striking each in the head. Turning in a full circle, he discharged several more bolts in rapid succession to discourage the dragons that were still in the air. They turned to flee in sudden terror.

Though the cape of the Fire Wizards had proved to be a miserable failure, Thelvyn thought he had recovered well, taking the dragons unprepared when they had come to finish him off. Even so, he had no idea just what else he could do to defend the Highlands forces if he didn't regain his power of flight. When he looked about, he saw that the leader of the dragons had come through the brief battle unharmed and was again flying around him in wide circles. The contest was still far from turning to his favor.

At least he had succeeded in diverting the attention of the dragons to himself and away from the Highlands army. While he watched the remaining dragons circle slowly, he became increasingly convinced that what he needed most was to regain his power of flight. Breaking the magic that prevented the cape from working as it should seemed unlikely, but there was a chance he could fly by either magical or clerical means. Flight wasn't a common clerical spell, but in the past he had been able to command some rather unusual clerical abilities.

He took a moment to clear his mind, permitting the spell to come to him. Fortunately, he was usually able to acquire clerical spells almost as quickly as he opened himself to his powers, unlike other clerics, who had to meditate for some time before they gained the ability to use a spell. He didn't even know if such a spell existed, but he knew he had to try. He felt the power of the spell of flight enter him only moments later, and he knew he had one last chance to defeat the dragons.

A movement from one side caught his attention as he circled to watch for sudden attacks. One of the stunned dragons had revived and was sitting up, shaking his head. A the massive bolt from one of the catapults caught the young dragon in the shoulder. He leaped up like a startled cat, roaring in pain and outrage. Twisting his long neck completely around, he drew out the bolt and tossed it aside. The wound was less serious to the dragon than an arrow would have been to a man, but nevertheless the fight was over for him. Limping awkwardly, he was able to launch himself into the air and soar out of range of the Highland weapons, coming to rest on a distant hill where a second injured dragon was waiting.

In the meantime, Thelvyn had been deliberately trying to give the appearance of inattentiveness, hoping to bait the remaining dragons back into range. His spell of flight would be useless to him if he had to chase down the dragons; he needed to take them by surprise. He continued to work his way out into the open field, farther and farther from the support of the Highlands forces.

For once, his strategy worked to perfection. The leader of the red dragons turned suddenly and rushed toward him, a move that led several of the others to break off their circling and dive to the attack. Thelvyn waited patiently as they came closer, still feigning a lack of awareness. He knew the dragons' own disadvantage from his long familiarity with Kharendaen. Their vision was extremely effective at long distances, but they could hardly see anything moving just under their noses.

Thelvyn employed his spell of flight and shot into the air. He noticed immediately that he was moving even faster than before. He stayed low at first, moving quickly just over the surface of the ground, then hurtled straight up between the dragons as they converged toward the place where he had previously stood. As he had expected, the dragons failed to see him coming, and most of them still didn't know where he was as he began to use his sword to strike at them, throwing them into confusion. He had to be careful to use just enough power to stun the dragons without actually knocking them out, which would have sent them crashing to their deaths to the ground below. The dragons scattered, roaring with the pain of the bolts and with their frustration.

Suddenly Thelvyn found himself enveloped in flames. Fortunately, his armor protected him completely. Guessing that the unseen dragon was making a pass from behind on his right, he moved sharply to the left. An instant later the leader of the red dragons shot past him, and the dragon's whipping tail just missed him. He brought up his sword and discharged a rapid succession of bolts, three of them striking the large dragon squarely in the back.

With that, the dragons seemed to have had enough. They withdrew to the hills across the field where their injured companions waited and proceeded to have an animated discussion with the leader of their band. Many of them had felt the sting of Thelvyn's sword, leaving their muscles cramped and painful. Four had been struck by bolts from the catapults; two had tears in their wing sails, while two others had taken damaging injuries to their bodies. But dragons were sturdy; they would recover quickly enough, Thelvyn knew, although for the time being they were no longer willing to risk themselves.

Thelvyn returned to the ground, fearful of losing his spell of flight to hostile magic. He removed his helmet and put away his sword, giving him his first chance take account of the situation. The Flaem had done reasonably well in holding their own with the dragons. Even so, they had suffered more casualties than they had inflicted. Portions of the line of freight wagons had been set aflame, and explosive blasts of dragonfire into the ranks of soldiers had left many burned or dead. The dragons had done their best to direct their attack toward the catapults, the only weapons they had to fear, destroying three.

Captain Gairstaan rode over to join his commander, leading Thelvyn's horse, Cadence. As he pulled himself into the saddle, Thelvyn was glad the king had given him a new horse. This mount was larger and sturdier than the two previous mares by the same name and breed, and thus better able to bear his weight when he was in armor.

"Have they given up?" Gairstaan asked.

"I believe so, although I intend to stay in my armor and remain visible until they leave," he said. "You seem to have everything under control."

"We've done the best we could," the captain said. "Since the archers were ineffective against dragons, I put several companies of them to work keeping the fires from spreading among the wagons. We've lost perhaps a hundred men, possibly less. Considering what we were trying to fight, things could be worse."

"Things would have been a good deal better if we had been fighting them with catapults from established defensive positions. I'm encouraged by the effectiveness of the catapults against dragons. I want to send a message back to Braejr immediately requesting that all the catapults that can be spared be sent north immediately."

They camped at the edge of the woods, so that the necessary repairs could be made to damaged wagons and catapults. Once they had salvaged what they could, the army prepared to continue on to the north. Only the wounded remained behind, waiting to be evacuated to a nearby garrison. Thelvyn believed that time was now a matter of great importance, and he had sent word back to Braejr that additional supplies, weapons, and soldiers were to be sent to the frontier as quickly as possible.

At least Thelvyn was spared the time involved in sending a messenger. There were wizards in their own company who were able to communicate with their fellows at the

Academy by magical means. The message came back only hours later that more supplies had been requisitioned from all across the Highlands and were already being prepared to be sent north, including as many catapults as the southern dukes would part with. A steady stream of men, weapons, and supplies would be coming up the main road from the south, beginning within the next few days and continuing for some time to come.

Because of this, Thelvyn had changed his plans by the time they reached the crossroads at Nordeen. He elected to establish a main staging camp at Nordeen for the purpose of distributing weapons and supplies necessary to establish a new fort or reinforce an existing one by sending wagons either east or west along the lesser roads as they were ready. In that way, their defenses could leapfrog along the northern border, the last fort in either direction secured before a new group was sent on to establish the next one. As soon as wagons and teams of horses had been relieved of their loads, they were sent back south immediately to prepare for another trip.

The first of the new shipments from the south, mostly catapults, began arriving only four days later. Since Thelvyn was now acquiring weapons faster than forts could be built to hold them, many of these catapults were dispatched to various towns and settlements along the frontier. Of course, there was neither the time nor the labor to establish true forts. The defenses of these forts were the weapons themselves, protected as much as possible by stone and earth embankments built by the soldiers while they awaited battle.

Soon the Highlands cavalry began to arrive and was divided into small companies to distribute among the forts and settlements. Thelvyn wanted as many mounted troops as possible at the front, which would give them the mobility to hitch teams to the catapults and move quickly to reinforce areas under attack. Even so, he hoped that there would be no further battles. He knew that the dragons were watching everything closely, especially his own movements. He hoped that they were content simply to watch and eventually become convinced of the truth of his promise that the Highlands army would not pursue them into the mountains.

On the tenth day since arriving at the frontier, Thelvyn rode back into the main camp at Nordeen to be told that the wizards had received a message that he was to report to Braejr. The king wished to see him in person, and he was needed also to coordinate the movement of additional supplies to the north, but only if he could spare the time. Thelvyn was reluctant to be away for long. He would have preferred to fly, which would have enabled him to go to Braejr and return again in a matter of hours. Unfortunately, the enchanted cape had never regained the power of flight.

"I won't be gone any longer than I can help it," Thelvyn assured Captain Gairstaan as he prepared to depart. "This is your show at any rate. I know you can handle things."

"The dragons seem content enough to wait for now," Gairstaan repled. "I'd feel a great deal better if you were riding with bodyguards."

Thelvyn shook his head. "You forget that I'm the Dragonlord. If dragons do attack, I'd only have to protect my bodyguards. Better I ride alone."

Convinced that the dragons were watching him from a distance, Thelvyn decided that he should slip out of camp as quietly as possible. His concern was not for his own safety. He suspected that if the dragons were to learn of his departure, they would seize the opportunity to attack and destroy the border defenses before he could intervene. He meant to ride alone, drawing no attention to himself in the hope that his journey would remain unobserved.

* * * * *

Recent days had been a bitter time indeed for Kharendaen. The attack upon Thelvyn and Solveig White-Gold's serious injury had caused her great concern. Sir George's disappearance had also caused her a good deal of anxiety, and then there was her personal nightmare of rage and shame over her capture by the renegade king. But her separation from Thelvyn had been especially difficult for her to accept, made even more so by their brief encounter in the ruins of the ancient city. Dragons didn't commonly form such close attachments, even to their own mates, but the Dragonlord had been her constant companion for the past five years. Times were changing quickly, and she wanted to be with him to protect him. There were many things she could have told him or done for him to make his life easier, but her duty as a cleric forbade her from doing them.

The Dragonlord would soon face the most difficult days of his life, and he was not yet aware of the demands that fate would make upon him. He simply didn't yet know enough about the events of his own life or the ultimate purpose of his existence to anticipate what might happen to him. Kharendaen was afraid she wouldn't be there when he needed her most.

Her heart was heavy as she rode the gentle winds above the mountains and forests of Wendar. Day was only just beginning to fade to night. The long summer days in these northern lands were slow to surrender to darkness. Returning at last to Shadowmere was like coming home, for this ancient sanctuary of the Great One had indeed been her home for many years when she was young, beginning when she was only a half-grown child. And yet a storm had seemed to rage over this place in recent years, when Shadowmere had seen some of the greatest yet also the most shameful events in the long history of dragons.

Shadowmere lay hidden in a great pocket of forest known as the Foxwoods, partially surrounded by the northern Wendarian Range. Here were trees unique from those found anywhere else in the world, even the enchanted forests of Alfheim. There were towering pines of such incredible height that a dragon could easily fly beneath their lowest branches. The sanctuary itself, a half-ring of hills where the lairs of dragons had been cut into the native stone long ago, was hidden deep within the woods. A rustic building of stone and timbers with a tiled roof had been built within that ring. It was in the shape of a horseshoe and set back against the hill so that it enclosed the older lairs.

Guided by instinct, Kharendaen dropped down into the

forest to glide slowly in the generous space between the ground and the canopy above. She approached Shadowmere from the east, passing above the icy stream that ran below the open end of the ring of hills. In a happier past, she might have seen dragons in the enclosed yard of the sanctuary, and many of the woodland elves who served the order of the Great One would have been gathering in the twilight of the summer evening. Her delight in returning to her old home turned to sorrow to see it as it had become, abandoned since that terrible day when the rogue dragons had turned on their own clerics. Long strokes of her wings slowed her descent as she glided to a landing in the yard before the main doors.

Kharendaen let herself in to the great hall through the main doors, stepping cautiously in the dusty darkness. Magic lamps hanging from the walls responded to her silent command, casting a soft glow, and she soon had a small fire crackling in the massive hearth at the far end of the hall. Her dinner that night came from a supply of cured meat she carried in the pack on her harness.

She dined alone that night among the shadows of her own past, reflecting upon a time when she had been little more than a child. She recalled winter nights when the dragons would gather in the great hall, many reclining on massive couches with open books resting upon stands before them. She remembered the nights of the dragon festivals, when they would roast elk in huge bonfires in forest glades and sing on windswept ledges in the high mountains of the Wendarian Range. The first time she had made love had been in these woods. But she had been away for a long time now, since before the day when the rogue dragons had come demanding an accounting for the prophecy they feared.

Kharendaen sat for some time and thought about old friends while the night grew deep and cool. She had missed the company of dragons, although she had been both quietly amused and a bit dismayed to find that her status as the companion of the Dragonlord had made her something of a legendary figure among her own people. The being all dragons feared most was her friend, and they naturally took that as a sign of boundless courage on her part. Only the clerics found it possible to believe that the new Dragonlord had not been sent to harm them but to serve them.

She felt the summons nearly an hour before midnight, sooner than she had expected. She slipped quietly out the main doors of the sanctuary into the night. The air was curiously cool and fresh for that time of the year, and the silver light of the moon seemed to flow down through the branches of the great trees. Kharendaen walked rather than flew, leaping the stream and following a path lined with white stones deep into the forest.

The dream began more abruptly than usual. She remembered having come to the glade, but she did not remember sleep overtaking her. It seemed to her that she stepped directly into the dream as she walked along the path. After a short time, the path returned to the stream and ran alongside it for a few hundred yards before coming suddenly to a great ravine in the middle of the forest. The stream plummeted downward in a series of short waterfalls, forming small pools on each ledge before spilling over to the next as if descending steps.

The path itself wound down into the great bowl of the ravine, snaking back and forth along the ledges of the steep walls. Trees lined most of the ledges, as if the forest above had spilled down into the ravine. The floor of the ravine was like a forest clearing illuminated in the silver moonlight, large enough for dragons to circle within the enclosing walls of stone. Images of incredibly large, graceful dragons carved from stone ringed the clearing.

She paused at the edge of the clearing, hardly daring to enter, for the Great One himself stood before her. He had shaped himself in his most commanding form, that of a powerful dragon, much larger than any living breed, with three heads all staring at her. Then his form shifted until he took the shape of a gold dragon of great size and strength, yet silver in color, with a beautiful, immense crest that extended well down past his shoulders.

The Great One had not manifested himself to any living dragon in the last quarter of a century. That he appeared to her now suggested something of the importance of his message. She also wondered if he might be returning at last to something of his former strength. Kharendaen approached him slowly, crouching on all fours with her long neck bent nearly to the ground so that she stared up at him.

"Stand, my child, and do not be afraid," he assured her. "You have served me well indeed. You sacrifice your own wants and needs, deny yourself the company of dragonkind, and stand apart from the one you love. I wish I could reward you as you deserve rather than ask more service of you."

"I have no regrets," she insisted, daring to lift her head slightly at his urging. The return of the Great One filled her with hope and delight, but she understood that as his cleric she was among those who bore the greatest responsibility for carrying out his plans.

"I know, little one," the Great One answered in a tone of infinite kindness. "Listen well, although there is much I cannot yet reveal to you. A time of transition is at hand. Old ways must soon be set aside and new ways embraced."

"Tell me what I must do," she entreated him.

"There is little that you alone can do," he told her. "There is little that even the Dragonlord can do. You at least should begin to understand the full meaning of what must come to pass. The time has come for the dragons to earn the future that I have so carefully prepared and set before them, and yet it is a future they fear."

"I understand," Kharendaen said meekly.

"This is the time of the coming of the Dragonking," the Great One explained. "Your role will be to serve and advise him, much as you have served and advised the Dragonlord. Soon he must take up the Collar of the Dragons and lead his people to the destiny that has been prepared for them."

Kharendaen lifted her head, hopeful and yet fearful of the promise laid before her. "I will serve him well. But what of the Dragonlord? Must he fight the dragons, or must that battle be avoided at all cost?"

"Your brother Marthaen knows more of this matter than even he is aware of," the Great One answered. "I believe that he will close up the rift of fear and mistrust that separates the Dragonlord from the dragons, but the Dragonlord must pay a bitter price for that. At least the price will be for the good of all dragonkind. This conflict has been unavoidable since before he was born, and it cannot be delayed much longer."

"I know," Kharendaen replied. "But he has been my friend. I would like to be with him at such an important time."

"You know that this is a time when a dragon cannot be in his company," the Great One told her. "The time is at hand for him to receive the companion that was promised him."

Kharendaen couldn't help feeling sad. She had known that this was about to happen; the spirit of Arbendael had warned her of it on the night of the dream she had shared with Thelvyn. She had been promised that she would return to him, and yet she couldn't help but fear that their relationship would never again be the same. Soon the Dragonking would come, and the time of the Dragonlord would be at an end.

"Do not despair," the Great One told her as his image began to fade. "When your days of hard duty come to an end, there will be time enough for rewards. I will speak with you again when it is time for the coming of the Dragonking."

The Great One slowly faded away until his immense form has disappeared in the gathering darkness. In time, Kharendaen stirred and lifted her head, only to discover that she had been curled up asleep at the edge of the clearing, her long tail wrapped around her. She looked up at the stars as they gleamed in the darkness of a moonless night. Then she lowered her head and wept quietly.

CHAPTER TEN

On the first day of his journey south, Thelvyn was beginning to think fondly of the simple life of an adventurer. He was reminded of his days in the village of Graez, wondering if Sir George was indeed the simple trader he claimed to be or the bold adventurer that everyone had suspected him of being. When he had been younger, he had eagerly anticipated coming of age so that he could finally go off with the old knight on interesting journeys and exciting adventures. Adventures were dangerous and travel was often dull, but he still would have preferred that to his present lot.

He was glad to be free and alone and no longer required to make a seemingly endless string of decisions that could mean life or death for armies and nations, even if he knew it was only for a few days. Thelvyn still disliked politics immensely. Learning how to play political games reasonably well hadn't helped him to like it better.

He almost preferred being out in the field with the

army, where at least he could have his way, to returning to Braejr and having to argue with an impatient king and scheming wizards. He was afraid that Jherridan might have decided to change plans now that dragons had actually attacked his army well within the borders of the Highlands.

He was beginning to wonder if the first Dragonlord had really possessed a magical device that had granted him the power of flight. According to the legends of the dragons, he had been a wizard of almost Immortal status. It was even possible he possessed such vast knowledge and experience in working with magic that he could fly or teleport himself at will. Thelvyn had heard tales of wizards so powerful they could fight even a mature dragon, without the need for enchanted armor or weapons, and hope to emerge victorious. He even suspected he himself might eventually possess such powers.

The novelty of riding alone in the wild was just as fresh the next morning, although he wondered if he would still be as pleased by the time he finally reached Braejr. The one thing he missed, he realized at last, was his companions. Solveig was still recovering slowly back at his house in Braejr, and Sir George was off searching for the Collar of the Dragons. Korinn Bear Slayer had long since returned to Dengar, and his steadily increasing duties no longer permitted him to travel. Thelvyn could only assume that the mage, Perrantin, was somewhere in the city of Darokin, almost certainly with his nose in a book. Kharendaen was at least in theory now his enemy, and he had no idea where she had gone.

It was middle of morning, and Thelvyn had been riding in the dense woods southeast of Traagen toward Braastar, the largest city in the Highlands. He had just entered a clearing in the dark woods when dragons seemed to leap out at him from every side. There were in fact only three red dragons, but in such close quarters, they seemed like an army.

Cadence's instinctive fear of dragons was the only thing that saved Thelvyn. Terrified, the horse screamed and reared on its hind legs, catching Thelvyn unprepared, and he was thrown backward over his saddle. Cadence fled in abject terror, and in the next instant, one of the dragons passed right over Thelvyn as he lay helpless on the ground, still struggling for breath after falling squarely on his back.

The dragon stood directly over him and seemed to have no idea where he was. The only thing he could do to protect himself was to teleport into his armor, knowing that it would protect him against being crushed. At the same time, he felt himself fighting on the very edge of his old panic at finding himself suddenly thrust into the close company of dragons. The protective shell of the armor was reassuring, calming him enough to think more clearly. He reached for his sword desperately, holding it above his chest with both hands as he engaged the hot cutting force of the blade against the leathery plate of the dragon's underbelly.

As he had expected, the sharp, searing sting got the dragon's immediate attention. It leaped forward so suddenly that it collided with a second dragon and knocked it aside. Then the third dragon saw him, thrust its head forward, and prepared to breathe its searing flames. Still on the ground, Thelvyn lifted his sword and discharged a bolt that struck the dragon full in the face. He seized the opportunity to climb to his feet. The dragons had scattered, pausing at the edge of the woods to turn back and glare at him through saucerlike eyes. But they had apparently decided the fight was over, disappearing into the shadows of the deep woods.

The attack was over in a matter of a few brief moments. The intent of the ambush was plain enough; the dragons had hoped to catch him unprepared and slay him before he could summon his armor. Once he had foiled their initial attack, they knew that continuing the fight was hopeless and withdrew before they got themselves hurt. The dragons obviously were learning to put aside their fury and fight him with cunning and stealth. Once they had tried something and found it did not work, they put it aside in favor of other plans.

Trying to anticipate their next move, Thelvyn felt certain

the dragons would make further attempts to catch him by surprise. He doubted that the next attack would come soon, and he was convinced it would take some other form than this last ambush in the woods. Their only real hope was to surprise him before he could get into his armor. Their legends left no doubt that they could never penetrate the magical defenses of the Dragonlord. There was only one obvious alternative. If they could not defeat the Dragonlord, then they would have to fight him as Thelvyn Fox-Eyes. Without the armor, he was nothing more than a cleric of rather unremarkable ability.

At the moment, Thelvyn's most immediate problem was recovering his horse. The last thing he wanted was to have to walk all the way to Braastar, especially since all of his supplies were in his saddle packs. Fortunately he found Cadence nibbling the grass less than a mile away, his terror already forgotten. Cadence possessed many virtues, but they did not include courage or cleverness. Having suddenly found himself on his own, the horse simply had no better idea of what to do with himself than to wait for his master to show up.

Since Cadence had already had time to rest, Thelvyn climbed back into the saddle and continued on his way. As he rode along the forest path, he no longer found his journey quite so peaceful now that he knew dragons could be watching his every move. He wondered briefly if he should head back north, fearful that the dragons would attack the army in his absence. But he believed that the full attention of the dragons was focused upon him. Whether or not that first attack upon the Highlands army had been sanctioned by the Parliament of Dragons, he was fairly certain that this last attack had been. The dragons seemed to have decided that their future depended upon ridding themselves of the Dragonlord.

* * * * *

On the third day of his journey, Thelvyn rode alone and unannounced through the gates of Braejr. Within a short distance, however, and much to his surprise, his solitary ride through the streets of the city became an unexpected parade of victory. He was recognized by groups of soldiers along the street, who cheered and saluted him. The noise caught the attention of people who worked in the shops, who in turn hurried out to wave and cheer. Word of his approach spread rapidly ahead of him, and people came running from all parts of the city to line the street and cheer him as he rode past. Thelvyn decided to teleport into the armor of the Dragonlord so that he looked properly heroic.

The celebration of his return had obviously not been prepared in advance, and Thelvyn couldn't think at first what he might have done to have earned such a resounding welcome. As far as he was concerned, his battle with the dragons had been fought to a draw, with both sides finding themselves at a greater disadvantage than they had expected, and the king's army had taken more abuse than they had inflicted. He could only guess that the people of Braejr must have heard a highly exaggerated version of what actually had occurred. He decided to accept the praise of the crowd with quiet grace, hoping that the people of Braejr would have as much cause to cheer him in days to come.

What concerned him now was not so much what the people of Braejr thought of him, but how the king and his wizards were going to react. His falling out with Jherridan over policy had placed a severe strain on an already volatile situation, and certain things the king had said had led Thelvyn to suspect that Jherridan was quietly envious of both his power and his reputation as the Dragonlord. An unexpected celebration of his return in the streets of the city might not help matters any.

Thelvyn was glad the day was already growing late, since that gave him an excuse to go directly home. The last thing he wanted was to lead a victory parade to the very doors of the palace, like a hero coming home to claim his reward. The cheers and shouts of the crowd only made the courtyard of his house seem all the more quiet and empty, a sharp reminder that Kharendaen was gone. A servant hurried out to take care of Cadence, freeing Thelvyn to go inside.

He bathed quickly to rid himself of the dust and smells of the road. It felt good to be in clean clothes once again. By the time he came down from his room, dinner was ready to be served. He was glad to see Solveig up and about once again, even if she still moved rather slowly and stiffly. Her injuries had been so terrible that she had been slow to recover, even with the best magical healing. They talked pleasantly over dinner, but Thelvyn waited until they had retired to the den before he related the events of the north in detail. He wondered how the true events differed from what had been told here in Braejr.

"Only in detail," Solveig explained. "Your battle with the dragons seemed to have gone so smoothly that I stopped worrying about you for a couple of days. Then I began to think that things are never all that easy, and I began to wonder what might have gone wrong."

"I'm not sure I follow your logic, but it led you to the proper conclusion," Thelvyn said. "That idiot cape never did regain the power of flight. I plan to have the wizards work on it to see if they can protect it against outside influence. I just wish Perrantin was here. I'm not sure those Fire Wizards are capable of making any magic that can stand up to a dragon."

"It sounds to me as if the dragons could be much more reluctant to agree to a truce this time," Solveig remarked, shifting in her chair to ease a lingering ache. "They won't be satisfied until they've done everything they can to destroy the Dragonlord."

Thelvyn knew he had to present himself at court early the next morning, no matter how reluctant he might be. Whatever else might be said, there were two subjects he had no intention of discussing at that time. The first was the attack upon him during his ride back to Braejr, the second assassination attempt within the Highlands and this time undeniably the responsibility of the leaders of the dragons. He was also determined not to discuss his growing suspicions that the true goal of the dragons was now to be rid of him at any cost.

His arrival at court was treated much as his arrival in

the city the afternoon before had been. Tables with pastries and breads with sweet drinks and juices were set out in the garden, and all the local worthies who could be persuaded to come at such an hour were present. The king was holding forth as gracious and delighted host, although Kalestraan seemed less pleased.

Thelvyn fervently wished the king would forego such foolishness as this celebration. He knew just how desperate the confrontation with the dragons might become, and he wasn't in the mood for this. Indeed, he had come to the palace that morning expecting to have a long, hard talk with the king and his wizards.

As soon as it seemed that everyone was present, glasses of fruited wine were passed about, and Thelvyn was toasted as the hero of the day. He was given a medal and granted new honorary titles, essentially meaningless but nevertheless impressive, and assurances of everlasting honor, trust, and support. Such proclamations had been bestowed upon him before, and he knew the words would be remembered only as long as he was doing what the Flaem wanted him to do.

Once things had settled down a bit, Kalestraan came over to join him. "I was informed about your difficulty with the cape. This will teach us not to underestimate dragons. Do you happen to know the spell he used?"

"No. He was too far away for me to hear or see anything," Thelvyn replied. "Dragons aren't very demonstrative about their use of magic. Whenever they do something, it just happens."

"I'm not certain it really matters," the wizard admitted. "I'm sure we can devise some kind of ward against the dragons' magic. My only concern is that the protection will begin to diminish as soon as you pass beyond the area of our influence. Unfortunately, that includes the northern frontier. I'll send someone around to get the cape so that we can get to work on the problem."

"I would appreciate that," Thelvyn said.

The wizard wandered away, leaving Thelvyn wondering how much good a cape of flight that only worked in the Highlands would do him. Long association with

Kalestraan led him to wonder if the wizard had contrived matters this way to keep the Dragonlord on a tight leash.

He saw Jherridan making his way toward Thelvyn, pausing for a brief word with various guests along the way.

"Could I speak with you alone for a moment?" Jherridan asked, indicating a secluded area on the far side of the garden.

Thelvyn seated himself on a stone bench that had been set back among the trees. Jherridan seemed excited and preferred to stand. "All of this ceremony aside, I need to have you speak plainly to me on this matter. I need to have this situation with the dragons resolved as quickly as possible, no matter how you do it. You needn't remind me that you've insisted from the first that we would have no luck fighting them. I think I understand what really happened in your confrontation with the dragons, no matter how it has been perceived by others. It was all that you and half the Highlands army could do to hold your own with a dozen dragons."

"Putting an end to the conflict might not be quite so simple," Thelvyn replied, his curiosity piqued by the king's sudden intense interest in peace. Or perhaps it was a sudden lack of faith in the Dragonlord's abilities. "After you've forced me to provoke the dragons into fighting, now you can't wait for me to make peace with them."

"I suppose that I should get to the point," the king said. "I've received some important messages from Emperor Cornelius while you were away. The Thyatians have been able to determine that the supposed alliance between the Alphatians and the dragons was in fact a treaty of peace. It was more a surrender on the part of the Alphatians, just as you said. Dragons were fairly crawling over Alphatia for several days. I daresay that they were looking for their lost treasure."

"I doubt that they found it. I think you know where they'll come looking next."

"I don't consider it a coincidence that Kalestraan is pushing me harder than ever to go to war with the dragons," Jherridan said. "I don't want to seem as if I have people spying on you, but I am aware that Kharendaen is still coming and going from your house. I suspect that you have her searching for the lost treasure of the dragons."

"That's not Kharendaen. It's a young male cleric named Seldaek. He was sent to help us find the . . . the thing the dragons have lost," Thelvyn said, electing to be as discreet as possible lest anyone was listening. "He's been out with Sir George trying to determine if any of the renegade dragons were involved. Because of the size of the thing that was stolen and the place it was taken from, we can be fairly certain that either the renegades took it for themselves or else they stole it for someone like Kalestraan."

"Then you think the return of the object would be enough to end the war?" the king asked, coming at last to his point.

"Frankly, I don't know," he admitted. "The dragons feel that the Flaem have insulted them and threatened them in their own lands. Also, you insisted that I take your side, and they aren't at all pleased about that. I don't know if they'd be willing to let go of their complaints so easily, but I can try. As soon as we have the chance to, I'll have Sir George negotiate for us. If anyone can talk a dragon out of anything, he can."

"The point is this," Jherridan began. "The discovery that there is no alliance between the dragons and the Alphatians has placed our own alliance in question. Thyatis is still interested in a treaty against Alphatia, but the general belief is that the dragons are now a greater threat. Our problem is that we must settle our disagreement with the dragons before there can be any alliance against Alphatia, and we must move quickly while the Alphatians are still reeling from their own conflict with the dragons."

"I'm not certain I can promise you anything," Thelvyn had to admit. "If you want to begin discussing peace with the dragons as soon as possible, we'll have make some gesture of reconciliation. I would suggest giving them something they want. Pull back the Highlands army from the northern frontier."

Jherridan considered that briefly, then nodded reluctantly. "It would seem there's nothing else to do, wouldn't it? We'll begin drawing up new plans for you to institute when you return to the north in a couple of days."

* * * * *

A messenger from the Fire Wizards arrived at Thelvyn's house that morning to get the cape. Although Thelvyn was still at the palace, he had anticipated such a visit and had the cape ready for him. When he returned home that night, Thelvyn found a letter from Byen Kalestraan. It seemed that the wizards were frustrated; whatever the dragons had done to the cape, it had permanently removed the enchantment of flight from the cape. They would have to start all over again with a new cape before they could attempt to find the proper wards to prevent future interference. That would take at least three or four days.

Thelvyn was concerned about the delay. He had assumed that he would be returning to the frontier and his duties with the army right away. He was fearful of what the dragons might do in his absence, and also of what might happen if they made another attempt on his life while he was in Braejr. He wondered if Kalestraan was using the problem with the cape as a means to keep him in the south a day or two more, even though it seemed a couple of days was unlikely to make any difference. When Thelvyn returned to the frontier, he would be drawing back the army in the hope of establishing a new truce, and Kalestraan was apparently very much interested in prolonging the war.

Thelvyn would have liked very much to know what Mage Kalestraan was planning. It was becoming increasingly obvious that the Fire Wizards had been involved in the theft of the Collar of the Dragons, since that alone would explain their present policies. If they had a burning desire for battle, it should have been with their ancient, hated enemies, the Alphatians.

For the time, Kalestraan seemed content to be quietly helpful but leave all matters of policy and planning to the king and the Dragonlord. Since the wizards now had a way to communicate magically among themselves, Thelvyn requested to have a wizard skilled in this technique made available to him at all times, so that he would know immediately if the dragons attacked while he was absent from the north. He expected excuses about why that wasn't possible, but instead Kalestraan promised him that a wizard would be made available to him by the next day.

By chance, Sir George returned from his most recent journey that same night. Seldaek settled into the yard shortly after nightfall and moved quickly to the cover of Kharendaen's lair. Even though the king knew a dragon was still coming and going in the service of the Dragonlord, discretion still seemed wise. Seldaek himself seemed quite concerned about the arrangement, obviously feeling that he was hiding behind enemy lines.

Sir George had been especially anxious about returning to Braejr as quickly as he could. He had been away at the time of the attack in which Solveig had been badly wounded and learned about it only after his return from his rescue from Darmouk. Shortly afterward, the urgency of locating the Collar of the Dragons had taken him away once again. He was relieved to see that Solveig was improving steadily.

Although the hour was late, they retired to the den to talk, but only after Sir George had raided the kitchen. Having been cruelly deprived for some time now, he had Thelvyn open a bottle of his favorite cherry liqueur. Once he was settled comfortably, he listened carefully to a detailed account of all that had happened in his absence.

"What interests me is that Kalestraan seems to have had a falling-out with Jherridan," Sir George commented. "As you say, his determination to fight the dragons when war with Alphatia seems such a promising venture only makes sense if he was involved in the theft of the collar. He's in a difficult position, unless the Dragonlord somehow defeats the dragons so decisively that they are in no position to ask for anything. He must know that if he doesn't mend his fences with the king, Jherridan might be willing to give him to the dragons to do with as they please if that would restore the truce."

"That sounds like a very good idea," Solveig commented sourly.

"How were the dragons able to determine that the Alphatians don't have the collar?" Thelvyn asked. "Assuming, of course, that they have indeed answered that question to their satisfaction."

"I really don't know," Sir George had to admit. "Alphatia is too big a place for them to have turned over every stone so quickly, as the saying goes. If the dragons had some magical means to trace the collar, you would think they would have used it by now."

"Unless the range of detection is very limited," Thelvyn offered.

"That could be. It might be good to know such things. Then we could offer to let them explore the Highlands for themselves, with the promise that they get to keep all the conspirators they catch. The problem is, I really don't think the collar is here."

"Is the collar really all that important to us?" Thelvyn asked. "If we had it to give back to the dragons, would they be satisfied and abide by the truce? Frankly, I'm beginning to get the impression that their greatest interest in this war is that they see it as a chance to get rid of me."

Sir George looked thoughtful as he considered that. "I'm sure Marthaen doesn't agree with that policy. Unfortunately, he happens to be a scrupulously honest and conscientious dragon. He may consider himself obliged to do whatever the dragons demand of him, even if he knows it's a bad idea. Did you have a chance to talk to him about it at Darmouk?"

Thelvyn shook his head. "Not really. But I'm sure he considers war something to be avoided at almost any cost, since he knows what the consequences would be.

I've always thought that was one point very much in our favor."

"Personally, I suspect you haven't yet matched wits with Marthaen," the old knight said. "That battle with the dragons was too ill-planned. They obviously didn't know you had the power of flight, but Marthaen knew from having seen you in Darmouk. The ambush, on the other hand, might well have been his doing, since the dragons involved left you alone the moment you teleported into your armor. That was a very simple and direct test, with very little risk."

"Meaning that Marthaen is going to be much better prepared to deal with me when the time comes?" Thelvyn asked.

Sir George thought about that a moment, staring at his glass. At last he sighed loudly and set it aside. "The trouble is that when a dragon is clever, he tends to be very clever indeed. Marthaen knows he can't fight you directly. Either he ignores you and makes war on the rest of the world, which doesn't really suit his purposes, or else he finds another way to defeat you. When he has explored all his options, he might be content to agree to restoring the truce."

That was actually very much what Thelvyn had already figured out for himself. It meant that he now needed to consider Marthaen his enemy. That was a daunting prospect indeed. Marthaen was very much like his sister—wise, calm, and patient. In addition, he could be cold and cunning in battle. He was young, but he was also a fighting dragon and a sorcerer of extraordinary ability. Yet Marthaen had made mistakes in the attack on Kardyer's lair.

Sir George told the others about the latest developments in his search for the Collar of the Dragons. He seemed to have flown the wings off Seldaek in the last couple of weeks. He was still seeking clues among the renegades, convinced that a band of renegades must have been involved in the theft. More specifically, he had been trying to find the band that had attacked Thelvyn and Solveig in Braejr, assuming that those same dragons may also have been involved in the theft. But in the end, he still had no idea where the collar was. All he had learned for certain was a few places where it was not.

Thelvyn wished he could be more directly involved in the search, but his other duties simply didn't allow him the time to be away. He had to admit that Sir George was better suited to conduct the search, having spent decades tracking down antiquities and other rare items. If it became necessary, at least Thelvyn could deal with the renegade dragons.

* * * * *

Thelvyn arrived at the palace early the next morning to begin conferring with the king about withdrawing the army from the northern border of the frontier. When he presented himself at Jherridan's private chamber, he was annoyed to see that Kalestraan had already arrived before him. The wizard was seated in a chair in front of Jherridan's desk. The king sat at the desk with his chin in his hands, looking rather put out. Kalestraan had obviously been pushing the necessity of the war again, although his efforts appeared to be doing him little good. The moment Thelvyn arrived, the wizard rose to leave.

"A brief word if you please, Dragonlord," Kalestraan said before starting for the door.

"Certainly," Thelvyn replied guardedly. The tone Kalestraan had used reminded the Dragonlord rather uncomfortably of a stern adult who was about to lecture an errant child.

"The wizards I sent to serve the Highlands Army have sent me reports of your battle with the dragons," he said. "From what I have seen in those reports, I have determined a mistake you have been making that is causing this situation to be much more difficult than it should be."

"Indeed?" Thelvyn glanced at Jherridan. The king looked mildly curious; he must not have known of this matter, although he seemed not to have much trust that the wizard actually knew what he was talking about.

"In your battles with dragons, you obviously make every effort to insure that you do not slay or seriously wound them," Kalestraan explained with great self-satisfaction. "You have complained that you do not possess the powers of the first Dragonlord, but I wonder now if the difference is simply that he did not concern himself with the welfare of his enemy as much as you do."

"I'm certain that he did not," Thelvyn agreed. "But I hardly consider my concern to be needless. If I start killing dragons with impunity, I'll force them to feel that they have to defend themselves at any cost. That would only start a war that would not end until every dragon in the world has been destroyed, and it would all be happening right here in the Highlands. I hardly think that's something you want, since there wouldn't be many of your own people left when it was all over."

"I'm perfectly satisfied that the Dragonlord is acting properly," Jherridan spoke up. "And I'm sure you must see the wisdom in what he says as well."

Kalestraan bowed his head. "Perhaps you are right. The object of battle is to destroy one's enemies, but I tend to forget that the common rules do not always apply where dragons are concerned."

"I'm still determined to defend the Highlands," Thelvyn said. "I can do that best if you can manage to fix that cape of flight for me."

Kalestraan bowed his head once more, never taking his eyes from Thelvyn as he did so. "I have not forgotten your needs. The cape will be ready soon."

The wizard took his leave quietly, closing the door behind him. Thelvyn thought that Kalestraan had put up surprisingly little argument on what he obviously considered a very important matter, and that left the Dragonlord suspicious. Of course, Kalestraan was actually quite correct; Thelvyn was making his task far more difficult by trying to avoid harming dragons any more than he could help it, but his response had been equally correct. Under no circumstances could he afford to begin killing dragons until he knew that war had become unavoidable.

Thelvyn spent most of the day in private consultation with Jherridan on the matter of drawing back their line of defense from the northern border of the frontier. Of course, the solution was hardly as simple as that. Some thought still had to be given to the northern lands to insure that the people there, especially the dukes, didn't feel they were being abandoned to the dragons. Thelvyn's answer was that the line of defense should be drawn not in the northern wilderness but farther south, in the towns and villages where most of the population was concentrated.

Thelvyn retired to his own chamber later that afternoon to finish making plans alone after the king had been called away to other duties. Since the garrison at the north gate was remote, Thelvyn elected to work in his private chamber at the palace, which was just down the hall from the king's chamber.

In the past, when he hadn't been occupied with duties of court, this had been where he entertained himself by reading or studying his oft-neglected spellbook. Hardly anyone other than the king ever had business with the Dragonlord, but now that he was in direct command of the Highlands army, he had more than enough to keep himself busy.

He was surprised that afternoon when a young lady came to his door. He guessed from her appearance that she was slightly older than he and obviously a daughter of the Flaemish nobility. She was copper-skinned, with long, full hair of the deepest red. She possessed the lean, aristocratic features that were especially striking on Flaemish women. Her attire was simple yet quietly elegant. She leaned forward to peer through the door, which had been standing partly open.

"Dragonlord? My name is Alessa Vyledaar," she said amiably. "Kalestraan sent me to assist you."

As she stepped through the door, having decided that she was invited inside, Thelvyn stared in growing astonishment. She was tall, nearly as tall as he. Her manner was confident yet friendly, intelligent and noble, yet bold and lively. Everything about her was so unlike the usual dour character of the Flaem, a vast improvement as far as Thelvyn was concerned.

"Yes," he answered weakly at last, seeming to find it hard to think of what to say. "I was expecting someone who could, uh, stay with me, so I'll never be out of contact with the wizards when I travel."

"I'm quite prepared to go anywhere you ask of me," Alessa insisted, seating herself in the empty chair beside him. "Or do you not want the company of a sorceress? So many of the experienced wizards have already been sent north that there are few left to serve you."

"No, I have no complaints with you," Thelvyn replied, beginning to recover his composure. "I just wanted to be sure you were aware of what you are in for. I think you should understand one thing. The dragons have already attempted to assassinate me once, and I have every reason to believe that they will make further attempts, as often as they can think up some new trick. I have my armor to protect me, but it could be dangerous for anyone else in my company."

"I understand," she said calmly. "And I know that one of your companions has already been seriously wounded in such an attack. But these times are desperate, and we must all take risks. I've had little training with weapons, but I am a sorceress of the seventh level of expertise."

From what Thelvyn had heard, that meant she was experienced enough to be considered one of the senior wizards at the Academy, and also that she was perfectly capable of taking care of herself. A wizard in possession of advanced spells, with the power to execute them quickly, accurately, and with devastating force, and with the wits to handle herself in danger could be a greater threat than a whole company of warriors. Alessa might even be able to hold her own against a dragon of moderate size and experience.

Thelvyn had to admit that he was rather intrigued by the thought of her company. Of course, he had been thinking more in terms of a servant than a companion or friend, someone who wouldn't always be about to hear conversations that Thelvyn would rather not have overheard by the Fire Wizards. He would have to watch himself, since he found it hard to think of her as belonging to Byen Kalestraan's lot.

"Do you have everything you need for a long journey in the wild?" he asked. "We could be called away to the north at any moment."

"I believe that I do," Alessa replied. "I've traveled some in the past, so I know what I need to know. I can collect my belongings and move into your house by late afternoon."

"Move into my house?" Thelvyn repeated, alarmed.

"It seems likely that you would need me at hand to serve you day and night."

He was inclined to wish she hadn't used quite those words. "You're right, of course. I suppose you'll be at the house in time for dinner?"

"Oh, excuse me," Sir George declared as he came through the door. He was already starting to back out.

"That's all right," Thelvyn insisted. "Come right in. This is Alessa Vyledaar. Byen Kalestraan sent her."

"Indeed? We really must thank the old boy."

"Alessa is a sorceress of the seventh level," Thelvyn explained.

"Is that a fact?" Sir George asked, taking her hand gallantly. "You must be a very capable sorceress indeed."

"And you must be Sir George Kirbey," Alessa remarked, rising from her chair. "I don't wish to sound critical of the qualities of my fellow wizards, but I suspect that I will be spending my time in livelier company than I am accustomed to. Now, if you will excuse me, I should attend to my preparations."

Sir George watched with interest as she left, then waited a moment longer to be certain she couldn't hear. He scratched his head with his hook. "Another one of those scheming, self-centered, power-hungry Fire Wizards?"

"Yes . . . probably one of the worst," Thelvyn replied. "She's gone to move her things into my house."

"Oh, my. That should be interesting," the old knight remarked. "At least she is a powerful sorceress, and

Solveig is still recovering. It should be a fair fight."

"Yes . . . Solveig," Thelvyn said ruefully. "I had forgotten about her. My only consolation is that Kharendaen is no longer about."

"The two of them would kill her for sure," Sir George ventured.

"She's not to know our secrets," Thelvyn reminded him. "She's still a Fire Wizard, quite possibly selected personally by Byen Kalestraan to spy on us. She might have been sent to serve me, but her first priority is going to be to her people and to her order. By all means, she's not to know that you're a wyvern or that I'm a cleric."

"I think I'll be able to remember that," Sir George told him. "After all, she's not likely to want to seduce me, and I'm not a lonely virgin."

CHAPTER ELEVEN

Solveig took the news that a sorceress was moving into the house very well. Although her recovery was proceeding quickly, she still wasn't able to be about much or leave the house, and she was bored. As far as she was concerned, having a young woman about the house to entice and frustrate Thelvyn would be entertaining. It might not be as delightful as being an actual participant in the chase, but it saved her the bother of doing it herself. At any rate, it seemed quite unlikely that either the sorceress or Thelvyn would actually become interested in a deeper relationship, since Alessa Vyledaar was human and Thelvyn was of uncertain origin.

At least there was no reason to worry about what the neighbors might think. After barbarian women and dragons, they would look upon the addition of a Flaemish sorceress as a decided improvement. Alessa arrived late that afternoon with a servant from the Academy pulling a cart that carried her belongings. Considering the fact that she was coming to live here for an indefinite period of time, she really didn't bring much. Being a Fire Wizard, she had a fair number of books and magical items, but otherwise she brought only the clothes she needed in the city and for travel in the wild. She had her own horse and tack, which were taken to the stables behind the house. The servant and the cart returned to the Academy, and the sorceress spent the rest of the afternoon in her room unpacking.

When Thelvyn and Sir George returned from the palace early that evening, they were rather surprised to find Solveig and Alessa in the den immersed in conversation. Solveig was hardly antisocial; she simply had no patience with people she considered silly or superficial, having had entirely too much of that while she was growing up in Thyatis. Alessa was intelligent and serious about her work, but she was fairly easygoing about life in general, and she seemed honest. Solveig could relate to Alessa for many of the same qualities Thelvyn liked about her.

Dinner was served shortly after Thelvyn and Sir George returned. Alessa accompanied Thelvyn to the dining room but sat some distance from him at the table, whether by chance or design, with Solveig between them. Thelvyn couldn't help but feel a bit disappointed, although he kept reminding himself that it was best that he keep his distance.

"I must admit that I had often wondered what life was like in the house of the Dragonlord," Alessa said conversationally.

"It must seem terribly strange to you, I suppose," Thelvyn commented.

"No, not at all," she insisted. "It's a most welcome change after living these last few years with a lot of dour wizards. And even the wizards were fascinating company compared to my family and the town where I grew up."

"If you'll excuse me for saying so," Sir George remarked, "on the whole, the Flaem aren't the most exciting people in the world. In my experience, the wizards are the dullest of the lot."

"Excuse you? As a matter of fact, I quite agree with you. They say that travel is a broadening experience. It allows one to recognize the deficiencies of home."

Solveig smiled; her experiences had been much the same.

"I must confess to having personal motives in asking to be assigned to assist the Dragonlord," Alessa continued, becoming more serious now. "I had heard much about his companions, especially the old knight and the northland girl who come and go, leading the lives of adventurers. Frankly, I may never go back to the Academy. I wanted a chance to have a closer look at your lives, to see if such a life might be more rewarding to someone of my temperament. Perhaps even to see if I might join you in your business, Sir George—when your business returns to normal, that is."

"There's no harm in looking," Sir George said. "As it happens, our resident wizard is no longer interested in travel."

"I am a daughter of minor nobility in the southwestern part of the Highlands," she explained. "My parents were not supportive of my study of magic, having other plans for me, but my talent for magic and other intellectual pursuits could not be denied. So when the wizards insisted it was their duty to the realm to permit me to attend the Academy, I jumped at the chance. As you may know, the Flaem consider failure in even the least duty to the realm to be almost an act of treason."

"I suppose that your talent for magic must be impressive, considering the level of expertise you've achieved at such a young age," Sir George remarked.

"I suppose so," Alessa said. "For a wizard, advancement must always accompany experience. But for me, it seems to bring only discontent. The senior wizards take no delight in their magic. All they think about is power and prestige; magic is merely a tool for them. I cannot live that way, and that leaves me feeling rather out of place."

She paused and glanced quickly at each of them in turn. "Of course, I know you can't just accept my word as easily as that. I'm aware that you have been the subject of Byen Kalestraan's manipulations in the past. Even if you find that you cannot take me into your confidence, I can always leave the Academy on my own. I have traveled in the world enough so I can find my way on my own."

"Being on one's own can be a highly satisfying experience," Thelvyn said, speaking for the first time. "For all my life, I've had someone either trying to control me or destroy me, from dragons to kings and wizards."

"Well, there is something that you should know," Alessa said, looking rather uncomfortable. "This time I hope you believe me. I am not motivated by the greed for power and conquest that my fellow wizards find so all-consuming, nor do I share their hatred of the Alphatians. Because I have recently come into the higher authority of the wizards, I am aware of many of their schemes. I'm sorry that I don't know everything, but I must tell you that I fear something terrible could happen at any time, something contrived by Byen Kalestraan."

"I've been suspicious that he was up to something," Thelvyn said. "He's seemed entirely too cooperative and eager to please lately. It's never been like him to allow the king or me to decide policy without him having his say on the subject."

"He has been working on something in secret," Alessa said. "As you must surely suspect, he has been trying to provoke the king into war with the dragons. The wizards want to commit the army and the Dragonlord to all-out war, which they cannot hope to win in the face of overwhelming numbers. Then when things begin to go badly, both the king and the Dragonlord will be discredited, assuming that they survive the conflict. That is supposed to create an opportunity for the wizards to seize power and then negotiate an end to the conflict with dragons, whom they expect will have been weakened considerably by the war."

Both Sir George and Thelvyn were all ears now. "That plan certainly supposes a lot," Sir George said. "But it's typical of the schemes that the wizards have hatched in the past."

"Their arrogance blinds them," Alessa went on. "They can't conceive of being wrong in their estimates. And to make matters worse, assassins may make attempts against both the king and Thelvyn to speed up the process."

"There have been attempts against me already," Thelvyn said. "I wondered at the time if the attack on the night of the Ambassador's reception had been contrived by the wizards. I was becoming uncomfortably influential at court, and Byen Kalestraan seemed to resent it bitterly. I take it that you don't think Kalestraan can defeat me."

"You presume correctly," she said. "After all, the Immortals seem to support you almost as if you were one of their clerics." She arched her eyebrows questioningly at Thelvyn, but when he didn't say anything, she went on. "I cannot say that the Flaem don't believe in the Immortals, but they certainly don't understand them."

When dinner was over and both Solveig and Alessa had retired to their rooms, Thelvyn and Sir George had a private discussion in the den. The old knight brought out a bottle of his best cherry liqueur and poured them both a large drink. Thelvyn was so upset he didn't even mind. He the glass up to his nose, sniffing the liquid but not drinking it. He had always thought it smelled good, however it tasted.

"I'm almost compelled to believe her story," Thelvyn said. "I wouldn't put it past the wizards to warn us of one thing to divert our attention from their true plans. But this warning was too vague. Simply putting us on our guard wouldn't seem to serve any purpose. She didn't really tell us anything that we hadn't already guessed."

"No, she didn't, did she?" Sir George observed. "And that could be suspicious in itself. It could also mean these wizards are just as transparent as we always thought they were. Since we already knew that someone was trying to kill you, our plans don't really change. The only thing we hadn't expected was that the king himself might be in danger."

"So now I have to look out for both the wizards and the dragons," Thelvyn said. "Well, I'm not surprised. I thought from the first that Kalestraan was behind the king's abrupt change in policy, from obsession over destroying the

Alphatians to desperation to fight the dragons."

Sir George settled back in his chair with his drink. "For my own part, things have gotten so complicated that, under other circumstances, I would have considered it time for us to pack our bags and sneak out of town."

Thelvyn had been thinking about the same thing for some time. For his own part, he privately thought he could trust Alessa. She didn't seem at all like the other suspicious and self-serving Fire Wizards, and he could understand her desire to part company with them. And she suspected that he was a cleric; if Byen Kalestraan had been told of her suspicions, he would have used the Flaemish distrust of clerics to discredit the Dragonlord long ago. Thelvyn decided the wisest course was to suspend judgment of Alessa Vyledaar. He would have to know her some time yet before he trusted her further.

He sat up late that night with his spellbook, committing as many new spells as he could to memory. He was fairly adept at magic, perhaps even more so than Alessa, although his other duties had always interfered with his studies. He knew he couldn't expect enough improvement in time to do him much good against the dragons, but his situation was so desperate that he felt anything might help. Sir George sat up with him, taking advantage of the time to attend to his own neglected business accounts.

Thelvyn was lost in his thoughts and his studies when he heard an insistent knock at the front door. The hour was very late, after midnight, and he assumed it must be very important to bring someone to his door at such a time. The servants had since retired, so he hurried to answer the door himself. He was surprised to discover that it was Taeryn, King Jherridan's young valet. His eyes were as wide as saucers, and he was obviously terrified of something.

"Dragonlord, you must come quickly!" Taeryn pleaded. "There are dragons in the palace! I'm sure of it. I think they've got the king. Only you can save him now."

"Is anyone else there?" Thelvyn asked, wondering how many guards would be there at such a time. Most able-bodied troops had been sent to the frontier.

"The wizards know about it," Taeryn explained. "Byen Kalestraan arrived a short time ago with a couple of his wizards. They said they don't have enough power to fight dragons. He asked me to summon you."

Thelvyn glanced over his shoulder at Sir George, who had followed him to the door. "Do you want to go along?"

"I think I should. I seem to be the ranking authority about dragons around here." He hurried off to find his sword.

"I want you to stay here," Thelvyn told the young valet. "You know that Solveig's still recovering and not ready for a fight, and I need you to keep her from following us. I'm also concerned that the dragons might come here looking for me. If that happens, get everyone out of the house as fast as you can."

"You can count on me," Taeryn insisted bravely.

"Believe me, I am," Thelvyn said grimly.

A moment later Sir George came running down the stairs, hurrying to fit a wicked-looking short pike to his left cuff. "It's not exactly the way I would prefer to go off to fight dragons, but it will have to do."

"I suspect they've already gone," Thelvyn said, pausing to close the door so that the young valet wouldn't hear him. "What concerns me is what they might have left behind."

* * * * *

There was no question that something was very wrong. The main doors of the palace were thrown open, and the bodies of two guards had been crushed and tossed aside into the yard. Thelvyn paused a moment in the deep shadows just inside the gate, watching for any sign of danger. No light shone at any of the windows, and that was remarkable in itself even for that late hour. Although he could see in the dark as well as any elf, he couldn't detect any sign of movement, nor could he hear the slightest sound.

By all appearances, the attack was already over and the dragons were gone. Just the same, Thelvyn knew better than to accept anything at face value. The dragons might still be lurking somewhere inside, waiting for him to rush in like a fool in the belief that they were gone. He was also somewhat worried they might attack his house, although he doubted that. It would do them no good to infuriate him even more; they just wanted him dead.

"It looks quiet," Sir George whispered. "For what it's worth, I don't sense any dragons."

"There's no sense delaying it, I suppose," Thelvyn said. "I have to go in there alone and search the place. I'm the only one who can do it in relative safety."

"I'm going with you," Sir George insisted. "I'm not afraid of dragons."

"Under no circumstances," Thelvyn told him firmly. "There's no reason for you to risk your life. You stay here and keep anyone else from going inside until I say it's safe."

Thelvyn knew Sir George would come running at the first hint of trouble, but he hoped to be able to deal with any problem he encountered before the old knight could get there. He intended to enter not through the main doors, which stood invitingly open, but at the north end of the palace where the guards were barracked. He thought that he could get in through the back entrance gate unseen, which was unlikely if he entered through the front.

He wasn't surprised to find that the north gate stood open. At least one dragon would have had to come that way in order to deal with the small garrison housed there. There was no sign of anything amiss in the yard, but the door to the garrison had been blasted to splinters and the barracks inside was scattered with broken bodies. The dragon had attacked swiftly, catching the men totally unprepared. They probably hadn't even had time to raise an alarm. Thelvyn moved through the barracks quickly, knowing that the objective of the invaders was farther within.

He didn't expect the dragons to be anywhere upstairs, where the corridors were too small to allow their passage. The king's private chamber and his suite were both located downstairs, close to the center of the palace. Thelvyn moved as quietly as possible, holding his sword before him in both hands so that he could swing it around quickly to face any sudden attack. The palace was in complete darkness, as if every lamp and magical light had been deliberately snuffed out by some powerful spell. Although Thelvyn could still see despite the darkness, his helmet restricted his vision somewhat. He had to keep turning constantly to see off to the sides.

The king's suite and his private chamber were both empty. There was no sign of an attack. The dragons must have found Jherridan in some other part of the palace, unless he had somehow been able to get himself to safety. Thelvyn recalled that Taeryn had said Byen Kalestraan and some other wizards were here, or at least they had been at the beginning of the attack. Perhaps the Fire Wizard had managed to get the king to safety before the dragons got inside. In that case, the dragons might be in the palace even yet, still quietly seeking their prey.

Turning slowly at a juncture in the hallways, Thelvyn became aware of the movement of a dark figure in the side passage and stepped back quickly into the concealing shadows. Whoever it was, he was certain it hadn't been a dragon. Then he remembered that the first attack against him had been by dragons who had magically assumed human form. Restricted by their great size, these dragons might also be taking enchanted form in order to move more freely through the passages of the palace. On the other hand, it could be the Fire Wizards or someone from the palace trying to find the king in the darkness. Thelvyn would have to be careful.

His second guess proved closer to correct. When he leaned forward to peer around the corner, he saw that it was Sir George, walking softly with his sword in one hand and the vicious-looking pike on his wrist raised ready to stab. Thelvyn pulled the old knight around the corner.

"Nice of you to wait outside the way I asked," Thelvyn remarked quietly.

"I saw a dragon look out through the front door," Sir George explained. "He was standing inside in the shadows, but I can see fairly well in the dark. He seemed to be expecting someone, so I thought I should see what he was doing. I also thought you'd want to know there are dragons in here."

"That's just what I wanted to hear," Thelvyn said sourly. "To make things worse, I can't find the king. Taeryn said that Kalestraan was here. I hope he found Jherridan and they were able to sneak out."

"Would they have left?" Sir George asked. "It would be just like Jherridan to want to stay and fight."

"Yes, but Kalestraan knows that he can't fight dragons, and he's also a pretty experienced sneak. With any luck, those two are running through the streets of Braejr on their way to the Academy. Just the same, I have to look. What are the chances that these dragons might be taking enchanted form to search the palace?"

Sir George had to consider that briefly. "Shape-changing is a specific talent in drakes, but a latent one in dragons. I'm used to it, but most dragons aren't. They don't know how to fight with weapons. Frankly, they don't even know how to walk upright very easily. Changing forms only makes the situation that much worse for them."

"So you're telling me that you don't think that they have assumed another form?"

"I don't consider it likely, no. There might be dragons in human form in their company, if they anticipated the need. They might have slipped in earlier to evaluate the situation, to find out where the guards were, perhaps even to locate the king. That's why you need me. I can recognize dragons on sight, and I might even be able to sense their presence before I see them if they're close enough."

"Let's get on with it then," Thelvyn said.

He thought it would be best to approach the larger chambers and halls of the central area of the palace from above. From the second floor, they could look out from the galleries on areas such as the great hall, the reception hall, the throne room, and even the vast entrance hall just inside the main doors. The second level was the location of the private chambers of a few servants and administrators who lived within the palace. At most, there were no more than a dozen of them.

On the second floor, they found additional signs of

dragon attacks. Many of the doors had been blasted apart, just as Thelvyn had seen in the garrison. Most of the rooms had been occupied, and they saw that the bodies of the slain crushed and tossed aside. But something puzzled Thelvyn from the outset. The victims had obviously been crushed or hurled against the walls hard enough to kill them, which would require strength far beyond that of a man. And yet dragons could have pushed through these passages only with the greatest difficulty, and they never could have gotten through these small doorways to get at their prey. Even more puzzling, the attackers seemed to have known which rooms were occupied, ignoring most of those that stood empty. He was beginning to suspect that something terrible was inside the palace besides the dragons, something with uncanny tracking abilities.

As Thelvyn saw more and more of that quick, precise destruction, he began to feel vaguely afraid. He wasn't afraid for himself, knowing he was secure within his armor. Instead, he felt the strange, tenuous fear that something was very wrong, something he did not understand. He was becoming possessed with the need to hurry, to confront the enemies hidden in the depths of night and drive them away with the darkness. The most important thing now, he knew, was to not give in to such impulses, which would only lead him into making mistakes.

The end of the corridor brought them to a short passage that led to the gallery above the north side of the great hall. Thelvyn paused at the doorway and moved forward slowly until he could look over the parapet of the gallery into the hall below. Something large was moving in the hall just below him, a black form that was indistinct in the darkness. He was sure it wasn't a man, and yet it wasn't nearly large enough to be a dragon. Whatever it was, Thelvyn knew it must be the creature that wreaked such violent death through the corridors of the palace.

"Down," Thelvyn insisted softly, pointing downward with one forefinger. "I have to find out what that thing is."

"It could be a wyvern," Sir George suggested, although he seemed uncertain. "A large one can be very nasty. And being dragonkin, they can be swayed to submit to the will of a true dragon."

They reached to a small stairway that led down to the first floor, almost directly across from the great hall. When they reached the bottom, Thelvyn moved cautiously forward, trying to stay within the deep shadows of the stairwell until he could lean forward far enough to see around the corner. The unknown creature was moving away from them along a wide corridor that led toward the larger open areas near the middle of the palace. All he could see was a large, dark form. It certainly looked like a dragon from behind, but it was hardly half the size it should have been.

He decided to follow, staying close to the wall, while Sir George slipped along quietly just behind him. Thelvyn was determined to discover what this creature was, to confront it and destroy it or force it to flee. After a time, it came to the vast entranceway before the main hall. This area was more open, with pale moonlight streaming in through the windows and open doors. When Thelvyn came to the same place, he carefully avoided the moonlight, retreating into a dark alcove next to the wall on the side of the entrance. Peering toward the corner, he discovered that the mysterious creature had turned toward the main doors.

Thelvyn's couldn't have been more surprised. It was indeed a dragon, a gold dragon in appearance, although its exact breed was uncertain. He knew enough about dragons that he was able to tell the difference between a male and female, but this small dragon seemed to have the qualities of neither. When he drew back to let Sir George take a quick look, he suddenly had a terrible thought.

"Could it be a child?" he asked softly. "Would the dragons be desperate enough to send half-grown children because they're small enough to make their way through the corridors of the palace?"

Sir George took a quick look., When he turned back, he looked shocked. "I . . . I don't believe it. The only thing dragons treasure more than their own lives is their young. They would never risk such a thing."

"It certainly looks like a gold dragon," Thelvyn insisted.

"You've never seen a young dragon. There's something about the appearance of that one that doesn't seem quite right. It looks like a gold, but it has characteristics of the red dragons as well. It's quite a bit smaller than a gold, but it's not any smaller than some of the white or blue dragons."

"Then you're satisfied that this isn't a child?" Thelvyn asked.

"It couldn't be," Sir George assured him. "A child wouldn't have the same proportions as an adult, as this one appears to. It would be shorter in the neck and muzzle, with a smaller crest and tiny horns. I'm not even satisfied that it's a real dragon. Something doesn't feel right."

Thelvyn knew he had to do something to drive these raiders from the palace, but he was determined not to risk slaying or seriously harming a child. It made him think of Kharendaen, although he had no idea why. He decided to do whatever he could to frighten this dragon away. Holding his sword before him, he stepped out from the shadows.

That proved to be a mistake. The small dragon had been peering out the main doors, careful not to allow itself to be seen from the outside. Suddenly it whipped around to face him, then paused to stare for a moment as if considering its tactics. Thelvyn hesitated when the dragon did not attack immediately, still uncomfortable at the thought of harming what appeared to be a child.

At that moment, a second small dragon charged out of the darkness from Thelvyn's left, catching him completely by surprise. Defending himself almost by instinct, he quickly his sword around and aimed it almost directly in the dragon's face. The first bolt discharged violently into an invisible shield, ripping apart the magical barrier so that the second shot struck the dragon just above its large, glittering eyes. Stunned by the blow, the dragon collapsed in midstride. Carried by the speed of its charge, it slid heavily across the smooth stone floor and crashed into Thelvyn where he stood, throwing him violently back against the wall behind him and pinning him there with its weight.

Thelvyn struggled free of the bulk of the stunned dragon

and turned back to face the other one, but he was too late. The dragon struck him in the side with force enough to send him sliding across the smooth stone floor, knocking the sword from his hand. Before he could pick himself up, the dragon was on him again, trying to pin his arms behind his back. Thelvyn was startled by the tactics. In previous encounters, dragons had never once attempted to capture him. Unfortunately, it proved to be perhaps the best tactic the dragon could have used against him. The magical shields of his suit could protect him from blows or crushing force, but it had no ability to give him the extra strength he would have needed to break the dragon's hold. Lacking any weapon or even the freedom to use one, he was utterly defenseless.

The small dragon knew it had the advantage over him, aware that Thelvyn was now a helpless prisoner. Turning him over on his back, the dragon held his arms tightly in one handlike claw while it used the other to probe the clips that held his helmet in place. The mechanism eluded the dragon for a moment. Its claw was too large to get a good hold on the small clips, but it was finally able to snap open first one and then the other, pulling loose his helmet and tossing it aside. For the first time since he had become the Dragonlord, Thelvyn had been defeated by a dragon. It needed only to twist his exposed neck, and the problem of the Dragonlord would be solved once and for all.

Suddenly the dragon straightened, roaring in pain. Thelvyn took advantage of the distraction to break free from its hold, and he rushed to collect his sword. When he turned, he saw that Sir George had driven the pike he was wearing on his left cuff deep into the dragon's belly. He had chosen an especially vulnerable opening between the leathery plates. Taking firm hold of the handle of the pike with his other hand, Sir George braced himself to draw the weapon back as the injured dragon pulled away, staggering back on its hind legs for a moment before it fell heavily over on its back. Sir George had accomplished the seemingly impossible. He had slain a dragon single-handedly.

Thelvyn looked around quickly. The dragon he had stunned was recovering and seemed ready to renew the attack. Instead of charging, however, it held back in the deeper shadows of the far side of the room, sitting up on its haunches to use its claws to form arcane gestures. Thelvyn realized that the dragon was trying to fight him with magic, not the usual subtle magic of the dragons but the gestural spells of mortal wizards. For a moment, Thelvyn was almost curious enough to want to discover what the dragon was doing, but he knew he dared not risk it. He lifted his sword and stunned the dragon, which once more collapsed to the floor.

Thelvyn glanced around quickly, probing the shadows. Although no other dragons had come to the attack, he felt certain there were more dragons somewhere in the dark passages of the palace. He would have to move quickly now and go on the offensive.

"This is strange. Both of these dragons—even the one you merely stunned—are dead," Sir George said. "Even an immature dragon should be heartier than that."

"This is strange all the way around," Thelvyn said. "When it had hold of me, that dragon didn't seem to be as strong as a dragon should be. And that second one was about to use mortal magic, I'm sure. I'm rapidly becoming convinced that these aren't real dragons at all, just as you said. I suspect they might be wizards in enchanted form, and I can guess who."

"Remember, we were warned about something like this only a few hours ago," Sir George said, then suddenly grabbed him by the arm. "Look!"

The dragon Sir George had slain was changing shape, its form shrinking rapidly until it became that of a man. By his features and his thick red hair, he appeared to be of the Flaem and almost certainly a Fire Wizard. Thelvyn saw that he had guessed correctly.

"Alessa was right," he said. "I have to move quickly now. If the king is still alive in here somewhere, I'll have to hurry to I have any chance of rescuing him. This time I want you to stay back and watch yourself. Things are going to get nasty now. I'm sure that they must have some surprises in store for me, or they wouldn't still be waiting around."

He hurried to the largest corridor leading into the southern half of the palace, certain now that his enemy must be somewhere in one of the larger halls where he had not yet looked. Knowing that he did not face true dragons but wizards, he couldn't imagine what manner of trap they might have arranged for him. The wizards had always overestimated their own abilities, and he was counting on his guess that they had probably underestimated him. He suspected he had no reason to be afraid, but he would have to be very careful.

As he came around a corner, he saw a pale light coming through the open doors of the throne room. Again he hesitated, approaching the doors cautiously from the shadows along the inside wall until he was able to peer carefully around the edge of the door. A massive ball of pure, clear crystal, nearly two full yards across, stood on a tripod of black iron. The light was coming from the crystal itself, a steady glow of cold, glaring white, yet dim enough that the corners of the room remained in shadows. Behind the crystal, standing on the dais of the throne, was the largest gold dragon he had yet seen that night.

Holding his sword before him, Thelvyn stepped through the door into the throne room. He noticed that there were two other dragons in the room, hiding in the deep shadows on either side of the door, where he hadn't been able to see them before. Another crushed body had been tossed carelessly to one side of the wide throne dais; Thelvyn suspected it must be King Jherridan.

Holding his sword higher, he advanced several steps along the carpeted runway leading to the throne, the massive crystal ball standing directly in his path. He knew that the crystal was almost certainly a device to amplify magic, adding greater strength or endurance to normal spells or enhancing the effects of a magical artifact. That warned him that any attack against him would likely be magical in nature; all he could do in turn was to trust the powerful enchantments of his armor.

The two smaller dragons moved in behind him, cutting off his only escape, while their leader stepped down from the dais to stand directly behind the vast crystal. Thelvyn stood ready, knowing that the attack would come at any moment. Then he saw Sir George peering around the end of the south gallery, waiting for the chance to remove the king to safety. Somehow Thelvyn had to delay a few moments longer.

"I know who you are," he declared. "I call upon you to surrender. You must know that your magic is no match for the power of ancient Blackmoor."

"But what are you without that power?" the dragon asked. "Are you able to fight me if you are no longer the Dragonlord?"

Suddenly Thelvyn felt the weight of his armor settle more heavily about him, almost as if its strength had gone out of it. Then he understood the tactics of his enemy only too well. In all the time he had been the Dragonlord, no adverse magic had ever been able to affect the armor. Somehow this crystal was powerful enough to overcome the enchantments of the armor, in some way either blocking or draining most of its own strength. The attack of the three dragons came almost immediately in the form of invisible blasts of force, which struck him like the massive bolts of a catapult.

The armor responded as well as it could, but its power was so diminished that the shields could only blunt the force of the blasts. Thelvyn was knocked to his knees from the first blow. He braced himself against the tremendous force of the barrage. Each blow felt as if someone were striking his armor with a club, and he began to grow uncomfortably hot as the searing blasts caused the exposed backplate of the armor to smoke. Yet somehow he had to endure this for a few moments more in order to give Sir George time enough to get the king to safety. If the dragons had physically attacked him at that moment, trying to crush him with their weight or overcome him with their strength, he knew that he would not have survived. Fortunately they respected the power of the Dragonlord too much, preferring to attack magically from what seemed to them a safe distance.

Defending himself the only way he could, Thelvyn desperately called upon his own magic to raise an invisible barrier, hoping to divert the worst of the attack away from the failing defenses of the armor for at least a brief time. He needed to hold what power of the armor remained in reserve for his counterattack. If he didn't somehow counter those blasts of energy to his back, he knew that he would soon be burned. He needed all the force of will he could command to hold the barrier about him, knowing that if it failed he couldn't get it back until he relearned the spell. When he dared to raise his head at last, he saw that Sir George and the king were already gone.

Now he had his one chance to attack, and this time the strength and magic he needed would have to be mostly his own. Moving slowly and carefully against the assault of the dragons, he called upon the last of his failing strength to force himself to stand and raise his sword. He felt his magic shield give out, and now he must rely only upon the remaining strength of the armor to protect him for the short time he needed. He lifted his sword to his full reach, facing the sphere of crystal. The leader of the dragons responded, moving quickly around to the front of the crystal to protect it.

Thelvyn knew that he couldn't expect to win a battle against wizards if he had to rely upon his own magic. He simply didn't have the experience. His greatest strength was as a cleric, commanding powers within himself that he knew were powerful enough to subdue a dragon. Teleportation wasn't commonly a clerical ability, but he was no common cleric. Suddenly he vanished and reappeared in the next instant on the far side of the crystal, behind the dragon. Startled by the unexpected move and suddenly fearful of what the Dragonlord might do, the dragon whipped around and charged directly at him.

Trusting only in the failing powers of his armor to protect him, Thelvyn commanded the full remaining force of the sword and brought the blade down with all his strength across the top of the sphere of crystal. The surface of the crystal was immediately crisscrossed with countless cracks, and in the next instant it failed altogether in a tremendous explosion of flame. Blinded by the blast, Thelvyn was hurled backward with tremendous force until he crashed hard against the inside wall of the throne room. Fortunately the power of the enchantments of his armor had begun to return at the moment the crystal was destroyed, protecting him from the full impact.

He was stunned all the same, and for a time all he could do was struggle to regain his breath. His head seemed to pound with pain, and he could barely move. For several seconds he could see nothing through the flames and the smoke. He was aware only that something heavy, like pieces of stone, was falling about him. He closed his eyes, waiting for the pain in his head to subside. Then, as he began to struggle to stand, a hand took him under his right arm and helped him to his feet. He returned the sword to its clip at his belt, then removed his helmet.

Sir George stood at his side. The blast from the destruction of the crystal had completely wrecked the throne room, rushing upward and blowing away the roof of the palace and tossing the debris in every direction. Many of the interior walls had also been ripped away as well, devastating the surrounding halls and chambers in that entire section of the palace. Only the wall behind him remained standing, and that was only because it was also the massive outer wall of the city. Everywhere wood from splintered rafters and beams and the ruins of the galleries was in flames.

When he looked around, he saw that none of the three dragons had survived the attack. Their broken bodies had been tossed aside and lay half buried in the debris.

"That was a bit extreme, I must say," Sir George commented.

Thelvyn shook his head slowly. "That wasn't my doing. They were using that large crystal to channel some vast reserve of power, great enough that it nearly overwhelmed the enchantments of my suit. I suppose we should consider ourselves fortunate it didn't devastate this entire side of the city. Did you get the king to safety?"

"He was already dead," Sir George told him. "They had crushed him just like the others. I left his body down the hall."

The fires seemed likely to spread throughout the entire palace, and they were in danger of being overcome by the smoke and dust. Although Thelvyn was still somewhat unsteady, the old knight helped him pick his way through the rubble. When they came to the body of the largest of the dragons, they found that the enchantments had failed and it had transformed back into its true nature.

As Thelvyn had expected, it was Byen Kalestraan.

CHAPTER TWELVE

When Thelvyn and Sir George finally emerged from the smoke and flames, they saw that the explosion of the crystal sphere had devastated at least a quarter of the palace. The spreading flames, which had been advancing slowly, suddenly began to burn vigorously and were in danger of consuming the rest of the palace. Once he had rested a few moments, Thelvyn cast a clerical spell to suppress fire to contain the damage. By that time, he was completely exhausted and in pain from the injuries he had sustained in his battle. He very much needed to rest for a while. Just the same, he thought it best to stay close and help sort out the mess that was sure to follow. Sir George wouldn't allow him to remove his armor, fearful of additional attacks, but at least he was able to sit down for a few minutes.

Needless to say, the destruction of the king's palace awoke the entire city, and help was quick in coming. The captain of the garrison at the north gate discussed the matter briefly with Thelvyn, finally sending most of his garrison to put out the remaining flames and stationing the rest at the gate and along the walls of Braejr to guard against further attack. When more soldiers arrived, Thelvyn sent them to secure the wizards' residence at the Academy, with instructions that no one was to be allowed to leave the premises until further notice. Then he sent a message to the captain of the garrison to begin searching the palace for survivors and remove the dead. Once he felt reasonably certain that nothing more could be done until morning, he went home to bed.

Thelvyn felt no better the next morning. He had taken quite a beating during the time that his armor had been unable to fully protect him, and again when the explosion had thrown him violently against the wall. His back and neck ached, and his head still throbbed. He was also concerned about his armor, which had come through the attack badly scorched. A good night's rest, however brief, seemed to have done the suit more good than it did him. When he put it on morning, there was already little sign of damage. The enchantments of the ancient armor seemed to cover all contingencies, including self-renewal.

As much as he hated to consider it, Thelvyn knew that he needed to return to the palace as quickly as he could. As the Dragonlord and the commander of the Highlands Army, he now commanded the highest authority of anyone in Braejr. Until he was able to determine who had been named Jherridan Maarsten's heir and successor, he would have to assume command himself. He knew that ancient Flaemish law required certain assurances from any new king. One of those laws required every new king to name his successor in his will, but Thelvyn couldn't recall Jherridan ever saying anything about whom he had chosen as his successor.

Only then did the reality of the situation begin to sink in. King Jherridan was dead, and Byen Kalestraan as well. A country that was at war with an enemy it could not fight was suddenly without direction, and by chance the welfare of the Highlands seemed to be his responsibility. He washed and dressed and then ate quickly. Then he asked Sir George to accompany him to the palace and sent a message to Alessa Vyledaar, who had been summoned to the Academy, to meet him there as soon as possible. As far as

Thelvyn knew, Alessa was now the senior ranking Fire Wizard. There might be other wizards at the Academy of higher rank and greater experience, but there was no way of knowing yet just how many of them had been involved in the plot to assassinate the king.

The morning was bright and clear, with only a few clouds hovering over the mountains to the east. But as innocent and pleasant as the morning seemed, the king's palace still looked dark and forlorn in the morning sun. A large area of the palace, fully a fourth of its length, had been devastated by the explosion of the crystal, although the damage didn't appear so bad from the courtyard because the front wall remained intact. The soldiers of the city garrison had begun to salvage what could be saved from the damaged areas.

Thelvyn's first concern was to uncover every smallest detail of just what had happened. Every member of the palace staff and some forty men of the palace garrison were dead, most of them slain as they slept. Of those who had been in the palace when the wizards had arrived, only Taeryn had survived, and then only because he had been sent by Kalestraan to summon the Dragonlord into the trap that had been prepared for him. Thelvyn hadn't intended to ask the young valet to return to the palace so soon, knowing that the death of King Jherridan had upset him, but Taeryn had insisted. The young valet didn't want for courage, and he was determined to remain calm at a time when he knew that he was needed.

There seemed to have been five wizards involved in the attack, and none of them had survived. Alessa returned from the Academy just past midmorning to report what she had learned so far. Knowledge of the conspiracy seemed to have been limited to the eighteen most senior Fire Wizards; of those, five had been slain in the attack, and the rest had fled in spite of Thelvyn's attempt to prevent that. For now, the Academy was under the direction of Alessa Vyledaar, supported by one older wizard who had agreed to take time from his books only until a replacement could be found.

Needless to say, the events of the previous night had already done serious damage to the prestige and the credibility of the Fire Wizards as the guardians of Flaemish law and tradition. King Jherridan had been generally well liked and respected. Worse yet, the wizards had attacked and slain him because of their own ambitions. Byen Kalestraan's plan, of course, had been to slay both the king and the Dragonlord and then seize power in the resulting crisis, laying the blame on the dragons, whom he then expected to defeat with his new power. Now that the depths of his treachery were generally known, the remaining Fire Wizards shared in his disgrace. The fury of the Flaemish people was so great that the wizards might never again reclaim the standing they had once enjoyed.

Indeed, the only one who seemed to have benefitted from this tragedy was the Dragonlord himself. Thelvyn was regarded as a hero for having exposed the traitors and for his desperate attempt to save King Jherridan. By that evening, there had already been public calls to make him the next king. It was unprecedented for the Flaem, considering their natural suspicion of foreigners, to even contemplate such a thing. At first, Thelvyn deemed such calls the least of his problems. He wasn't able to speak privately with his companions until that evening at dinner. By that time, he had two very important questions that he needed to have answered.

"I have a very nasty suspicion," he began. "I am reminded that the dragons accused the wizards of stealing something they very much want back. I know what it is, and the thing I destroyed last night wasn't it. Still, if Kalestraan had stolen the Collar of the Dragons, then he apparently wanted it for its supposed ability to direct great powers, much as he was using that crystal."

"Kalestraan stole something from the dragons," Alessa admitted reluctantly. "I don't know what it was, although it apparently never did him any good. Now, with all of his associates either dead or fled, I'm not sure we have any way now of finding this thing."

"This has got to have something to do with that great source of power that your Fire Wizards have discovered," Thelvyn said.

Alessa looked surprised. "You know about that?"

"Kalestraan himself told us about it the first time we were here," Sir George told her. "Its limited range was his excuse for why his wizards were having no luck fighting the dragons, and also for why Thelvyn's cape wasn't supposed to function outside of the Highlands. I suppose he thought it was safe enough to tell us, since he thought he was sending us to our deaths anyway."

"Byen Kalestraan was an absolute idiot," Alessa declared sourly. "The source of power he told you about is called the Radiance. Only experienced wizards are supposed to know about it, and even they aren't allowed to know the secret of its nature. Only the most senior wizards are allowed to know the secrets of its power, if anyone does. I wasn't among them, but I've pieced together enough to have some idea."

"What do you think it is?" Thelvyn prompted.

She shrugged. "It's a great, inexplicable source of latent magical energy. The wizards discovered it even before our people came into this world, at the time when they were still searching through the worlds for traces of the Alphatians. They immediately saw the Radiance as a source of the power we needed to defeat our ancient enemy, so they brought us here to take advantage of it. At first they wanted it left here, when this place was mostly wilderness, so they could have it to themselves. Later, when they began learning to use the Radiance, they decided that it should have better protection. They encouraged the first archduke to move the capital of the Highlands here from its first home in Braastar."

"But they still have no idea what it is?" Sir George asked.

"No, although there's a good deal of speculation about what it might be. The most logical assumption is that it must be some natural source of magic of a type we don't yet comprehend. Many of the wizards prefer to believe that it was a gift from the Immortals in recognition of the value of our quest to destroy the Alphatians."

Solveig rolled her eyes. "The self-righteous never cease to amaze me."

"As you already seem to know, the Radiance is tremendously powerful, yet limited in range," Alessa continued. "That was what got Kalestraan in trouble during the last war with the dragons. His wizards were able to assemble magic powerful enough to subdue a dragon, at least here in Braejr where they were working on it. But when they went into the northern frontier, the magic failed."

"Then how did he expect to deal with the dragons after he had assassinated Jherridan and me?" Thelvyn asked. "Did he expect to just sacrifice the frontier and wait until the dragons had come within the effective range of the Radiance in the central Highlands?"

"I suppose that was it," Alessa said. "If he had other plans, I have no idea what they might have been. That's why I greatly regret the escape of the conspirators who have fled. They are the ones who best understand the Radiance, and before the trouble with the dragons is over, we may need its power. Also, they alone may know the location of the treasure that was stolen from the dragons."

Thelvyn shook his head. "Kalestraan's plans were flawed. He presumed too much in thinking that the Radiance was powerful enough to defeat an army of dragons, just as it couldn't completely negate the enchantments of my armor. It didn't prevent my using either my magical or clerical powers."

Alessa looked surprised. "I had suspected you were a cleric, but do you mean to say you are a wizard as well?"

"The term wizard might be a little extreme in describing my abilities," he said, aware that he had already told her too much. "But we can speculate on the motives of dead wizards some other time. The problem facing us now is finding a new king. Jherridan had no direct heir. By ancient Flaemish law, he was supposed to name his successor in his will. Naturally, one of the first things I needed to do this morning was to find that will. And I wanted to do it in the presence of the most credible witnesses in the city, so there could be no accusations by the dukes that I had changed it. That turned out to be a good thing."

"What do you mean?" Sir George asked. "Jherridan named a successor, didn't he?"

"Oh, yes, he certainly did," Thelvyn admitted reluctantly, crossing his arms on the edge of the table. "The trouble is that he named me."

"Well, well. Congratulations, old boy!"

"Do try to be serious," Thelvyn told the old knight. "I certainly don't want to be King of the Flaemish Realm, and I'm sure that my duty as the Dragonlord doesn't permit it. I might be willing to watch over things temporarily, but the Flaem are going to have to find themselves a real king. The trouble is, I'm not sure there's a mechanism in Flaemish law to decide upon a new king. The dukes made Jherridan archduke as a matter of convenience; he later made himself king. Ordinarily the wizards would be the arbitrators of Flaemish law, but their order is in utter disgrace for the foreseeable future. That seems to leave only the dukes to decide, and I doubt they could. They're too suspicious of each other to want another duke made king."

"I'll put the remaining wizards to work reviewing the law," Alessa offered. "Perhaps there's a precedent from ancient times for the formation of a larger conference that has the power to name a king. The obvious solution, of course, is that Thelvyn should remain king until the war with the dragons is settled, then name his own successor."

"Oh, fine," Thelvyn said sourly, then thought of something. "I have firsthand knowledge of how exclusionary Flaemish law is regarding people not of their race. The question I have is whether or not the law would permit me to be made king in any event."

"Again, we would have to research that," Alessa said, lifting her empty wine glass to stare at it. "If Jherridan had named you a citizen of the realm, perhaps so. There might be nothing said on that subject one way or the other. The question of a foreigner becoming king may have been regarded as so inconceivable that no one ever felt the need to write laws about it. But the will of the Flaemish people can supersede even Flaemish law. If everyone wants to have the Dragonlord as their king, they certainly can."

"Wait a moment," Thelvyn insisted. "I'm not arguing for my right to be king."

"The situation might be too critical for you to refuse," she told him. "There is no one alive except yourself who is respected enough to be granted the title. If the realm remains in a state of anarchy for very long, either the dragons will destroy us or else the dukes will split up the realm among themselves as they did before Jherridan took the throne, leaving the Highlands leaderless and vulnerable. If the Flaem will have you, then you must become king. Once things are more settled, then your successor can be chosen without fear of anarchy."

Thelvyn glanced at Sir George, who made a helpless gesture. "She's probably right," the old knight said. "And you already are the king in practice if not in name."

"I have the feeling I'm about to become king whether I like it or not," Thelvyn said ruefully. "I can't help but wonder how the dragons are going to react to such news. I wish Kharendaen were here."

* * * * *

By the next morning, Thelvyn was beginning to think the dragons were the least of his problems. The death or disappearance of so many senior Fire Wizards had caused their system of magical communication to collapse. Alessa Vyledaar was able to find enough wizards who were trained in the use of the Radiance to get the system back in operation by early afternoon. The problem was that the system enabled the news of the assassination of King Jherridan and the treachery of the Fire Wizards to spread quickly through every part of the Realm. By morning of the next day, the dukes had taken over the system to express their many opinions and demands not only to each other but to Braejr.

Authority in the Highlands was threatening to collapse, but not quite yet. Even the dukes had come to recognize the benefits of a unified realm, especially in times of danger. They wanted to know who had been named as Jherridan's successor and whether the Dragonlord was going to be around to handle the problems they already had. Realizing that he no longer could afford to be subtle, Thelvyn had it announced publicly that he had been named the successor, but he wasn't willing to hold the title permanently. He would assume duties of king only until the crisis with the dragons was over.

If the people of Braejr were any indication, Thelvyn had no cause for concern. There had already been public calls for him to accept the throne, which surprised him very much. What he failed to understand at first was the great sense of betrayal they felt, a betrayal so deep that they might never overcome it. While he had grown up excluded from much by Flaemish law, the Flaems had always felt complete trust in their law, the absolute unity of their race, and in the wizards as the defenders of their beliefs and traditions. Now all they had left to believe in was the Dragonlord, who alone had always acted selflessly on their behalf.

If he remained reluctant to accept the title of king, he couldn't escape the duties required of the leader of the Highlands. Whatever else, the problem of the conflict with the dragons still had to be addressed, and he had to move quickly if he still hoped for a peaceful solution. He had already begun conducting business at the palace, occupying Jherridan's former private chamber. As soon as he could, he called in both Sir George and Alessa to discuss certain confidential matters.

"I know you were about to leave again to continue your search for the Collar of the Dragons," he said to the old knight. "I wonder if there is any point to continuing the search. I'm doubtful we can spare the time. Alessa says Kalestraan was involved in the theft, and you could spend months trying to determine which of the renegades was involved with him. The only important question is what he's done with it, and our best chance of finding a quick answer to that would seem to be here at the Academy."

"I don't believe it could still be there," Alessa said.

"Yes, we know that already," he agreed. "But there might be some clue to its whereabouts. Sir George got only as far as the basement before."

"We were desperate," the old knight explained when Alessa stared at him suspiciously. "The only thing I got from it was a quick lesson in architecture. Now that Kalestraan isn't about to protest, I'd be very interested in poking about among his private papers."

"I've begun searching already," Alessa said, obviously reluctant.

"Sir George is something of a professional, you might say, in finding things," Thelvyn told her.

"Yes, of course," she agreed hesitantly. "I don't have any reason to refuse, beyond a wizard's instinct for privacy. Under the circumstances, I don't think our order is in a position to claim any special privileges. Besides, Kalestraan had some secrets that I would very much like to get my hands on just now, possibly some that may prove very helpful if we do have to fight dragons."

"If there's anything to be found, we should have it fairly quickly," Sir George said. "What about that dragon of yours, Thelvyn? We can't keep him around forever when we're supposed to be at war with his people."

Thelvyn frowned. "I'd like for him to stay close for a while longer, if he's willing. We might need him to retrieve the collar, if we can ever determine where it is. Do you suppose the renegades who stole it for Kalestraan decided to keep it for themselves?"

"That could be," Sir George said thoughtfully. "I've also just realized that he might have stolen it himself, since he was able to assume the form of a dragon. His disguise obviously didn't hold up to close scrutiny, since any dragon would have recognized him on sight. But if he was able to keep at a distance, it might have been good enough for him to sneak inside the city of the dragons and carry away the collar. I still can't imagine how he knew about the collar or where to find it unless a dragon told him."

"His powers were tied to the Radiance," Alessa said. "He might not have been able to maintain the shape of a dragon outside the Highlands."

"I have to leave that problem to the two of you," Thelvyn told them. "We would benefit from having the collar to offer the dragons, but I don't hold much hope we can find it in time. I have to prepare for the worst, which now means preparing the Highlands for invasion."

"You asked me to investigate what Flaemish law has to say about your ability to serve as king," Alessa reminded him. "I've been able to discover a few interesting things. First of all, there seems to be nothing in Flaemish law that says that you have to be Flaemish to be king. Only one who is foreign-born, Flaemish or otherwise, cannot be king."

"I was born in the village of Graez," Thelvyn said. "I wasn't a full-fledged citizen, but Jherridan made me one five years ago so he could appoint me his advisor because only a citizen can be in the pay of the king."

"That seems to satisfy that requirement," Alessa agreed. "But refusing the title of king when you've been named successor is another thing. Apparently you are bound by duty, since it was the final command by the previous king. The only way to avoid it is if someone charges you with being unfit and can prove it. No such charges apply to you, I'm sure."

"But I can surrender the title when I like, and to whom I like?" Thelvyn asked.

"There appear to be no obstacles to that."

"Fine," Thelvyn agreed, settling back in his chair. "Still, I prefer to wait until I discover what the dukes think before I decide anything. We can't afford the distraction of being caught up in a battle of succession while the dragons are preparing for war. The dukes can squabble over who gets to be king all they want if they're willing to allow us to run things until then."

"My concern is that the realm very much needs a new king just now, when so much our people once believed in has been betrayed," Alessa said.

"Yes, I'm aware of that," Thelvyn admitted, staring for a moment into the dark fireplace. "My other great concern just now is for the dragons. Have there been any reports from the north about any sign of movement? I don't know how soon they might learn of recent events here in Braejr, but I'm afraid they're going to look upon them as something they can use to their advantage."

"I've heard nothing about any such reports," Alessa answered. "But I have learned this: We have found evidence that the attack of the dragon assassins on the night of the ambassador's reception was devised by Byen Kalestraan. We also learned he had dealings with a band of renegade black dragons who attacked you while they were in enchanted form. That's now absolute proof that the dragons did not break the truce first."

Thelvyn shook his head slowly. "It may be too late. Now that the dragons feel threatened, they won't be quick to forgive and forget. I suspect they still want to test the limits of my abilities, to find out whether or not they really have to fear the Dragonlord. Which brings me to the next problem. I very much need that cape."

Alessa looked at the floor and sighed. "I have people working on that, but the wizards who made the cape are gone now, and they had done no work on it since you brought it back. They expected you would never need it again."

Thelvyn had never considered that he might not have the powers of the cape of flight to give him the mobility he needed to fight the dragons. "Can your wizards start all over again, and this time not tie the enchantments of the cape to the Radiance? I can't have it fail me just because I've ventured too far into the frontier."

"We can certainly try," she agreed, rising to leave. "If nothing else brings me back, then I will see you tonight."

"Tonight?" he asked, confused.

"I still live at your house," she reminded him as she left.

The matter of the cape continued to worry Thelvyn a great deal. He didn't hold any great hope that the Fire Wizards would be able to come up with anything that could withstand the magic of the dragons. Without the ability to face the dragons on their own terms, he would have to fight a far more defensive battle, withdrawing the troops from the north to fortify positions in the larger towns and cities. The dragons could easily ignore him if he had to chase after them.

He would be even more restricted if he had to deal with the responsibilities of the king of the Highlands at the same time. He was no longer free to rejoin the army in the northern frontier. He now found it necessary to remain in the central Highlands, where he could most easily direct the defense of the entire realm. That led him back to the question of whether it was best for him to agree to become king, or ask to be granted the authority only for as long as the war with the dragons lasted. Or perhaps it would be best to ask that a new king be named so he could concentrate on his pressing duties as Dragonlord. All he knew for certain was that he would have to decide soon.

* * * * *

The first problem Sir George and Alessa faced in finding any secrets Byen Kalestraan might have kept was determining where they should look first. Sir George wanted to begin with his private chamber. Alessa considered that entirely too obvious, but Sir George pointed out that Kalestraan had always been quite obvious in his schemes. Finally Alessa relented, although she had already searched the chamber carefully and was at a loss to know where else to look. Sir George attacked the room energetically as a challenge he appeared to enjoy, checking off in his mind an entire list of hidden doorways and drawers he knew about from his experience as a thief.

"You're young yet," he explained as he searched the edges of the mantelpiece. "You have to be on your own for a while before you begin to learn some of the really sneaky little things associated with magic. Wizards always have secret places, and they prefer magical hiding places to mundane ones. In that case, you almost have to know the type of thing you're looking for before you can find it."

"Do you think Thelvyn will agree to become king?" Alessa asked idly, content to watch patiently while he continued his search.

"Yes, I expect that he will," Sir George agreed. "He really doesn't have much choice, does he?"

"He leads a rather lonely life, doesn't he?" she asked. "I mean, he's alone in that big house most of the time while you and Solveig are away, with no real friends except that dragon."

"He gets along very well with `that dragon,' as you put it," Sir George told her. "Are you asking if he's likely to need the company of someone like you? I really don't think that I would hold my breath if I were you. He's the Dragonlord. His duty pretty well precludes any long-term plans or commitments. To tell you the truth, I really don't expect that we'll be around here very long after this problem with the dragons is over. Things are changing, and his responsibilities will probably lead him somewhere else. You probably shouldn't hold any personal expectations involving him."

"That's being candid," Alessa remarked.

"Just a moment," Sir George said. "I think I've got it."

He had been studying the door in the back of the room that led into a smaller chamber. Aside from a common latch, a lock was set into the door just above it, which could be secured from the inside by turning a small handle so that a key was needed from the outside. Turning the handle in one direction set a bolt that locked the door. Turning it all the way in the other direction didn't seem to do anything at first, until Sir George shut the door and then opened it again. This time the door opened into a completely different room, hardly more than a closet of shelves stacked with books and papers.

"Hit with your pick right here, as the dwarves would say," he remarked, quite pleased with himself. "One of the classic interdimensional tricks. Any competent thief knows all the variations on this one. This top shelf appears to be notes the old wizard kept on his political enemies. By the looks of the stack, he didn't trust anyone."

Sir George took the first stack of pages off the very top and began reading. Alessa tried to look over his shoulder, but he was too tall for her to see. After a moment, he made some noises of great interest.

"He even kept reports on his own people," he explained. "This is about one of the wizards. She's described as being thirty-four years old but looks younger, uses a spell of weight reduction, a permanent but reversible spell of infertility, and once used a spell to augment her bust."

"What?" Alessa's face reddened, and she grabbed the paper from his hand, staring at it in disbelief. "This is about me! How did he know all of that?"

"He must have pulled it out when he was considering you to serve the Dragonlord. It was on the top of the pile,"

Sir George said, riffling through the stack of pages quickly. He found one and pulled it out. "Yes, here's one on Thelvyn."

"It's pretty small," Alessa observed.

"Well, there's not much even Thelvyn knows about himself," the old knight explained. "It seems that Kalestraan was forced to guess about a good deal of what he does have. It says here that Thelvyn is of unknown race, but he is most likely a creature of magic as well as a mortal, and that he is possibly a dragon in enchanted form."

"Is that true?" she asked, bending her head forward to look at the page.

"Well, it's true that he is both a mortal and a creature of magic," Sir George said. "That's obvious enough. And given his various qualities, it's also a fairly reasonable guess that he could be a dragon in enchanted form. The only problem, as you may know, is that all creatures, including dragons, must be born in their natural form. Even true shapechangers have to come into the world in their real forms. Thelvyn was born as you know him, and his mother was obviously of the same race. I was there."

"Which is why you wouldn't encourage anyone to become very close to him?"

"All I can is that he's twenty-one years old—a good deal younger than you are, I might add—and he's never had any attachments with members of the opposite sex," he said, taking the paper from her hands and placing it with the others. "Please don't destroy evidence."

"Yes, we do have quite a bit to look through, don't we?" Alessa said, glancing at the stacks of papers.

"And this might be just the start of it," the old knight told here. "Now that I have the run of the place, I need to check for more such hidden chambers. There could even be one large enough to hold the Collar of the Dragons."

* * * * *

By the end of that day, Thelvyn found that he had underestimated just how frightened the dukes were of the dragons. They had all been through the attacks of the rogue dragons before, and present events reminded them only too much of their previous fear and inability to defend themselves. Their responses had arrived masked by many elaborate excuses and dignified phrases, but the essence of what they all had to say was that Thelvyn should do whatever he thought best just as long as he took care of the problem with the dragons. None of them seemed at all interested in being king, and they had no other suggestions regarding his rule.

Thelvyn was beginning to see that he was only delaying the inevitable. This was end of the second day since the death of King Jherridan, and the people of the city were becoming rather concerned with the fact that their country had no leader at a time when it was at war with the dragons. He could imagine how worried the people of the north were becoming, now that their king was dead and the Dragonlord was no longer there to protect them. As much as he dreaded it, Thelvyn allowed the announcement to be made that he would be acting in the king's place, at least for the time being.

He still had to deal with the dragons, of course. Alessa had found evidence that the first attack upon Thelvyn hadn't been the work of the dragons but of Byen Kalestraan, who had been working with some renegade black dragons. The point of the attack had been simple enough and was designed to work to Kalestraan's advantage almost any way it might have turned. If the assassins succeeded, it hardly mattered to him whether or not the dragons were implicated. The only objective to all of his schemes had been to find some way to be rid of the Dragonlord and King Jherridan, leaving the Highlands in a state of chaos, which would allow him to seize power for the wizards.

The fact that Thelvyn could now prove the details of that treachery was less useful to him than he might have wished. Under the circumstances, no one in the Highlands doubted the existence of a plot. The problem for Thelvyn was to get the Parliament of Dragons to forgive the Flaem for the accusations that had been made. To that end, he issued the order that the line of defensive forts was to be drawn back from the northern border to the southern frontier.

How the dragons responded to that move would determine what he would have to do next. There had been no indication yet whether the dragons even knew of the treachery of the wizards or the death of King Jherridan. Individual dragons continued to patrol the frontier, but there had been no actual attacks upon either the towns or settlements or upon the army itself. Even so, Thelvyn was certain that they would know of the events in Braejr soon, within the next few days at most, and he was just as certain that their plans would change accordingly.

Thelvyn was working in the king's private chamber when there was a knock at the door and Taeryn entered. "My lord, there is an elf lady here to speak with you."

"A representative from the elvish holdings in the south?" Thelvyn asked. His first thought was that the elves were withdrawing their support, having decided that they weren't in any trouble with the dragons as long as they didn't ally themselves with the Flaem. He wondered if he actually dared to hope that he might be getting more support.

"It's not one of the Highlands elves," Taeryn explained. "This is an elf lady out of Alfheim . . . a cleric."

Thelvyn knew who it was even before Taeryn had stepped aside to permit her to enter. In all the dangers and concerns of the last few days, he had completely forgotten about the spirit of his mother telling him that someone would be sent to assist him in Kharendaen's place. He realized now that he should have guessed who that would be. Aside from the dwarvish clerics of Kagyar, who would never have left their own land, Sellianda was the only other cleric he knew.

Even so, he almost didn't recognize her at first. She hadn't changed in the least; indeed, she appeared to be dressed the same as she was the last time he had seen her. It had simply been such a long time that he had nearly forgotten the details of her appearance. She was tall for an elf, although still much shorter than he. Her face was long, with delicate features, and her flowing hair had the color of burnished gold.

"I told you we would meet again," she said simply. "Were you not told that I would be coming?"

"Not specifically," he said. "I was told only that a new advisor would be sent to replace Kharendaen."

Sellianda paused a moment to look at him; she seemed pleased. "I said you would grow up to be someone very remarkable, and I see that I was not mistaken. I have been sent to assist you in any way I can. I have been told much of your situation already, but I will have to know everything. The question now is how we can defuse the problem with the dragons. If it is already too late, we must prepare for war. Our time is brief."

"I've been doing what I can," Thelvyn assured her. "I can prove now that the dragons never broke the truce. The problem is getting them to listen."

"We will do what we can," she said. Then she glanced about the room. "Do you live here at the palace?"

"I'm trying to avoid that as long as possible," he replied. "You probably noticed the mess from the battle. But I have a room for you at my house."

Then he recalled that Alessa Vyledaar was there. He could see already that it would be a very interesting time at dinner. He also thought that he had better lock his door at night.

CHAPTER THIRTEEN

Nightfall came late as the season moved toward midsummer, and the evening shadows were growing long when Thelvyn and Sellianda came to the courtyard of his house. Thelvyn no longer had to be concerned about closing the gate; even though, strictly speaking, he was not the king, he already had a small garrison on hand to watch his house and grounds at night. Sellianda paused a moment in the courtyard, staring at the warehouse that had come to be known as Kharendaen's lair. There were lights in the windows again; the young cleric Seldaek was now in residence.

"Is that where the dragon stayed?" Sellianda asked.

"I wish she were still here," Thelvyn replied, then flushed with embarrassment as he realized how that must sound. "That's not to say I'm sorry to have you here."

Sellianda glanced at him. "You love her very much."

He shrugged. "She's been a remarkably good friend, and I've never had many friends. She was always there for me, always and completely a friend. Her only concern was what was best for me. I suppose I became entirely too used to that, although I hope she never thought I took her for granted."

"I'm sure that you did not," she assured him. "Perhaps I cannot put you on my back and fly you to other lands, but I will do what I can for you."

Thelvyn gave Sellianda's horse to a servant and helped her carry her things to the room where she would be staying, which was next to his. There wasn't much to carry; she had traveled light, her luggage containing mostly clothing of the elvish style and a few books. Unlike wizards, clerics carried no spellbook or magical devices, although they sometimes bore talismans or artifacts of their order. As a cleric of Terra, Immortal spirit of the living earth, Sellianda's sacred artifact was the land itself.

As he had expected, things began to get interesting when they came down to dinner a short time later. Sir George was surprised by Sellianda's sudden appearance; Thelvyn had apparently forgotten to tell him a new advisor would be taking Kharendaen's place. Solveig was less surprised but obviously quite amused; she knew already what to expect, and she wasn't going to complicate the situation by entering the competition for Thelvyn's attention. Alessa Vyledaar was caught completely by surprise and didn't know what to make of Sellianda's sudden appearance, since none of the stories she had heard about the Dragonlord had ever mentioned a female elf cleric. Indeed, she had no idea just how matters stood between Thelvyn and Sellianda, and she remained quite subdued for some time.

All through dinner, Sellianda listened carefully as the others explained the situation to her. She seemed familiar with the events leading up to the death of King Jherridan, but she had only a general idea of what had followed. After dinner they retired to the den, where Sir George insisted upon passing out glasses of cherry liqueur to celebrate the occasion.

"I can appreciate your problem," Sellianda told Thelvyn. "I do not see how you can avoid accepting the title of king, and yet that would only hinder your ability to function as

Dragonlord at a time when you need complete freedom to act. Have you considered what you will do if the dragons force you to fight?"

Thelvyn shook his head helplessly. "All I could do is fight a purely defensive battle. I'm not interested in placing Braejr at risk, but this is where we have our greatest concentration of strength. If nothing else, the presence of the Radiance is strongest here, and the wizards will be able to give me some support in battle. But I still hope to avoid war if I can. The Flaem are willing to concede that they have no complaint against the dragons. The problem is that the dragons feel they have been accused falsely and have been the victims of aggression by the Flaem."

"That is true," Sellianda agreed. "However, I suspect that their greatest concern now is with the Dragonlord. They believe they have the means to deal with you now if they can use your disadvantages against you, and they want the question settled. That is the position they are least likely to back down from, and the only real issue as far as they are concerned. The Flaem are incidental."

"Then how should I be trying to negotiate with them?" Thelvyn asked.

"I'm not certain that you can," she told him, sniffing her cherry liqueur with a rather confused expression. "There is nothing you can say to them short of offering to surrender. Your gesture of drawing the army back from the border is quite irrelevant to them. Perhaps the best you could do is to make a demonstration of the powers of the Dragonlord to convince them of the hopelessness of fighting you."

"That's probably only going to happen in battle," Thelvyn said. "I have the impression that the Immortals still support me, even the Great One. Could he have his clerics, like Kharendaen, intercede to stop this war?"

Sellianda shook her head. "You must recall that the Great One has been required to distance himself from the affairs of dragons to insure that other plans are not compromised. Remember also that, while we ourselves might not want to go to war, such events may suit the purposes of the Immortals perfectly. If you can defeat the dragons, then they will know that they simply cannot expect to have their way in the world."

"Then it seems to me that war is almost unavoidable," Alessa observed. "We could waste a great deal of time in pointless negotiations when we should be preparing for battle."

"I'll do what I can to avoid war, but I'm also doing what I must to prepare for battle," Thelvyn insisted. "Even withdrawing our forces from the northern border works to our advantage now as well. We can't hope to fight the dragons with our strength spread out across the entire northern frontier. And I can't be everywhere at once, even if I should regain the capability of flight. Our greatest strength lies in concentrating our defenses in one place. I want those catapults back here, where they'll be of most benefit."

"There is much virtue in that," Sir George agreed, holding his glass up to the light to peer at it. "But I'm not sure that the northern dukes are going to like the dragons going through their lands to get here."

"I'm beginning to believe they have nothing to worry about," Thelvyn said. "It does the dragons no good to ravage the north."

"I agree," Alessa added. "War is a desperate matter, and there are no perfect solutions. While it goes very much against my pride to leave the northern lands defenseless, I know that we must not be so concerned with winning every battle that we lose the war."

"The wizards must do their part," Thelvyn said. "I still need that cape of flight, and the remaining senior wizards have got to learn to use the Radiance effectively. And this time, they can't afford to be overconfident. That was Kalestraan's undoing."

"We won't fail you," Alessa assured him.

As much as she hated to leave, which put her at a distinct tactical disadvantage in courting the Dragonlord's attention, Alessa had to spend time alone studying her spellbook. Once she had learned just how briefly Thelvyn and Sellianda had actually been together in the past, she decided that she was still very much in contention. Thelvyn had been watching her, trying to determine whether her interest was personal or there was something else she was after. To her credit, she had seemed genuinely hurt by the elf cleric's unexpected arrival.

Of course, Thelvyn had no idea himself about Sellianda's intentions regarding him. She had been rather forward the last time they had been together, but that was five years ago. He realized that she hadn't come to Braejr because she had chosen to; whether she desired his company or not, she was there only because her patron had sent her. He could be just as sure that her patron hadn't sent her to him for the sake of companionship or affection, but to offer him advice and to help him interpret the will of the Immortals. She also knew that Kharendaen would eventually return, and when that time came, Sellianda would almost certainly be sent somewhere else where she was needed.

Thelvyn wondered if it would be best for him to keep his distance from the elf cleric. His duties as Dragonlord could involve him for years to come, taking him to other distant places. It would be best if he didn't become attached to someone who either could not or would not accompany him wherever he needed to go.

For that reason, he was even more surprised when Sellianda hurried after him when he went to return his glass to the bar. "Your affairs are entirely your own, of course, but I must ask why, of all people, that ardent sorceress is staying at your house."

"It was none of my doing," he insisted, suddenly feeling guilty. "I asked Byen Kalestraan for a wizard to stay with me at all times to warn me of any developments in the north. With so many of the former senior wizards either dead or fled, Alessa is one of the highest-ranking wizards in Braejr. She's served me well since the attack on me."

"Yes . . . she is eager to serve," Sellianda remarked mysteriously, then paused and smiled to herself. "Just listen to me. I must sound terribly jealous, and I have not even seen you in such a long time. Except for the circumstances, we would not be together even now."

"And the circumstances being what they are, we still do

not have time for each other," Thelvyn observed sadly.

"Come outside with me for a time," she said.

They stepped out the front door into the courtyard. The summer night had finally given way to darkness; the moonless sky was clear and dark, and the stars glittered brightly overhead. They walked together out into the yard to a small wooded corner away from the front gate. The elf maiden seated herself on a bench beneath a large tree and indicated for him to sit beside her. After he was seated, she took his hand in hers.

"I have only myself to blame," she said softly. "I chose to become a cleric, and for a long time I was certain that there could never be anything else important in my life other than my work. But you had no choice in the matter. The circumstances of your life left you no choice about becoming a cleric."

"Except for the occasional use of some very remarkable magic, I'm not sure I'm much of a cleric," Thelvyn confessed.

"Do not worry about that," she told him. "As Dragonlord, you are doing the service required of you by the Immortals. Few clerics can say they accomplish half as much as you do."

"I do regret being so alone," Thelvyn admitted. "I'd feel better if there were other clerics loyal to my patron."

"There are," Sellianda told him, much to Thelvyn's surprise. "But it would not be entirely accurate to say that they belong to the same order as your do. The Dragonlord is a clerical order unto himself. Although the dragons say the first Dragonlord was a wizard of such power that he was almost an Immortal, he was not a cleric. In that, you are different. I do not know how you came to bear the right to claim the armor of the Dragonlord or command its enchantments, but it means that your circumstances are more unusual than you may think."

"They seem strange enough as it is."

Sellianda laughed. "I suppose they must. All I can tell you is this: You possess certain unusual qualities. Your association with your patron is based upon the fact that those remarkable qualities are something you share together, qualities that draw you to one another. Also, your patron is one of the more unusual Immortals. Normal rules do not apply, either to your patron or to you. For that reason, it is not entirely accurate to say that you are a cleric. The association may appear the same, but you are something more than a cleric."

"I suppose I'm still not allowed to know which Immortal is my patron," Thelvyn said.

"No . . . not yet," Sellianda replied regretfully. "That knowledge would influence decisions that you must make alone, and it is something your enemies could use against you."

He sighed audibly. "I've been told that before."

* * * * *

Alessa came to the palace in the middle of the morning bearing news from the wizards in the north. Dragons of all types were gathering along the border, although so far they were staying in the mountains and not crossing into the Highlands. Thelvyn recognized the implications of the message from the first. This was the worst possible news short of actual invasion. He was running out of time much sooner than he would have liked.

Obviously he was facing some very important decisions, and he wanted to have a hasty meeting with his advisors. The problem was that he presently had a shortage of advisors; Jherridan had never confided in many people, and most of those had either died the night of the attack or were in the north with the army. Aside from the captain of the city garrison and the mayor of Braejr, the only advisors he could call upon were his own companions. Solveig had insisted that she was able to move about now, and so she had accepted a position as a captain in the king's army. Gairstaan, who was still in the north, would remain as captain of the larger Highlands army.

They gathered in the palace at the long table in the meeting room, this group being too large for the king's private chamber. Alessa Vyledaar was there to represent the Fire Wizards. Although the Academy was officially in the hands of a senior wizard who had returned from retirement because of the present need, he was an elderly gentleman and rather frail. He concentrated on keeping the demoralized wizards working on the problems they faced, while Alessa handled duties outside the Academy, including serving as the king's advisor.

"The message tells us more than it might seem to," Thelvyn stated when Alessa had reread it aloud. "The most alarming part is that it specifically states 'dragons of all types.' I asked Alessa to confirm the wording, which she has done. Now red dragons, even greens and blacks, are one thing. But the presence of gold dragons can only mean that this action is being taken on behalf of the entire Nation of Dragons and was ordered by the Parliament of Dragons. It means, in short, that they are ready to go to war."

Sir George nodded. "I'm sure you are correct. That's not the same as saying that they actually intend to invade the Highlands, however. They could simply be testing us to see how we'll react. It might also be a trap to lure the Dragonlord north, where they would prefer to wage this war. They know their advantages, and they're quite clever enough to anticipate what we might be thinking."

"Do you think this means they've heard about the troubles here?" Solveig asked.

"Perhaps, but not necessarily," Sir George explained, leaning back in his chair. "I have to admit, with no actual king, this is the worst possible time for Thelvyn to leave Braejr. Granted, if Thelvyn does become king, he's going to be more reluctant to leave than ever. At the same time, this might simply be the natural progression of the dragons' plans and have nothing to do with the situation here."

"The Dragonlord won't leave us now, will he?" the mayor asked fearfully.

"I have no intention whatsoever of leaving," Thelvyn declared emphatically. "Going into the north would only divide our defenses, more so than the dragons might realize. I believe our best response is to try to lure them here. If we do have a battle ahead of us, I want it to happen here in the fields outside the city. We can concentrate our forces on the walls, where the wizards can be of assistance."

"Then are you saying war is inevitable?" Alessa inquired.

"Not entirely, although there's not much else I can do," Thelvyn said. "I've already ordered our forces to draw back from the frontier. This might be taken as their response. Now we'll continue drawing our forces into the middle Highlands, back toward Braejr. That's a purely defensive attitude, and it's about as far as we can go. It tells the dragons that we won't fight unless they insist on it. That leaves the final decision about going to war entirely up to them, and I suspect that they'll be reluctant to go that far."

"It will be difficult for them to make that decision," Sir George agreed. "The Nation of Dragons has never chosen to go to war. Defending themselves is one thing, but deliberately pursuing war is another. They know if they ravage the Highlands or destroy Braejr, all the other nations in this part of the world are going to react very negatively. Dragons aren't very popular as it is."

"Of course, all this must be weighed against their great fear of the Dragonlord," Sellianda added. "The ire of the rest of the world is irrelevant as long as they destroy him. They can deal with any other problems later."

Thelvyn nodded. "All we can do is to give them every reason to leave us alone, then see how they react. At this time, I want to send orders to the north that our forces are to begin to withdraw to Braejr one regiment at a time. And I want to send word to the dukes that I expect that the dragons will not be ravaging their lands, at least for the most part. They're going to be coming for me."

Alessa bowed her head. "The orders will be relayed to our wizards in the north at once."

The sorceress left for the Academy to take care of the messages at once, and most of the others departed to attend to preparing the city for battle. That left Thelvyn alone with Sellianda and Sir George.

"I wanted to discuss something with you in private," Thelvyn said. "I've realized that if the dragons are primarily interested in me, then perhaps I can lead them away from the Highlands."

"I do not believe that it would be as simple as that," Sellianda explained. "The dragons have specific complaints with the Flaem, not the least being the theft of their treasure. If Alessa Vyledaar cannot find it, I'm not sure anything we do will appease them. The only alternative is to defeat them in battle, and the Flaem need you for that."

"I have to agree," Sir George added. "You could probably get the dragons to follow you, but I suspect that they'll be coming through Braejr first."

"I suppose you're right," Thelvyn agreed uncertainly. "I just can't help the feeling this war is largely my responsibility."

"I seem to recall that you've done everything in your power to avoid it," Sir George reminded him. "Jherridan and his wizard were determined to begin their little war with the dragons. No one would listen to you until it was too late, and now you're the only one left to handle the problem."

"In a very real sense, this is their fault," Sellianda added. "They were so caught up with themselves and their schemes that they came to believe that any means justified the end they considered so worthy. I hope the Flaem have learned something from this. As the elves would say, they are entirely too small a dog to bark so loudly."

"So now it's time to get busy, I suppose," Sir George commented.

"I was under the impression that I already was rather busy," Thelvyn said as he led the others toward the door. "I need to have a candid talk with the ambassadors from Darokin, Rockhome, and Alfheim to see if anyone wants to help us fight the dragons."

* * * * *

Marthaen settled himself beneath the trees on a high hilltop, where he could look down across the forest to the road more than two miles in the distance. As far away as that seemed, his dragon's vision was sharp enough to easily see every wagon and every rider as they passed slowly on their way from the frontier to the central Highlands. The sky was clear and the morning bright, almost too warm for the taste of a northern dragon. He remembered that his sister Kharendaen had somehow managed to endure this for the sake of her duty for the last five years.

He wasn't concerned about being seen; the Flaem knew fully well that they were being spied upon almost constantly, and they hadn't allowed that to concern them greatly. When Marthaen had heard the first reports of this latest withdrawal, he had wanted to see it for himself. He desperately needed to make sense of the situation so he could make the right decision about whether or not the dragons would go to war. He realized this was perhaps the most critical time his people had faced in centuries, and a wrong choice now could have disastrous consequences. He was also only too well aware that dragons had a long-standing reputation of for making bad choices, despite their legendary wisdom.

The Dragonlord was trying to send him a message, and apparently it was that the Flaem were no longer interested in a fight. Marthaen understood the message well, but the only thing he liked about this situation was that he could end it anytime he wished by simply going to the Dragonlord and asking to negotiate—but only if he could convince the dragons to continue to follow his lead. His people had lived in great fear and uncertainty since the Dragonlord's return, and their instinct was to destroy anything they feared. If the dragons were absolutely determined to fight the Dragonlord, then he would have to lead the way. They faced an enemy who could easily destroy them all. Before he could allow that, he would have to find some way to defeat the Dragonlord.

Marthaen understood how the other dragons felt. He himself felt trapped by his own obligations, and his instinct as a dragon was to respond with impatience and fury. His duty was to protect the dragons from their enemies, and yet he also had the duty to lead them if they wanted to fight. He also felt obliged to the Great One; he didn't believe that the guardian of the dragons was gone forever. Instead he felt the presence of the Immortal in the background, still quietly directing his clerics. The Dragonlord somehow appeared to be a part of his plans. If so, Marthaen had no wish to interfere with the wishes of the Great One. The matter had been hopelessly complicated when the Immortals had directed the Dragonlord to protect the Flaem even if they were wrong. Kharendaen had told him that, and even she did not understand why.

The thing that worried Marthaen most was that the dragons simply didn't seem to understand the true scope of the power of the enemy they proposed to fight. In his few battles against dragons, the Dragonlord had always made every effort not to kill or seriously harm his enemies. Marthaen suspected that the dragons mistook his compassion as a sign of weakness. Marthaen knew better. He had seen the Dragonlord fight the renegades in Darmouk, and he had a much better idea of the true powers that Thelvyn commanded. No matter what, he had to be certain the dragons never tried to fight the Dragonlord on his own terms, forcing him to abandon his past compassion. Marthaen believed that the dragons had forced the first Dragonlord to fight them, resulting in their own near destruction. He wanted to be certain that they did not repeat such a foolish mistake.

Nor could he easily forget that he owed the Dragonlord for Kharendaen's life, a debt that he did not wish to repay with treachery.

Marthaen watched for a short time as a line of mounted catapults passed in slow procession, the horses nickering and raising a cloud of dust. Ever since he had heard of the attack in which the Flaemish king had been slain, he couldn't forget that the Fire Wizards, misguided fools that they were, had nearly succeeded in killing the Dragonlord. He believed that he knew how to keep faith with all sides, heeding the fears and desires of the dragons while maintaining the trust of the Immortals and the Dragonlord himself. The time had come for him to return to Windreach and summon the dragon kings to meet with him in parliament to decide what they should do.

* * * * *

The funeral of Jherridan Maarsten was to take place that afternoon. Because there were so many other concerns during this time of crisis, he was to be laid to rest in a small tomb in the center of the city. Befitting his position as the first king of the Flaem in their new world, he would later be given a larger, more ornate tomb and monument.

The people of Braejr were beginning to slip toward panic, for it seemed to them that their very world was falling apart. Not only had they had to part with their first king, but now the rumor was flying through the city that the dragons were invading, preparing for a great battle that would take place right there at Braejr. It was becoming increasingly difficult for Thelvyn to remain firm in his plans; he wasn't a politician or even a warrior, but a protector. If he could have fought the dragons somewhere else, he would have.

Matters were only worse the next morning. Every hour of preparation was now vital, and yet not enough was being accomplished because of the fear that held the citizens of Braejr in its thrall. Thelvyn realized that the fault was partly his own, and the time had come to do something about it. He asked Alessa to remain with him at the palace, since she would be having new proclamations and orders to carry when she left. He called for his other advisors to join him in the king's private chamber. Lastly he summoned Taeryn.

"What are you planning to do?" Alessa asked, waiting attentively beside the chair where Thelvyn sat.

"I think I'm going to make Taeryn very happy," he said simply.

Solveig arrived almost at once, having already been on her way, and both Sir George and Taeryn arrived together a few minutes later. Thelvyn glanced up as they entered. "Taeryn, would you happen to know how to go about turning someone into a king?"

The valet paused a moment to let the implications of what Thelvyn had said sink in. Then his face broke into a huge smile. "When Jherridan became king, there were a great many celebrations and receptions. They probably aren't strictly necessary, although you might want to consider some type of public celebration to make the people feel better. Otherwise, I recall that Kalestraan looked in the books of Flaemish law and came back with some papers that Jherridan signed, and that was that."

"I think I've found those papers," Thelvyn said. "Why don't you run off to see the mayor and ask him what type of celebration we could manage."

"I will," Taeryn agreed eagerly, then paused at the door. "What time should I say the ceremony will begin?"

"I was hoping to take care of the formalities tomorrow morning. I'll leave the rest up to him."

Crossing his arms, Thelvyn sank back in his chair. Becoming the Dragonlord had been a simple matter compared to this, perhaps because he had been so caught up in the quest to find the armor. He might have been fearful of the destiny he had been shown, but it had never seemed as if it were his decision to make. Agreeing to become the king, on the other hand, had been entirely his own decision, without the guidance of any Immortals or prophecies, and it was very much against his wishes.

"I know how much you dislike this," Sir George said as he took one of the seats in front of the desk. "There just weren't many alternatives."

"I know," Thelvyn agreed. "The only alternative I liked was making you king, but then I realized I'd never be able to get you to let go of it once you had it."

Solveig laughed out loud in a way that made the old knight turn around and glare at her. Then he shrugged. "Taeryn is a bit more clever than most people think. He knows how important it is for the people of Braejr to know that they have a champion at a time like this."

"Which is also why the announcement needs to be made right away," Thelvyn said. "Alessa, I suppose it must be up to the wizards to consult the law and find out just what we need to do. I seem to have all the papers Taeryn described."

"It would be best if we could consult them," she said. "I'm sure we can have everything prepared by tomorrow morning. The most important thing just now is to make that announcement. The dukes are beginning to fret about the lack of clear leadership the past few days. This should make it easier for them to lend the support we need from them."

"I've also been wondering if there is some way of getting the news to the dragons," Sir George added. "If so, the announcement that the Dragonlord is about to become King of the Highlands will give them something to think about—something they instinctively respect, I might add."

"I suppose that this will give me greater advantage in trying to solicit help from other lands," Thelvyn said. "I'm beginning to feel like Jherridan, constantly wheedling support from others for a hopeless war."

"Is it too early to ask about our chances of getting any help?" Solveig inquired.

Thelvyn shook his head. "Actually, it's not so much a question of whether or not help will be sent, but if it can get here in time. Needless to say, the dwarves will send all the strength they can spare, and I'm sure we can count on Darokin. Alfheim may or may not see fit to send help. Even Sellianda agrees they're just as likely to sit in their woods and pick their pointed little ears."

News of the announcement that Thelvyn Fox-Eyes was to assume the title of King of the Realm fanned through the city like the spring wind. The effect was immediate. The sense of fear and despair, the feeling that going to war with the dragons was hopeless, seemed to lift at once. Suddenly the people felt certain that they could defend themselves if they were only given the time to prepare. Now they were in a race against time as they worked at the city's defenses in anticipation of the army's return.

A battle with dragons would differ in many respects from an ordinary siege. Fortunately the Flaem had always been in the habit of building things solidly, with heavy stone and tile roofs, which offered protection against dragonfire. Any buildings that were vulnerable, especially the warehouses, shops, and smithies in the southern part of the city, would have to be protected in some way. Piles of firewood or anything else that burned easily, such as wagons and crated goods for shipping, would have to be moved indoors, and supplies of water would have to be made available in all parts of the city. There was great concern for the wooded areas in the center of the city, but those were probably too wet and marshy to burn.

Sir George was given the responsibility of getting the catapults into their defensive positions along the top of the city wall, and also providing some protection for as many of the catapults as he could. The best defense he could devise against the threat of dragonfire was to surround each catapult with large shields or screens lined with tiles or sheets of tin. The protection was far from perfect, but at least it might offer the crews the chance to retreat to cover and return to their catapults with a minimum of damage. Any surplus of catapults would be positioned throughout Braejr in places where they could shoot upward, discouraging dragons from flying over the city.

The trouble was that a dragon was more than just a warrior. It was in effect a powerful weapon of war in itself. Each dragon combined the highest qualities of destructive potential, magic, speed, armor, strength and simple bulk. Thelvyn had never fought more than a dozen dragons at any one time, and that had been with the support of a small army. He expected this battle to involve hundreds of dragons, possibly thousands. He knew he did not dare underestimate the determination of the dragons in their one great bid to defeat the Dragonlord.

Late that afternoon, Thelvyn joined Sir George on the city wall near the north gate to see how the preparation of the defenses was getting along. Fortunately the walls of the city were thick enough that the wheel-mounted catapults could be maneuvered along the top. Permanent stone ramps had been erected on either side of the north gate and where the sections of walls ended at the river to allow access of the heavy machines. Unfortunately, Thelvyn had moved nearly all the catapults in the Highlands to the frontier, and these would not begin returning for several more days.

"At least the dragons aren't likely to try to bring down a section of the city wall," the old knight said as they walked together along the top of the wall, as wide as a city street. "They don't have to. Most likely they'll just whack away at the defenses until we can't keep them out any longer, and then land in the streets and begin ripping apart anything that's left."

"Is that their usual tactic?" Thelvyn asked. The stones of the walkway felt warm in the afternoon sun, even though he was used to being barefoot.

"There are no usual tactics for a situation like this," Sir George said. "Dragons haven't attacked a major walled city in all of recorded history. Of course, taking the city is only a secondary concern. Their first objective is to deal with the Dragonlord. Once they've accomplished that, they'll tear apart the city at their leisure."

"Then I'm really providing nothing more than a delaying tactic."

"I prefer to think that they'll never get to the second part," Sir George replied. "What are the plans for tomorrow? Is everything ready?"

"Alessa says that the necessary papers will be ready tonight," Thelvyn said, watching the young sorceress as she stood at the outside parapet several yards away, looking out across the fields. "I'll sign everything at a reception at the palace tomorrow morning. There will be a procession tomorrow afternoon through the main streets, followed by a general celebration throughout the city."

"I suppose that you'll have to name at least a temporary successor," Sir George observed. "Would it be presumptuous of me to ask if you have anyone in mind?"

"All things considered, I plan to name Solveig."

"Ah, wise choice," the knight agreed, greatly relieved. He glanced in the direction of the north road. "Three more days before the first of the Highlands army begins to return from the north."

"Perhaps four," Thelvyn corrected him. "And perhaps as long as two weeks before all our forces are here and everything is ready. If the dragons come sooner than that, and I expect they will, then there's really nothing else I can do.

I'll challenge their leaders and fight for as long as I can. Then I'll submit. You've always said that dragons are usually magnanimous to their enemies in defeat."

"Surely it won't come to that," Alessa insisted as she joined them. "Part of our forces will be here soon. Then we'll be able to hold out for a time, and more help will arrive."

"When the battle finally does come, it's not likely to last long," Thelvyn told her. "Even if we were as ready as possible, the dragons are still going to have the numbers to overwhelm us. I still see no hope for victory. My main goal is to put us in a strong enough position to negotiate to our best possible advantage. It would certainly help if we could give them back their treasure."

"We still haven't discovered any clue as to its whereabouts," Sir George admitted. "I'm beginning to suspect that Kalestraan had the treasure taken somewhere outside the Highlands. And of course there's something else the dragons will demand."

"I'm prepared to surrender to them under the proper terms, if that's what you mean," Thelvyn said. "If I'm going to influence their future according to the prophecy, I'll eventually have to go among them. The obvious way for that to happen will be as their prisoner."

"I should be able to go with you, under the circumstances," Sir George said.

"You can't be expecting defeat so easily," Alessa protested. "I always understood the Dragonlord was invulnerable."

Thelvyn paused to stare out from the wall across the fields. "The problem is that the dragons still have the advantage of speed, mobility, and numbers. I expect that several hundred, perhaps even several thousand, dragons will gather for the siege. If I'm forced to surrender, it won't be to save myself."

"But you should be able to do something," she insisted.

"I still have some hope of negotiating a new truce," Thelvyn said. "I'm prepared to offer them the promise that I will remove myself completely from the affairs of the outside world if they will do the same, and from then on we'll keep our disagreements entirely between ourselves. I realize now that I should have kept myself isolated from the first."

"So that's the reason why you were so reluctant to become king," Sir George said. "I say, you do seem to have things thought out fairly well. What you say just might suit the dragons after all. We just have to be careful that things don't turn against us, and the best assurance of that is to be as prepared for this battle as we can be. It would help a lot if some of the nearby countries could send us support."

"I'm not even sure our own army will get here in time," Thelvyn said. "The dragon army could leave the Wendarian Mountains at any time and be upon us within hours. How much time they give us is entirely up to them now."

CHAPTER FOURTEEN

The gold dragon Marthaen rode the cool winds above the Wyrmsteeth Mountains in the wilds of Norwold on his way to the hidden city of Windreach, the citadel of the dragons, hundreds of miles northeast of the Highlands. In spite of his concerns about the threat of war in the west, he was dreaming of autumn. The high, rugged mountains, most of them still wearing a cap of white even into the middle of summer, would all be buried deep in fresh snow. The winds would be cold and brisk, and a dragon could ride the swift currents in and out among the peaks and valleys. Hunting was actually easier in the winter, when elk and deer, driven by hunger out into the open, would stand in plain sight against the fields of white.

Marthaen was soaring through the mountains, letting the warm southerly winds carry him the final miles of his long flight home. He did not regret his journey to the Wendarian Mountains above the Highlands; he could appreciate the attraction of that ancient land, especially the old, forgotten forests on the north side of the mountains where men did not come. There was an ancient sanctuary hidden deep in the wooded hills of Wendar, an uncomfortable memory of a time when the dragons had denied the Great One. The red dragons, always fierce and quick to anger, had turned on the clerics for prophesying the return of the Dragonlord, yet they had refused to help seek him out. The Wendarian Range had been a place of trouble for dragons ever since.

But Marthaen was more clever than any red dragon, and even they deferred to the wisdom of his leadership. He recognized the deeper meaning of things. For one thing, he knew that if the clerics of the Great One refused to actively oppose the Dragonlord, then there must be a good reason. He would never ask his sister Kharendaen about the secrets of her order, but he had seen enough to know that the Great One still maintained some contact with his clerics. If the Great One had simply gone away without a trace or a word of explanation, as most dragons believed, then there would be no further need for his clerics. Why, then, were those same clerics still so busy?

Some questions found their own answers. Marthaen could see that the Great One had protected the dragons from themselves, from their violence and lust and the same desire for power that drove the renegades insane. The Great One had given them their one great city and had forced them to sit together in parliament, gently guiding them away from any action that was ultimately not to their best advantage. Intentionally or not, the Great One had left the dragons to make their own decisions at a time when those decisions would be especially critical, and Marthaen felt that it was his responsibility to make certain that they chose correctly.

The question of the Dragonlord both intrigued and frustrated him. The obvious answer to the problem he presented was to find some way to slay the Dragonlord and capture or destroy that accursed armor. Yet even that wasn't as simple as it seemed. If killing the Dragonlord was the proper solution, then why did the clerics refuse to help? He realized he was trying to determine the Great One's will by inference rather than making a decision for himself, but the matter was simply too important to risk making a mistake. He wished he could talk to Kharendaen about it, not necessarily to get direct answers but just to seek her advice. But Kharendaen had been called away by her duty, proof enough that the Great One still played some part in this affair. And while Marthaen was loath to distrust his sister's judgment, he knew that her heart was filled with love and devotion for Thelvyn Fox-Eyes.

As Marthaen came out through the mouth of a wide, forested valley, he could see the great peak of Windreach rising into the sky directly before him. From this distance, the peak appeared to be nothing more than the snow-covered summit of an especially tall, steep mountain rising from a group of high, rugged peaks. In truth, the city of Windreach was built within the ring of an ancient volcano. The white cap wasn't snow but the spires and towers of the great buildings, all built of purest white marble, that stood on the floor of the ancient volcano.

Marthaen rose steadily as he approached, finally passing low over the rim of the volcano before he began to circle wide, searching for the wide ledge of his home. Windreach was a large city, especially since everything was built on a scale to accommodate dragons, but it was large even by draconic standards. Individual lairs had been carved deep into the stone of the wall of the volcano, with openings like large balconies. The lairs were all interconnected by passages and vast chambers within the mountain itself.

The floor of the volcano was occupied by a city of great beauty, with simple, elegant buildings of carved white marble. The center of the city was dominated by the towering Hall of the Great One, easily the largest structure in the known world, with great towers and slender spires rising above the top of the ring of the volcano's caldera. Other great edifices clustered about the Hall of the Great One, each as impressive as the next. The dragons had erected their own school of magic and science, mostly under the direction of the golds and a few of the more clever reds and blacks. There was a magnificent library containing books from a time unknown to scholars and wizards of the outside world.

Marthaen found the ledge of his home and banked sharply, descending with long, slow backsweeps of his wings before dropping onto the wide shelf of stone. He folded his wings, then turned his head and looked back for a moment across the city. Windreach seemed curiously empty and quiet, with only a few dragons gliding among the white towers. Many of the dragons were already away in the west, especially the young dragons eager for adventure, waiting to see if they would invade the Highlands and fight the Dragonlord. He opened the wide door and stepped inside, crouching to clear his wings, then paused a moment to slide the door shut behind him.

The interior of his apartment was large and comfortable, even by gold dragon standards. Contrary to the rough-hewn cave dwelling of human legend, these apartments were of dressed, polished stone, with floors and fixtures of the hardest marble. The marble had been cut and brought to the mountain, since marble doesn't occur naturally in volcanic lands. The ceiling of the main chamber was high enough for Marthaen to sit back on his haunches, using his claws to release the straps on the harness that carried his weapons and pouches.

Setting the harness aside, he left his lair through the inner door to follow the interior passages to the bathing chambers. He spent some time soaking in one of the great heated pools deep within the volcano, feeling the tired muscles in his shoulders and chest relax after his long flight. He was still young for a dragon of his authority, but he was no longer an adventurous and carefree adolescent. He still enjoyed short visits to the wild, but he no longer relished sleeping on cold stone night after night or eating venison cooked in his own dragonfire.

When Marthaen returned to his own lair, he wasn't surprised to find the old wizard, Alendhae, waiting for him. Alendhae wasn't a dragon but one of the Eldar, the most ancient of elven races. The Eldar were more heavily built and taller than other elves—taller even than most men—with black hair and large, dark eyes. They were also extremely long-lived, their average lifespan closer to the thousands of years of the dragons rather than the mere hundreds of other elves. Their kind had been all but forgotten by the other elves and were thought to have disappeared long ago. The last remaining survivors of their race lived with the dragons of Windreach.

"How are things in the west?" Alendhae asked.

"Confusing," Marthaen admitted. "There seems to be no need for us to fight the Flaem. For now, they seem to be too busy killing each other."

"We heard news to the effect that some wizards had taken the form of dragons and had tried to slay their king and the Dragonlord."

"They succeeded in killing their king," Marthaen said. "They tried to kill the Dragonlord by some means that restricted the enchantments of his armor, but their magic proved not strong enough. At times like this, I wish we had a more effective way of knowing what is happening. Life was easier when Kharendaen was among the Flaem to tell us everything we needed to know."

"So the king of the Highlands is dead?" Alendhae asked as he seated himself in a chair on one side of the chamber. Because Marthaen had frequent guests of both dragons and elves, he had furnishings adapted to fit both. "That must change things considerably."

"I'm still not sure if it changes anything," the dragon admitted as he lowered himself to the ground. "The Dragonlord was in command, and he had already ordered his forces to draw back from the northern border in an obvious gesture of appeasement. Now he is withdrawing his forces all the way back to their capital. I interpret the message to be that the Dragonlord and the Flaem no longer wish war, but if there is to be one, then they want it to be fought on their own ground. They are fortifying their city and concentrating their forces even now."

"Yes, but they have half the Nation of Dragons staring at them from the north."

Marthaen laid back his ears and lowered his head. "The Dragonlord has put us in a position in which the decision to fight must be our own. Obviously we must weigh the advantages against the disadvantages. We want desperately to be rid of the Dragonlord, but I respect his abilities and I am fearful of how many lives a battle with him will cost us even if we do succeed in defeating him. Kharendaen insists that we can trust the Dragonlord as long as we do not make war unavoidable, and I am inclined to agree with her. I do not believe that the destruction of the Dragonlord is necessary as long as we can keep a solid truce with him."

"Most dragons are not going to agree with your position," Alendhae pointed out.

Marthaen sighed. "I know that. I doubt I can stop the dragons from going to war, and if I try to stop them, then my arguments must be very sound. But I must also weigh the consequences of an attack. We presently have a just claim against the Dragonlord and the Flaem. It hurts our pride, but we must face the fact that going to war with the Highlands is going to leave all other nations fearful of us and angry with our aggressions. Our reputation cannot bear much more harm. This action will have consequences for all dragons for a very long time to come."

"The dragons are strong," the elf commented. "They could rule the world if they wanted to—or at least until the Immortals interceded. Only the Immortals are stronger than the dragons. With the return of the Dragonlord, I believe that the Immortals have already interceded once. Will they allow the dragons to defeat their champion?"

Marthaen sighed again loudly. "Sometimes I think our size, our strength, and our powerful magic are also our curse. Even the Immortals fear and despise us."

"The Immortals do not fear and despise you," Alendhae insisted. "But because of your potential for evil and destruction, you must prove to them that you can control yourselves. Perhaps that is what this Dragonlord has been sent to teach you."

"If so, it is a lesson most dragons must be taught the hard way," the gold dragon replied. "Still, my first duty is to protect my people. If I can defeat the Dragonlord, and the price is not too high, then it must be done."

* * * * *

The next morning, Marthaen stepped out onto his ledge and paused to look around. The sky above was clear and blue, although the depths of the crater remained mostly hidden in shadows, as they would until late in the morning. Just as he had the previous evening, he saw that there seemed to be only perhaps half the usual number of dragon flying over the city or sitting out on their lofty ledges. Windreach seemed strangely empty and silent, producing an almost disconcerting sense of abandonment.

If he had been inclined to believe in omens, Marthaen might have taken that as a warning of the dire consequences of the decision he must make should it prove to be the wrong one. Dragons didn't normally believe in omens, and he suspected that if the Great One had something of such importance to tell him, he would have been considerably more plain. The truth was that most of the young dragons were away in the west preparing for war, which was ominous in itself.

Marthaen stepped to the front edge of the shelf and spread his wings, then leaped outward into the air. He descended slightly until several powerful sweeps of his wings brought him level again, then glided swiftly over the deserted streets as he made his way toward the center of the city. As he came nearer the towering mass of the Hall of the Great One, he began to climb, rising steadily in a tight spiral just beyond the huge building's smooth, white walls. His destination was one of the lower halls. Spotting his objective, he turned suddenly and landed on one of the ledges.

The passages of the Hall of the Great One were wide and the ceilings were high, offering ample room for even the largest of dragons to pass unhindered. This was important, since two dragons trapped together in a tight space would instinctively turn on one another. His own chamber was only a short distance inside, just around the corner from the ledge where he had landed. Although he hadn't expected it, he wasn't surprised to find the gold dragon Daresha was waiting for him. She lowered her head to rub her nose and cheek against his chest, a draconic display of affection he promptly returned. It was an extreme gesture of trust, since the base of one's neck was exposed to the teeth and horns of another dragon.

"I trust that you will not be here long?" his mate asked,

still pressing her cheek lightly against the side of his neck.

"I must return to the west very soon," he answered, "perhaps as soon as this council has come to a decision. I do not trust all of those young dragons to be left alone for long with their enemy in plain sight."

Daresha looked quietly amused. "You forget, you are still a young dragon."

"I have concerns enough to make me old before my time," he told her.

"Then I regret having to bring you yet another concern," she said, becoming serious as she lifted her head to look at him. "The report came during the night. The Dragonlord is to be proclaimed King of the Highlands this very morning."

"King?" Marthaen asked, sitting back on his haunches. "That does surprise me. Kharendaen has always insisted the Dragonlord doesn't want that type of power. It was my own impression as well."

"You know who and what he is," Daresha reminded him. "Considering that, is it really surprising that he would be tempted?"

"Perhaps I have given him too much credit," Marthaen said. "I still cannot see that this makes any sense. Kharendaen has always said that he didn't want power or authority, and I trust her judgment. If he had wanted power, he could have had it years ago. What could have changed in the last few days?"

"As I understand it, the death of the king and the wizards made it a matter of necessity," Daresha observed. "I would guess now that he has had a taste of authority, he has developed a healthy appetite for it. You will have a difficult time convincing the parliament that a peaceful solution is still possible."

"I will have a difficult time convincing myself," he admitted. "I've been telling myself that we might be able to negotiate a new truce now that we hold a stronger position. But if the Dragonlord wants to make himself king, then he is becoming too ambitious for my peace of mind. I regret I do not have more time to ponder this."

"Indeed," Daresha agreed. "We must hurry to the Hall

of Dragons at once, or the reds will be debating this matter in our absence."

Marthaen waited for his companion to depart, then locked the door of his chamber behind him. The Hall of Dragons, the meeting place of the parliament, was a vast chamber in the center of the Hall of the Great One. A corridor encircled the outside of the hall, and each representative had his own chamber directly across the corridor from his place in the circular gallery. Each representative sat on a ledge, enclosed on either side by dividing walls with a partial roof overhead. The enclosure, too small for most dragons to spread their wings, was a precaution against a display of their fiery tempers.

As First Speaker of the Parliament, Marthaen's ledge was larger and higher than most, with a stone walkway leading out above the floor of the Hall of Dragons where he could be seen clearly by the others. In all the centuries of the history of Windreach, he was only the third to sit in this place of honor. In the past, in times of great need, the Great One himself had sometimes manifested himself on the highest ledge, far above the gallery, a place where no other dragon dared to go. But the Great One had been absent from the mortal world and the affairs of dragons for a quarter of a century now, and more than twice as many years had passed since the time he had last presided over a meeting of the parliament.

Marthaen had been a only child when he last saw the Great One. He felt almost like a child now, wishing in his heart that the true Lord of the Dragons were there to guide him in perhaps the most important decision the dragons would ever make. As he glanced about the hall, he could see that barely a fourth of all the representatives were present. That might make this discussion shorter than it would have been otherwise. As he had expected, the speakers for the red and the black dragons, Jherdar and Thalbar, were present. Gheradaen of the gold dragons and Lhoran of the blues were there as well. He noticed that both representatives of the white dragons were on hand; they would play no part in the battle unless matters turned particularly desperate. They were tied to the cold lands of the far north, and they would not willingly come down into the southern lands in the summer.

Marthaen watched the others, anticipating the beliefs that each would be prepared to argue. As the First Speaker, he was required to be responsive to the desires of all dragons, not just his own golds. Jherdar and Thalbar, leaders of the headstrong reds and blacks, would be prepared to argue in favor of the death of the Dragonlord. As a blue dragon, Lhoran's opinion could easily go either way. The rest would be waiting to see what Marthaen himself had to say. Marthaen was held in high regard by all dragons for his wisdom and cunning, and even the reds and blacks admired him because of his youth and eagerness. As in a great many such debates, Marthaen would likely have his way on this matter, unless his plans were so abhorrent to a large number of the others that they couldn't support him.

Things had changed quickly that morning. Marthaen had been prepared to test the dragons to see how determined they were to go to war. If possible, he would have suggested sending a delegation to negotiate with the Dragonlord rather than risk an invasion. Now he no longer intended to debate the matter; an invasion of the Highlands had become unavoidable. All he wanted now was for the others to agree to follow him without question, allowing him to deal with the Dragonlord.

He saw his mate Daresha enter, taking her place almost directly across from him. With her arrival, in accordance with a prearranged signal, he assumed that all the representatives who planned to attend were already present. He rose and moved to the very front of his ledge.

"We have gathered today to decide a matter of the greatest importance to the fate of all dragons," he began. "The Highlands army is drawing back from the north, apparently with the intention of establishing a defensive position for a final stand at their city of Braejr. The Dragonlord now decides their policy, and both he and the Flaem clearly no longer wish to continue the conflict with the dragons. How then are we to respond?"

"Are you aware that the Dragonlord has made himself King of the Highlands?" Jherdar asked challengingly.

"I am aware of that," Marthaen said. "I assume we have all heard the news by now. And I admit that I find it very disquieting. This is not the act of the Dragonlord I knew five years ago. You knew him yourself, Jherdar. He was wise and merciful, unimpressed with his own power."

"I knew him," Jherdar agreed reluctantly. "He showed the dragons mercy and forgiveness."

"I feel that we owe him a debt," Marthaen continued. "I had thought that we could best repay that debt by being patient and open-minded. But the security of all dragons must come first. The Dragonlord had authority thrust upon him by chance with the deaths of the old king and the wizards. Now he seems to have decided that he likes that power and wishes to keep it. What else will he desire? His strength and invulnerability are such that no one could deny him whatever power he desires. If he wishes to be a conqueror, only the dragons could ever hope to defeat him."

"The Dragonlord must be destroyed," Jherdar insisted, thrusting his neck well out over his ledge. "And that time must be now! We know of the ways in which he is vulnerable, and we know that he seeks to find new enchantments that compensate for these vulnerabilities. We must act now before he becomes even stronger."

"I agree," Thalbar declared. The black dragon was standing poised at the front of his ledge. "We should not be discussing whether or not we must fight the Dragonlord, but how his defeat can best be accomplished."

"I agree completely," Marthaen said calmly, sitting back on his haunches. "Jherdar, you say that the Dragonlord is vulnerable. I remind you that his vulnerabilities and limitations are entirely of his own making. He may seem less powerful than the first Dragonlord only because he has not, out of compassion, used the full power of his weapons against us. I have seen for myself what he did to Kardyer, who was considered the most powerful of the renegade kings. I saw him slay six renegades with a single bolt from his sword. If we force him to forsake his compassion, he has the potential to be every bit as dangerous to us as the first Dragonlord."

Jherdar opened his mouth to answer hotly, then paused to consider. At last he laid back his ears, seething at the inescapable truth of Marthaen's. "You are correct, First Speaker. If we press the Dragonlord to the point that he must fight for his life, then he may well be forced to call upon his full powers."

"Both his own powers and the awesome powers of the Dragonlord, for they are indeed separate," Marthaen said. "A combination far greater than those of the first Dragonlord. Our only blessing is that he is not yet aware of his true strength. We dare not force him to that realization."

The dragons remained silent, sitting back on their ledges as they appeared pensive, even confused. Because of their awesome size, strength, and magic, dragons were in the habit of solving problems by simply destroying their enemies in the most convenient manner available at the moment. Patience and cleverness were qualities reserved for when they fought among themselves. The First Speaker had shown them that they were not as ready for this battle as they wanted to believe, and that they would have to think of the Dragonlord in much the way they would any other dragon, and an especially dangerous one at that.

"Then you think we cannot hope to fight him?" Jherdar asked at last.

"I think we must make some response to the present situation," Marthaen answered. "And yet we must be cautious and cunning with an enemy this dangerous. I do not wish to see a single dragon die in this effort, but we cannot deny that an attempt to destroy the Dragonlord in combat would cost us many lives. I believe that the most important thing is not so much that we slay the Dragonlord, but that we find the means to leave him powerless and no longer of any concern."

Jherdar had been prepared to argue, and he was caught by surprise. He sat back on his haunches and craned his neck forward, listening carefully. "You sound as if you have a plan."

"I believe that I do," Marthaen replied. "Thelvyn Fox-Eyes has made himself a king, contrary to his own duties as Dragonlord. He has had a taste of power and has found that he desires it. He is becoming like a renegade dragon, consumed with a boundless belief in himself and an unrelenting need to command the entire world. That must not be allowed to happen."

"The Dragonlord must be destroyed at any cost!" Jherdar declared.

"No, not at any cost," the gold dragon insisted. "I will not waste the lives of dragons needlessly. We have no assurance that we could ever defeat him in battle. I remind you that he is the Dragonlord and he commands the power of ancient Blackmoor, which almost succeeded in destroying us once. He also has the favor of the Immortals. We cannot be certain of prevailing against either of those, and certainly not both. Is that not so?"

"And yet we must try," Jherdar insisted. "We may well die, but we will not live as slaves."

"That is not my intention," Marthaen replied. "Bear in mind the words of the prophecy. We fear that prophecy terribly, yet have we ever really understood it? The prophecy tells us that, with the return of the Dragonlord, he will become the ruler of all dragons, and that he will set into motion certain events that will shape the destiny of dragons forever. His decision to make himself King of the Highlands seems especially ominous to us because it foreshadows the day when he will conquer us as well. But have we understood the prophecy correctly? There is no inherent threat in those words beyond what we chose to see. That prophecy can just as easily be seen as a promise of hope and glory to come."

Jherdar laughed aloud. "Would you have us believe that the Dragonlord is here to help us?"

"According to the cleric Kharendaen, that is exactly what the Dragonlord himself has always believed. I remind you that the clerics of the Great One have not worked to protect us from the Dragonlord as we expected. Rather, they have seemed almost to help prepare for his return."

"Are you suggesting that the Great One intends for the Dragonlord to rule over us?" Thalbar asked, outraged. Nearly all of the dragons were standing on their ledges now and glaring or muttering in fury.

"No, I do not believe that," Marthaen explained. "Not in the sense that he will conquer us to make us his slaves. I do not believe the Great One or his clerics would betray us. I am saying that I have reason to suspect that the Dragonlord has something yet to do in our benefit, and to destroy him may be to destroy the key to our own future. But if he must be fought, then it must be on our terms. I believe that we must not destroy him yet if it can be avoided."

Jherdar sat back on his haunches and laid back his ears, looking bemused. "Easier said than done."

"We know who and what he is; even he does not know that," Marthaen insisted. "We know his strengths, but we also know his weaknesses. I believe I can fight him, and if I cannot make him submit, then I will destroy him. All I ask is that you follow me, that you do not question my plans at this critical time. I will do my best to explain the reasons for all that I do. I fear that we may face a desperate time, and our dispute with the Dragonlord could be only the first of many battles."

"Are you trying to frighten us into submission?" Jherdar asked suspiciously.

"I only want you to understand the reality of what we face, so that you will know why I find it so important to look beyond our immediate concerns. All other races fear us. Just as we look upon the Dragonlord as a threat that we cannot ignore, others look upon us as a threat they cannot ignore. If we slay the Dragonlord, perhaps others will decide we must be destroyed, just as the men of Blackmoor did long ago."

"Pah! We can take on the entire world," Thalbar asserted proudly.

"At what cost?" Marthaen demanded. "Are we likely to win such a war, or will the Immortals intervene? Every tyrant who has tried to rule the world by force has been destroyed. When Blackmoor fell, the face of the world was changed forever. Nithia was so utterly destroyed that even the memory of its existence was wiped from the slate of history, so that only we now recall that such a place ever existed. Are we so special that the Immortals would not do the same to us?"

"I understand your arguments for not wanting to destroy the Dragonlord," Jherdar said in a more reasonable tone. "If you can defeat him otherwise, then I will support you willingly. What I cannot comprehend is how such a seemingly impossible thing might be accomplished."

Marthaen dropped his head, his ears laid back. "The wizards of the Flaem nearly defeated him by taking away the enchantments of his armor and weapons. That greatly encourages me, for I firmly believe that we as dragons can do better. We must not attempt to defeat the Dragonlord in battle, since everything about him was specifically designed to have every advantage over us. Our contest must be one of magic, to see if our powers are greater than the enchantments that created him. To this end, I will call together the greatest of all the dragon sorcerers to assist us in this battle."

Jherdar lifted his head. "I believe I finally understand you. If we cannot fight the Dragonlord, then we will defeat him by other means."

"And once the Dragonlord no longer commands his powers, then there is no longer any need to destroy him. He will be ours."

"I am content to have you lead us as you see fit," the red dragon conceded. "My pride argues that we must fight and destroy the Dragonlord, but I am not willing to pay the price with the lives of those dragons who look to me for their protection. If you can tame him by some more clever and less costly means, so be it. But if you fail, then we will battle the Dragonlord to the death."

Jherdar sat back on his haunches in the center of his ledge, as if waiting for others to have their say. But Marthaen knew that the decision had already been made. Now that the Speaker for the red dragons was in agreement with the First Speaker, the others weren't very likely to be in dissent. The vote would continue, but it was only a formality.

"The gold dragons agree," Gheradaen announced after glancing first at Daresha and then at the only other gold representative present.

"The black dragons agree," Thalbar said almost sullenly. He probably didn't understand the arguments that Marthaen had made and wanted only to destroy as many of his enemies as he could, but he would follow Jherdar's lead even against his own will.

"Then it is decided," Marthaen declared. "And if there is no other matter of importance to be considered, I call this session to a close. I must return to the west at once."

He waited for a time in the corridor outside his ledge, knowing that Daresha would join him as soon as she could. He was surprised to see both Jherdar and Thalbar following her, although he knew he should have realized the red dragon hadn't yet had his full say on the subject of the Dragonlord.

"If you are leaving for the west, then we will go with you when you are ready," the red dragon said.

"I will be ready within the hour," Marthaen answered. "There is someone I must see before I go."

* * * * *

Marthaen didn't have far to go to make his call. He circled the Hall of the Great One higher and higher until he reached the upper reaches of that immense edifice. The upper portions of the hall were dominated by towers and delicate spires. Soon he had risen high above the rim of the volcano; from this dizzying height, the city below appeared no more than some tiny ant village. He had to be careful as he moved in and out among the towers, knowing that the winds here were often unbelievably strong and treacherous. Over time, more than one dragon had found himself dashed against those walls of white marble, only to plummet to his death on the streets far below.

Marthaen knew his errand probably wouldn't be successful, although he had to try all the same. This matter was too important for him not to seek out the advice of the Great One, especially since he was now convinced that the Great One had been one of the principal architects of the Dragonlord's return. And if the Dragonlord was indeed so important to the future of the dragons, then Marthaen simply did not dare to destroy him. He needed to know how to deal with this problem to the best advantage of the dragons. And if he had guessed wrong—if the Dragonlord was indeed the enemy of the dragons and would do them great harm—he needed to know that as well.

At last he found the right ledge and landed, having to come in quickly before the wind could carry him away. He opened the door and passed inside. The upper levels of the Hall of the Great One were nearly as spacious as those below, but they were more bright and open from being so high above the shadow of the volcano, for here there was light through the windows of transparent crystal all day long. But the passages were also bitterly cold, since the upper reaches of the hall were constantly exposed to the chilling winds. He had only just closed the door when a young blue dragon hurried to meet him.

"I must speak immediately with Saerna," he explained. "It is a matter of the greatest importance."

The young dragon nodded and turned, and Marthaen followed her through the corridors to the inner chambers. There was no question that Saerna would see the First Speaker; whether or not she would answer him was quite another matter, and a choice that wasn't really hers to make. Saerna was the most senior of all the clerics of the Great One, the leader of her order, and quite possibly the oldest dragon in the world. Although she wasn't old enough to remember the first Dragonlord, she had survived the fall of Ancient Blackmoor and the Rain of Fire. Because of her great age, Marthaen would have preferred that she didn't spend so much of her time in this high part of the hall, where it was always cold and the air was thin.

He waited a moment outside the door of her chamber while the young cleric hurried inside to announce him. The small blue dragon returned a moment later and held the door for him, closing it behind him when he had passed inside. Saerna lay reclining on the cushions of her couch, a book of draconic proportions resting on a stand before her. The ancient dragon hardly looked her age, for her eyes were bright and her armor was still firm, with perhaps only the slightest blunting of the tips of her crest. And yet she was so old that she belonged to no modern breed of dragon, vaguely resembling a gold in features but more gray in color. Her size was no more than that of a blue.

"First Speaker Marthaen," she said, recognizing him. "Tell me if the rumors are true. Are the dragons going to war?"

"The dragons are going to war," he told her, sitting on his haunches beside her couch. "It is now inevitable. Whether or not we are required to fight, however, remains to be seen. My hope is to avoid that if I can."

"And how will you do that?" she asked.

"I must find a way to place the Dragonlord at a disadvantage," Marthaen explained. "The dragons must somehow overcome the enchantments of his armor and weapons. We must find the means to fight the Dragonlord on our terms, not his, and if possible it must be a way that does not destroy him. For it seems to me that the Great One intends that he should play an important role in our future."

"Does he indeed?" Saerna asked, feigning surprise. "I was under the impression that everyone believes that the Great One has gone away."

"I pray you, do not be obtuse with me now," Marthaen told her plainly. "The future, perhaps even the survival of our kind, may be at stake, and there are not so many of us as it is. I believe that the Great One still communes with his clerics. The members of your order seem to have entirely too much to do for clerics who no longer have an Immortal to guide them. You cannot both maintain your secrecy and perform your duty."

"You are a clever dragon," Saerna remarked. "Why did you not become a cleric yourself? You hear the voice of the Great One within you. What is the voice telling you?"

Marthaen laid back his ears and lowered his head. "It tells me that I must not harm the Dragonlord."

"And there is a problem with that?"

"There remains one very large problem," he insisted. "I am compelled both to fight the Dragonlord and yet not to slay him. My hope is that the Great One can tell me how to accomplish what the wizards of the Flaem almost succeeded in doing—nullifying the enchantments of his armor and leaving him vulnerable."

Saerna looked uncertain. "I think you seek complicated answers when you already have a simple and obvious one. You know what the Dragonlord is."

"I had hoped you would tell me his disadvantages rather than play games with me," Marthaen said impatiently.

"You do not have to do anything to the Dragonlord except to tell him what he has always wanted to know," she explained. "He will not willingly make war upon the dragons after that, will he? Make his past known to him, and he will lose all heart for the fight. Tell him who his mother really was, and he will be forced to reconsider his service to the Immortals."

Marthaen considered her words briefly, then looked up at the old dragon. "What you are saying is that I will not have to fight him at all, then. I can render the Dragonlord powerless with a word."

"You will not have to fight him," Saerna agreed. "But you will inflict upon him the greatest pain that he will ever know."

"I see," Marthaen said softly. "Is this the will of the Great One?"

"Such an inquisitive dragon!" Saerna declared, indicating for him to leave. "I have said too much already. Go and do what you must."

CHAPTER FIFTEEN

No matter how uncomfortable it made him, Thelvyn realized that it was time for him to do something he both regretted and detested. Since he was now the king of the Highlands, it was time to leave his comfortable home and move into the king's palace. He had a number of problems with that, not the least of which was that work on repairing the damage to the palace was proceeding very slowly because of the countless other demands caused by the preparations for battle. Dust was everywhere, a fresh cloud of it rising each day when more debris was cleared away, and there was still a vague smell of smoke throughout the central portions of the palace.

Much to his surprise, though it probably shouldn't have been, he found that he missed Kharendaen even more when he was away from his own home. Since he would no longer be staying at home, he realized that the time had also come to dismiss the gold dragon Seldaek. The young cleric needed to withdraw from the Highlands so that his duty to the Great One would not be in conflict with his obligations as a dragon.

Of course, moving into the palace had certain advantages as well. For one thing, he could give his various companions their own suites among the dozens of abandoned chambers, and things suddenly seemed much less close and cozy than they had at home. Better yet, Alessa Vyledaar would be moving back to the Academy. The death or disappearance of so many of the traitor wizards had left her much in demand as one of the most senior wizards in residence. She had many duties to attend to until a new head of her order could be elected. That came as something of a relief to Thelvyn, who preferred not to have temptation quite so close at hand. He still had enough temptation in the form of Sellianda, who at least seemed to feel that discretion was required in her role as an advisor.

The situation with Sellianda remained unresolved for the present. She possessed a quiet, natural dignity, with great depth and maturity. She and Thelvyn were alike in many ways. Sellianda was dark, tall, and rather hearty for an elf, although she was actually more attractive to him for those qualities because of his own size and strength.

At least their moving into new quarters brought a sense of life back to the king's palace, which had seemed dark and deserted since the night of the attack. Knowing that Byen Kalestraan and his wizards had gone through the palace from one end to the other, methodically twisting the necks of everyone there, was a decidedly uncomforting thought to a prospective tenant. Nevertheless, a regular staff and a garrison returned to the palace for the first time. Even so, it often felt like living in a house that was still being built.

That same afternoon, Sir George came to Thelvyn's private chamber to take him out for a brief ride. When they came down to the north door, they found that not only Sir George's horse but Thelvyn's Cadence had been saddled and were ready. They rode alone through the streets near the west wall until they came to the north gate.

Sir George led them through the gate and along the dusty road for over a mile, until they came to one of the higher hills in the fields north of the city. When they paused at the top of the hill, Thelvyn could see a line of wagons approaching along the road perhaps two miles in the distance, making slow yet steady progress as they rolled along in a cloud of pale brown dust. When he allowed his sharp eyes to cross the distance, he could see clearly that most of what he had taken for wagons were in fact mounted catapults, the key to Braejr's defense. Each catapult was drawn by a team of two draft horses, barely adequate for the task and even then only because the roads were dry and firm. With so many catapults being moved south, there were only two horses to spare for each.

"How many catapults are there?" he asked.

"I believe there are two dozen with this first group," Sir George answered. "A fair number of soldiers are in the train as well, and just now we need all the manpower we can get to help prepare the city for battle. If everything else is ready, we can roll the catapults into place as they arrive."

"I just want to get as many catapults here as we can before the dragons attack. The problem is, I don't know when that will be," Thelvyn explained, patting Cadence's dusty neck to calm him.

"I understand your concern. Frankly, it will probably be another week before the entire Highlands army can withdraw from the frontier. We should have more catapults and supplies arriving from the middle and southern Highlands sooner."

Thelvyn shook his head hopelessly. "I just can't believe that's going to be soon enough. The dragons have to realize it's to their advantage to move against us as quickly as they can."

"That depends upon how large a force they want to assemble before they make their move," Sir George said. "There aren't all that many dragons in the whole world, and they live somewhat scattered about. It could take a while for all of them to get here."

"All of them?" Thelvyn asked. "How many do they think they need? No, I know the answer to that. To destroy the Dragonlord, they probably would assemble every dragon in the world."

"I'm not certain they can destroy the Dragonlord," Sir

George commented. "The enchantments of your armor are so powerful that there might not be anything they can do to you once you're inside it. I have this odd suspicion that, in the worst of all likely events, the entire city of Braejr will be reduced to rubble and all the dragons of the world will be dead or in full retreat, and only you will be left."

"Oh, fine," Thelvyn remarked sourly. They turned their horses to ride back to the city. "I worry about you and Solveig. Neither of you have to be here, you know. The best thing for you would be to pack your bags and leave before the dragons get here."

"Perhaps," Sir George said uncertainly. "But to tell you the truth, I still don't believe we'll actually have to fight this battle, no matter how close we might come to it. The Immortals are very much in control of these events if you ask me, especially your patron. They have their own goals in mind, but I don't think they want to see the destruction of either the Flaem or the dragons."

"I wish I could have that much trust," Thelvyn said. "I still feel that I have to consider myself very much on my own in finding a way through this, and I have to be prepared for the worst."

"Well, of course you do."

The problem, of course, was that Thelvyn doubted that he would be given nearly enough time to prepare for the worst. He needed at least a week yet, and in spite of Sir George's assurances, he felt certain that the dragons didn't need nearly that long to prepare to attack. He suspected the question might be irrelevant no matter how much time he was given to prepare. He was afraid that all the resources of the Highlands, together with his own abilities, might not be enough to stand off an invasion of dragons.

At least the people of the Highlands remained optimistic, and the preparations for battle were proceeding quickly. Thelvyn felt rather guilty about that; he needed their trust to be able to protect them the best he could, and yet he was afraid their trust would only be betrayed. His one assurance was in knowing how fiercely independent the Flaem were. They would prefer to do everything they could to prepare for a battle that they couldn't win rather than surrender or flee, not when it was their own homes they were defending.

He thought it was time to decide upon a definite course of action so that he wouldn't be caught by surprise if the dragons came sooner than he liked. The time had come to make some very cold and deliberate choices. He preferred not to consult with any of the Flaem on this matter, knowing that the choices he intended to make would place their safety above their pride. For that reason, he chose to discuss it alone with Sir George, Solveig, and Sellianda that night in the king's private chamber, which was now also doing temporary service as their den. Sir George had already stocked the bar with bottles of cherry liqueur.

"I don't know if I've ever seen you look so tired," Solveig told Thelvyn after she had taken one of the seats by the hearth. "Or so worried. I'm reminded of that time five years ago when we had something like two weeks to cross the western half of the continent in time to intercept the invasion of the rogue dragons. You didn't look nearly so worried then."

"I was young and foolish," Thelvyn told her as he paced the floor. He understood now why Jherridan had always paced when he was thinking. "I was in the middle of a great adventure. I might have been frightened, but I didn't have to make the decisions. The most frightening part of something like this is when you have the responsibility to make all the choices, and they have to be right because the consequences are so great if you're wrong. I find myself wishing my patron was taking a more active part in directing me, sending me all the instructions and advice I need in dreams."

"Even the Immortals don't want *that* responsibility," Solveig remarked in jest.

"Either that, or they also don't know what to do," Sir George said as he prepared himself a drink at the bar.

"I'm beginning to understand why the Immortals don't seem to like us," Thelvyn said darkly, then sat on the edge of his desk to stare at the elf maiden. "I don't suppose your patron is willing to let you know how things will turn out."

"My word, no," Sellianda insisted. "That would take all

the fun out of it. If you want such reassurances, then place your trust in the prophecy of the dragons. You are important to their future, and that would suggest that your involvement with them will not end here."

"Meaning that it's still my problem," he said, taking the chair beside Sellianda. "That seems to be the trouble with being a cleric. First the Immortals decide everything about your life for you, and then they abandon you with the responsibility."

"You are not a cleric," she insisted. "I've told you that before. You do not serve any of the Immortals; you are simply related in many ways to one of the Immortals. That is why you seem to have all the abilities of a cleric except the ability to commune, plus many powers that do not seem typical of a cleric. Your powers do not come to you through an Immortal; they are your own. You are a bridge, partly a powerful mortal and partly an Immortal of limited powers."

"Are you serious?" Thelvyn asked, too startled to know what he should think.

"That is the truth, as far as I know," Sellianda assured him. "But it still does not tell us just what you really are, or where you came from."

Sir George looked surprised, setting aside the bottle he was holding. "That means he could become an Immortal himself, I suppose. You know, lad, between the enchantments of your armor and your own powers, you should be able to do just about anything you want."

Sellianda nodded. "If he had been allowed more time, he could easily have been far more powerful than the first Dragonlord, and the dragons would never dare to confront him. Unfortunately, Thelvyn is still very young, especially by the standards of his race, and he will need more experience before he will be able to command his higher powers. And no mage or cleric can give him that experience—only a true Immortal."

Thelvyn sat very still and listened, wondering if he was supposed to hear this. As vague as all of these hints were, he had still learned more about himself and what he would become this night than he had ever known. Once again he wondered about that strange and remarkable race to which he belonged, where they were and why beings who commanded powers second only to those of the Immortals were not better known in the world.

Then he thought he understood. His race might not be of this world, like other unusual, powerful creatures that had come to haunt these lands. That would explain why his mother had seemed to come from nowhere into the wilderness of the mountains of Wendar. And it also explained why the dragons feared and hated him so—not just him personally but all of his race. The thought that he might indeed be the only one of his kind in the world was a rather lonely and frightening prospect.

"Unfortunately, I have more to worry about than discovering the answers to the secrets of my origins," Thelvyn said at last. "I need to know what to do if the dragons come sooner than we can be ready."

"Yes, I know that you're worried about that," Sir George agreed as he leaned back against the bar. "I think perhaps you're letting the dragons, or at least the reputation they have, intimidate you. Because they are so large, so powerful, and so fast, you assume that they must be very sure of themselves. If you were in their position, you would attack right away while most of the Highlands army is scattered about in the wild. All you can see are the advantages that dragons possess."

"I suppose you're going to remind me of just how frightened they are of me."

"I don't know if you've ever understood just much they fear you," Sir George insisted. "The Dragonlord haunts their dreams. To fight you, according to all they know, means that they will be destroyed. Their fear of you compels them to fight in the hope of being rid of the menace you represent, but the terror of facing you in battle makes it almost impossible for them to act. I believe they will wait so long gathering their forces that they will give us all the time we need."

"I agree," Sellianda said, nodding. "Do not assume the dragons are acting from a position of superior strength, for nothing that they have done shows that they are. In fact, it's quite the contrary. Your two battles with the dragons, and the fact that they have stayed in the mountains this time rather than raiding the frontier, shows that they are afraid of you."

"I'm not arguing," Thelvyn insisted. "Perhaps I have allowed events to make me see my situation as more desperate than it really is, and feeling so helpless trying to play politics has led me to forget the true power of my abilities. My strength lies in the ability to accomplish deeds that no mortal could otherwise hope to achieve."

"Exactly," Sellianda agreed. "Also, you must remember just how frightened and irrational the dragons are, enough to cause them to fly headlong into their worst fear and make war inevitable. I must confess that the Immortals themselves are very concerned."

What it all meant, Thelvyn realized, was that he was in the same position he had been from the start. He understood his own situation and that of the dragons better than he had, but he still had to prepare for the worst and hope for the best. He was still waiting for the dragons to take the first step, to see if they were indeed prepared to go to war with the Dragonlord. Granted, there were already a great many dragons in the Wendarian Range, and yet they had yet done nothing could be taken as their first response. If the dragons had been raiding throughout the frontier, he would have had a hard time justifying the retreat of his forces to Braejr.

The others went to their rooms soon after that, although Solveig remained behind. After a time, she rose from her chair in the shadowed corner by the bookcase and stretched, then took her empty glass back to the bar.

"I need to move about for a bit," she said suddenly. "My injuries are healing, but I'm still a bit stiff much of the time. Would you like to go for a walk on the wall with me?"

Because the back of the king's palace rested directly against the west wall of the city, they could take one of the inner stairways all the way up to the roof of the palace and step out onto the walkway of the wall itself. A watch was now kept all along the city wall, but extra guards were stationed above the palace itself to make certain that no assassins would try to come in that way. Thelvyn was interested to see that stacks of Sir George's tiled screens were already there, waiting for catapults to be brought from the north.

The guards recognized them at once and retired immediately to the parapet, where they could look out across the dark fields beyond the city. The night was deep and dark, with only a small moon in the western sky, and the light summer breeze was cool and fresh. The sky above was dusted with stars, all glimmering against the blackness of the night. Lightning flashed repeatedly far to the distant south, so far that even Thelvyn's eyes could barely see the billowing stormclouds in the dim light.

"It seems strange to think that these hills might be overrun with dragons of every kind in only a few days, yet we haven't seen one yet," Solveig said as they strolled slowly along the top of the wall. "It would be easier to believe in war if we could see the enemy."

"I have no complaint," Thelvyn replied, glancing over his shoulder to the dark fields beyond. "When we see the first dragons, the rest won't be far behind."

"So what do you think of Sellianda?" she asked. "She let a few surprises slip out tonight."

Thelvyn paused a moment. "I doubt she let anything slip. In my experience, a cleric won't tell you the time of day until the Immortals have decided that you should know. That she told me anything means that it must be time for me to be aware of certain things."

"I was beginning to wonder if she was ever going to make herself useful," Solveig admitted as they continued walking. "To tell the truth, I never expected an elf who lives in a big house in a forest a long way from here would have much to tell us. She certainly seems to know more about dragons than I would have expected."

"Not from personal experience," Thelvyn said. "I suspect that most of what she knows she learned from her patron. The only reason she was chosen to be my advisor, I believe, was that she already knew most of my secrets anyway, which meant there was no need to tell another cleric things that were better left unknown."

Solveig shrugged. "She's still clever enough. Are you

going to go away with her when this is over?"

Thelvyn shook his head slowly. "I can't imagine that I'll have the chance. Sellianda will go back to Alfheim, and I'm sure my destiny will keep me busy elsewhere for a long time to come."

"You don't think you deserve a bit of a rest?"

"Whether or not I deserve it doesn't matter," he said wryly. "Sellianda was permitted to tell me part of the secret of who and what I am, and I doubt she would have been allowed to do that unless the rest was soon to follow. Whatever the Immortals may want of me isn't coming to an end; it's actually only about to start. I feel as though I'm rushing forward into my future so quickly that it's difficult to concentrate on the present."

He paused, lost in thought, staring at the lightning flashes in the distant south. After a moment, he climbed up in the parapet so that he could see more clearly. His eyes couldn't accurately judge distances from so far, especially in the dark, but he thought that he could see flashes of lightning briefly illuminate the rugged hills beyond the mountains of the Highlands Range some fifty miles distant. He couldn't hear even the faintest grumble of thunder.

Near the middle of every summer, the winds usually changed direction, and wet air from the sea was drawn up into the Highlands from the south. Then late every afternoon, thunderstorms would build quickly in the Colossus Mounts to the east, the southern Highlands Range, or the rugged lands far to the north. sometimes these storms would hang over the mountains and drop torrents of rain; at other times, they would wander over the wide valley of the central Highlands like dark invading armies.

What Thelvyn was seeing was the advancing summer rains, and they had not come early.

* * * * *

Thelvyn sent for Alessa Vyledaar early the next morning, with advance warning that the matter was urgent. She arrived within a half an hour. She entered his office tentatively, wondering what the problem could be and obviously expecting the worst.

"Did you notice the storms to the south last night?" he asked, looking up at her from his seat at his desk.

Alessa looked rather confused. "No. I spent the evening engrossed in my spellbook."

"The midsummer storms are coming," he explained. "You can see clouds hanging over the mountains this morning, a clear sign that the storms will be here to stay soon. There could be storms here in Braejr by tonight, and all through the Highlands soon afterward."

"I would assume the rains could work to our advantage in the event of an attack, to help put out any fires started by the dragons."

"Yes, I certainly hope so," Thelvyn said, rising to stand beside his desk. He could see that she didn't understand. "The problem with the storms is that they'll turn the roads to a sea of mud, and those catapults are going to take a lot longer to get here. So far, the roads have been fine, but if they turn to mud, those weapons won't be going anywhere. We could be forced to abandon half the wagons to double up the horse teams, and even then things are going to be slow."

"Yes . . . I'm beginning to see your point," Alessa said thoughtfully. Heavy rains could be a disaster.

"We have to do something about it at once," he continued. "The wizards are our only hope. They need to come up with some way to divert those storms and keep the roads dry."

Alessa frowned. "We're Fire Wizards, not Air Wizards like the Alphatians. That type of magic is not our specialty."

"Then you'll have to come up with the spells they'll need," he told her. "There's got to be something."

Alessa went away feeling frustrated. She could recognize the importance of keeping the roads dry, but she wished they had a good deal more time to research the matter. But the Fire Wizards were eager to prove their usefulness and do what was expected of them. They set to work on the problem furiously.

There were other problems before the day was out. Word came from the north that dragons were beginning to follow the movements of the Highlands army as they made their way south, and that there were more dragons than ever in the mountains above the northern border. Thelvyn took that to mean the dragons were becoming very serious about the invasion, but there was nothing he could do about it. He could only hope the dragons didn't interfere with their efforts to keep the roads dry.

There was also some good news later that morning. Alessa Vyledaar hurried back to the palace within the hour to report that a spell for diverting thunderstorms had been found. Instructions for the spell were being relayed to the wizards who accompanied the army. Since the spell depended on the power of the Radiance, tremendous power could be transferred to where it was needed and directed by the wizards in the field.

Thelvyn turned his own attention to other matters, trusting that the solution to the problem of the summer storms had been found. As it happened, it was not the only turn of good fortune that he was to receive that day. Early in the afternoon, Taeryn hurried to his private chamber to tell him excitedly that there was a surprise waiting for him in the courtyard of the main gate. The young valet refused to say more, wanting to surprise Thelvyn.

Solveig and Sir George reached the courtyard just ahead of them, alerted by the noise and confusion. Thelvyn paused a moment when he approached the main gate, not certain whether he wanted to get any closer. What he saw was that well over a hundred fighting griffons and their riders had arrived from Thyatis, the only force that could have reached Braejr in such a short time. The great, fierce creatures filled the courtyard to overflowing, with others settling wherever they could in the garden. At least three dozen griffons sat perched like crows along the outer wall. Thelvyn was grateful for the assistance, but he would have to find somewhere to put them right away.

The nearest of the griffon riders dropped down from his saddle, grasping the nose ring of his beast in one hand. He was wearing a somewhat more decorative version of a Thyatian dress uniform bearing the gold insignia of a captain, indicating that he was no common griffon rider, but a visiting dignitary of some kind. He was already removing the massive leather gloves the riders wore, and he pulled off his helmet to reveal a strikingly handsome man, rather young for his station. He was also surprisingly tall, nearly as tall as Thelvyn, although he was clearly of the somewhat darker Thyatian stock.

"Darius?" Thelvyn asked, coming down the steps to greet him.

"Dragonlord!" the Thyatian called back. "We haven't missed anything yet, have we?"

"My word, what a question," Thelvyn exclaimed. "But if you're referring to the dragons, then you're just in time."

Solveig had also descended the steps to stand at Thelvyn's side, although she had been staring at Darius Glantri in silent fascination since the moment he had removed his helmet. Then, to Solveig's complete astonishment, he turned to her and bowed in the Thyatian manner, his gesture almost too gallant for words. He was aware of her discomfort and tried to come to her rescue.

"You must be Solveig White-Gold," he said. "Allow me to introduce myself. I'm Darius Glantri, Captain of the Thyatian Imperial Army. You'll have to excuse me for being late, but my griffon seemed to think I looked good enough to eat."

"Quite understandable," Solveig said, then caught herself. "I mean, griffons are so fierce. . . . Oh, my. Am I blushing?"

"And very attractively, I must admit," Darius assured her. Then, to spare her any further embarrassment, he turned to the old knight. "Sir George Kirbey?"

Sir George nodded. "You seem to know all about us."

"You are the companions of the Dragonlord, the subjects of legend," he said. "But I must confess that Thelvyn is a good friend of mine, and he's told me about you. Anyway, I've brought all the Thyatian griffon riders except for the diplomatic messenger service."

"Can your griffons actually fight dragons?" Thelvyn asked.

"That's something we've never tried," Darius confessed. "But allow me to show you something."

Releasing his griffon's nose ring, he took firm hold of the reins and leaped back into the saddle. The beast turned its great head, snapping in irritation, but Darius got it back under control with a firm tug on the reins. Then he released some clips that held a massive crossbow to one side of the saddle. The weapon was considerably larger than most crossbows. The bow itself was like a great spring of bright steel, and the bowstring was a length of thin wire. The weapon shot steel-tipped bolts of equally massive proportions, the heads wickedly barbed.

"This is the best we could do on short notice," Darius explained. "If we can get in close enough to penetrate a dragon's armor, the head of that bolt will catch itself under the plate and be decidedly difficult to remove. I can't imagine it killing a dragon, but it would be a blasted nuisance."

"Can you cock a crossbow that large in flight?" Sir George asked.

"We've taken that into account."

Drawing up his left leg, Darius caught the bowstring in a metal clip mounted on the side of the stirrup. By holding the handle on the top of the crossbow firmly, he was able to kick down, extending the bowstring far enough for it to catch. Being secured in the saddle made the move much easier for him to accomplish.

"I admit we probably won't do much good with the crossbows," he said, handing Thelvyn the weapon before he climbed down from the saddle. "I think that we'll be more useful later in the battle. If dragons try to come over the wall or land directly in the city, our griffons will be more of a match for them on the ground."

"I only wish your griffons could encourage the dragons to talk to us instead of fighting," Thelvyn said, handing the crossbow to Solveig. "If it comes down to a fight, we could use the entire Thyatian army."

They were all startled by the snap of the steel bowstring; Solveig had been examining the massive crossbow, holding it by its shaft. Her hand was nowhere near the trigger. It was her good fortune that her hand hadn't been in the way of the bowstring. Everyone looked up to watch in silence as the large bolt climbed straight into the sky, higher and higher for what seemed an incredibly long time. It hesitated a moment, bobbled slightly, and then the heavy barbed head dropped over and the bolt began to fall point down with alarming speed. They all leaped back just before the bolt struck the stone steps where Solveig and Sir George had been standing a moment before. Stone chips sprayed outward, and the steel head rang a rather flat note as it bounced back up. Thelvyn reached out and caught it in midair.

"Jolly good show," Darius declared. "Is that what you people do for sport?"

Somehow they had to find stables for more than a hundred and twenty griffons. Griffons required more room than horses, in order to prevent them from snapping and fighting each other. Fortunately, the barracks of the king's army at the north gate was nearly deserted, and the cavalry stables were empty. The griffon riders took their beasts away at once, rising into the air only a few at a time so the griffons didn't become nervous. Thelvyn, too, felt considerably less nervous once they were gone.

The first opportunity for the Fire Wizards to demonstrate their ability to divert the summer storms came that same evening. Thelvyn was at dinner with his companions when Taeryn rushed in to report that the guards on the wall above the palace had been watching a large storm developing just south of the city.

By the time Thelvyn and his companions had taken the stairs up to the wall, the storm was moving quickly northward, almost directly toward the city. This was a large and impressive summer storm, filling the southern sky almost from the Colossus Mounts in the east to the Highlands Range in the west. The shadow of the black clouds brought on an early nightfall, which usually came late in the northern lands in summer, and dark sheets of rain were already moving across the fields beyond the juncture of the Areste and Aalban rivers.

"I hope the wizards at the Academy are ready for this one," Thelvyn commented at they stood at the parapet.

"The wizards are supposed to be keeping someone stationed about every fifteen miles or so along the major roads,"

Sir George explained while they waited. "That should be enough to make certain the rains don't wander anywhere they shouldn't. I suggested to Alessa that they should divert the storms off to the mountains to annoy the dragons."

Solveig glanced up at the lightning ripping between the dark clouds. "I daresay the dragons are fast enough to get out of the way."

"Perhaps, but it will annoy the heck out of them all the same," the old knight remarked.

Sellianda laughed aloud, obviously finding that very funny. "Sir George, you really should have been put in command of the defense of the Highlands. You could probably find a hundred ways to pester the entire race of dragons into submission."

He bowed gallantly. "My dear, I have the talent to pester anyone into submission. That's my secret to success in matters of romance."

Thelvyn was about to point out that he'd never heard anything about Sir George's forays into romantic affairs, but he realized that the old knight had been around long enough to have done many things the younger man wasn't aware of. There seemed to be enough romance in the air to keep him quite entertained. Thelvyn had never expected to see Solveig reduced to a state of confusion over an infatuation, but that was precisely what had occurred from the first moment she had laid eyes on Darius Glantri. After years of maintaining an aloof dignity, she had chosen an awkward time to make a complete fool of herself over a young man. After his initial amusement with her behavior, Darius had apparently decided he was quite as interested in her. They stood apart from the others and were talking quietly.

"Solveig seems to have finally found her match," Sir George commented quietly. "I was beginning to wonder if there would ever be a match for someone like her."

Thelvyn hadn't realized it, but he must have been looking a bit sad and lonely as he watched them. Sellianda moved to his side and took his hand. He appreciated the gesture, although he couldn't forget that they both had duties that would keep them apart.

"Have you been able to discover anything about the Collar of the Dragons?" he asked Sir George, changing the subject.

Sir George could only shake his head helplessly. "Kalestraan certainly left us some extensive records about his schemes. We even found enough references to the collar itself to be certain that he did have it for a time. The trouble is, he was so afraid of the dragons that he didn't dare to put many of the details in writing. I'm planning to go back to the Academy to look for more hidden storage compartments, but my only real hope is that one of the other conspirators had something specific to say about the collar in his own secret files."

"I wonder if it even matters anymore," Thelvyn commented, almost to himself. "Even if you did find it, we don't have the means to move it. I've already sent Seldaek away."

"We could at least tell the dragons where they can find it," Sir George offered.

They suddenly became aware of an odd movement within the storm. The dark bank of clouds immediately south of the city began to flash with great sheets of lightning, illuminating the blackness from within. The movement of the storm was almost imperceptibly slow, but over the next few minutes they could see that it was breaking into two uneven parts, which began to move off to either side of the city. The larger mass was heading toward the rugged hills below the Colossus Mounts, while the smaller portion seemed to be dispersing quickly.

"It looks as if the wizards can handle it," Thelvyn observed. "In all my experience, this is the first time I've ever seen them do anything exactly right."

"They never did come up with a functional cape of flight, did they?" Sir George asked. He had seated himself in an opening in the parapet.

Thelvyn shook his head. "I need to ask Alessa about that, but the fact that the wizards haven't sent it back yet probably means they're having trouble with it."

He paused as he spotted the distant forms of three dragons drop down from the dark, roiling clouds to the southwest, hurtling directly toward the city as they descended rapidly. The others had also seen them. The dragons approached Braejr from the southwest as fast as they could fly, driving themselves forward with quick sweeps of their wings, then slowed suddenly to pass low over the very middle of the city. As soon as they passed above the north gate, they began to climb steadily while increasing their speed. In less than a minute, they had disappeared again.

The incident's significance didn't escape Thelvyn. He had seen clearly that the dragons had been a pair of young reds under the lead of a mature gold.

"That was exciting," Solveig breathed.

Sellianda turned to Thelvyn, looking concerned. "Did you notice that they were led by a gold dragon?"

He nodded slowly. "I saw. I've always said I would know that war has become inevitable when the gold dragons became involved. And now that they've taken their first look at Braejr, we can be certain they'll begin moving their forces closer very soon now."

CHAPTER SIXTEEN

Marthaen rode the gentle winds of evening as he sailed slowly over the wooded lower slopes of the Colossus Mounts. Darkness was already deep enough that he could see the faint glitter of the lights of the Flaemish city of Braastar well to the west. Banking sharply, he turned east toward the black shapes of the mountains. He was harboring thoughts of a warm dinner, perhaps the only comfort to be found in the wilderness.

Complete stealth was no longer as important now that he had been allowing some of the patrols to show themselves deliberately, but he still didn't want the Flaem to know the true size of the forces that had been gathered against them. Dragons had been gathering from throughout the continent of Brun in response to his summons, until there were now nearly two thousand in the mountains surrounding the Highlands. Marthaen didn't know how long they might have to wait, so he had kept them in reasonably small bands so they wouldn't hunt all the game in any one area.

A large part of his forces were in the Colossus Mounts, a

rugged cluster of towering peaks where the men of the Highlands did not go. Hundreds of dragons could lose themselves in the maze of towering peaks and long, steep ridges. He weaved his way through several deep valleys until he saw several fires in the distance. As he approached, he circled the camp briefly before descending to land in a clear area of the wooded slope. He moved aside as the two gold dragons who served as his bodyguards landed after him, the broad sweeps of their wings lifting clouds of dust and dry pine needles.

At least the nights were cool here in these remote, high mountains. He walked through the camp until he came to a sheltered place amid trees and great boulders, where the red dragon Jherdar was tending a fire. Some small animal was roasting on a spit over the fire while Jherdar was quietly dining on a second, sitting up on his haunches and holding it on a spit of wood in his hands.

"What do you have for dinner?" Marthaen asked.

"Roasted sheep," the red dragon said, holding up his partially devoured dinner. "I saved the little one for you."

"Sheep again?" Marthaen settled back on his haunches and reached for the one still on the fire. "Is there nothing but sheep in these mountains?"

"Most of this range is too steep and rugged for elk and deer," Jherdar explained. "That's why this place is unpopular with dragons, as nice as it seems otherwise. Did you tell me that Kharendaen used to do most of her hunting here?"

"It must have been in the forests below the mountains," Marthaen said, sniffing at the slightly burned meat. "Hunting should be better very soon now. I believe the time has come for us to begin our siege of the city before any more of their army can arrive."

"We've waited a long time," Jherdar commented.

"It has suited my purposes to keep them guessing about our intentions, letting them wonder if they dare to hope. Now we'll trap them in their hole and let them spend some time wondering when we plan to attack."

"Lord Marthaen!"

The great gold dragon lifted his head at the sound of a voice, looking back over his shoulder. Although he hadn't even been aware of the arrival of a messenger, he saw that a young gold dragon was approaching his camp, still breathing heavily from a long, hard flight. He set aside his dinner, then rose to stand before the young dragon.

"I have just now come from Windreach," the messenger explained, still panting for breath. "The Alphatians have broken the treaty and are invading Norwold in great strength. A fleet of ships five hundred strong has been seen approaching the Great Bay. Gheradaen has sent word that a part of the army of the dragons must return at once if we hope to repel this invasion before the Alphatians can return to their abandoned strongholds."

"Five hundred ships," Marthaen said to himself, unsure just how many men that meant. "Are these invading ships all war galleys, or are some of them supply ships?"

"I have not seen them myself. I do not know," the young dragon admitted.

"What difference does it make?" Jherdar asked. "It's bad news either way."

"It would tell me something of how they expect to fight," he explained. "If they are sending mostly galleys, they can only make a quick attack before they run short on supplies. If they are bringing in ships full of supplies, perhaps they mean to dig themselves in at their former strongholds. Was that the entire message?"

"Only that they will probably need another two days if they mean to make landfall in the back of the Great Bay."

"Rest by the fire and eat," Marthaen told him, indicating his own dinner. He turned and walked away slowly, passing aimlessly into the darkness. After a moment, he noticed that Jherdar had remained close at his side. "They must have heard of our present conflict with the Flaem, and they saw that as a chance to return while our greatest strength is away here in the west."

"Treacherous weasels," the red dragon remarked in dark fury. "Not that we can't handle them. If we can catch their ships still at sea, dealing with them would be more like sport than battle. But how will it affect your plans concerning the Dragonlord? Do you think it best to deal with the problem here first?"

"Do they think that we cannot return to the east?" Marthaen said irritably, pausing a moment before looking back at his companion. "What do the Alphatians hope to gain? They amaze me at every turn."

"At least the Dragonlord is reassuringly predictable," Jherdar agreed.

"Unfortunately, I'll need some time to deal with the Dragonlord," Marthaen continued, sitting back on his haunches to consider the problem. After several long moments, he arose, his mind made up. "This is our plan. We will deal with both of our enemies in their own best time. You must leave at once for the east, taking half the dragons with you. Your task will be to destroy the Alphatian invasion fleet as quickly and completely as you can, with as little risk as possible to our forces. When you are done, return here at once."

"I will not be gone any longer than I can help it," Jherdar promised.

"I will gather together the remaining dragons here," Marthaen said. "As soon as we get organized, I will besiege Braejr and keep the Dragonlord occupied until you are able to return with the rest of our forces. Unfortunately, it will cause some delay in our plans here."

"The Flaem will have time to prepare for a siege," Jherdar said.

"It cannot be helped," the gold dragon said, then shook his head slowly. "Not that it matters. It was never my intent to fight the Dragonlord in battle anyway."

Jherdar hurried away to send out the summons for half the dragons to join him in the east. Marthaen was left alone, still lost in his own thoughts and concerns. The matter of the Alphatians did not greatly change his plans. He knew how to deal with the Dragonlord, and a delay did not make any real difference.

He didn't like to see the dragons forced to resume their war with the Alphatians. Just the same, it might yet work to his advantage. Once the dragons had destroyed much of the Alphatian navy, the nations of the west might be tempted to descend upon weakened Alphatia like wolves moving in for the kill. An invasion of Alphatia might help divert the fear and mistrust of the western nations that the dragons would earn by defeating the Dragonlord.

* * * * *

The dragons began to make their presence known over Braejr by the next morning. One or two would fly in slow circles over the supply trains streaming in from the north, or else they would settle themselves to watch in some high place where they could be seen clearly. Their actions caused a certain amount of panic at first as the soldiers guarding the wagons and the mounted catapults would prepare furiously for battle. Soon it became obvious that the dragons had no intention of attacking yet, although they were always close at hand. The soldiers tried their best to ignore the dragons, and eventually came to take the great creatures almost for granted.

Dragons were seen over most of the cities and towns of the Highlands, and at Braejr they soon became hard to ignore. At first they were content merely to fly over the city, but late in the fourth day they began to gather in the lightly wooded hills beyond the fields to the north of the city. There were dozens at first, but within a couple of days, at least several hundred dragons had gathered. At night, the blazing fires of their camps could be seen from atop the city walls. Thelvyn had expected the dragons to close off all access to Braejr as soon as their numbers were sufficient to enforce their will, and yet they did nothing to interfere with the steady stream of supply trains from the north.

That left Thelvyn with the difficult problem of trying to figure out what they were planning. Their lack of an aggressive response seemed to make no sense, especially considering that they had every advantage. He thought at first that their strategy was nothing more than a gesture of contempt, demonstrating a complete lack of concern for the Highlands defenses. Then he recalled Sir George explaining how much the dragons feared the Dragonlord, and he began to wonder if they were trying to bait him into making some ill-advised move. He knew his position would be less strong if he went out to meet them.

Soon the last of the supply trains arrived, and the north gate of the city was closed for the final time. Catapults were now stationed along the wall of the city every few yards; more had been set up throughout the city in such a way that they could shoot upward and turn quickly to track a dragon in flight. There were also companies of archers along the wall and in many of the towers and other high parts of the city. The archers, of course, would be far less effective than catapults except at extremely close range. The elves of the southern Highlands had sent even more archers, whose skill with their bows was such that even a dragon dared not approach them too close.

There were dragon encampments in the hills north of Braejr and also on the other sides of the two rivers east and west of the city. When Thelvyn went up on the wall to inspect the defenses, he became distracted watching the dragons. Although their numbers were impossible to count, there were at least a thousand in all. They filled the sky in all directions during the day as they passed back and forth into the hills to hunt, and at night their fires encircled the city. They had shown remarkable restraint so far, refraining from destroying the abandoned farms surrounding Braejr.

"They're playing with us," Thelvyn commented as he stood at the parapet with Sir George, watching the dragons.

"I hate to say it, but I'm beginning to think you're right," Sir George conceded. "That worries me, because I would have never anticipated the dragons would be that confident, knowing they have to face the Dragonlord. It leads me to wonder what they've got up their sleeves."

"They couldn't be planning to starve us out, could they?" Thelvyn asked suddenly.

"That many dragons?" the old knight responded. "They would starve themselves out first. You might have noticed that they have to fly to the mountains to do their hunting. Kharendaen had little trouble finding an elk or deer nearly every day, but that's changed now. Soon they won't be able fly far enough to find game and return. They'll turn to raiding the farms and villages for cattle and sheep. They won't eat horses or goats if they can help it. I would say by two weeks from now there won't be any edible game left within flying distance."

Whatever problems the dragons might be having locating food, they were willing to let the Dragonlord ponder the situation for another day. The only change in their tactics was that, with the arrival of the last of the supply trains from the north, they had cut off the city from any direct contact with the outside world. Anyone leaving was allowed safe passage, but no one else was coming into Braejr from the outside.

To his surprise, Thelvyn found himself strangely drawn to the dragons and watched them whenever he could. He had never thought much about the creatures beyond his almost instinctive fear of them, although he had always appreciated their remarkable grace and beauty. He found it ironic that he felt so close to them now, when in the coming days they might destroy him or vice versa.

For the first time, he began to understand the despair and fury of the dragons. He was more determined than ever that the lesson of the first Dragonlord should not repeat itself, yet in many ways that was not his decision to make. He was very much a servant to the dictates of his patron. His response would be by the actions of the dragons themselves, and he would fight only as long as they insisted upon fighting. He wouldn't hurt or kill a single dragon unless he must, but at the same time, he couldn't sacrifice the people of Braejr.

With that thought in mind, he spoke later with Sir George and Sellianda. Both were knowledgeable about dragons. Thelvyn didn't want the Flaem to get the idea that his concern for dragons made him any less concerned for their well-being. He was still the King of the Flaemish Realm, and he took that duty very seriously.

"I've been thinking a great deal about the possibility that I will have to fight the dragons," he told them as they paused a moment in his private chamber on their way to lunch. "I was wondering if either of you knew the best way to render a dragon helpless but not endanger its life."

Sellianda closed her eyes and sighed. Clearly the thought

of slaying dragons bothered her as much as it did Thelvyn. "I think the best tactic would be to use the cutting force of your sword to rip through their wings. The most vulnerable part of a dragon is its wings, although the sails and ribs have the ability to completely regenerate from almost any damage. But that takes time; a dragon with damaged wings wouldn't be able to fly for at least a week or two. It would be a painful wound, considering that your weapon will be burning through their sails. You must be careful not to cut through the main bone, or part of the wing might be sliced off completely and the dragon will never fly again."

Sir George nodded. "That's what happened to me. I was attacked by assassins at a time when I lacked a proper weapon to defend myself, so I assumed my drake form. There were quite a few of the brutes, and one of them brought his sword down on the outside joint of my left wing. Only the Great One himself could give my wing back to me after that."

Thelvyn had never known how Sir George lost his hand, beyond the fact that he had been a knight of Darokin at the time. Still, he knew that in the fury of battle, it would be difficult not to injure more dragons than he intended. He would be inflicting tremendous pain under any circumstances, even if he tried to spare as many of their lives as he could.

He realized he should be more concerned about what the dragons might be planning to do to him. They certainly seemed confident, and he was sure they wouldn't repeat Byen Kalestraan's error in underestimating him. They had one obvious advantage. They had fought a Dragonlord before, one who had probably commanded even greater powers than he, and they had three thousand years to contemplate their mistakes. He couldn't help thinking they knew something about him that he was unaware of, some hidden vulnerability that he had never suspected.

* * * * *

The warning that the dragons seemed to be preparing for attack brought Thelvyn and his companions to the top of the city wall late in the morning, although they were a bit confused by what they found. The dragons didn't seem to be gathering for an attack on the city itself. Instead, their attention was directed to the woods on the east side of the river, just beyond the new stone bridge which crossed the Aalban. Many dragons were already on the ground, as if drawing a battle line, and scores of other dragons were either circling above or hurrying to join the effort to hold the bridge.

"They seem to be trying to prevent someone from crossing the river," Sir George remarked as he stared intently.

"Several thousand someones," Thelvyn said, taking in the distant scene with his keen eyesight. He smiled with wry amusement. "It looks to me as if the hordes of the Ethengar are coming to our rescue. I need to do something to help them out."

"I can have the griffon riders ready in minutes," Darius Glanti offered.

"There aren't enough griffon riders to take on that many dragons," Thelvyn told him, quickly considering his options. "You might have them standing by in case they're needed, but I'm the only one who has a chance to go out there and provide enough of a distraction to get the Ethengar over the bridge into the city."

Thelvyn hurried down to the palace stables where the horses for the messengers were kept, taking the only mount that was already saddled. The horse was unfamiliar with him and protested his presence, reacting with the curious fear that all horses seemed to have of him, but he was able to master it by his strength and force of will. Within a few short minutes, he had raced through the streets of the city and out into the fields beyond.

The dragons were still gathering to repel the Ethengar, trying to prevent them from gaining the bridge only a few hundred yards beyond the safety of Braejr's north gate. Thelvyn hoped to intervene quickly and scatter the dragons before they had the chance get organized, catching them by surprise and turning their fury upon him so the nomads could reach the safety of the city. He was glad to see that the dragons were continuing to act with restraint rather than openly attack, using their flames and great size and speed to try to frighten the Ethengar into giving up their attempt to reach the bridge.

Thelvyn had donned his armor at the outset, although the rather frightened horse seemed not to notice the extra weight as it bolted across the fields. The race to the bridge was a short one. When he reached the scene, he planned to release the horse, since he doubted that he would be able to fight dragons from the saddle. He kept hidden as much as possible behind a line of small trees that lined the road. He managed to come up behind a dragon without being seen. He brought the horse up onto the road at the base of the bridge, its iron horseshoes ringing on stone as horse and rider charged into the midst of their enemy.

The dragons couldn't have been more startled at his sudden appearance. Those on the ground scattered like a flock of birds flushed by a hound. Their broad wings snapped as they struggled to climb into the sky, lifting great clouds of dust and leaves. As dire as the situation was, the sight amused Thelvyn. Encouraged, the Ethengar pushed on through the break created by the fleeing dragons. Shouting their thanks to the Dragonlord as they passed, the riders charged over the bridge in tight ranks. The Ethengar rode straight for the gates of Braejr, needing no encouragement to get themselves under cover.

Thelvyn knew it was up to him to cover their retreat, permitting them to ride on ahead for some distance while he waited behind at the bridge, facing the dragons if they dared to attack. Most of the dragons were circling, scores of them watching him balefully, although they kept their distance. He wondered if they would try to attack the moment he turned to ride back to the gate. Perhaps they didn't dare challenge him, even in such great numbers, or perhaps they were under orders from their leaders to leave him alone for now. He looked around as well as he could, his vision limited by his helmet, but he failed to see Marthaen or Jherdar among them.

When the last of the Ethengar were more than halfway to the gate, Thelvyn turned his horse to follow. He thought it best to get away while he could, before the dragons had a chance to organize an attack. He kept the horse at a slow trot, mindful that the beast was shivering and panting with the weight of the load he carried and his fear of both the dragons and his rider. The run back to the gate would be a long one for them both.

He was still several hundred yards from the gate and beginning to think his retreat would go unchallenged when the attack came. Something flashed past the edge of his vision to crash into the road only a couple of yards to his left, exploding in a shower of dust and stone. The horse shied, stopping suddenly and rearing in terror, although Thelvyn was able to stay in the saddle. After a moment, he urged the horse forward again. He was curious about the nature of the attack; it obviously hadn't been a blast of dragonfire. He glanced behind him, but the dragons were still holding back, far enough away to offer some protection from his weapons. At the same time, he was well out of the range of their flames.

Then a second explosion of rock and dirt erupted from the ditch beside the road, and a third, and this time Thelvyn was certain of what he had seen. The dragons were snatching up large boulders from the riverbed and dropping them from great height. There wasn't much he could do about it except to urge the horse into a full gallop. Almost at once he found himself caught up in a deadly hail of boulders, dozens crashing relentlessly in a tight cluster all around him as the horse galloped in panic-stricken fear, needing no urging from him.

Despite the attack with the boulders, Thelvyn wasn't overly concerned for his own safety, trusting the enchantments of his armor to protect him. Besides, there was a limit to how large a stone even a dragon could throw. But he had underestimated the weight of the stones. A sudden sharp blow caught him squarely in the upper back as he rode low in the saddle, driving him to the ground with such crushing force that his vision went dark for a desperate moment.

Fearful that the dragons would take advantage of him while he was down, Thelvyn crawled a short distance to retrieve the sword that had been knocked from his grasp before struggling to his feet. The horse was dead, crushed as the weight of both Thelvyn and the boulder had been driven into its back. He turned quickly to see that he was still at least a hundred yards from the gate. The dragons were still holding back, seeing that he had only been momentarily stunned by the blow, although they continued their barrage of heavy stones.

Thelvyn lifted his sword with both hands and released a series of short blasts of power from the enchanted weapon. While there was little chance of actually hitting a flying dragon from such a long distance, at least he forced them to scatter and retreat. Then he turned and ran as fast as he could toward the gate, taking advantage of their momentary confusion. While the armor of the Dragonlord was not especially heavy, it was restrictive. A hundred yards was a long way to run, especially when he expected the dragons to resume their attack at any moment.

But they seemed content to allow the matter to end right there. Thelvyn teleported the armor away the moment he slipped through the gate, standing aside so that the soldiers could close and bar the massive portal. Solveig and Sir George were waiting for him, although all he could do for the moment was pant with the effort of running in his armor.

"I feel sorry for that poor horse," he said at last. "He nearly made it."

"He died well," Sir George said, "if such a thing has meaning to a horse. What about you?"

"I'm as well as can be expected after having a boulder the size of a fat sow fall on me," Thelvyn said as he rose stiffly. "Where's Darius? I don't want him taking his griffon riders out there for me to have to rescue as well."

"He won't go past the wall without checking to see if he's needed," Sir George said as they walked toward the inner gate. "The more immediate problem is what to do with all those Ethengar warriors. We can't expect to feed that many extra horses for very long. I'm not certain, but I would guess something like six thousand of them came through that gate."

"They must have gone through the pass below the

Colossus Mounts and come up through the forests," Solveig said. "I don't know how else they could have caught an army of dragons by surprise."

They paused a moment at the inner gate, which stood partly open. The paved square and the streets beyond seemed filled to overflowing with Ethengar warriors and their horses—especially horses, since the warriors always traveled with a change of mounts and switched horses during the day. The barracks inside the north gate could handle some of them, but Thelvyn suspected that most would have to camp in the city park, which would probably suit the nomadic Ethengar just fine.

"Now that they're here, I'm not sure why I thought I wanted them in the first place," Thelvyn remarked.

"They'll be of use," Sir George insisted. "The Ethengar are nearly as deadly with their bows as the elves are. We can use them along the wall. And just having their numbers should be worth something if it comes to bargaining a truce with the dragons."

* * * * *

The next morning, Thelvyn and his companions were still at breakfast when the news that they had been dreading came at last. Captain Gairstaan, who had taken command of the city defenses after his return from the north, sent warning that the dragons were preparing for something. They had gathered in orderly ranks in the open fields several hundred yards out from the city walls, a move that made it appear they were preparing for battle.

Followed by the others, Thelvyn hurried up the stairs to the roof of the palace and onto the wall, where horses were regularly kept saddled, awaiting urgent errands. The passage behind the parapets was now crowded with mounted crossbows and shields, but a narrow passage large enough for a horse to pass through was kept clear. Following the path, they reached the north gate in short order

Ranks of dragons had been drawn up in the fields on either side of the main road beyond the north gate, although Thelvyn sensed that this was almost certainly not a preparation for attack. For one thing, he didn't believe dragons would ever organize themselves in companies like soldiers on the ground when their attack would surely come from the sky.

"I suspect they're just trying to get our attention," he said as Captain Gairstaan hurried over to take his horse. "Do they want to talk?"

"That seems to be the case. I would have been surprised if they had rushed straight into battle without wanting to discuss things first."

They followed the walkway out from the main wall, passing through the towers of the gateyard to the parapet above the outer gate. Her wounds almost completely recovered now, Solveig leaped up into an opening in the parapet to see better. Sir George and Sellianda remained back behind the stones where they could not so easily be seen. Considering the sharp vision of dragons, they might even have been able to tell that Sir George was a drake from that distance, and it would have been an extremely awkward time for a dragon to announce that Thelvyn's oldest friend and advisor was in reality a mandrake.

Thelvyn and Solveig had only just shown themselves at the wall when a gold dragon leaped into the air from the hills far beyond, gliding sedately over the main road to pass above the ranks of the waiting dragons. Thelvyn was certain it was Marthaen. He looked a good deal like his sister Kharendaen, except that he was larger, his crest and horns longer and his face less narrow. The dragon landed some distance from the wall and then approached in a slow, rather stately pace. When he had come close, he sat back on his haunches, his long neck held high enough that he could look down slightly upon his opponents, even though they were high on the parapet above the gate.

Before the dragon could speak, Thelvyn stepped into the opening in the parapet to face him. "Hear me, Marthaen. The time has come for us to put an end to all these gestures and talk. It is plain that neither of us wants to go to war, knowing what the consequences would be for both sides."

"What you say is true," the dragon agreed. "And yet

what am I to say? The dragons have done no wrong in this matter, and we have just complaints that must be addressed. We have been falsely accused of breaking the truce, and the former king of this land sought to expel our people from the mountains that were given to us by the terms of the truce."

"The truth of that matter has been determined," Thelvyn insisted. "The Fire Wizard Byen Kalestraan had joined with renegade dragons in an attempt to assassinate me. The dragons were blameless in that, and King Jherridan was hasty and extreme in his response. Surely that is something we can discuss."

"It is a beginning," Marthaen conceded. "But no more than a beginning. We have other complaints that must be addressed before there can be peace. First, I must tell you that your recent ambitions have been a cause of great concern to the dragons. We demand that you relinquish the title of King of the Flaemish Realm, and we further demand that from this time forth you must never again enter the service of any country or person, take any other titles or positions of power or authority, nor swear any loyalty beyond what is directly a part of your duties as Dragonlord."

Thelvyn looked surprised, suddenly realizing how his recent actions might seem to others. "There has been some misunderstanding here, and I'm afraid it has been my own fault. I have no wish to be king. I agreed to take the title only during the duration of this time of crisis. Then a new king will be found."

Marthaen laid back his ears and glanced toward the sky, making a silent appeal to the Great One. Then he puffed through his cheeks and brought his head forward to glare at the Dragonlord, speaking very softly. "Of all the incompetent, idiotic bumbling! If I had only been informed what you were doing, I could have kept this confrontation much simpler. As it is, I have no choice but to finish what has been begun."

"Was I supposed to write you letters about my plans?" Thelvyn asked in turn. "What more do you want?"

"We ask that there be no new settlements in the northern Highlands," the dragon continued. "The mountains and the wooded lands of Wendar are home to many dragons, and certain places there are sacred to us. As long as the people of the Highlands continue to move into that area, they will continue to interfere in our affairs."

"Is this point negotiable?" Thelvyn asked, thinking of how the dukes of Aalban and Ardelan were likely to react to that.

"Perhaps there can be some accommodation," Marthaen agreed vaguely. "But the last issue is beyond negotiation. If you desire to make amends for the insult given us and establish a new truce, you must return the Collar of the Dragons."

Thelvyn sighed, realizing that he could never satisfy the dragons if they were determined on this point. "We've been looking for the collar since the night Byen Kalestraan proved himself to be a traitor. We fear that the only ones who knew of its location are no longer alive. If you would be willing to declare a truce, then perhaps we could work together to find it."

"Then you deny that you stole it?"

"You know perfectly well that I personally didn't steal anything," Thelvyn declared, becoming impatient now. "Kharendaen would have told you if I had. I've never asked her to betray any of your secrets, and we both know that she wouldn't have in any event. She was the best of friends and companions, but she serves the Great One and not me."

Marthaen considered that briefly. "I can only refer your proposal to the other leaders among the dragons, but I see little hope. Of the three things that we have asked for, you are able to give us only the first. I make this offer: If you will surrender to me the armor and weapons of the Dragonlord, and if you promise to seek the Collar of the Dragons, then we will be satisfied and withdraw."

Thelvyn could only shake his head. "I can't give you the armor, since it's not mine to give. I would need the consent of the Immortals, and they're not in the habit of speaking to me."

"Then for now I suggest that you return to your companions and advisors and discuss what you can do to satisfy our demands," Marthaen said as he turned to depart. He glanced back over his shoulder. "I will grant you three days to meet our demands."

Thelvyn knew now that he was still a long way from finding a peaceful settlement, since a truce seemed to be dependent upon his granting the dragons things that were not his to give. As Marthaen had suggested, he called for his companions to join him at once in his private chamber to discuss Marthaen's demands and discover which of his terms they might be able to meet. The dragons had already returned to their camps in the distant hills and in the forests on either side of the rivers opposite the city, apparently content to wait out the three days that had been promised.

"I suppose I have to take it for granted we won't be able to find the Collar of the Dragons in the time we have," he began. "Can we put the matter of finding the collar back on the dragons themselves, considering that dragons were surely involved in its theft?"

Sir George looked dubious. "I have my doubts about that. Marthaen seems determined to demand something of you that you can't give him, as if he's trying to make war inevitable. Even so, I'm certain the last thing he wants is a fight, so he must be up to something. If we can, our best response now is to find some way to give him exactly what he wants."

"But can we?" Solveig asked.

"Well, let's see," the old knight remarked, wondering about the possibility of opening a new bottle of cherry liqueur. "Thelvyn is willing to relinquish the title of king, but he always meant to do that anyway. I'm sure we can reach some accommodation about the northern settlements. Now if we can just give them back the collar, or at least tell them where to find it, we should have nothing to worry about. The dragons have named their terms, and they will keep their word."

"Unfortunately, finding the blasted thing seems to be my job," Alessa commented, looking uncomfortable. She could only shake her head. "I just don't know what to say.

We've searched for a clue everywhere we can think of. We just don't know what Kalestraan did with the collar once he took possession of it, nor do we know which renegades helped him steal it."

"Unless we happen to get exceptionally lucky in the next three days, that brings us to our final alternative," Thelvyn said. "I am prepared to surrender the armor of the Dragonlord on the condition that I go with it."

Sellianda glanced up suddenly. "What an interesting thought. Putting the Dragonlord and the leaders of the dragons together in the same place would be the ultimate stalemate."

Alessa looked surprised, almost offended. "Surely you are jesting."

"I'm sure he's not," the elf insisted. "The Dragonlord's duty is tied to the dragons. Where else should he be?"

Sir George also looked rather surprised by the suggestion. "Do you honestly mean to say that you expect the dragons to allow him to keep the armor?"

Sellianda turned to face him. "I am certain that Kharendaen and the clerics of the Great One would be willing to bring their considerable influence to bear on this matter. Knowing what you do about this situation and about dragons, do you expect any contention to remain unresolved for long?"

"No, I suppose not," Sir George agreed. "All Thelvyn will have to do is knock a few heads together, and then everyone will get along like old friends."

Alessa looked impatient. "I'm beginning to think we would be better off trying to fight."

Thelvyn found himself wishing that Alessa hadn't said that. It reminded him that she was of the Flaem; like Jherridan and Kalestraan and so many others, she was only too eager to commit to battle. She was the only one who could possibly find the Collar of the Dragons in time to avert this war, and Thelvyn needed to be able to trust that she was doing her best. His almost instinctive distrust of Fire Wizards had returned to temper his judgement. It was a lesson he had been taught only too well all his life.

He had a quiet dinner that evening with his closest

friends. Afterward he went alone to the top of the wall above the palace. Night was nearly upon the city, with only a pale glow in the west where the sun had set long before. The campfires of the dragons glittered through the trees of the stands of woods beyond the fields, miles away and yet seemingly close to Thelvyn's sharp eyes. The day had brought no new answers; that left him only two more days to find some way to appease the dragons, and the only solution he had come up with was to offer himself.

Thelvyn turned, suddenly aware that someone was approaching quietly from behind him in the enclosing darkness. He had been on guard against unexpected attacks for some time now, knowing the dragons were willing to try anything to get rid of him. Of course, he knew he was hardly alone on the wall. Elvish guards, with their ability to see in the dark, kept watch on the walls all night, and a crew was stationed at every fourth catapult at all times to respond to any sudden attack. Still, Thelvyn was surprised to see that Alessa Vyledaar had followed him.

"Have you learned anything?" he asked, always hopeful.

She shook her head. "There is nothing new. Kalestraan kept his secrets well."

Alessa stood deliberately close to him at the parapet. Thelvyn had almost forgotten about her attentions toward him in the last few desperate days. With the reawakening of his distrust of Fire Wizards, she had chosen a bad time to make a play for him. Ignoring his lack of response, she moved still closer to him.

"I don't know how we can avoid this battle," she said.

"I plan to do everything I can to prevent it," Thelvyn assured her.

"You can't mean it when you say you'll surrender yourself to them if you have to," Alessa insisted, looking up at him.

"It wouldn't really be surrender," he explained. "At least, not under the terms that I intend to propose. I would keep the armor, and I would live among the dragons, but not as their prisoner. As Sir George said, under such circumstances, we would settle our differences very quickly."

"Or else kill each other," she said bitterly. "I don't want

you to leave. Why should you? You're the Dragonlord and the King of the Highlands. If these dragons want a fight, then give them one and be done with it. Don't worry so much about hurting them; they've asked for trouble. Stay here with me."

"I don't have that choice," Thelvyn insisted. "And I have no desire to remain king."

"And you do not want to stay with me. I know," Alessa said sadly. "I admit you don't have much reason to trust me, considering who I am. In your eyes, I've inherited the reputation of those who have always been your enemies. I know you find it easier to believe that I care far more about becoming a queen than about you. And I don't know how to prove to you otherwise, since I won't have the time to show you. Everyone seems to believe that soon you'll be going away, one way or another."

Thelvyn frowned, uncertain for a moment just what he should say. When he didn't answer at once, Alessa looked up at him. "There's only one thing I can say to prove myself. When the time comes for you to go, wherever you have to go, I'll go with you."

"It's not just that," he told her. "You talk about time. I haven't had time to get to know you well enough yet."

"They say that you know Sellianda from years ago," she said. "Is it that you feel closer to her?"

Thelvyn could only shake his head hopelessly. "I don't know what to say."

"Dragonlord!" It was the voice of Taeryn, running along the wall to join them.

Alessa moved discreetly away. Thelvyn hardly knew whether to chastise the young valet or shake his hand.

"Sir George sent me to find you," Taeryn explained, out of breath from running. "He says a dwarf has come to speak to you—an emissary from Rockhome."

Taeryn led the way to Thelvyn's private chamber, while Alessa Vyledaar followed in brooding silence. Sir George had already poured drinks to celebrate the occasion. Next to Solveig and Sellianda, in the middle of the room, stood a young dwarf dressed in dark, well-worn leather and cloth, his pack and weapons deposited just inside the door.

Thelvyn stared for a moment before he realized who the visitor was.

"Korinn Bear Slayer!" Thelvyn exclaimed. "I'm delighted to see you, but I have to admit that it seems like a bad time."

"I never expected there were so many dragons in all the world," the young dwarf remarked. "I had to wait until it was dark to find a way to slip inside the city. But the dragons are why I'm here, as you may have guessed. I have two thousand of the best warriors in Rockhome with me."

Korinn paused a moment, staring in dismay at the glass of cherry liqueur Sir George handed him.

"Anyway, while we were waiting for night to fall, danged if about four thousand elves from Alfheim didn't show up," he continued, taking a seat near the corner. "If you can use the help, we need to start moving them into the city at once to get everyone inside by morning."

"Yes, of course," Thelvyn insisted, still very much at a loss. "I just never expected this. The defense of Braejr hardly seems important to the dwarves, much less the elves."

"I can't speak for the elves," Korinn said. "I heard their captain say something about defending their kinsmen in the Highlands. I suspect he just doesn't want to admit that even the elves are alarmed at the thought of an army of dragons attacking anyone, even the Flaem. But that's exactly what brought me, I don't mind saying. The dwarves are convinced the dragons will be after our mines and treasures next, so King Daroban thought it best to get involved right now rather than wait for them to come to us."

Korinn didn't add that, as his father's likely heir, he had been given command of the dwarvish forces as much for the experience as for the fact that he had been a friend and companion to the Dragonlord.

"Then the dragons don't know you are here?" Solveig asked.

Korinn shook his head. "They wouldn't have let me in if they had, would they?"

"We're still trying to avoid an actual battle," Sir George

said. "The addition of your forces and the elves will make our position just that much stronger."

"More so than you might be aware," Korinn added. "The elves told me they saw at least half the army of Darokin only five days south of here. The dragons have to be aware of it by now."

"That's the best news I could have hoped for," Thelvyn said. "I think Marthaen will be a little more reasonable the next time he wants to talk."

"We'll make certain they don't have everything their way," the dwarf declared. He rose and set aside his still-full glass. "If you'll excuse me, I need to begin bringing my people inside the city. Two thousand dwarves and four thousand elves surrounded by a thousand dragons seems like the perfect combination for trouble."

Korinn bowed and departed without another word, pausing only a moment for Solveig and Sir George to join him. Thelvyn smiled to himself. The young dwarf had matured a great deal in the last five years. He had become more like other dwarves, confident and occasionally boisterous, but also commanding. Thelvyn was glad to have so many of his old companions gathered together at such a time; he wouldn't even have been surprised if Perrantin arrived with the forces from Darokin. Only Kharendaen was absent, and greatly missed.

"If I cannot be of additional service, then I should return to the Academy," Alessa sounding frustrated.

Thelvyn nodded to her but remained silent as she departed. He was still uncertain whether he regretted or was relieved that her attempt to seduce him had been so opportunely interrupted, although he suspected that he would have refused her flat if it had come down to that. He still couldn't escape the feeling that she had secret motives in wanting to be intimate with him, something that would work to her advantage if not actually to his disadvantage.

"Is something wrong?" Sellianda asked, rising from her chair in the corner to approach him.

"Just Alessa," he explained. "She was trying to tempt me into staying here and remaining king. She says she wants me to stay with her—even offered to come with me if I have to go away. I'm inclined to think that she was just trying to convince me of her sincerity. I wish I had more experience at this sort of thing."

"Alessa is a sorceress with strong ambitions," Sellianda answered. "Her ambitions are not necessarily evil or even selfish ones, but ambition is the passion that shapes her life. She may be trying to use you, or it may be that she simply sees a person of your power and abilities as the perfect match for her. I cannot say. Does she tempt you?"

"No, not really," he insisted, then laughed at himself. "I suppose I'm just wondering if I should be flattered or offended. I'm used to being treated as a stranger in this land, an undesirable."

"They've taught you to question everyone's motives because they always have hidden reasons for their actions," she said. "And yet what can I say? I encouraged your affections five years ago, and I still want you to think fondly of me. But I also feel that you belong with your own people, and that you should not make any lasting decisions until you are given the chance to discover who you really are."

"Yes, but when will that be?" he asked.

"Very soon now, I believe."

CHAPTER SEVENTEEN

A griffon rider arrived in the middle of the day, coming in so quickly from the east that he was already upon the city before he was even aware of the siege. That was probably just as well, since he might not have dared attempt to pass the dragons otherwise, and the dragons might not have allowed him to pass if they hadn't been taken by surprise. The messenger flew his beast low over the city, then made a hurried landing in the main courtyard of the king's palace. Several dragons were following him by that time, although they seemed merely curious and made no attempt to attack him.

The message he had carried all the way from Thyatis was delivered promptly to Darius Glantri, who had gone out to meet him. The messenger found himself pressed into service with the other griffon riders, since his only alternative was to try to depart through the ranks of the dragons. Darius brought the written message to Thelvyn's private chamber immediately. Thelvyn was in the middle of a discussion with Sir George and Captain Gairstaan.

"It's a report from Emperor Cornelius himself," Darius explained, placing the pages of the message on the desk. "My impression is that it's good news. It seems the Alphatians found out that the dragons had been gathering for the invasion of the Highlands. Since the dragons seemed to be otherwise occupied in distant lands, they decided to launch a massive fleet to invade Wendar. Their apparent intent was to occupy the holdings that the dragons had driven them from earlier this year. But an army of dragons met their fleet at sea and destroyed it."

"A second army of dragons?" Sir George asked, his interest suddenly piqued. "When did all of this take place?"

"Three days ago, according to the report," Darius explained. "We've had griffon riders watching the lands of Wendar discreetly since we first learned of the Alphatian trouble. That's how word of it was able to reach us so quickly."

"A second army of dragons indeed," Sir George mused. "The dragons are apparently so up in arms that they can have one army here and a second in Wendar at the same time. I'm not so sure I would call that good news. It means we could be up to our necks in twice as many dragons if it weren't for the stupidity of the Alphatians."

"Yes, I see what you mean," Thelvyn said. "I assumed they had sent every dragon they had here to deal with me. If they kept a second army in reserve back in their own lands, they must be very confident of themselves indeed."

"Unless they never meant to fight in the first place," Sir George reminded him. "In that case, they have all the dragons they need right here."

Gairstaan could only shake his head. "I'm not sure about this. The fact that we could be facing twice as many dragons is actually the good news. The bad news is that the dragons don't feel they need the extra numbers."

"At least I understand the situation a little better now," Thelvyn said. "My guess is that Marthaen had to send away half of his army to deal with the Alphatians. That's why he had to give us time to complete our defenses, and that's why he has seemed to be moving so slowly and cautiously. I thought he was playing games with us, and I assumed the worst. The truth is that he needs to buy time."

"Will this affect the way he plans to negotiate with us?" Darius asked.

Thelvyn shook his head helplessly. "I just don't know. Eventually we will reach an end to negotiations, and Marthaen has to tell me what he really wants. I suspect it has to happen soon, or he's going to have an army from Darokin to deal with as well."

"I'm not so certain he has to worry about that," Darius said. "An army that isn't where it needs to be is worthless. The dragons should find it easy to prevent the Darokin forces from crossing the river."

When all was said and done, Thelvyn felt the message explained to him the meaning only of events that had already occurred. At the most, it allowed him to feel a bit more certain that the dragons hadn't come to fight. He wondered if Marthaen had in fact already laid all his cards on the table, and what he really wanted was the surrender of the Dragonlord. That helped to explain the siege; it was all just an act of intimidation. The problem was that Thelvyn was still only guessing.

As the final day of the truce came to a close, Thelvyn knew that he couldn't give the dragons what they wanted. He was never going to find the Collar of the Dragons soon enough to avert the coming battle, and he had to admit that they were reasonable in their desire to have it returned. His alternatives were becoming increasingly limited. Soon he would either have to fight the dragons or surrender to them. He was no longer hopeful that the dragons would accept his counterproposal to surrender himself to them but keep his armor. While Thelvyn believed that Marthaen personally would agree to such terms, he realized that the First Speaker was subject to the will of all dragons and they wanted to see the Dragonlord defeated.

At least the arrival of a large force of dwarves and elves, something the dragons did not know about, might make them a bit more reasonable about coming to terms—especially now that the companies from Darokin were only two days away. A thousand dragons was a tremendous force, but even they could not easily fight both the Dragonlord and a combined army of well over thirty thousand men. Still, as Darius Glantri had pointed out, the army from Darokin was useless as long as they were on the wrong side of the river.

With the first light of dawn, plans were already under way to prepare for the very real possibility of battle. Thelvyn was certain that he would have a final chance to speak with Marthaen, and he hoped to be able to give the gold dragon something to think about. He suspected there would be no battle again that day, just another exchange of offers and promises and threats in a final effort to avoid war. Still, he had to be prepared for the chance that the dragons were beginning to feel pressed to resolve the matter in combat. He wanted to keep their attention there at Braejr rather than have them attack the approaching forces from Darokin.

The city of Braejr seemed as prepared for battle as it could be. The Fire Wizards had continued to manipulate the summer storms; either the dragons could not or chose not to interfere with the powers of the Radiance. Although the approach from the south had been kept dry, anticipating the arrival of the companies from Darokin, there had been rain over the city itself the last two nights and everything was fairly wet. Ample supplies of water for fighting fires were at the ready throughout the city. All the Highlands forces were prepared, and there was a crew at duty with every catapult.

Alessa Vyledaar was ready to relay orders to the wizards at the Academy to do whatever they could in defense of the city. The dwarves and elves remained in hiding behind the city wall, waiting to present themselves at a time calculated to surprise the dragons. Darius Glantri had the griffon riders standing by at the north barracks, ready to lead the fierce beasts against the dragons.

The dragons had also been busy during the night. As Thelvyn stood at the parapet above the gate, he could see that they had gathered hundreds of bundles of branches and straw, tied together like stacks of hay, on top of several hills in the distance. There was hardly a dragon to be seen in the sky, but entire rows of the vast creatures waited silently in the fields beyond the city wall. The sight of them waiting patiently on the ground was almost more unsettling than seeing them crowding the air.

"What are they doing?" Thelvyn asked.

"Dragons are not in the habit of mounting attacks against cities," Sir George explained. "I think they're improvising their tactics. The bundles of sticks and straw can be set alight and dropped from considerable height, out of range of our catapults. That allows the dragons to attack us without exposing themselves to danger."

"They won't be out of range of my weapons," Thelvyn said.

"Or from bolts of force projected by the Radiance," Alessa added. "We believe we can weave a net of lightning over the city, but only for several minutes at a time. I believe we can time the use of the magical lightning for when we need it most."

"If the dragons won't talk, then our best hope is to hold out until the army from Darokin can get here," Thelvyn said.

Perhaps Marthaen had seen them gathered on the walkway above the gate. At any rate, at that moment he leaped into the morning sky, gliding slowly along the road leading to the gate. The gold dragon landed about a hundred yards away and folded his wings, then stepped closer to the gate. Once more he sat back on his haunches and lifted his neck so that he could look down upon those who faced him.

"Dragonlord, have you considered our terms for peace?" he asked.

"We have," Thelvyn answered. "As I told you before, I have always intended to surrender the title of king as soon as a suitable replacement can be found. That term will be met. Unfortunately, we haven't been able to locate the Collar of the Dragons. We do not believe that it has been here for some time now. I remind you that renegade dragons were involved in this affair. They most likely were the ones who stole the collar, just as they were the ones who betrayed its existence to the Fire Wizards. Only they know where to find it."

"You are the Dragonlord," Marthaen said. "Our first

treaty gave you the authority to deal with renegades however you see fit."

"And you could have asked for the return of the collar long ago," Thelvyn reminded him. "The same treaty would have obliged me to help you find it. I will help you to search even yet."

"That is no longer the issue," Marthaen said. "I gave you alternate terms for peace. Have you considered those?"

"I have. My response is that I will surrender myself to the dragons, to accompany you to your stronghold and remain in your company, but I will keep the armor and weapons of the Dragonlord. Only in that way can I maintain my duty to the Immortals. The dragons will always have the assurance that I am not somewhere out in the world plotting against them."

Marthaen drew back his head in surprise, lifting his ears. "Your proposal does possess a certain remarkable merit. But I do not believe that the dragons will agree to such terms at this time."

"I cannot forsake my duty," Thelvyn insisted. "I cannot give you the armor of the Dragonlord. Before I would ever surrender, I would be required to fight you, and I think you know the Immortals support me. Perhaps you would prefer to take yet another day to consider that."

Marthaen paused in his response, suddenly aware that companies of dwarves and elvish archers were filing out through the towers along the city wall to take their places behind the parapet, joining the Flaemish defenders and the Ethengar archers already there. The dragon couldn't easily guess their numbers, but he could see that they were spreading out all along the wall. Then, to the dragon's obvious dismay, the griffon riders began to take to the air from the barracks just beyond the main gate, less than a hundred yards away. Thelvyn had to resist the urge to smile when he saw Marthaen lay back his ears to reconsider the matter.

"Yes . . . perhaps we will discuss your offer," he said at last. "Your plan has much to recommend it, not the least being that it is likely to force the dragons and the Dragonlord to make peace. You will have our answer in the morning."

Marthaen turned and withdrew, flying back across the fields. Thelvyn was glad no one along the wall cheered or taunted the dragon as he departed, suspecting that it could only have had a detrimental effect on a potential truce.

Thelvyn didn't deceive himself into believing that the dragons would conclude that they no longer possessed the strength they needed to take Braejr. Marthaen would wait only until he could make some determination about the number of elves and dwarves now within the city. Possibly he would also make certain that there were no companies hidden in the forests waiting to attack them from behind. But the dragons would not be discouraged from their plans simply because of the presence of the dwarvish and elvish defenders, or even the griffon riders. The best he could hope for was that it would influence their decision about whether or not to accept Thelvyn's latest offer.

"Well, at least we've bought ourselves another day," he told the others. "That leaves us tomorrow to worry about. If we can hold out till then, the forces from Darokin should be here. I'm just not sure what we can do about getting them across the river and inside the city. Korinn, I never did find out how you were able to get your own people across the river, especially after the Ethengar slipped through only the day before."

"It was simple enough," the dwarf insisted. "The elves tied a rope to an arrow and shot it into a wooden post on the other side of the river, down along the docks on the south side of the city. After that, they needed no time at all to get a couple of rope bridges in place."

Thelvyn said nothing. That might have worked for the ingenious elves and dwarves, but it wouldn't get the soldiers from Darokin across the river. The dragons had been taken by surprise the first time, but they knew of the approach of the forces from Darokin, and they weren't about to allow another entire army to slip across the river.

"Are the dragons likely to accept your offer?" Solveig asked.

"I have no way of knowing," Thelvyn admitted. "Marthaen will go along with it, I'm sure, but the others won't be so easy to convince. That's the trouble with dealing with a dragon of integrity. A red dragon like Jherdar would have simply told his followers what he had decided. Jherdar wouldn't even consider moving the Dragonlord into his own home unless Marthaen was there to argue the matter."

Korinn made an impatient noise. "I don't like the thought of you going off alone with these dragons."

"He won't be alone," Sir George interjected. "I plan to go with him. The dragons don't have to agree to take me; I have the rare privilege of being able to claim that right. And Kharendaen will be there as well."

"I never much trusted her either," Solveig remarked softly.

"You wouldn't want her to hear you say that," Sir George warned her.

A watch was kept at all times now in case the dragons attacked without warning. Thelvyn suspected privately that it would do no real good. The dragons were so swift and they were camped so close, at least by dragon reckoning, that they could be over the wall before anything could be done to stop them. But the dragons had never yet pressed their advantage since they had first come into the Highlands, and he didn't believe that they would now. Either they remained supremely confident or else they knew that they wouldn't have to fight.

The day passed slowly, with nothing to do but wait. There was no longer any hope that the Collar of the Dragons would be found and their enemy would be appeased, and there was nothing more they could do to prepare the city for battle. Thelvyn wished that there had been more optimism among his companions and advisors, but they understood the reality of the situation only too well. Sir George seemed to believe that battle was now unavoidable, and Thelvyn was increasingly inclined to agree. Korinn, like Alessa, Captain Gairstaan, and the other Flaem, actually preferred to have a chance to bash the heads of a few dragons. Only Sellianda still seemed to believe that the dragons didn't want to fight, and since she was privy to the guidance of the Immortals, Thelvyn wondered if she knew something that the others did not. That wasn't to say she was hopeful about the situation; indeed, her mood was best described as one of weary resignation.

The dragons made their response to the arrival of the dwarves and elves that same evening. Thelvyn and the others had been called to the wall because the dragons were gathering again in the fields, waiting patiently. At first Thelvyn wondered if Marthaen was ready to give his answer early, but the First Speaker never approached the city.

Then, just as the first stars were beginning to appear, rank upon rank of dragons began to approach from the north, more golds and reds, and more blue, black, and green dragons than ever. As the defenders watched from atop the walls of the city, an entire second army of dragons arrived in a matter of only minutes, sweeping down from the north in wave after wave, like the autumn migration of birds. In a matter of minutes, the force of dragons had doubled. The army that had been in the east to deal with the Alphatians had returned, and Thelvyn felt certain that Marthaen was through waiting.

The dragons weren't through demonstrating their strength, however. While they had done nothing more than show themselves in the past, flying well within sight of the city, they had never before engaged in any openly destructive or threatening gestures. Now they prepared a more violent demonstration of their fury, to remind the defenders of Braejr just how fierce and dangerous dragons could be.

Through most of the early night, waves of red and gold dragons hurtled out of the darkness to sweep in low over the hills, striking with their flames against any target they could find. Barns and homesteads were swept by deadly blasts of dragonfire so intense that the buildings actually exploded from the sudden buildup of heat. Soon all the farms surrounding the city, previously spared, were in flames, and the lights from their fires ringed Braejr on all sides.

The attacks on the countryside finally began to diminish, and the people of Braejr at last began to retire to their beds. But just when things had been fairly quiet for a time, a new and more deadly attack commenced. Late that night, several hours after midnight, fire began to drop from the sky to crash in small explosions of sparks and flame on the roofs and streets of the city. Sir George had guessed correctly. The dragons were taking the bundles of straw and branches they had gathered up to a great height, then setting the bundles aflame with their breath and dropping the burning debris more or less at random throughout the city.

Fortunately most of the roofs of the city were made of slate or clay tiles, and much that might have fed the fires had already been moved to safety. At first it was little more than a nuisance as the flaming bundles hurtled down from unseen heights. But then the deadly barrage became unexpectedly intense as the city came under a hail of flame, hundreds of bundles of fire descending like shooting stars. As well protected as Braejr had been, flames soon began to shoot up throughout the city, especially in the more vulnerable workshops and warehouses near the rivers. For nearly an hour, it was as if the legendary Rain of Fire had descended upon Braejr. Fear began to spread faster than the flames themselves. Although great stores of water had been set aside to battle this very threat, no one dared go outside to fight the fires while so many of the burning bundles were still falling.

Unfortunately, there was little that either Thelvyn or the Fire Wizards could do to stop it. The dragons were flying extremely high, so high that even Thelvyn's sharp eyes and night vision could not easily identify them, and they were beyond the effective reach of the weapons of the Dragonlord and the Radiance. And yet, Thelvyn knew, this was merely a statement, not a full-fledged attack. The dragons ended their barrage after about an hour, having proven the point that they could act against Braejr with relative impunity.

Once the danger had passed, the people of the city hurried to put out the fires before they could spread. Because of advance precautions, and also because the Flaem had built the city mostly of heavy stone, the flaming bundles had started relatively few actual fires. No more than three or four dozen buildings had burned throughout the city, although some of the fires had spread from lack of attention. The flames cast an eerie flickering light across the city, illuminating the bottom of the dense curtain of smoke that hung over Braejr.

"I don't know what else I can do," Thelvyn told his companions as they watched from one of the towers of the king's palace. "I should have expected that Marthaen would call in reinforcements if the odds were no longer strictly in his favor. I'm still not certain this is an indication of his willingness to fight as much as an added incentive for me to accept a settlement on his terms."

"You don't plan to surrender yet, do you?" Alessa asked, concerned.

Thelvyn shook his head. "I told Marthaen that I could never simply relinquish the armor and weapons of the Dragonlord, and I'm sure he believes me. What I expect is that he put on this show tonight to remind us of what the dragons are capable of. He'll make his own counterproposal in the morning. At least I hope so. The others, especially the red dragons, might demand more than I can give them, and if Marthaen can't convince them otherwise then we will have a battle."

Korinn frowned fiercely, still staring at the dragons as they resumed their attacks on the countryside beyond Braejr. "We've been in some rough places before, and we always came through. I thought that the Immortals protected you."

"It's not so much that they protect me as they have plans for me," he explained as he sat wearily in an opening in the parapet. "I've always expected that I would eventually end up among the dragons, which is apparently where I have to be to fulfill their prophecy. Perhaps now is the time for that to happen. My duty doesn't require that I win all my battles, only that I do what is best to suit the ultimate goals I have been given. My only concern now is that we must not go to war over this."

"That depends a great deal upon the stubbornness of dragons," Sir George reminded him. "Marthaen might be fairly reasonable, but the last thing most dragons want is for you to become directly involved in their affairs."

Thelvyn nodded. "Unfortunately, I know that only too well."

As the night of danger and fear deepened toward a dawn of uncertainty, the defenders began to hope the dragons would grant them at least a few brief hours of peace. Thelvyn sent his companions home to rest, knowing that the next day would begin early and might prove to be an especially long day. He himself found it impossible to rest; not being human, he had discovered that a good night's sleep was far less important to him now that he was older. He had too many questions yet to confront, and the time had come that his decisions had to be the right one. He couldn't predict whether Marthaen would accept his proposal or demand war, and he had to know the best way to respond however things turned out.

More than ever Thelvyn regretted that the Immortals wouldn't advise him as they would true clerics. There was so much he needed desperately to know. He had provoked the dragons, mostly on the advice he had received from his own mother in the dream he had shared with Kharendaen. As a result, he had inflamed their deepest fears, and now he was afraid they would not rest until they had defeated him. If it had been his choice, he would have given them the armor of the Dragonlord if that's what it took to placate them. And yet he knew that only the Dragonlord could stop them if they once again went on the rampage as they have five years before.

For that reason, Thelvyn felt certain that he had to retain the armor no matter what. He wasn't afraid to fight dragons, but he was very reluctant to inflict the injury and death such a battle would require of him. He was just as reluctant to allow the destruction that Braejr would be forced to endure.

After a time, he went back up to the wall to watch the dragons. The fires they had set earlier had since burned themselves out, although dragons continued to circle and dart in mock attacks, their flames flashing in the darkness. He was surprised to find Sellianda sitting in one of the openings along the parapet, calmly watching the dragons. She glanced at him as he approached, then rose to face him.

"Are you worried?" she asked.

Thelvyn shook his head. "Just impatient. I won't know what to do until Marthaen gives me his answer to my proposal. I just don't know whether or not the other dragons are going to allow him to come to any peaceful solution."

"I doubt that there is any such contention among the dragons," Sellianda told him. "They made their decision even before they left the mountains to come down into the Highlands. They know Marthaen's policies, and they have long since given him their trust. Contrary to what everyone thinks, that dragons are fiercely independent and driven by violent impulses, they would not undertake such an important matter as going to war without first being very certain of their intentions."

They turned back to the opening in the parapet to watch the dragons for a time. Sellianda sat close beside Thelvyn, not to deliberately distract him but as a natural and unintended expression of her affection. She had been an enigma to Thelvyn since her arrival in Braejr. He felt certain that she loved him, but she was obviously waiting for the conflict with the dragons to conclude, never permitting her personal interests to interfere with her duty as a cleric.

"I know you do not want to fight the dragons," she said at last.

"I just wish I knew what Marthaen is going to do," Thelvyn said wearily.

Sellianda glanced down, as if considering a difficult decision. "Perhaps I should not be saying this, but I think you are looking for complex answers when the obvious one is correct. Do you not suppose that the dragons know what you can do to them if they force you to fight them without constraint?"

"Of course they do," Thelvyn answered. "That's why my first inclination is that they have no intention of fighting me. The cost to them would be too high."

"Then what alternative do they have?" she asked. "They know that the Fire Wizards nearly defeated you by impeding the enchantments of your armor. They know little about the Radiance, but they know their own magic. The magic of dragons is unlike all others, and the greatest of the dragon sorcerers command powers nearly those of an Immortal. Perhaps they think they can subdue or even destroy the enchantments of the Dragonlord."

"I hadn't considered that," Thelvyn admitted thoughtfully. "Is this something your patron has allowed you to know?"

"No, I am only guessing. But—" she hesitated, glancing down—"I do love you, and I intend to stay at your side and share your fate."

* * * * *

Once again the city of Braejr began to prepare for battle before dawn. The crews readied their catapults, and archers lined the parapets. All the wooden roofs were wetted down with water from the river, and the water set aside for fighting fires was refilled. At sunrise the dragons responded with a new tactic. They gathered in ranks according to breed in the field before the main gate, just beyond bow shot. They appeared from a distance almost like the squares of a chessboard, all in different colors, with red and black squares but also many of gold, green, and blue. More bundles of wood and straw had been laid out in rows before them.

In spite of Sellianda's assurances, Thelvyn still didn't know whether they had come to fight or to talk. If they had come to fight and he tried to force the dragons to retreat with a minimum of death and injury, then the battle would only be prolonged and Braejr would suffer all the more. Or, like the first Dragonlord, he could wreak ruthless destruction upon the ranks of the dragons and settle the matter quickly. He considered all he knew about dragons, about how much they feared the Dragonlord and how much they valued life, and he couldn't believe that they would drive themselves to certain death in a hopeless battle. And yet they had once before, a very long time ago, almost to the destruction of their kind.

Thelvyn went up to the main gate as soon as the dragons began to assemble. Marthaen would want to talk with him one last time, if for no other reason than to demand his surrender. He had been watching them for some time, trying to see what they were doing, when Sir George joined him.

"An elvish scout entered the city just before sunrise," the old knight said. "He reported that other bands of elves have been watching the approach of a small army of orcs and goblins out of the Broken Lands. They're up in the hills across the river, still hours away."

"Have they been summoned to serve the dragons?" Korinn asked.

Sir George shook his head. "Only renegades make alliances with orcs or other such creatures. Other dragons consider them beneath their dignity. I would say that our new friends have gotten wind of the upcoming battle and are waiting to pick through the spoils of Braejr after the dragons have taken what they want."

"Well, I certainly don't need to ask them what they think of our chances," Thelvyn remarked dryly.

"You don't seem too concerned, lad," Sir George observed.

"Me?" Thelvyn asked. "I feel as if the world is about to end, but I've been expecting it for so long that there seems to be nothing left for me to do but wait for it to happen."

"You don't believe that we can win?" Solveig asked.

"Oh no. On the contrary, I don't see how we can lose," he said, turning to wave his arm from west to east across the field. "I could draw my sword and rain so much destruction down upon them that a third of them would die before they could scatter, and they know it. They aren't here to fight. Look at them. They're just waiting, as if they've been brought here to witness something. What does Marthaen plan to do that has them so satisfied?"

The First Speaker of the Dragons was approaching at last, gliding slowly toward Braejr. He circled low over the city once in a bold display, knowing he was within range of the catapults. Then he turned, landed lightly with powerful sweeps of his wings, and stepped up to the gate.

"Dragonlord, are you prepared to surrender your armor?" he asked as he settled back on his haunches and lifted his head level with the parapet.

"I am not," Thelvyn answered. "My duty forbids it. Have you considered my offer to come and stay among the dragons?"

"There is nothing to consider," the dragon replied. "Whether you come or go is no longer relevant after this day. I cannot fight you, and I cannot take the armor from you by stealth or by force. But what I can do is defeat you with words. I know something about you that you do not even know yourself, a truth so terrible that the knowledge of it will destroy all the trust you have earned. It is the only weapon that I have against you, and now I must use it."

Thelvyn braced himself, understanding too late. He saw both Sir George and Sellianda look away, unable to face the dragon, and he realized that they had always known but were unable to tell him. Korinn looked skeptical, certain in his belief that nothing could turn him against his friend. Hundreds of defenders along the wall had fallen deathly silent, waiting for the dragon to speak even if they were not prepared to believe his words.

"All these grand gestures have been but the stage that I have set," Marthaen continued. "I have been in absolute command of this situation since before the dragons entered this land, and all of these ploys have only served to prepare for this moment. But I confess that the only joy I take in this is in the knowledge that no one will be made to suffer or die for our victory. I regret that the price will be paid in your own pain and in that of your companions, who have been devoted to you. Even the pain of my own sister Kharendaen, who has loved you for years."

He glanced briefly over his shoulder to the north, to where the dragons waited in silence. At last he sighed, laying back his ears, and turned back to the Dragonlord.

"Several years ago, a time of great trouble and uncertainty came upon the dragons," he began. "Part of this you know already. The Great One had left us. For the first time in centuries, the dragons were without guidance. We had not been required to make decisions for ourselves in a long time and thus we were not especially good at it. No one knew whether the Great One had left us by his own choice or if the other Immortals had taken him from us. No one knew when he would return, and many feared that he was gone forever."

Thelvyn nodded. "I know of this."

"That was only the beginning," Marthaen said. "Into this conflict came the prophecy of the Dragonlord, a prophecy that told us that the Dragonlord would return, and that he would become the ruler of all dragons, and that he would set into motion events that would shape the destiny of the dragons forever. Perhaps it was foolish of the dragons to see the prophecy only as a portent of doom. I am inclined to believe that if you change our destiny, it will likely be for the better. But the name of the Dragonlord was a part of that prophecy, and that has always been a name that held nothing but terror for us.

"The Nation of Dragons was in a state of chaos, and a faction of rogue dragons panicked. They did something terrible, turning not upon their own kind but upon our clerics. They learned that the Dragonlord was to be born of one of the clerics, and they felt betrayed by not only the clerics but by the Great One himself."

"My mother was a cleric of the Great One?" Thelvyn asked in amazement.

"As are you, I believe," Marthaen agreed. "Your mother was Arbendael, a senior cleric of the Great One and a gold dragon. I cannot tell you who your father was, whether he was also a dragon or of some other race. Your mother was enchanted into human form so that you would be born the person you needed to be to become the Dragonlord, not hatched as a dragon from an egg."

"Then what you are saying is that I am a dragon?" Thelvyn asked. Of all possibilities, this was the one thing that he hadn't expected. He had always understood that dragons could only give birth to their young while both mother and child were in their true form, and so he had never dreamed that he was, by some unknown means, an exception to that rule.

"Strictly speaking, you are not a dragon and never have been," Marthaen told him. "The form you wear is that of the Eldar, the ancient ancestors of the elves, after the dragons themselves the strongest, heartiest, most powerful race of sorcerers and clerics this world has ever known. But you possess the heritage of a gold dragon from your mother, and I suspect you command the power to break the enchantment and assume your true form."

Thelvyn shook his head slowly, looking up at the dragon. "But—but—"

"Of your history, I am sure that you can surmise the rest," Marthaen went on. "The rogue dragons came to destroy your mother in the most sacred of sanctuaries of the Great One in the mountain forests of Wendar. But she had already taken the only form you knew her by, and she had fled into the mountains. They hunted her ruthlessly. They even fought her in a desperate battle of flames and magic in which five red dragons died and your mother suffered her fatal injury. Perhaps it was chance, or perhaps it was the intervention of the Great One himself, that Sir George was there to care for you. He has served you better than you may know, and you must not begrudge him for keeping your secret from you."

"I speak the language of the dragons, lad," Sir George explained. "I understood everything your mother told me, even your name—your real name, that is."

"My real name?" Thelvyn asked, his mind reeling.

"Your true name is Thelvaenir of the gold dragons," Marthaen told him. "Consider all that you know about yourself, and you will see the truth. Have you never realized that you have the same black on blue eyes as the gold dragons? Do you not know that you have the same farseeing vision as a dragon, sharp enough to spy an elk in the woods from five miles away, able to pierce the darkest night? Are you not both a wizard and a cleric, a remarkable situation known to exist only among dragons? Does not the close approach of a dragon cause you to instinctively draw back in alarm, as it would any dragon?"

Thelvyn shook his head slowly. "No . . . you misunderstand. I don't doubt anything you've told me. Now that the truth is out, it's as if I've always known. I don't deny anything; I just want to know more."

"Perhaps, but this is not the time," Marthaen replied.

"Kharendaen will return to you soon, and she will tell you what you must do next. All I know is that circumstances have changed radically. You must not come among the dragons unless you are prepared to do so as a dragon."

"Then I will seek Kharendaen," Thelvyn said meekly.

"My part is now finished. Perhaps I have done it entirely too well," the leader of the dragons continued. "We were afraid that you would become a king and a conqueror, and we feared that the distrust all other races have of dragons would gain you their support and following. Since then I have learned that you never wished to be king, but the damage is done. Now the Dragonlord will have no place in the world except among dragons. According to prophecy, that is where you belong."

Thelvyn looked up at him. "I don't understand. . . ."

"That is why I have betrayed you publicly. You may have lost the trust of all the rest of the world, but you have taken the first step in earning the trust of the dragons. We no longer fear you. You know that you are one of us, and the dragons know that you will not harm us. Whether you come to us remains to be seen. You must now have some time to consider all that you have learned, to see what your place will be in the world after this day, and perhaps even to realize that being a dragon is not such a bad thing after all. Unfortunately, at this moment you must feel that you have become your own worst enemy."

"No, that's not it," Thelvyn said. "I think perhaps there are a few things even you do not understand. Just because I am the Dragonlord has never meant that I hate or fear dragons. You associate me with your legends, comparing me to someone I've never known. I have never considered myself the enemy of the dragons. I have always understood that I was given the powers of the Dragonlord to prevent the dragons from doing harm to others and bringing harm upon themselves. The first Dragonlord was a warrior. I am a cleric."

"That is something the dragons could never believe until it was proven," Marthaen said.

"Then they should also understand that the Great One never betrayed them," Thelvyn continued. "As you said, a time of chaos had come upon the dragons. The Great One saw that the dragons should not, in their fury and fear, put themselves at odds with the world. Only the Dragonlord could prevent the dragons from going to war, and who better to perform that task than a dragon?"

Marthaen remained silent.

"There is one other thing you should understand," Thelvyn went on. "I am still the Dragonlord, and I still have my duty. Learning my secrets does not change that."

"No, I don't suppose it would," the dragon said. "But now I must go."

Marthaen turned and, in three powerful leaps, thrust himself into the morning sky and rose steadily as he flew to the north, withdrawing to the wooded hills many miles beyond the city. Rank after rank, the dragons all spread their wings and ascended to follow him, passing in waves over the city before they banked sharply to pass in a seemingly endless line to the north. In a matter of minutes, the last of the dragons had withdrawn to the forests and hills beyond the fields, where they settled in once again to wait.

CHAPTER EIGHTEEN

By that evening, the balance of power was already beginning to change drastically. Seeking forage for their horses, the Ethengar had moved out into the open fields north of the city between the two rivers, where the dragons had gathered that very morning. The army from Darokin arrived at sundown and made camp on the south side of the Areste River, where it seemed perfectly content to remain. The dragons themselves were now camped well to the north, beyond the camps of the Ethengar. Dragons continued to scout the region, but less frequently and in fewer numbers, and they were flying higher to appear less threatening.

At first Thelvyn thought they would depart for their own lands now that their task was complete, but on further consideration, he knew what they were waiting for. Marthaen had planted the seed of dissension; the news that the Dragonlord was himself a dragon in enchanted form had been calculated to destroy the trust of his allies. Marthaen was waiting for a sign of confirmation that his plan had worked, and the ultimate sign was the departure of the allied armies. The quickest way for him to be rid of the dragons, Thelvyn realized to his wry amusement, was through the collapse of his own fortunes.

Ironically, none of this had really been necessary. If he had only been in communication with Marthaen, the gold dragon wouldn't have found it necessary to discredit the Dragonlord in the eyes of all the world. He couldn't blame Marthaen, since he understood how easy it would have been for the dragon to assume that his becoming the King of the Highlands had been the actions of a person hungry for power. His only consolation was that perhaps things had turned out for the best. The dragons would not be going to war, and he was free of all past ties and could confront his true duty.

The dragons had correctly anticipated a loss of faith in the Dragonlord, but it did not come all at once. The trust of most people in the Dragonlord to protect them had been so great they resisted the news that he was a dragon at first. Relatively few of the defenders along the wall had been close enough to actually hear the words of the gold dragon, so that most learned the news only by way of a rather astonishing rumor that swept through the city that afternoon. For the time being, at least, nearly everyone was so boundlessly pleased that there would not be a battle that they hardly cared whether their king was a dragon, an elf, or a pig-faced orc.

Even so, Thelvyn had a lifetime of experience with the Flaemish distrust of foreigners, and he knew that they would turn against him sooner or later. The only immediate result was that the army of marauders from the Broken Lands gave up and returned home in disgust.

Thelvyn disassociated himself from taking an active part in the leadership of the Highlands, leaving the planning for bringing Braejr down from a state of siege to Captain Gairstaan and Solveig. The tall barbarian woman had earned a certain fondness with the Flaem from her part in the attack the night of the reception for the ambassador from Darokin; the popular story held that she had received her wounds in a noble sacrifice to save the life of the Dragonlord. She was already well known in that part of the world as one of the companions of the Dragonlord, and her reputation did not suffer because of his disgrace.

Curiously, Sir George didn't take advantage of his own reputation to assume a role of leadership. When Thelvyn considered this fact, he realized what the old knight had already figured out. Thelvyn would likely be leaving the Highlands soon to begin a long journey that would eventually take him to the dragons. And Sir George meant to go along.

"Are you upset, lad?" Sir George asked that night as he and Sellianda sat with Thelvyn in the king's private chamber.

"Upset?" Thelvyn asked, leaving his quiet thoughts to look up. "Should I be upset?"

"Well, you've had a bit of a shock," the old knight said. "Dragons killed your mother, and they've tried to kill you even since they discovered that you were still alive. Being told that you're secretly a dragon must be quite a surprise under any circumstances."

"No . . . I can't really say that I'm upset," Thelvyn answered thoughtfully. "I suppose that it isn't any great surprise to be told something you've always known in your heart. I don't hate dragons, so that doesn't distress me. I admit that I'm feeling a bit sad, though."

"How is that?"

Thelvyn shrugged helplessly. "You know all of the stories I invented to tell myself who I was, mostly that I was descended from the race of ancient Blackmoor. Of course, you knew the truth all along."

"There was no special race of ancient Blackmoor," Sir George explained. "They were perfectly ordinary people, common mortals very much like those who live in this part of the world today. The only difference was that they knew a great deal about magic and science, and they were able to put the two together."

"Which is why you always knew that I wasn't one of the legendary half-elves," Thelvyn said to Sellianda. "You always did know who I was, didn't you?"

She nodded. "I knew from the first, which is why the question of who you really were has never made any difference to me."

"Solveig could hardly care less," Thelvyn said. "Although I'm sure this is going to create a political mess for Korinn. Or did they know as well?"

"No, I never told anyone," Sir George insisted. "You might recall my telling you that a dragon or dragonkin will almost always recognize another on sight, no matter what form the dragon might take. That's how the dragons knew who you were from the first time they saw you at Torkyn Fall. And that was why I recognized your mother for who she was the moment I saw her. Of course, she knew who I was at once as well, which was why she trusted me with the truth. I swore a promise of duty very much the same as that of a cleric that night, a promise that I later found increasingly hard to keep. I knew how much you wanted to go home, but I was always afraid that you wouldn't like the truth."

"I always imagined my people lived in some faraway land so remote and forgotten that no one had ever heard of them," Thelvyn continued sadly. "For years I've lived with a fond dream of a grand homecoming. I remember the first time I met my mother's spirit, the day we ascended World Mountain. I assumed the spirit of the gold dragon chased her away before she could reveal any important secrets, but now I know that the gold dragon was her in her true form."

"World Mountain is the gateway to the spirit world," Sellianda explained. "She would have found it easier to manifest herself there, although she obviously didn't find it so easy to maintain the illusion of her enchanted form."

Thelvyn looked at Sir George. "Now I'm more curious than ever why you didn't betray me at once to the rogue dragons. You knew they were in the mountains that night looking for me. I daresay they would have given you a great reward for your assistance."

"I had promised your mother not to betray you," the old knight said, looking a bit embarrassed. "From the moment she first looked at me, I could never say no to her. Besides, the Great One had told her you were very important to the future of the dragons, which she repeated to me. I wasn't about to cross the will of the Great One."

Hiding a smile, Thelvyn said no more about the matter. He knew Sir George well enough by that time to be aware of his secret admiration and respect for dragons. The wishes of the Great One were law to him, a loyal drake. He had been honored and enormously pleased to serve.

"What will you do now?" Thelvyn asked Sellianda. "Your duty here must be nearing an end."

"It is also my duty to remain with you until Kharendaen returns," she said. "And she cannot come to you while you remain here in Braejr."

* * * * *

Things were beginning to change even by the next morning, and very much along anticipated lines. A rumor was already going through Braejr that the recent troubles with the dragons had been entirely a struggle between the dragons and the Dragonlord for control of the Highlands, and that the Flaem wouldn't have been involved at all but for them. It was likely that very few people actually believed that rumor. They remembered only too well how determined King Jherridan had been to go to war with the dragons and that Thelvyn had actually opposed such drastic actions. And no one had forgotten the treachery of the wizards.

Still, there was a growing suspicion that Thelvyn was in some way responsible for recent events, at least by implication. The general opinion was that the Dragonlord was dangerous to have about, no matter how benevolent his intentions. Unfortunately, there was some truth in that. The only thing Thelvyn could do at that time to avoid a crisis of confidence was to let it be known, by formal decree, that he would be relinquishing the throne as soon as a capable replacement could be found, and that he was calling together a council of special advisors to select the next king. Under the circumstances, he would not be naming his own successor.

Thelvyn found that he was not the only one who had been left in a difficult position. The demands of both politics and prejudice required Korinn Bear Slayer to break all ties with Thelvyn, betraying their long friendship, something a dwarf was especially loath to do. Korinn was trapped by his own duty. He couldn't afford a blemish on his reputation, since it might threaten his claim to the throne of Rockhome. His brother Dorinn had been gravely wounded in battle in the Broken Lands, and he seemed unlikely to recover enough to be considered fit to be king, so it was becoming increasingly likely that Korinn would be his father's heir. Because dwarves considered dragons their special enemies, his association with the Dragonlord had abruptly changed from being an asset to being a potential liability.

Thelvyn could understand Korinn's need to distance himself from the Dragonlord, and he didn't blame the dwarf in the least. But he was not completely without friends. Solveig hardly cared what anyone thought about her, yet curiously the Flaem thought rather highly of her. Thelvyn's other chief supporter was Captain Gairstaan, who remained loyal and devoted both publicly and privately. He knew better than anyone how hard Thelvyn had worked to spare the Highlands from devastation, and he felt that there was a debt to be paid.

At least Thelvyn did not yet have any open adversaries, although he expected the Fire Wizards would turn against him in the hope of salvaging something of their own damaged reputation at his expense. He also wondered if one or more of the dukes would turn against him in a bid to claim the throne, although he considered that unlikely. The problem wasn't so much in deciding upon a successor as in finding someone both willing and capable of being the next king. Any one of the dukes could have probably been king by the end of the week simply by coming to Braejr and asking for the job.

When Solveig and Gairstaan came to the palace at noon, at least they had something encouraging to report. With an army of dragons only a few miles to the north, they had been required to maintain the city in a fairly high state of readiness for battle. The threat of war was greatly reduced, but the siege itself was not yet lifted.

"Our scouts have noticed something odd," Gairstaan explained as they conferred over a hasty lunch. "It seems that there aren't nearly as many dragons in this area as there were. Perhaps as many as half of them have gone."

"That was to be expected," Thelvyn said. "They might have won a battle, but the dragons are still at war with the Alphatians. I'm sure Marthaen felt the need to get an army back east as quickly as possible. We knew that many dragons couldn't remain in this area for long. Dragons are fairly active and they eat a lot. Obviously game is becoming scarce."

"I wonder why they don't just leave altogether," Solveig remarked.

"They might just as well, frankly," Thelvyn said. "But they won't leave until they see what happens next, whether or not our alliance is going to fall apart. Of course, no one else is going to leave while the dragons are still there."

"I suspect the dwarves are seriously tempted to go home under any circumstances," Gairstaan commented. "I think the elves from Alfheim want to go home as well, since they don't see much possibility of a fight."

"If we want to get rid of the dragons, we need to encourage the others to leave," Thelvyn said.

Part of the problem with having so many armies at hand was that they were even more inclined than the people of Braejr to grumble, and no one was louder at grumbling than the dwarves. Open resentment and suspicion directed toward the Dragonlord was becoming commonplace by that night, and it appeared to have started with disgruntled dwarvish fighters who had been trying to find entertainment in a city full of people nearly as reserved and suspicious of strangers as themselves. Although the Darokin forces remained firmly encamped on the far side of the Areste, soldiers from their army were also coming into Braejr in small bands, and they were quick to express their own opinions.

The people of Braejr hardly knew what to think at first. They had given their trust to the Dragonlord, and he had never betrayed them in any actual deed. But the betrayal by their own wizards and the violent death of their first king had left them suspicious and angry, and their trust was fragile. Their fear of dragons was second only to their ancient hatred of the Alphatians, so when others began to condemn the Dragonlord openly, their words did not fall on deaf ears.

For these reasons, Thelvyn was surprised when Korinn came to speak with him that night. The dwarf seemed especially uncomfortable, knowing that he must seem faithless to his old friend. It undoubtedly made it easier for him that Thelvyn was alone in his private chamber with Sellianda. Neither Sir George nor Solveig were there.

"You probably shouldn't have come," Thelvyn said as he welcomed the young dwarf. "Do any of your people know you are here?"

"Only those few I trust best," Korinn said. "You seem to know what the problem is."

"Of course I do," Thelvyn insisted, passing him a cup of ale. "I know better than to think that you would ever turn against me."

"It was a difficult choice," Korinn said sourly, taking an empty chair and staring at his ale. "Either I betray my friends or I fail my family and clan. If keeping my reputation weren't so critical to the future of Rockhome, I would never be acting this way. I've learned that my own warriors are spreading false rumors, and I'm in no position to stop them."

"They haven't done any real harm," Thelvyn assured him. "The wizards are going to be spreading rumors and turning the Highlands against me soon enough, if they haven't already. It's not as if I'm fighting to keep the throne. I'm just trying to hold on long enough to get things settled and find a suitable successor. But the dragons won't leave until they see what happens, and no one else will go home until the dragons do. I had rather hoped the dwarves felt put out by the whole affair and were ready to leave."

"They are," Korinn said. "But it's a matter of pride. No dwarf wants to be the first to walk away, especially while the dragons are still out there. That would seem faithless and cowardly. Of course, it never occurred to me that you actually needed us to go."

"I do," Thelvyn said, "but not if it would harm your reputation in any way. Besides, I wouldn't be surprised if the Ethengar head for home in the morning. They were never as ready to fight dragons as they thought."

"Well, I should be going," Korinn said, rising. "I'm sorry it's had to come to this. I hope things settle down in a couple of years so that you can return to visit me in Dengar. But you have to promise to keep your dragon's claws off my treasure."

Thelvyn laughed. "I promise. But don't expect me to call until after the matter of the succession of the next king is settled. That might be some time yet. I don't want to risk upsetting things."

Korinn bowed and left quietly. Taeryn had been waiting outside the door to show him out. Thelvyn had to wonder if he would ever see the young dwarf again. He had taken Kharendaen on errands to Dengar in the past, but he knew it would be a long time before he would be welcome in Rockhome again. Once Korinn was gone, he noticed that Sellianda seemed to be quietly amused about something.

"You already possess the hoard of the greatest of the renegade kings," she said. "Any dwarf would pull out his beard with envy over such a treasure."

"I'd forgotten about that," he admitted. "I suppose Marthaen was deliberately doing me a favor when he insisted that the treasure belonged to me."

"He is trying his best to support you even yet," she said sincerely.

"I was also wondering if the assumption that I really am a dragon might be a bit premature, regardless of the fact that my mother was a gold dragon. It might be easy to assume that my father was also a dragon, but we don't know that for a fact. Or do we?"

Sellianda shook her head. "No one but your mother, your father, and the Great One himself knows who your father is."

"I don't have the faintest idea how to assume the form of

a dragon," Thelvyn said.

"Of course not. You are under a powerful enchantment that prevents you from taking your true form. The circumstances of your birth required it. Your mother could not have given birth to you if the enchantment holding both of you in this form had not been very secure. You will not be able to become a dragon until the enchantment is removed. Perhaps only the Great One can do that. But there is much to suggest that you are a dragon nevertheless, not the least being that the command of magic has always come easy to you in spite of the fact that you are also a cleric."

"You told me once that I'm not a true cleric," he reminded her. "You said my status is almost that of a lesser Immortal."

"The status of any powerful dragon cleric is almost that of a lesser Immortal," she explained. "Marthaen told you the other clues to your nature."

"That's true," he conceded. "But there's one thing I wonder about. In my present form, I'm twenty-one years old, and I know that dragons mature very slowly. When I take the form of a dragon, will I be a mature dragon of perhaps a hundred or so, or will I be a twenty-one year old dragon child?"

Sellianda looked rather startled. "I had never thought of that. I really do not know. Frankly, your situation is unprecedented, for no dragon has ever been born in enchanted form. I expect that you would remain mature. It's sad, in a way, that a duty you never asked for has required you to miss a hundred years of childhood."

* * * * *

As Thelvyn had expected, the Ethengar warriors decamped early the next morning, filing across the Aalban Bridge just north of Braejr. That led them into the wild lands east of the river, lands held by the elves of the southern Highlands but sparsely inhabited. Soon they would pass through the hills between the Colossus Mounts on the north and the Broken Lands on the south, both rugged and dangerous lands. But their numbers were too great to worry much about being attacked by orcs or other evil folk, and the Ethengar probably would have welcomed a fight in any event. Since the war with the dragons had turned out to be rather disappointing, they needed a good battle to restore their pride.

The dwarves intended to start for home as soon as they could. To observe formalities, Korinn and his captains approached Thelvyn that morning to ask if their presence was still required. The general in command of the forces of Darokin made his intentions known later the same day, pointing out the urgency of returning to the south before the summer rains made the wilderness roads unpassable. Only the elves of Alfheim seemed in no hurry to leave; the truth of the Dragonlord's heritage had never concerned them in the least.

Thelvyn's reputation took a rather serious turn for the worse that day, if that were possible. The new rumor was that he had always known he was secretly a dragon, and he would have continued to deceive his allies and the people he was sworn to protect if the dragons hadn't revealed the truth. Most of the people of Braejr didn't believe that, but they were beginning to feel that the Dragonlord must have betrayed them in some way. If nothing else, he was an orphan of unknown origin, suspicious in itself.

The Fire Wizards complicated the picture even more by deciding that it was time to denounce the Dragonlord publicly. They now knew his secrets, and that gave them the ammunition to attack his reputation as effectively as the dragons ever could. They reminded the people of Braejr that he was secretly a cleric, a highly suspicious calling as far as the Flaem were concerned, and most likely a cleric of the Great One, at that. They pointed out that he was a traitor to his own kind, that even the dragons hated and distrusted him. And they were quick to insist that they had always been aware of his hidden evil and had opposed him for that reason.

By late in the day, the wizards were calling upon Thelvyn to surrender the crown at once, suggesting that, by right of Flaemish law, they should rule the Highlands until a new king could be found. This was one matter that Thelvyn would not tamely accept. He didn't care so much about the attack upon himself, but he was still the King of the Highlands, and he took his duty very seriously. The last act he could perform for the good of his realm was to defend the people from themselves. He was determined that the callous, self-serving wizards would never again get close enough to the throne to even dream that they could seize it for themselves. Since there still didn't seem to be any clear leader among the Fire Wizards, Thelvyn called Alessa Vyledaar to his private chamber that evening.

Alessa came willingly, but she was cold and dignified. She was dressed in the stately robes of a sorceress of great power, accented by the stiffened collar worn by the Flaemish aristocracy. Thelvyn didn't rise to greet her, and she remained standing near the door.

"So are you still interested in climbing into my bed?" he asked.

Alessa looked only mildly surprised, recognizing his sarcasm. "Frankly, I think I would find that a delightful experience, but it would hardly be expedient to either of us. Things have changed a good deal in these last few days. Now you are the lord of the dragons, and I know better than to cross you. Perhaps we've been a bit too bold already."

"If you had been patient and waited for me to depart quietly, you could have had your way with the Highlands once I was gone," he told her. "I was going to leave anyway, and you aren't getting rid of me any sooner by spreading malicious lies. In honesty, I think that you would have to admit that I've served the Flaem well. Your wizards certainly can't say that much. So I'm going to pull your fangs before I go. Just as the dragons knew how to deal with me, I know how to deal with you."

Alessa frowned. "You wouldn't be telling me this if there were anything we could do to stop you. I don't suppose you would mind telling me just what you have in mind."

"I really wouldn't want to ruin the surprise," he said. "You should really thank me, although I daresay you won't.

Without the distraction of playing at politics so much, your wizards might actually accomplish something. Would you object to a little advice? Do sit down."

"Why should I object?" she asked as she took a chair across from him. "The wisdom and cunning of dragons is legendary."

"Then try more wisdom and less cunning," he told her. "Your people have been in this world for well over a hundred years now, and quite frankly, you wizards have yet to accomplish anything. You have one of the greatest libraries in the world, and you've learned nothing from it. You possess the power of the Radiance, but you don't know how to command it beyond a few simple parlor tricks. You spend great quantities of time worrying about the reputation you have with your own people, and now you have none. If you spent half as much time being useful, you would never have to be concerned about your reputation."

"You're a foreigner," she said defensively. "You don't understand us. We're the guardians of Flaemish law."

"Don't try that logic on me," Thelvyn told her. "I've lived here all my life. I understand the Flaem perhaps better than they understand themselves, because I've had to make a concerted effort not to be like you. As far as that goes, you need to sit down and rewrite large portions of your book of Flaemish law. Everything you profess to believe in just keeps getting you into trouble. You've destroyed one world, and I hesitate to guess how many more you were chased out of."

"Is the lecture finished yet?" Alessa asked.

"I don't believe in spending too much time wasting my breath," he explained. "And saving the Flaem from themselves isn't my concern. Actually, that's what I'm supposed to do for the dragons."

"Yes, you've handled that well," she said mockingly.

Thelvyn shrugged. "The dragons didn't fight, which would have been to no one's advantage. It might seem that I lost, but I'm inclined to think that everything turned out for the best."

Alessa made a gesture of indifference. "That's just the point, isn't it? I'm rather pleased with the way things turned out. The dragons have been handled without destroying half of Braejr in the process, we'll soon have a new king who will be less suspicious of his wizards, and I've personally profited from it all."

"Indeed? What was your involvement in all of this? Or would you rather not list your schemes?"

"Not in the least," she said, rather pleased with herself. "As you so obviously suspected from the first, Byen Kalestraan himself selected me specifically to keep an eye on you and to influence you in any way I could. And I do mean that literally. Of course, I knew already that Kalestraan and his chosen few were up to something, some bid for power meant to get rid of you and possibly even Jherridan in the process.

"That left me in a rather enviable position. If Kalestraan had succeeded and I had proven my loyalty, I would have moved higher in his favor. But I had realistically considered the chances of even a senior Fire Wizard taking on the most powerful enchantments of ancient Blackmoor, and I realized that you were most likely to win. I did warn you, and I might have told you more, but I expected Kalestraan to try to deal with you before he went after Jherridan, and so I never thought that anyone was in any real danger."

"At least you have some loyalty to your own people," Thelvyn commented.

"Of course, I never expected that you would become the next king," she continued. "Once again I found myself in a position in which I stood only to gain. If you fought the dragons and won, I thought I could convince you to remain king. I would not have minded being your queen, and at the least I expected to use my association with you to help me gain authority in my order now that all of the senior wizards were gone. Of course, once the dragons embarrassed you, I had to cut my ties with you to retain my standing. In fact, I've gained even more power at your expense."

"Very clever," Thelvyn commented. "Have the wizards been able to determine who will become their next leader, or are the politics still too thick to judge?"

"Actually, I'll probably be able to hold on to that position," she told him. "The next few days should tell. There are some wizards with greater experience, but I'm young enough to take best advantage of the current situation in the Highlands. So even if you do have some way to leave us at a permanent disadvantage, I already have nearly everything I could ever hope to have within my own order."

"How remarkable," Thelvyn said. "I should have come to you for lessons in politics five years ago; my own life would have been a great deal less complicated. So what do you plan to do now? You seem to think you've plundered the situation for all it's worth. Do you think you might try to make yourself useful, or are you waiting to see what else you can get?"

Alessa looked perplexed for a brief moment, then glanced up at him. "You think you can leave us in political disgrace?"

"Putting the wizards in political disgrace is not my intention," he told her. "They've already done that to themselves. My intention is to change the way the realm is governed so that no one person or faction can ever again use this country for their own personal ambitions. And you can't oppose me. Whether or not you like to admit it, people still trust me more than they do the wizards. What remains to be seen is whether the wizards have a place in this new government or if they're to be excluded altogether."

"And you never felt yourself capable of playing politics," Alessa said with a sigh. "What else can I say? I am perfectly aware of the magnitude of our disgrace, and they say that discretion is the better part of valor. Therefore the best thing for me is to be gracious in defeat and support you in your plans. Contrary to what you seem to think, I am not without devotion to my land or my people. We have a great deal to rebuild."

"What about the Alphatians?"

She frowned. "Like you, I always knew that we weren't ready to take on the Alphatians, and I'll not allow that to be one of my chief concerns. Your dragons have made any alliance against Alphatia nearly impossible for the foreseeable future. The dragons have so completely destroyed the Alphatian navy that they're no longer much of a threat anyway. No one believes there is a real need for an invasion of Alphatia anymore, and they want to keep their armies close to home. Ourselves included."

"You had better keep looking for the Collar of the Dragons," Thelvyn added. "If you ever trusted me on anything, then believe the dragons will be back for it, and this time I won't try to stop them."

* * * * *

The dwarves left early the next morning, following the trail of the Ethengar as they crossed the Aalban Bridge and marched toward the pass below the Colossus Mounts. The forces from Darokin also prepared to leave, having never once crossed the Areste River to enter the city of Braejr. With considerable numbers of wagons and cavalry and whole ranks of infantry, they needed half the morning to get themselves packed and organized, and it was shortly before noon when they were finally on the road.

The departures of the various contingents of troops apparently satisfied the dragons, and the last of their numbers left late that same morning. Thelvyn went up to the city wall above the palace to watch them, rank upon rank of dragons rising from the woods beyond the fields and circling once before flying off toward the north. They made an impressive sight, a long column of dragons that seemed to take forever to pass. There appeared to be more dragons than there actually were, but he thought that only four or five hundred of their original two thousand were in this final group.

The departure of the last of the dragons brought the siege of Braejr to a formal conclusion, and the city was at last able to begin a slow return to normal life. And life would indeed be returning to normal, but Thelvyn was not to be a part of it. He could almost laugh at himself for finding it a sad parting, considering how impatient he had been most of his life to be away from this land and its people.

But it was still the only home he had ever known; here he had been everything from an unwanted orphan to a hero and then a king, and then full circle until he was unwanted once again. He thought that the time was ripe for him to leave.

Still, he had to wonder if life in the Highlands would ever again be quite the same. He hoped that things might be better for what he had done, and especially for what he had yet to do before he surrendered the crown later that morning. While he had never wanted to be king, he had accepted that duty with a deep sense of responsibility. Whatever else, he was determined to leave the Highlands in better condition than when he had found it. That would be no small trick. The Flaem had always been in more danger from the wolves within their own fold than from any foreign enemy.

He found Solveig waiting in his private chamber when he returned from watching the departure of the dragons. She had been looking into the single large trunk in the middle of the floor containing the possessions he had brought here when he moved from his house. Her interest was not idle curiosity; she seemed quietly dismayed.

"I'm glad you could come early," he said, taking a seat at the desk. "I'll be going before the advisory council to declare my formal abdication this morning, and I have much to arrange."

"I daresay," Solveig agreed, seating herself in the chair across the desk from him. "The council hasn't even begun its search to find a possible successor. If you abdicate now, the person you named in your will would have to take the crown."

"I've never asked you what you think of all this," he said, as if deliberately changing the subject.

Solveig looked confused. "I'm not certain what I'm supposed to think. The Fire Wizards have had their feathers trimmed back so far that they won't recover any time soon, although they'll always remain a threat. Your new king had better be strong enough to handle them. At the same time, none of the dukes seem to want the throne. It would be easier for you to name your own successor. It's your right."

"Any king I choose would be bound to inherit a share of the ill-will directed toward me," Thelvyn said. "In that respect, his authority would be weakened from the first. You've said yourself that the next king has to be strong enough to face his enemies. But I was wondering what your plans are now that Sir George and I will be leaving."

"You might be welcome to leave as soon as you want, but you've tied me down with responsibilities to this council," she said. "After that, I have no idea. I won't be working with Sir George until he returns from wherever you take him, and I doubt that I can go with you. I suspect you'll soon be heavily involved in the private affairs of dragons. Are you going away soon?" she asked. "Are you planning to leave the Highlands to your named successor?"

"I named you to be my successor."

"Oh, that's clever," Solveig said sourly, then stared at him. "You're serious, aren't you?"

"Well, I do have an alternative plan," he said. "The alternative is to leave the Flaem without any king. As long as they have a king, the dukes and the Fire Wizards will always be fighting for power. At best, all they seem to be able to think about is finding trouble, like making war with enemies they can't hope to defeat."

"That's certainly true."

"I was thinking of a two-part council or parliament," Thelvyn continued. "A full-time assembly of elected representatives who would always be on hand here in Braejr to deal with common problems and unexpected difficulties. Then, at certain times of the year, the full assembly would meet, which would include the dukes or their surrogates and a representative of the wizards. They'd decide the major policies of the Highlands. The council would have a senior representative, comparable to the First Speaker of the dragons, who would act as the leader of the council and the representative of the Highlands in political affairs."

Solveig looked a bit confused. "Why? You could just as well have a new king to lead the council."

"I was thinking of the matter of implied power. A First Speaker would be more aware of his position as a keeper of trust. Anyone bearing the title of king might become too concerned with the powers usually associated with a king. The foundation for the system already exists. The advisory council can simply expand to become the new representative council."

"What makes you think the Flaem will agree to this?" Solveig asked, still looking skeptical.

"If they don't, I'll sit here in the palace until they search the Highlands for someone wise enough and honest enough to become king. I think we both know how long that might take."

Thelvyn hoped his threat was only an idle one. The full story of his origin was now generally known, and his popularity was lower than ever. Everyone had become firmly convinced that trouble with dragons had always followed him and would continue to do so wherever he went, and they wanted him out of their land as soon as possible. It was apparently a reaction he could expect anywhere he went. With the news that he would soon be moving out of the palace, various diplomats had been presenting themselves to him. They still respected the power of the Dragonlord, and they wanted to have him about if dragons ever threatened, but they made it clear that they preferred not to have him in their lands otherwise.

Under the circumstances, the advisory council agreed with Thelvyn's proposal. They needed some time to work out the details of their new representative government, but they were prepared to assume nominal control of the Highlands until then. Much to her surprise, Solveig was elected to be the first Prime Minister of the Parliament of the Realm. She would remain in the house that Thelvyn was vacating. The palace was to be renamed the Hall of Parliament. For the time being, no one would live there except the staff and guards.

The wizards remained unusually quiet through it all. Alessa Vyledaar had apparently taken Thelvyn at his word. She hadn't opposed his plan but instead became one of

Solveig's chief supporters. Thelvyn couldn't begin to guess whether or not she had really learned her lesson or if she was just biding her time until the wizards regained some of their lost popularity. He was certain, however, that if Alessa tried anything with Solveig, she was in for an unpleasant surprise.

CHAPTER NINETEEN

Now that all other concerns were settled, Thelvyn abdicated quietly, without ceremony or speeches. He simply packed the last of his bags and moved back into his own house later that afternoon, together with Sir George and Solveig. Taeryn was eager to help and carried out all his possessions to the waiting cart, although he was obviously sad and concerned at the same time.

"I don't care what people think," he insisted. "You're still the best king the Highlands could ever have."

"I appreciate that," Thelvyn assured him, "although I'm sure others might disagree with that."

"Yes, I know they would. But they're so busy talking, they don't bother to consider what they really think."

At first Thelvyn was glad to be home again, although he soon found that there was little here to remind him of happier days. Kharendaen was gone, and the old warehouse remained dark and empty. He thought of a time when he had been proud to be the Dragonlord and travel throughout the known world with the dragon cleric. He had never felt much like the Dragonlord since she had left.

Since he no longer had any staff on hand, Thelvyn had to cook dinner that night. The problem of finding a new staff would have to be Solveig's, and she would probably wait until he had left, since the people of Braejr believed trouble followed the Dragonlord wherever he went.

"I can find help easily enough when you've gone," Solveig said as they sat together in the den that night. "I'm not sure why, considering how unpopular you are just now, but I seem to be rather popular. I think they would have made Sir George king if he had been willing to stay."

"Not that I would want to be the king of these people," Sir George said. "If they ever found out what I am, it would absolutely be the end of them. They could never stomach the thought of another dragonkin on the throne."

Thelvyn had been sitting back in his own chair, listening to the others talk. Sellianda was seated near him, also listening quietly. The old knight was contemplating a bottle of cherry liqueur as if it might be his last for some time, which, in fact, it could be. Solveig had poured herself an especially large glass of the stuff, which was surprising considering that she normally detested it. It seemed to indicate an awareness of just how much trouble she had bitten off that day.

Thelvyn had been watching Solveig, knowing the problems she would have after he was gone. In some way, she seemed to have changed. When he had first met her years before, she had expressed disgust for politics. Perhaps it was because she was indeed older now. Solveig White-Gold the adventurer was no more; she was ready to become Valeria Dorani once again, the adopted daughter of one of the first families of Thyatis. For now, she seemed part of both the cold, quietly menacing barbarian woman and the calm, calculating empress.

"Will you be staying here long?" Thelvyn asked her suddenly.

Solveig looked confused, as if she hadn't thought about it. "I really don't know. It seems like as good a place as any, and the Flaem seem to want me. I might just stay here until I get tired of them or they turn on me, whichever comes first."

"What about Darius Glantri?" Sir George asked. The young Thyatian had recently returned to his own land.

"I'll have to see," she answered vaguely. "But what about you, Thelvyn? I know that you want to find that dragon of yours."

"Marthaen said Kharendaen would let me know what I must do next," Thelvyn replied. "I assume the Great One is guiding her. In the past, everything was always laid out before me, and it seems that it will continue to be so in the future."

"That depends upon when your patron decides to put you back to work," Sellianda pointed out. "You waited five years for this turn of events. How long will you wait until the next one, and what will you do until then?"

"Well, what about it, lad?" Sir George asked. "It seems to me that if we just take to the road and head north toward dragon country, Kharendaen should find us soon enough. What else is there?"

Thelvyn turned to Sellianda. "Do you have any useful advice to offer?"

"Sir George is correct," she told him. "The time has come for you to become more involved in the affairs of dragons. Tomorrow I must take you into the north."

"But I thought that your duty here was done," Thelvyn said, confused.

"I said I would stay with you until Kharendaen returns," she said. "When you leave, I will go with you."

* * * * *

Always mindful of such things, Sir George had kept very busy the last few days making certain that both his own wealth and Thelvyn's had been converted to a secure form and transferred into safekeeping in Darokin. Thelvyn had also arranged for the ownership of his house to be transferred to Solveig's name. She insisted on paying for it, having profited substantially over the last five years as Sir George's business associate, although Thelvyn wasn't concerned about that. Solveig was actually rather pleased with the thought that she was the only person in the world whose house had a guest room for a dragon.

Thelvyn was glad Sir George didn't have to sell a house too, or they would have never gotten out of Braejr before the people of the town decided to help them on their way. Sir George reminded him that no one was going to try to cheat the Dragonlord, but he took the point. He insisted that he would be ready to go by the next morning.

"You really don't have to go with me, you know," Thelvyn insisted. "I'm not sure the dragons are done trying to get rid of me permanently, and my company could be dangerous. You could stay here with Solveig, or return to Darokin and go back to your former life. At least it was relatively safe and comfortable."

"Well, I'm not so certain of that," Sir George commented. "You'll always be involved with dragons, and I can't say that I've had my fill of them just yet. Besides, we're practically related—two dragons who never have been dragons, caught between two worlds and wanted by neither. You don't mind having me along, do you?"

In fact, the need for Thelvyn to be out of Braejr no longer seemed quite as important as it had. Now that his departure was imminent, the wizards no longer felt the need to stir up sentiment against him. His departure from the palace and the formation of the new representative council had also provided something of a distraction. Indeed, the establishment of the new government of the Highlands had caught everyone by surprise, and once the people began to understand the reason for the change, they were inclined to be grateful to Thelvyn for finding a way to spare them the constant political battles between the king, the wizards, and the dukes. At least Thelvyn wouldn't be leaving Braejr totally despised, after all that he had done to save the city. Being held in general suspicion and fear was depressing enough.

Thelvyn was reminded oddly of his first adventures on the road with Sir George years before, when he had been a mere boy with no idea what to expect. This was the first time in a long while that he had felt the old familiar excitement about the prospect of adventure and travel, leaving behind all of his old duties and concerns to face new challenges and responsibilities.

Of course, Sir George's remarkable life had been spent with a whole sequence of companions and associates whose lives changed relatively quickly. From time to time, Thelvyn had heard many of their names and adventures—people like Sir David Southworth, Adrian Kelius, Roar Njalsson, and the master thief, Bartholomew Mellow. There had been the mage, Tennet, and the beautiful sorceress, Lerian, who may or may not have spent some time as Lady Kirbey. Sir George was deliberately vague on that account. All had eventually gone off on adventures of their own, some never to return. Others had simply grown too old for a life of adventure long before Thelvyn or Solveig had even been born.

They awoke a couple of hours before dawn and went out to the stables behind the house to saddle their horses. Thelvyn brought their packhorse to the front of the house. Sellianda rode the same graceful elvish horse that had first brought her to Braejr. Solveig was to ride with them as far as the north gate to see them on their way and, if the gate happened to be shut, to make certain that they were allowed to leave without incident. Thelvyn was quietly amused, explaining that if he was trying to leave, there was no one in Braejr who would want to stop him. The shoes of their horses rang against the paving stones of the dark, deserted streets, echoing in the cool night air.

As it happened, the north gate was open, and the guards on duty rather pointedly ignored them as they approached. They rode through the gate and a short way down the road before they stopped, pausing in the open field several hundred yards beyond the city wall.

"Where will you go from here?" Solveig asked.

"North, following the dragons," Thelvyn explained.

"Meaning that your plans are always subject to the will of the Immortals," she observed.

"I've always ended up exactly where I was supposed to be, often in spite of my best efforts to do otherwise."

"You're starting to sound like a real cleric," she told him. "You trust completely in your patron, I suppose."

"Not at all," he said. "Whatever qualities I possess, devotion has never been one of them. I've just learned to do what's expected of me because I know I'll have to eventually anyway. I'm stuck with the job and all the enemies that go with it."

"You sound as if you've given up."

"Not in the least. I've simply weighed what I want against the price, and I'm willing to continue."

"Now that I'm starting to think of you as a dragon, I'm beginning to see I've never really understood you," Solveig said, then turned to Sir George. "I know this is a waste of breath, but try to keep Thelvyn out of trouble."

Solveig returned home alone, while the others followed the main road northward. They were well beyond Braejr by sunrise, but they found travel slower than they had expected after that, since they chose to avoid the villages and farms as well as any travelers they met along the road. The only way to manage that was to leave the road altogether at times and travel within the woods, often leading their horses for miles around the edges of fields.

There were a great many travelers on the road, with so much to be done to bring the Highlands back to normal now that the dragons were gone. Soldiers who had come to the defense of Braejr were now returning to their garrisons throughout the realm. Families who had evacuated their farms were returning, and traders were moving slowly back into the north.

Thelvyn hardly noticed, riding in a deep silence that Sir George mistook for brooding. The old knight did what he could to lighten the mood, singing tavern songs and telling terrible or outrageous jokes. But his concern was wasted; Thelvyn wasn't really upset by anything that had happened. Instead, his mind was exploring his life, recalling everything that he had ever found out about himself. He regretted that he had never fulfilled his long-cherished dream to return to his own people, filled with a sense of belonging and the delight of discovery.

Because their first day had begun at such an early hour, they stopped well before nightfall in a hidden clearing in the woods across the Aalban River from Braastar, although the city was so far east of the river that it couldn't be seen. Thelvyn had been riding Cadence, the same horse he had ridden when he went to the frontier with the Highlands army. The powerful war-horse was holding up well, and Sellianda's elvish horse seemed tireless. But the long hours on the road had left their packhorse much in need of a good rest.

"Do you want to start the fire or tend the horses?" Sir George asked.

"I'll have you know that I'm the Dragonlord and the King of the Flaemish Realm," Thelvyn replied, although he was already stripping the weary pack horse of its gear.

The next day of riding brought them into the frontier. These northern lands were wilder and less inhabited, and the travelers were able to make better time because the local farms and villages were more widely spaced and there were few other travelers on the road. They crossed the bridge over the Aalban River at the town of Traagen at dusk that night.

They were now entering the deep pine forests of the frontier, land where Thelvyn had been born. He would have liked to stay that night at a comfortable inn, especially since there were pockets of storms wandering across the valley, and he was sure his companions felt the same way. But they knew there was nowhere in the Highlands they could stay without being recognized. Even though it was late, they rode on through the darkness until they had passed well beyond the fields around the town and reentered the forest.

Once they were well north of Traagen, they were able to find a secluded place to camp in the forest a short distance from the side of the road. Sir George started a campfire immediately, and he had begun preparing their dinner before Thelvyn and Sellianda had finished with the horses. Dusk was fading by that time, and the first stars appeared through the breaks in the trees overhead as the sky turned dark. A storm flashed with lightning as it moved through the rugged foothills many miles to the west; Thelvyn had forgotten about the summer storms hereabouts, but overhead the sky was mostly clear, and he thought they had no need to be concerned that night.

"Do we keep going north?" Sir George inquired.

"Our path leads north and west, as far as the roads will take us," Sellianda explained. "We will be going over the mountains into Wendar, to a place called Shadowmere."

"Are you going to stay with us all the way?" Thelvyn asked. "Now that we're out in the wilderness, I expect Kharendaen to join us any time now."

Sellianda frowned. "Will you take a walk with me?"

She took him by the hand and led him away into the forest. As dark as it was, they could both see well enough to make their way through the trees. Thelvyn knew this was a difficult time for Sellianda. Soon Kharendaen would join them, and then the female elf cleric would return to her home at the elvish sanctuary of Silvermist, in the distant forests of Alfheim. After a hundred yards or so, they came to another opening amidst the trees.

"Sellianda, I don't want you to think I'm in a hurry to be rid of you," he assured her. "I was only wondering if it was wise to delay the inevitable. Your duty does not permit you to remain with me much longer, and I doubt you want to remain in the company of a dragon."

"Kharendaen is also a dragon," Sellianda reminded him.

"Is that what's wrong? Are you jealous of her, just because we're both dragons?"

"I think you are very fond of her, and you have missed her very much."

"Yes, I have missed her," he admitted. "More than I would have ever expected. But until you mentioned it, I never once thought it was anything more than a close companionship of two friends who have shared a great many experiences together. It never occurred to me to look upon her as anything more. If Sir George is correct, that a dragon will always recognize another one, then I realize now that she must have always known what I was. But I can't guess what she might have thought."

"She loves you very much, and that has made her afraid to return," Sellianda told him. "She cannot guess how you will react to a dragon who loves you."

Thelvyn considered that briefly. "I think I would consider myself very fortunate. But what about you?"

"I am no longer concerned for myself," she said. "You see, I am Kharendaen."

For a moment, Thelvyn hardly understood what she meant. She stepped away from him to the center of the clearing, then turned to face him. A sudden flare of brilliant white light enveloped her form, so that all he could see was her figure outlined in black against the brilliant white of the radiance. She made a sudden movement like the spring of a cat, and as she did, the dark form within the core of light shifted, flowing and expanding to become that of a young dragon, lean and graceful. The glare of light faded, and suddenly Kharendaen stood before him, her wings half-furled. She brought her head forward and rubbed her nose gently against his chest in the old familiar gesture that he had missed so much. He rubbed her muzzle.

"Among dragons, that is a gesture of affection between lovers," she explained. "It may have been presumptuous of me, but until now you did not know its meaning, and it has helped me to wait until we could become even closer."

"It's so good to be with you again," he told her gently. "I only wonder if we can dare to assume that we'll always be together now."

"I cannot say," Kharendaen replied. "But if we must wait until there is no uncertainty, then we will never be together. Let us enjoy whatever time we have. Now we must return before Sir George begins to feel our absence is unseemly. I do not wish to endure his comments."

Thelvyn knew she was right. Kharendaen changed form once again, but this time her appearance was not in the form of the elf Sellianda but one more like his own. She was nearly as tall as he, with thick, black hair and large, dark eyes. Somehow she reminded him of Kharendaen.

"You must understand that there is no Sellianda; there is only Kharendaen," she told him as they walked back to the camp. "Sellianda was not a separate person so much as a convenience, a guise to keep the elves of Alfheim from being concerned that there were dragons in the service of the Great One living among them. I was hesitant to allow you to become too close to me as Sellianda because I have always known that we are both dragons."

"But I thought Sellianda was a cleric of Terra," Thelvyn said. "Then again, I recall you telling me long ago that Terra and the Great One were closely allied at one time, and that they remain close even yet. I also recall someone once telling me there are elvish clerics of the Great One."

"That is so," she replied. "Silvermist, where we first met, is in fact a sanctuary of the Great One, not of Terra. I have always served the Great One."

Sir George had dinner ready by the time they returned. The old knight noticed that Kharendaen had changed her form, but as a dragonkin, he had always known her true identity whatever form she assumed.

"Well, I like what you've done with your appearance," he remarked. "The only problem is, now you look like Thelvyn's sister."

* * * * *

Kharendaen wasn't as much help in finding their way through the mountains as they had hoped. She knew this land well from her childhood, but her familiarity was limited to flight. A dragon flying over the mountains would be looking for great ridges and towering cliffs to deflect and direct the winds she would ride. She knew very little about trails and passes that might lead them to the other side of the mountains, and she wasn't certain there were many trails to be found anyway. The Flaem had always stayed south of the mountains, and the elves of Wendar had always remained to the north. Very few people ever ventured among the mountains themselves.

The best the young cleric could do was to assume her dragon form and fly ahead, scouting out the best path. But she soon became increasingly reluctant to leave her companions. Dragons were watching their every move, as many as six or eight of them, maintaining a discreet distance in the heights as they passed among the valleys and high meadows. Thelvyn had wondered whether or not the dragons considered that his dispute with them settled, but unless they actually attacked him, there wasn't much he could do about it. Certainly they were well aware he was still the Dragonlord.

"They'll leave us alone once we reach Shadowmere, won't they?" Thelvyn asked when they stopped that night. In the distance, they could see the fires of the dragons' camps burning in the darkness.

Kharendaen looked worried. "If you are thinking that they would not dare violate the Great One's sanctuary, then you should know that they have done it once before. When the rogue dragons first learned of the prophecy of the return of the Dragonlord, they descended upon Shadowmere in force to slay you before you were even born. The sanctuary has remained abandoned to this day."

"Marthaen told me about that," he said pensively.

"The Great One had already warned your mother," Kharendaen continued. "She escaped into the mountains, and they followed her as she fled south all the way to the village where you were born. When she was wounded, the Great One intervened as much as he could by deceiving the rogue dragons with a false image so that they left her to search farther south."

"I always wondered why they never came back," Sir George remarked.

"I am not certain that they intend us any harm," Kharendaen said. "But I can understand why they are curious. They are waiting to find out what the future holds for them."

Indeed, the dragons seemed to have no interest in interfering with their journey, but they were careful to keep the Dragonlord in sight at all times. Kharendaen informed them that she expected that they would be coming down from the mountains into Wendar by the end of the next day, although she could not be absolutely certain of that without flying on ahead to check the distance. Later that morning, they topped a high pass and could see the lines of ridges and hills of the Wendarian Range falling away before them, eventually fading into the green tide of the deep forests of Wendar.

Kharendaen indicated a place almost directly ahead of

them, where a great pocket of forest lay encircled in the lower arms of the mountains. This was the Foxwoods, she explained, the location of the sanctuary of Shadowmere. A second large area of forest lay entrapped by the mountains just to the east of that, barely visible from where they stood, while a long spur of the Wendarian Range stretched to the west of the Foxwoods. It was still many miles distant, and they had some rough terrain to cross before they got there.

Standing atop the high pass, where they could see for great distances along the range of mountains, they were able to see dragons in every direction, gliding alone or in small groups all along the line of the Wendarian Range. There were probably no more than two dozen in all, and yet that many dragons in one relatively small segment of the wilderness was unheard of. Thelvyn was beginning to wonder if they were going to try to prevent him from reaching Shadowmere, as if that would somehow defeat the prophecy. Kharendaen couldn't deny that possibility.

Storms began to gather in the mountains by early afternoon, slowing their travel in the wind and rain before finally forcing them to make an early camp for the night. They were coming down from the mountains rather quickly by that time, and the edge of the Foxwoods was not many miles ahead. The next day the dragons seemed determined to make their journey difficult, or at least disconcerting. Mostly young reds, the dragons repeatedly flew low over their heads to make the horses shy, or else circled tightly overhead.

Kharendaen was becoming frustrated with the situation by the middle of the afternoon, and she had been contemplating for some time whether she should return to her true form and chase away the young rogues. The dragons knew who she was and respected her, but more and more dragons were watching and following from a distance as their journey continued.

After a time, Thelvyn hardly even noticed the dragons anymore. He was becoming filled with a sense of urgency. He was concerned about the intentions of the dragons but he did not fear them, nor did he feel driven by them to seek the safety of Shadowmere. Although this had never happened to him before, he knew that he had been called. The Great One had summoned him here to the Foxwoods, and somehow he knew he had to be there by nightfall. By late afternoon, they passed into the deep forests of the Foxwoods, although they still had a journey of a couple of hours ahead of them before they reached Shadowmere.

There was something familiar and comforting about this hidden place deep in the cool shadows of the immense trees. Kharendaen had led him here without explanation, and he had never questioned her choice. He had never considered himself much of a cleric, but for once he had to trust the guidance of the Immortals. There was nothing more he could do for himself.

Kharendaen had assumed her Eldar form when they entered the forest, and it was she who led the way. The afternoon was fading quietly into evening, and the shadows were lengthening in the depths of the forest when they came at last around the open end of the ring of hills and rode into the sanctuary of Shadowmere. Thelvyn paused a moment to look about, since this was the first time that he had ever seen a place built by dragons. The sanctuary was a rustic structure, built of great, solid timbers of dark wood, its heavy doors barred and its windows tightly shuttered. Great drifts of leaves mounded against the structure's sides. The immense proportions of the sanctuary left Thelvyn feeling small and insignificant.

Only the stables and other parts of the building apparently reserved for the elvish clerics of the Great One were of a size more familiar to him. They led their horses to the stables at the east end of the sprawling stone structure, tending to the beasts quickly before they moved to the main hall of the sanctuary.

Kharendaen performed a spell to bring the magic lamps to life the moment she stepped inside the hall, although the dim glow did little to brighten the depths of the massive chamber. Sir George hurried to light a fire in the huge hearth along one outside wall. They kept their packs beside them as they settled before the fire to wait.

They had ridden mostly in silence that day, but now they

all shared the same sense of anticipation. Thelvyn sat alone at the edge of the ring of light from the fire while Sir George prepared their dinner.

"Do you know what's going to happen?" he heard the old knight ask quietly.

"I'm not certain," Kharendaen had to admit. "I spoke with the Great One here before I left for Braejr, and I'm very afraid."

"For him?"

"For us," she explained. "The Great One is regaining his former powers. He told me that the time of the Dragonlord is coming to an end, and that I would soon be serving the new Dragonking."

"That should make the dragons happy," Sir George commented wryly.

"Unfortunately, the dragons do not know about any of this," she said. "All they know is that they no longer fear the Dragonlord. They have foreseen what is likely to happen here at Shadowmere, and they mean to be at hand when the Dragonlord becomes vulnerable."

Thelvyn sat in silence, seeming not to listen. He wasn't particularly concerned for his own safety. There was hardly any need for the dragons to fight him now; he had always served as well as he could, and if he was asked to do so, then he would surrender the enchanted armor and cease to be the Dragonlord. But he felt certain that the time of his service was not yet at an end, that his role as champion of the dragons was only just beginning. He thought he knew why he was here. There was one thing he had to have before he could continue his service.

The time of the summons came several hours later, near the middle of the night. Thelvyn had been leaning back against his pack while Kharendaen slept in his arms, but she awoke suddenly and rose to her feet. She stepped out into the middle of the room, returning to her true dragon form before hurrying to settle herself into the saddle that she had left during her previous visit here. Thelvyn had summoned the armor of the Dragonlord, then removed the helmet and teleported it into safekeeping. He didn't expect he would need the armor for protection; it served more as a token of his title and his duty.

Kharendaen opened the doors and stepped out into the yard, pausing to allow Thelvyn to climb into her saddle. The night was deep and cool, with a fresh, gentle breeze stirring through the trees, and the stars were shining in the dark sky above the clearing. Once Thelvyn had settled into the saddle, the dragon leaped across the forest stream and followed the path through the darkness of the Foxwoods, coming soon to the edge of the great ravine that served as the Great One's sacred place. She paused for a moment, where they could both look out across the clearing below and hear the waterfall splashing down the steps of ravine wall just below them. Then Kharendaen gathered her strength and leaped out into the night air, her broad wings snapping out to bear her aloft.

She rose quickly above the forest into the night sky. As Thelvyn looked about, he recalled the dream in which he had spoken with his mother, and he knew that they had passed abruptly into another world. The forests and mountains about them were not the same he had seen from the high passes of the Wendarian Range. The land seemed to be illuminated by a wash of silver moonlight, but there was no moon to be seen in the star-filled sky. The wind against his face felt strangely cool.

Kharendaen banked northward, toward the dark line of the most forbidding mountains that Thelvyn had ever seen. Now he knew beyond all doubt that he was no longer in the same land, for there had been no mountains north of the Foxwoods. Kharendaen flew with little effort, hardly even beating her wings and never having to search for a favorable gust of wind to carry her, and yet many long miles of forest flashed by with each passing minute.

"Do you know where we are?" Thelvyn asked.

"I have never been in this place before," she answered, glancing back at him briefly. "I believe that we are no longer in the mortal world but in the place the Great One has set aside as his own. I also suspect we are here only in a dream, and in truth we are asleep in the clearing of the Great One's sacred place back in Shadowmere."

Whatever the case, they crossed a hundred miles or more

of wilderness in a matter of minutes. The shadowed forms of the great mountains rose swiftly before them, and Kharendaen allowed the momentum of her unnatural speed to carry them into the heights. They rose swiftly up the rugged slopes and suddenly encountered a massive castle, as large as a city, seeming not to have been built but rather carved from the very cliffs of the mountain itself. Soft golden lights shone in a few of the windows of the towers and halls, and there were no sentries or warriors standing watch. The castle appeared very dark and forbidding, although it also seemed deserted.

Kharendaen began to slow herself in the final moments of her approach, turning to circle for a time as she sought an entry into the castle. Thelvyn did not question how she had known to come so swiftly and unerringly to this great castle, but for the first time he began to feel helpless and afraid. He wanted to tell her he couldn't enter this place, but he seemed to lack the will to speak. Kharendaen found the main gate of the fortress after only a few moments of searching, a massive portal with doors of heavy timbers bound by steel. The only approach to it was a small ledge. No road, path, or steps led up to the place; it was obviously an entry reserved for dragons alone.

Kharendaen landed on the ledge, then turned to approach the gate. The two immense doors parted, drawing back before her. She entered without hesitation, walking slowly down a long, dark passage of featureless gray stone, drawn ahead by the promise of a warm light until she came to a large chamber that resembled a dining hall. Thelvyn looked around the room but saw no furnishings. Vast beams of dark wood supported the ceiling high above, and the walls were hung with tapestries bearing heroic scenes of dragons. The room was completely windowless, and a lone doorway stood directly across from where they had entered. Beyond it was nothing but darkness.

Thelvyn glanced up at Kharendaen, finding himself standing at her side, although he didn't recall climbing down from her saddle. As they waited, silent and motionless, Thelvyn once more felt afraid. He became aware that someone was approaching from the darkness of the passage on the far side of the hall, someone he could neither see nor hear. He wanted to run, certain somehow that this was a meeting he must somehow avoid, but he felt there was nowhere for him to go.

Slowly, from out of the darkness, a dragon emerged, a gold dragon that was the largest he had ever seen, larger even than Marthaen. He was the very image of power and grace, his chest deep and well-muscled, his horns elegantly curved, and his crest was long and full. His face was exceptionally noble, with a long, narrow muzzle, and the brows above his large, piercing eyes were broad and deep, so that he wore an expression that was calm, confident, and supremely wise. He stopped just inside the doorway and sat back on his strong haunches, lifting his proud chest with his neck drawn back in a graceful curve.

Kharendaen gasped softly as if she recognized him, taking a step forward as if drawn against her will. Thelvyn looked up at her, wondering what this strange dragon had done to her, but then he saw that her expression was one of supreme delight. And yet he knew beyond any doubt that this was not the Great One. Kharendaen glanced down at him, almost a gesture of farewell, before she looked up at the strange dragon and began to move toward him, step by step, before rushing suddenly to his side. Then, to Thelvyn's dismay, she stroked the side of her face against his breast, the same intimate gesture he thought she reserved for him, and for a moment the two dragons rubbed their cheeks and necks together affectionately.

"I've waited for you so long," she told the strange dragon. "I feel as if I've been in exile these last five years."

"I know you do," the dragon told her gently as he held her against him, although he lifted his head to stare at Thelvyn, his gaze neither compassionate nor proud but carefully neutral.

"I love you so," Kharendaen said, her eyes closing in delight.

Thelvyn could only stand there, staring in disbelief as his heart sank into his feet. Until that moment, he had never realized how much Kharendaen really meant to him. He knew it would be futile to fight for her affection. Her love was given freely; he couldn't hope to win it with the weapons of the Dragonlord. He was a dragon, and yet he was not, as long as he remained unable to assume his true form. He had never felt such burning shame and frustration in all his life, made all the more bitter because all he could do was accept it.

"Leave us now," the dragon said to Kharendaen, lifting his claw to gently stroke her neck. "I will return to you soon, and then we will be together always."

Kharendaen rubbed her cheek against his, then stepped back and turned to depart. Thelvyn couldn't watch her leave, his own gaze held by the large, penetrating eyes of the gold dragon.

"Who are you?" Thelvyn breathed at last.

"I am the Dragonking," the gold dragon replied.

"But what is your name?"

"I know you better than you know yourself, yet cruel necessity has made it impossible for you to know me," the Dragonking said. "You have served me well, and I regret that this one brief moment of both our meeting and our parting should be a bitter one for you."

"Then I will not be allowed to serve you further?" Thelvyn asked.

"You cannot serve me," the Dragonking told him, rising and walking slowly toward him. "The time has come for me to fight my own battles, to use my own cunning and my own powers rather than the enchantments of the wizards of a forgotten empire. It is tempting to have you about, to comfort me with old habits and defend me with your powers, but the time is at hand for the Dragonlord to return to his long sleep."

"Who are you?" Thelvyn demanded once more. "You must have a name as well as a title."

The Dragonking loomed over him, staring down at him. "I am the gold dragon Thelvaenir. I am what you were meant to be."

Suddenly Thelvyn's vision of that world of dreams vanished in a glare of light. Sensations he could not describe engulfed him in those few brief moments while he was blinded by that white brilliance, sensations of being drawn into some place he could not see and brought forth again. He felt like a piece of paper that was folded into a new form, yet without pain. Then the overwhelming flood of light faded into cool, soothing darkness.

Thelvyn found himself lying in the cool grass of the sanctuary of Shadowmere. He blinked and lifted his head, finding the effort strange and awkward, as if his body was unable to serve him as he expected. The night was deep and still, although the clearing was filled with a gentle golden light. Kharendaen moved quickly to his side, helping him to rise. He almost drew back from her touch, the memory of her betrayal still sharp and bitter. But when he sat back on his haunches and saw himself, he suddenly understood. The enchantment was broken, and he had assumed his true form, the same form as the noble gold dragon he had met in the dark fortress of the dream. Sir George stood before him, now as small in his eyes as a tiny child, looking anxious and quite at a loss for words for once in his life.

Then Thelvyn paused and lifted his head, suddenly aware that he and Kharendaen were not alone. The encircling ledges of the ravine were crowded with dragons of every breed, hundreds of dragons, all glaring at him intently and malevolently. More dragons pressed forward behind them as they peered over the edge of the ravine far above. Still more were perched among the boulders at the far end of the clearing, where the ravine narrowed abruptly. Only perhaps three dozen of the huge creatures had dared to enter the clearing itself, almost all of them golds, who were gathered about him in respectful silence.

"The clerics have returned to Shadowmere," Kharendaen told him very softly. "But there are not enough of us to fight, and I fear that the rogue dragons will force us to do so. They are very frightened."

"I don't understand," Thelvyn said hoarsely. Even his voice seemed loath to obey him. "What do they want?"

"They want to be reassured," she explained.

The dragons all rose, muttering in their fury and their fear. The clerics in the clearing responded by gathering about him in a tight circle, facing outward toward the growing tide of anger. For the time being, Thelvyn was uncomfortably aware that he was unable to defend himself. He could no longer transport himself into the armor of the Dragonlord, since he did not yet know how to assume his old shape. He certainly couldn't fight as a dragon. For the moment, he doubted he could even walk. The great bulk and power of a dragon was unfamiliar to him.

The dragons paused in their angry muttering and lifted their heads to look up. A gold dragon was descending swiftly down into the ravine, slowing himself with powerful sweeps of his wings to land a short distance away. He rose to his hind legs and reached over his back to draw forth an immense sword he carried in his harness.

"I am Marthaen, First Speaker of the Parliament of Dragons," he declared in a booming voice. "I warn you that you must not invade the sanctity of this place or defy the will of the Great One a second time, or by my word you will have to answer to me!"

Suddenly Thelvyn became aware that Marthaen had not come alone. Daresha and Gheradaen and other gold dragon kings had come as well, bringing their bands to support them. Several dragons gathered on the ledges above leaped down into the ravine to join the loyal dragons in the clearing, but far more still remained on the ledges, too angry to relent. The rogue dragons above still greatly outnumbered the defenders below. In spite of all of Thelvyn efforts to prevent the dragons from going to war, their most desperate battle seemed likely to be among themselves.

"What can I tell them to get them to change their minds?" Thelvyn asked his companions.

"I do not know if there is anything you can say," Kharendaen replied. "It has always been the bane of dragons for our wisdom to fail us when anger or fear takes over."

Thelvyn tried to rise, determined that he had to prevent the dragons from fighting. He stood unsteadily, still very shaky and uncertain. The renegade dragons fell silent and stared, as if they were unable to fear an enemy who could hardly even stand before them. Thelvyn was concerned that they would realize his vulnerability and take advantage of the moment. One of the larger red dragons glided down into the clearing and landed a short distance away before advancing slowly. The gold dragons gave way before him, permitting his passage. Only Marthaen refused to stand aside, holding the massive sword out before him. Thelvyn felt certain the red dragon was Jherdar; the others would fight, or not, depending on what he did.

"I know you," Jherdar said, looking at Thelvyn. "I recall that you showed me mercy a long time ago. My friend Marthaen would remind me of that, even if I had forgotten. But we do not know if you have come to serve us or to conquer us."

"Why should you believe that I have any wish to conquer you?" Thelvyn asked in his confusion.

"Because that is implied in the prophecy," the red dragon answered. "It is said that the Dragonlord will come in time to rule the dragons, and that he will influence our destiny for all time to come."

"I think you do not understand the prophecy," Thelvyn replied. "The time of the Dragonlord has come to an end. By the will of the Great One, I am now to become the Dragonking."

The dragons all rose, muttering in their fury and their fear as they stood at the stone ledges, staring down. Many flexed their extended wings as if they were preparing to leap down from the ledges and join in battle. The Dragonking was their last great hope, and the last thing they wanted to hear was that their legendary protector and their greatest enemy were the same. The dragons no longer trusted the prophecy, feeling it had failed them, and Thelvyn was afraid they would turn on him rather than risk being betrayed. Thelvyn saw that even his own companions had been startled by his statement, and he wondered if he should have kept the news secret for a time. His defenders closed even more tightly about him, placing themselves between him and the fury of the rogue dragons.

"Then you believe that your destiny is to rule us?" Jherdar demanded.

"It is not my intention to rule anyone," Thelvyn insisted. "My only wish is to serve."

"Why should we believe that? What proof do we have that this is the will of the Great One and not just your own desire for conquest?"

"Can you still doubt the will of the Great One in this matter?" Marthaen demanded.

"We must have some assurance," Jherdar responded. "If this is the will of the Great One, then why doesn't he tell us himself as he has done in past times."

"If that alone will satisfy you, so be it."

Thelvyn nearly jumped at the sound of the deep, commanding voice behind him. The dragons fell as silent as death, and he saw that his companions were staring in awe. Marthaen lowered his sword as the dragons about him all drew back, holding their long necks low to the ground in a gesture of the deepest respect. He turned awkwardly, although he had to brace his legs wide to keep himself from falling. A dragon stood just behind him, or rather the shimmering image of a dragon of tremendous size and strength. The dragon's three heads glared at the assembly. After a tense moment, the hostile dragons lowered their heads in almost childlike shame at the knowledge that the Great One himself had witnessed their lack of trust.

"You will not defy me!" the Great One proclaimed. "Nor will you defy my champion. I can forgive your doubts when I could not be there to serve you, but the time for fear and uncertainty is past. Now, leave this sacred place in the peace and solitude in which you found it."

The image faded, leaving the dragons in the darkness. Then, in clusters of twos and threes, they began to depart, spreading their wings as they leaped out from the ledges. For several long moments, the sky over the clearing was so full of dragons that Thelvyn wondered how they managed to avoid each other. They quickly climbed above the trees and turned to the east, flying back along the Wendarian Range toward home.

"That was too close for comfort," Sir George breathed. "It pays to have influential friends."

"It was a bad time to suddenly turn into a dragon," Thelvyn remarked as he seated himself on the grass. "I can't imagine learning to fly at my age. I can barely walk."

"You are a very handsome dragon," Kharendaen said, settling close at his side and rubbing her cheek against his own.

"He's rather fox-faced, if you ask me," Marthaen commented, returning his sword to its sheath on his back.

"I just wish I could have some warning before things like this happened," Thelvyn said. "I'm tired of adventures and changes, at least for a while."

"You have earned a time of rest and happiness," the voice of the Great One said, speaking from out of the night.

Thelvyn lifted his head. "But if I am now the Dragonking, won't my new duties keep me occupied?"

"There is little you can do right now," the Great One answered. "Before you can be the Dragonking, you must first learn how to be a dragon. And you must find the Collar of the Dragons, which is now yours. You may have until next spring as your own, but after that the dragons will need you."

"But why me?" Thelvyn asked desperately.

"Do you regret your service?"

"Indeed not," he insisted. "All that I have been through and all that I may have yet to face will be worth the price if the dragons are better off for it. But why have I been chosen? Why am I so important to the destiny of the dragons when I hardly know what it means to be a dragon?"

But the Great One did not reply, choosing to keep such matters secret for now.

Thelvyn lowered his head, for the moment uncertain even of his ability to walk back to the sanctuary. Marthaen followed the rogue dragons, to talk to them about the events they had witnessed and to be certain that they would obey the will of the Great One. Kharendaen and the other dragon clerics helped Thelvyn back to Shadowmere. He tried to return to his more familiar form, but it seemed that even that was something he would have to learn.

A chamber was prepared for him at the sanctuary, and he lay that night on the large cushions of the bed with his mate Kharendaen at his side. He found it difficult to sleep, however. He felt huge and awkward in his new body, although his greatest discomfort was more subtle. He felt as if all the life he had ever known had been stripped away—his home and friends, his pride in his duty as the Dragonlord, even his familiar body had been lost. He knew his destiny was not complete but only just beginning, yet he hardly felt prepared for whatever lay before him.

It seemed to him now that everything that had happened before had been easy compared to this. He had always been secure in his invincible armor, commanding the most powerful enchantments of ancient Blackmoor. Everyone had to respect him, since he could neither be fought nor ignored. Being the Dragonking would be far more challenging. He couldn't count upon being the largest, fastest, or most powerful dragon. His strength would have to come from within himself, and the respect he commanded from others would have to be earned by his wisdom and authority. By spring, he would have to learn not only how to walk and to fly and to fight like a dragon, but also he had to learn how to be a king.

His last thought, before he finally slept, was to reflect with wry amusement about how the first Dragonlord would have felt if he had known the true identity of the heir to his title.